D0198379

PRAISE FOR *EMBRACE*

"One of the best YA novels we've seen in a while. Get ready for a confident, kick butt, well-defined heroine." —*RT Book Reviews*

"You'll quickly be hooked on this new series." —*Girlfriend* magazine

"This epic novel feeds *Twilight* fans' thirst for another extraordinary supernatural tale." —*Dolly* magazine

"Well-written and worth a read." —*Cosmopolitan*

"*Embrace* is a dark and heart-racing tale, filled with action and secrets that will keep you on the edge of your seat and reading deep into the night…Jessica Shirvington's debut novel has something special. It's a combination of the badass-action of *Vampire Academy*, the complex love triangles of *Twilight*, and the angel mythology of *Fallen*, taken one step further." —*Book Couture*

"*Embrace* is fast-paced and exciting, answering some questions about the hierarchy of angels and opening up quite a few more questions with those answers. Filled with emotional turmoil and the eternal choices between good and evil, it's a book that hooked me from page one and never let go. Now I am waiting very impatiently for installment number two." —*Beauty and Lace*

"WOW. I was absolutely blown away at how much I enjoyed this debut novel! I was getting tired of reading angel stories, but this one was so blissfully different. I highly recommend it!" —*Nice Girls Read Books*

EMBRACE

EMBRACE

jessica shirvington

sourcebooks
fire

The author and publisher would like to thank the following for permission to use copyright material: Canongate Books, Edinburgh, for a quotation from "Love Poem" in *Rebel Without Applause* by Lemn Sissay; Princeton University Press, Princeton, for a quotation from *Collected Works of Carl Jung* by Carl Jung; St. Mark's Press, Pavenham, for a quotation from William Barclay; Transaction Publishers, New Jersey, for a quotation from *The Public Philosophy* by Walter Lippmann.

The author and publisher would also like to acknowledge the following works from which the author has quoted: *Zohar III, 19a* by Rabbi Shimon Bar Yochai; "The Desert Has Twelve Things" by Mechthild of Magdeburg; New American Standard Bible; God's Word to the Nations; the Holy Bible: International Standard Version; the Holy Bible: English Standard Version; and the King James Bible.

Every endeavor has been made on the part of the publisher to contact copyright holders not mentioned above, and the publisher will be happy to include a full acknowledgment in any future edition.

Published by Sourcebooks Fire, an imprint of Sourcebooks, Inc.
P.O. Box 4410, Naperville, Illinois 60567-4410
(630) 961-3900
Fax: (630) 961-2168
teenfire.sourcebooks.com

Originally published in Australia and New Zealand in 2010 by Hachette Australia.

Library of Congress Cataloging-in-Publication data is on file with the publisher.

Printed and bound in the United States of America.
BG 10 9 8 7 6 5 4 3 2 1

For Matt,

who showed me that true love is possible

(even at seventeen), and our girls, Sienna and Winter,

who shine new light on the world and make

every day better than the last.

For we wrestle not against flesh and blood, but against principalities, against powers, against the rulers of the darkness of this world, against spiritual wickedness in high places.

EPHESIANS 6:12

chapter one

"Outside, among your fellows, among strangers, you must preserve appearances, a hundred things you cannot do; but inside, the terrible freedom!"

RALPH WALDO EMERSON

Birthdays aren't my thing.

It's hard to get too excited about the day that marks the anniversary of your mother's death. It's not that I blame myself for her not being here. No one could have known she wouldn't survive childbirth. It's not that I miss her either. I mean, I never knew her in the first place. But it is the one day each year that at some point I'll be forced to ask myself, Was it worth it? Was my life worth taking hers?

I stared out the bus window, avoiding. Steph was blabbering on, something about the perfect dress, completely absorbed in what she was saying. She was relentless when it came to the science of shopping. I could feel her watching me, disappointed with my cheer level. Buildings flashed past through the frame of the smudged glass and I couldn't help but wish my seventeenth birthday tomorrow would slide by in the same hazy blur.

"Violet Eden!" Steph said sternly, sucking me out of my trance. "We have your dad's Amex, a green light, and no specified limit." Her mock rebuke morphed into a devious grin. "What more could a girl want as a birthday present?"

Technically, it was *my* Amex. My name, my signature. It just happened to be connected to Dad's account. A by-product of being the only person at home who actually bothered to pay any bills.

I knew Steph wouldn't understand if I told her I wasn't in the mood, so I lied. "I can't go shopping today. I…um…I have a training session."

She raised her eyebrows at me. For a moment I thought she was going to call me out on my fake alibi. But then she segued onto a topic we seemed to be discussing more and more often as of late.

"With Lincoln?"

I shrugged, trying not to let on how much just the mention of Lincoln affected me. Although the training part wasn't true, I *did* have plans to see him later on and was already doing my best not to keep a minute-by-minute countdown.

Steph rolled her eyes. "Honestly, one of these days I'm gonna tell him you'd prefer to get all hot and sweaty with him in a different kind of way!" She threw me her bitchy smile—something she usually reserves for other people.

I sat back and let her vent. It was easier that way. Steph didn't get it and I couldn't blame her—I'd never told her *all* of the reasons why training was so important to me. Some things are just too hard to talk about.

"You *do* realize you're turning into some kind of sports geek, don't you? And don't pretend you actually like them all. I know for a fact that you hate long-distance running." Steph couldn't understand how anyone would rather go rock climbing or boxing in place of shopping.

"I get a kick out of training with him," I said, hoping to put an end to the conversation, even though she wasn't completely off base about the running. If I didn't have Lincoln's butt to stare at the whole time, motivation would be a lot harder to come by.

I busied myself by rummaging through my backpack, which was jammed with all the books they force you to take home on the last day before break. Steph didn't seem put off.

"It's like he's training you for battle or something." Her eyes lit up. "Hey, maybe he has some underground fight club and he's grooming you!"

"That's it, Steph. Definitely."

I didn't want to be talking about this, didn't want to have to admit the round-the-clock desire I had to be with Lincoln. It was like something deep within me found comfort in his presence.

Crushing with the best of 'em, Vi!

Too bad it was a lost cause. It had been that way ever since the moment I'd first met him two years ago. He was a late entry into a self-defense class I'd signed up for. When he was partnered with me, what I thought was going to be another mediocre attempt on my part to get fit and strong became so much more.

I never found out why Lincoln had taken the class. He clearly knew more than the instructor, moving through the exercises with the kind of ease and grace that made it clear he was in another league. After the first couple of weeks, when I was finally able to string more than two words together around him, I asked him why he was there. He shrugged it off, saying it was always good to do a refresher class.

By the end of the three-month course, I was learning more from him than from the instructor, and he offered to give me some kick-boxing lessons. Now I get the best of both worlds. I get stronger every day—our list of activities has expanded to include rock climbing, running, even an archery course—*and* I get to hang out with Lincoln. It's perfect…almost.

"Well, I guess that means we're going shopping tomorrow then." Steph pouted but couldn't keep it up. She can never stay mad for long.

Unfortunately, she was right. I knew Dad had given her strict instructions, due to my lack of spirit and his lack of know-how, to make sure I had a new dress for my birthday dinner tomorrow night. The clock was ticking—shopping was inevitable.

"I can't wait," I said, flashing her a well-practiced fake smile from my birthday repertoire.

As the bus slowed for its next stop, Steph stood up from our seat, three rows from the back. She was convinced only the wannabes sat right at the back, the geeks at the front, and the goths/weirdos right behind them. That left about three rows we could work with, the ones that apparently put us in the not-trying-to-but-can't-help-being-cool section. The ironic thing was, if judged purely on academic achievements, Steph was the biggest geek I knew. Of course, she never publicized the fact that she was some kind of borderline genius.

She wrapped her narrow frame around the metal pole near the doors, donned her favorite pair of D&G sunglasses, and blew me a kiss. I laughed. Luckily for me, Steph wasn't only a label girl. For all the designer clothes she paraded around in, she was surprisingly balanced. The fact that she was from a seriously moneyed-up family and was usually wearing something that cost more than my entire wardrobe didn't adversely affect our friendship. I didn't *overly* care for material possessions and she didn't *overly* care that I didn't.

"Do me a favor?" she said, making her way out the door, unfazed by the logjam of kids sardined behind her. "While you're drooling over Mr. Fantastic, make sure you jab him in the gut a few times for taking up all your free time and depriving me of my bff."

"Sure thing," I said, blowing her a kiss back and ignoring the twinge of guilt I felt about lying to my best friend.

chapter two

"*I have set my bow in the cloud, and it shall be a sign of the covenant between me and the earth.*"

GENESIS 9:13

Instead of going home to an empty apartment, I found myself walking toward Dad's offices. I wasn't sure why. On my way up to the fourth floor, my phone beeped with a text message from Lincoln.

Running a bit late. Meet at my place around 7?

I smiled at the phone, my fingers fumbling over the keypad quickly.

Yep—see you there!

Then I deleted the exclamation mark and counted to thirty before I allowed myself to press send.

It was bittersweet, my relationship with Lincoln. Like always, as soon as the elation of hearing from him subsided, the reality of our "friendship" hit home. It would be nice if he *was* offering a date, but he was really only granting me entry to his warehouse abode—there was a gigantic wall there just begging to be painted and Lincoln had finally agreed to relinquish it to me. The most I could hope for in between coats of primer was a meal. Though I'd tried to reassure Lincoln that coffee and two-minute noodles are a well-balanced diet of dairy and carbohydrates, he remained unconvinced. Since Dad was never around at dinnertime, Lincoln had recently started inviting me back to his place for dinner before dropping me home. I had to admit, even though it wasn't romantic *at all*—we mostly just went over training exercises—it was nice to have someone to talk to instead of eating alone.

Dad's company took up the entire fourth floor. When the elevator doors opened, I spotted the familiar stainless-steel Eden Architects sign that had greeted me for the past eight years.

"Hi, Caroline," I said, walking up to the reception area. "Is he in?"

Dad's receptionist smiled at me and raised her eyebrows. "Where else would he be?"

I found Dad in his office, cemented behind his drawing desk, reams of paper unraveled in front of him. It was an image synonymous with my dad and one that I'd had to accept a long time ago. I used to fight it—or rather, fight for his attention—but the truth was, the minute I had his full attention, I always felt suffocated by it anyway.

He was completely absorbed in whatever he was doing, and by

the look of him, he'd been there awhile—tie gone, sleeves rolled up, ruler in one hand, pencil hanging loosely from his mouth. I was willing to bet that when he stepped away from the desk, he'd reveal shoeless feet.

I made it into the middle of his office without him even noticing.

"Hey, Dad," I said with a wave.

He looked up and smiled, running a hand through his salt-and-pepper hair as if it could somehow release him from a world of lines, angles, and light reflections. He pushed his pencil behind his ear and emerged from behind his desk—socks only.

"Hi, sweetheart." He cleared his throat. "This is a nice surprise. Ah…How was your day?"

I hated that I could hear it, but there it was, same as always: the voice that said, *I'm glad you're here, but I'm really in the middle of something I don't want to be distracted from.*

I swallowed and pushed through it. It was all I could do. I knew if he knew I could hear it, he'd be mortified.

"Great!" I said, beaming with my news. "I got into the Fenton art course. It starts just after graduation." Finding out had been the main motivator for going to school today. The last day before break is usually a blow-off, and Dad never enforced attendance. Well…Dad never enforced anything. But I had been waiting for months to find out if I'd gotten in, and seeing my name on the short list of two had made the day well worthwhile.

He gave me his genuine Dad-of-pride smile. "Of course you did! There was never any doubt. You take after your mom." His voice broke a little at the end. She'd been an artist too. He was rarely the one to bring her up. Like me, he preferred to leave painful things buried. It was easier that way…and harder. But the fact was, nothing was going to fix him. Her death had broken him completely.

"Thanks, Dad," I said, eager for a change of subject.

He straightened abruptly and came toward me, then, reconsidering, went back to his desk and sat behind it, gripping the sides as if to bolt himself down. Dad was finally losing it.

"I know it's technically not your birthday until tomorrow, but I'd like to give you something now." He clicked his jaw from side to side, something he does when he has a deadline approaching or a big proposal going on. Then he took a deep breath and put his hand down on the desk decisively. Nudging his wrist was the one personal item Dad keeps in his office: a sculpture of a white door with red graffiti over the front of it saying, *No nannies allowed!* It was the first and only artwork we had ever done together.

By the time I turned thirteen, Dad had caused seven nannies to quit by not getting home on time, forgetting to pay them regularly, and expecting them to work weekends. I had dispatched eleven. What can I say, they weren't up to the job. On the day nanny number nineteen threw a hissy fit and stormed out, Dad and I pulled out some clay and decided: no more. From then on, it's been just us. Or rather, just me.

"Dad, I don't want any more gifts," I whined. Dinner and the soon-to-be-bought dress were already more than I wanted. Tomorrow was the only day of the year I *didn't* want presents.

"It's not from me," he said quietly, looking away from me. He opened the bottom drawer in his desk—the only one that required a key. His movements were slow, almost pained. He lifted a small wooden box from the drawer and gently placed it on his desk. His hand trembled over the intricate carvings that decorated the lid.

My eyes began to sting and I had to blink quickly. Dad rarely allowed his emotions this kind of exposure. He raised his hand and, as it hovered in the air above the box, he made a fist and closed his eyes. It looked as if he were praying—something I knew he didn't do. I had only ever seen one thing make him look like that.

Finally, he looked up at me with a small smile. I blinked again.

"I was given instructions. I've waited seventeen years to give this to you. It's from Evelyn…It's from your mom."

My mouth gaped involuntarily. "But…how?"

Mom's death had been unexpected—a hemorrhage during childbirth that couldn't have been foreseen. She couldn't possibly have left something behind with instructions.

Dad pinched the bridge of his nose then rested his hand under his chin. "I honestly don't know, sweetheart. That night, after I came home from the hospital"—he motioned to the small box—"this was on the top of her chest of drawers. There was a note resting on it that said, *For our girl on her 17th birthday*." He took a deep breath. "Perhaps she was just organized; perhaps…I don't know…She was an extraordinary woman…She sensed things others couldn't."

"Are you saying you think she knew what was going to happen?"

"I'm not saying that, sweetheart," he said, absentmindedly caressing the box. "And anyway, that's not the point. She wanted you to have this and it was important to her that it be now." He pushed the box across the desk toward me, standing as he did. "I'll…uh…I'll give you some privacy."

He slipped into his shoes and quietly left me alone in the office. He had his hands in his pockets and looked so…alone. It occurred to me that Mom wouldn't be too impressed with where we had ended up.

The box was beautiful. It was a rich, dark mahogany with splices of illuminating gold breaking through. The carvings on the top were detailed and finely crafted to create not a picture but a pattern, a sequence of wispy feather tips. The artist in me appreciated it instantly.

I'd never been given a gift by my mother. She'd never made me warm milk, never wiped away my tears or put a Band-Aid on me. She hadn't saved me from the embarrassing outing with my nanny to buy my first bra, and she hadn't left me with a nifty stash of tampons in the bathroom cupboard that would never run out and that I'd never have to talk about. There were a lot of things I'd never get from her, but I'd accepted that a long time ago. Finally *receiving* something from her, something purposely left for me and only me, was…awkward.

I sat down in Dad's chair and ran my fingers over the top of the engravings as he had done. A shiver ran down my body. I wriggled in the chair and shook my hand out. "Get a grip, Vi."

When I opened the box, my heart sank. A tiny silver chain with a small amulet lay inside. The last time I'd seen my baby necklace, it had been tucked away in the trinket box on my dressing table. Apparently, Mom had it made for me while she was pregnant as some kind of good luck charm. In every one of my baby photos, I'm wearing this necklace. Dad had made sure Mom's wishes were followed—and then some.

Obviously, Dad had taken it from my dressing table. I started to wonder whether the rest of the contents of the box were from him, but then I dismissed the thought. He'd never felt the need for fake gifts before. It just wasn't his style.

I pulled two envelopes out of the box. Both were still sealed, though they were yellowed and worn with marks of consideration along the edges. It must have killed Dad to have known about them for seventeen years and not know what was inside them. I wondered how many times he had run his fingers along the seals, contemplating tearing them open. It was impressive that he hadn't succumbed.

I opened the first envelope. Inside was a page torn from a book. It was a poem.

You must love no-thingness,
You must flee something,
You must remain alone,
And go to nobody.
You must be very active

And free of all things.
You must deliver the captives
And force those who are free.
You must comfort the sick
And yet have nothing yourself.
You must drink the water of suffering
And light the fire of Love with the wood of the virtues.
Thus you live in the true desert.

It was pretty, I guess, in a sad and surprisingly religious kind of way. From what little I knew, Mom hadn't been religious. She'd hated anything that pigeonholed people's beliefs. I'd only been baptized because Dad's family had insisted and he liked the idea of my attending the same high school he had.

I opened the second envelope. Inside was a handwritten letter. The writing was confident: long letters, curling like old-fashioned calligraphy. My hands quivered slightly, holding the piece of paper last held by my mother.

My girl,

Happy 17th birthday. I wish I could be there with you, but I think if you are reading this…I am not. For that, I am sorry. The day your dad and I found out we were going to have a baby was the happiest day of my long life. I know the only day that will exceed that joy will be the day you are born—no matter how that day ends.

A big decision lies ahead. The burden of the covenant is a heavy one to bear. Choose with your heart, for I already know that you, my girl, must let your heart guide the way.

Believe in the unbelievable—for it will not wait for you—and know that nothing is ever as simple as good and evil, right and wrong. There are spirits in this world that are not like us, my girl. In their rightful place, they are wonderful and terrible, valiant and wicked—and that is okay, for we need both. Keep your eyes open, but do not trust everything they show you. Imagination is their highway; free will is ours.

Remember always, everyone has a place of perfect belonging, and if they leave that place without permission, sometimes they must be returned.

I love you. Please forgive me.
Mom

Methodically, I refolded the letter and the poem, placing them back into their respective envelopes, concentrating on each function carefully so as not to think beyond, focusing my mind to slow down and not go places I couldn't handle. Not yet. It was a skill I had taught myself through practice, practice, practice.

The last thing in the box was a wristband. It was made of thick leather, though it looked metallic, with some type of distressed silver finish. It was roughly an inch and a half wide and had similar engravings to the box. It was mesmerizing, more handsome than pretty. Beside it was an identical circular mark on the wooden base where the varnish had worn away. At some point, this box had held a twin to this band.

I picked up the wristband, ignoring the fact that my mouth and eyes were watering. My nose was running too, although I could swear I smelled perfume. Something floral? I wondered if it was *her* smell, impossibly contained in the box for all this time. I pushed the thought aside. And then, just as quickly, another took its place.

The letter. She'd known she was going to die.

No, I couldn't think about it. Not now. Dad would be back any minute. I needed to stay in control, not let this derail me. I wasn't sure what the letter meant anyway. *A big decision?* Maybe college? It could be anything. She probably just left it as a precaution—every mother wants her child to believe anything is possible. As for the bit about her long life, I didn't understand that. How could anyone think her life had been long? She was only twenty-five when I was born...when she died.

I wiped a hand under my runny nose and placed all of the items back in the box in the same order. When Dad came back, I'd packed it away into my bag and moved to the couch.

He hesitated. "Are you okay?" he asked.

"Yeah, good...fine...yep. There was a letter. Do you want to read it?" I really didn't want to give it to him. It was nice to have something of my own from her, even if it was strange, but I knew that seventeen years of suspense was enough torment for anyone.

Dad smiled, lines creasing in the corners of his eyes, but his shoulders dropped. "No, it's okay," he said.

Oh crap. I didn't know how to handle it if Dad actually cried. But he recovered, clearing his throat and tilting his head to the ceiling. "No, honey. It's between you and your mom. But…thank you for offering."

Apparently, the offer was enough.

"Well, like you said, I think she was just prepared. It was one of those…follow-your-heart letters." I said it like I got them all the time.

"Don't be cynical," he chastised me, though I knew he loved the fact that I was just as cynical as he was.

He sat next to me and put a hand on my knee. I put my hand on top of his. We were silent for a moment.

"So…" he said finally, as we both moved our hands away. "What are you doing tonight?"

"Going to Lincoln's. Got a wall to paint."

"Finally gave in, did he?"

"Yep." Victory was definitely sweet.

"Right…sure. So you'll be going there straight after this, then?" he asked, a lilt in his voice that normally meant he was about to tell me something I didn't want to hear.

"Yes," I said, dragging out the word.

"Oh, good. You know, actually, I bumped into Lincoln today when I was out getting a sandwich." His eyes drifted around the room and he stood up and went to his desk, suddenly very intent on a stack of papers.

"What did you do, Dad?" My heart skipped a few beats and I had an awful feeling I knew where this was going.

"Nothing. Nothing. We were just talking about you guys, you know, your training. Lincoln said you were running in a marathon next month with him. That sounds like fun." He strained a smile. "And…um…he asked me about work, which was nice of him and…you know…"

"No. You know *what?*"

"Well, I said, mentioned really, that you…well, that you'd been through a tough time at your old school and…ah, you know…that maybe he could bear that in mind…He *is* five years older than you, Vi. I just didn't want you to feel pressured. I didn't plan it, I just bumped into him and…Christ," he said, getting more and more flustered. "Your mother was on my mind and I thought she'd want me to, you know…*say* something."

Someone kill me now! From heartfelt moments to this!

I stood, moving to the far side of the room. The tension in the air was palpable. Neither one of us liked talking about the attack. In fact, talking about it was an agreed out-of-bounds. Even this slightest mention brought a familiar darkness into the room.

I stared at my feet, stubbing the toe of my sneakers into the carpet as if I could shift it if I concentrated enough. Why couldn't I be one of those kids with parents who actually knew what they were doing?

"You had no right," I said flatly.

"That's not entirely true, Violet. I *am* your father."

You picked a great time to start taking the reins.

"Dad, you're so far off the mark I can't even…Lincoln hasn't pressured me at all!" I grabbed my bag and heaved it onto my back. "WE'RE JUST FRIENDS! He's not even interested in me like that, and thanks to *you*"—I shook my head at him in utter disbelief—"he never will be now."

Dad's eyes went wide with surprise. Clearly he'd decided Lincoln and I were a couple.

"Oh…" He stumbled over his words, lost for any comeback.

Great, now my own dad thinks I'm pathetic.

"Oh…I just assumed. Sorry, Vi. I just…after everything that happened…I just worry."

I didn't respond.

"I'll stay out of things from now on," he added.

"I've gotta go. I'll see you tomorrow night," I mumbled, knowing that even though we lived under the same roof, we wouldn't be crossing paths before then—especially now.

"Yes! Great! I'm really looking forward to your birthday dinner. Meet at seven?" he asked overenthusiastically.

I was already heading for the door. I threw a hand in the air. "Whatever."

One good thing about Dad was that I knew he'd be happy to pretend this conversation never happened.

chapter three

"*There is an old illusion. It is called good and evil.*"

FRIEDRICH NIETZSCHE

I considered calling and making up some excuse to get out of going over to Lincoln's. But even though I didn't want to have to talk about the attack, I'd also decided a long time ago that I wouldn't let it rule my life. I wished Dad had kept his big mouth shut, but now that Lincoln knew, I wasn't going to run. It was one of the rules: I don't run and I don't quit. And since the attack, since the court case and changing schools, I'd stuck to them like a mantra. They were what got me through.

Even though I'd set a meandering pace, I was still early by the time I hit Lincoln's street, and I spotted him through the window of the corner shop. He had his back to me and was in training gear—black sweats and a white sleeveless T-shirt, which showed off his golden tan and sun-streaked brown hair. He had a covenant with the sun—unlike me, who it chased even under a cap and sunscreen. I took a moment, luxuriating in the rays of warmth that settled over me whenever he was around, and braced myself for what was ahead now that Dad had opened his trap.

I watched Lincoln loading food into a basket after first studying the nutrition table on the back of every package. All except my favorite cookies—he threw those in without a second glance. I took a breath for gumption and knocked on the glass, feeling a more nauseating version of the excitement I always felt in anticipation of seeing him. He turned, already smiling, as if he knew without looking that it was me, and despite my preparations, my breath caught and my stomach fluttered in a specific salute reserved solely for him. You'd think that after looking at his face almost every day for nearly two years, I'd be better at handling it.

Nope.

I scrutinized his smile, looking for signs of change as he put two fingers in the air to let me know he'd be a couple of minutes. When he turned his back, I stopped nodding like an idiot and wondered, for the millionth time, if he could see how awestruck I was. If he did, he never showed it. His smile hadn't given anything away either. It had been the same beautiful—platonic—smile as always.

Dusk fell while I loitered next to a couple of discarded milk crates—the makeshift break lounge for shop staff if the pile of cigarette butts around them was anything to go by. A cool evening breeze carried through the warm air and I turned to face it, closing my eyes, drawing it in. As I did, I became aware of the growing orchestra of crickets in the distance. It was that time of year when, even though there were no gardens in sight, their songs filled the night.

When I opened my eyes, orange streetlights were beginning to flicker on. The buildings that edged the pavement threw sharp, jagged shadows over the street, changing the mood instantly to a gloomy display of light overcome by shade. The mood snuck its way into me and I had to work to stop my mind from running away, from forcing me to relive things I didn't want to. But as soon as I pushed one disturbing thought aside, another took its place— namely my mother's wooden box. I was grateful I'd had so much practice compartmentalizing, because right now I didn't want to think about whether she might have known she was going to die. Yeah…not going there.

"All done." Lincoln was beside me and I hadn't even heard.

Not good, Vi.

I looked at him quickly, nervous to look for too long. "Hey. Are you cooking?"

"Yeah, I thought I might. Is that okay?"

"Sure. What's on the menu?" I said, tucking a few stray hairs behind my ear. We started to walk toward Lincoln's warehouse and I took one of the bags to lighten his load. Our fingers brushed briefly and it was enough to make my heart jump.

"Pasta, chicken, basil, feta," he said casually, listing the ingredients of my favorite pasta dish.

I bit my bottom lip. A sympathy meal.

Shit.

Walking into Lincoln's warehouse, a wave of contentment washed over me. It felt more like coming home than anywhere else. Lincoln had just bought it when we first met. It was small by warehouse standards but huge by one-person-living-alone standards. It was a dump when he got his hands on it, but he'd been gradually fixing it up, and—I had to hand it to him—he had good vision. He loved it. So did I. The most beautiful thing about it was the enormous arched windows at either end. During the day, they dropped waterfalls of light into the big open space, flooding it. It was the perfect place for art. That was one reason I loved it. The other had more to do with its occupant.

We silently unloaded the groceries in the kitchen. With every opening of the fridge or rustling of the plastic bags, my heart beat faster and I became more anxious, wondering what he was going to say. But he said nothing. Instead, he started piling up ingredients on the bench the way he always did and set about making dinner.

After he pulled out a chopping board and had everything ready to go, he looked up at me with raised eyebrows. "So…" He cleared his throat. "How was your day?"

I realized I had been standing silent and motionless in the middle of his kitchen like a lost kid. I unstuck my feet from the floor and walked over to the counter, resting my hip against it as casually as I could. "Fine. School was good. I got into the Fenton course."

Lincoln put down the knife and turned to me, grinning from ear to ear. My heart melted that he knew me so well, knew how much the course meant to me.

"Thank God! I was worried I was giving up my wall to an amateur," he teased, pulling me in for a hug. He smelled of baked sunscreen and his body radiated warmth. I relaxed into his arms. I loved the fact that I was the ideal height so that my head rested snugly into his shoulder. It was like we were two pieces of a jigsaw puzzle. We locked together perfectly. Of course, as soon as I relaxed, Lincoln was stepping away. It was just like the other million hugs we'd shared, and though every time I wished it meant more, his body language assured me it didn't.

"So," he said, "are you ready for the transfer of official ownership rights?"

"Yeah, definitely," I said, regrouping. "I was going to lay down a coat of primer first, if that's okay?"

"It's your wall—do with it as you please."

He smiled, turning back to his cutting board. I had been bugging him for over a year to let me paint a mural on one of his walls and had finally worn him down.

"How about we eat first?" he suggested. "I'm starving."

"Sure."

Could he truly be planning not to talk about it?

People always wanted to know the details. First it was the authorities. Then my supposed friends who wouldn't let me forget. Then it occurred to me—maybe he didn't care, didn't want to know. Before I let myself go down that slippery slope, I forced myself to decide. I either had to wait patiently to see if he said anything or just say it myself.

"I was fourteen," I blurted out.

Lincoln's eyes flashed up at me and his body paused for a moment, then he simply went back to chopping up the chicken. "Okay."

"I know Dad said something to you," I said more defensively than I had intended.

He looked up again, briefly. "We bumped into each other earlier, yes." Chop, chop, chop.

"Well?" I asked, increasingly confused. "Aren't you going to ask?"

"Do you *want* me to ask?" He threw the chicken into the frying pan and it sizzled and smoked.

"What does that mean?" I asked, tucking my hair behind my ears.

"It means there's a good reason you haven't told me about it before. If that reason still stands, then I don't want you to feel forced to tell me just because your dad said something in passing. We all have secrets, Violet. Trust me. We all have things we can't talk about."

He went back to his cooking, but then looked up again. "Anyway, you only do that thing with your hair"—he motioned to his own ear—"when you're worried. Nervous."

Wow. I hadn't seen that coming. Suddenly I had no idea what to say. I mean, I hadn't wanted him to know. I didn't want anyone to know. But now that he did, it felt weird not explaining as much as I could. And…if I ever wanted someone to know, it would be him. So now I was screwed because I didn't want to say anything…but I did.

Lincoln pulled the fresh pasta out of the boiling water and started tossing it through the cooked chicken, adding lemon, feta, and lots of basil. The aroma filled the air and I smiled, remembering the time he'd tried to grow his own basil in pots and failed dismally, killing all three plants within weeks and sending me into hysterical laughter. He got cranky any time it came up, and every time it made me laugh.

He sat me at the table and gave me a fork. I watched him eat. He watched me pick. I felt bad that I couldn't stomach much. He didn't complain though, just took the plates away and returned with a mug of coffee, which my hands went to like a magnet. Something about the bittersweet smell of roasted coffee beans always reminded me of when I was a little girl, when Dad actually made it home before I'd fallen asleep. He always smelled of coffee and day-old aftershave, and to me it was bliss. As soon as I could figure out how to use a coffeemaker, I started drinking coffee.

Finally, I looked up from my cup. "I want you to know."

His eyes watched me, my fingers gripping the mug tightly, my knee bouncing under the table.

"Are you sure?"

I nodded and willed myself to calm down, to go to that place, the one that would remove me just enough. It always starts the same way: choosing a spot to focus on—in this case, my coffee cup. Then I take a deep breath and steady myself so that when I start speaking, I'll be able to hold my tone, not crack and whimper.

"Who was he?" he said softly.

"A teacher from my old school."

"What happened?" he asked, treading carefully.

"He called me back after class to discuss an essay I hadn't done well on." And just allowing my mind to go there, allowing it the freedom I so rarely did, I was suddenly fourteen again, trapped in his classroom, trying pathetically to fight him off. I could feel his fingers digging into my arms, holding me down. Could see the look of relentless intent in his eyes; smell the cheap, spicy after-shave mixed into his slick, sweaty skin.

"Anyway," I said quickly, trying to jolt myself away from the images. "Another teacher walked in. It was weird, actually. She worked on the other side of the school and could never remember why she came all the way over. She said she just knew something was wrong and felt compelled to check that classroom."

"Wait. She said she felt *compelled*?" Lincoln asked, eyes wide.

"Yeah, something like that."

"Someone interfered," he said, almost to himself, shaking his head as if he couldn't understand. When he saw the question on my face, he snapped out of it. "What happened—I mean…to him?"

"He lost his job, can never work with kids again."

"That's why you'd just changed schools when we first met."

"Yeah." Becoming friends with Steph and starting kickboxing sessions with Lincoln had been my reasons to hope again. It was too embarrassing to admit to him that before I had them in my life, a cloud of nothingness surrounded me that I wasn't sure I would ever escape from.

He was quiet for a while, but I could hear his breathing deepen the way it does when he's upset. Then he asked what I knew he would. At least he tried to.

"Vi…did…did he?"

It's not easy asking someone outright if they've been raped. You would think it's just a question, but actually saying the words is different. It was a question I'd had the awful experience of watching a lot of people try to dredge up the courage to ask. Even people you'd think would remain completely matter-of-fact, don't.

"No. I mean, they stopped him in time but…" I stood. "I'll get more coffee."

While I hid in the kitchen, willing my hands to stop shaking, I heard Lincoln move to the living area. He was giving me some privacy. It helped.

When I finally joined him on the couch, without a word, he reached over and put an arm around me, pulling me in close for a moment. I relaxed and let my head rest against his chest, accepting what he was telling me in his own way—I was safe.

He pushed a strand of hair away from my face, tucking it behind my ear, and spoke quietly, his warm breath hovering over my neck. It smelled like sugared coffee. "I swear to you, he'll never hurt you again. You're…I'll never let him near you," he whispered. I believed him. Even if what we had was just friendship, I knew it was true. He knew me, got me. The way no one else had ever bothered to. He had always understood that I needed to be strong, that I couldn't run from things—even if, until now, he hadn't completely understood why. He never questioned it or made me feel stupid. Instead, he helped me, made me stronger.

"Linc?"

"Yeah."

"About the other thing my dad said to you." I cringed.

"What else is he supposed to think?" he asked, a smile in his tone. "You're over here all the time. If not training, we're hanging out. I'm surprised he hasn't warned me off sooner. It's good to see he's paying attention."

And like that, he finished it, simply and cleanly. But it only made me want him all the more and ask the question: *What else am I supposed to think?*

chapter four

"There are as many nights as days, and the one is just as long as the other in the year's course. Even a happy life cannot be without a measure of darkness, and the word 'happy' would lose its meaning if it were not balanced by sadness."

CARL JUNG

I loaded a paint tray with primer and set about starting on my wall. As much as I'd wanted to linger on the couch, the control freak in me won out. It was the best place for me to be right now—face to a wall, back to the world. It's one of the reasons I love painting so much.

I got into a good rhythm. But even a steady tempo couldn't push aside the memories. Tears streamed silently down my face. I hated that it could do that to me. Still.

Struggling to reach the higher parts of the wall, I started to lose patience. I could feel it all bubbling up and then a hand was on my arm and my whole body jolted in fear. It was a reaction I could not stop, and one that I hated myself for having—the reaction of a victim.

Lincoln's hand didn't release me. Instead, it moved softly down my arm and pried the paintbrush gently from my rigid hand.

"I'll do it."

"It's okay. I can—"

But he cut me off, moving around to face me. I couldn't look at him. "Let me look after you." He stroked my hair and I exhaled shakily, scared to let go. "Please. Just tonight. Before…" he said in barely more than a whisper. I glanced up and was caught by the intensity in his luminous green eyes. I felt my body melt in response. The last of the memories faded away.

"Before what?" I murmured.

He blinked and stepped away. "Nothing. Have you decided what you're going to paint yet?" He climbed onto the stool.

I sat on the floor and watched as he finished priming the wall, the muscles in his bronzed forearms flexing with each stroke. Just being around him made things better. It always did. I hadn't fully decided what I was going to paint, but I wanted it to resemble the way Lincoln's place always felt to me, and I guess I wanted him to know how he made me feel.

"Kind of. It's going to be like an…aura, I guess."

He looked down at me and raised an eyebrow. "Explain?"

"Like even though there are outside forces pushing through the walls, in here it's like a bubble of goodness. Like coming home." I could feel him smiling and it encouraged me to elaborate. "When I think of how others would see it, I imagine them seeing a force of goodness overshadowing a force of evil, protecting us."

Lincoln almost fell off the stool. He jumped to the floor with a look of shock.

I tried to reassure him. "Don't worry! It'll be subtle and soft, but not girly either. You'll really like it." Worried I was about to lose my wall before I even got started, I quickly added, "If you don't like it, I'll paint it back white for you. *Promise!*"

"No…No, it sounds great—perfect in fact. I was just surprised. To hear you explain it like that—the good and evil part. Do you…consider it much? Good and…evil?"

I blew out a breath of relief. I still had my wall.

"Umm…I don't know. Not really. I don't really know how I feel about the whole God issue." Although in truth I did. "You know I'm not religious."

How *could* I believe in God? What kind of bastard would leave me motherless the moment I was born? Would leave me alone in a room with a sicko who would mess with my mind forever? And that's just *me*; don't even get me started on the rest of the world. God? He's just for the very lost to question and the very found to praise.

He nodded as if he'd actually heard all the things I hadn't said. "Nor am I. But I believe there are forces of good and evil at work in our world and…beyond. I believe that between us and the 'God issue'"—he wiggled his fingers to indicate quote marks—"is another layer, so to speak."

"Another layer?" I asked.

"Like…" He jiggled his hands by his side, as if he was considering whether to go on. "Other realms, other…beings."

"*Really?*" I said, a little annoyed. "What is it with everyone and otherworldly stuff?"

"Huh? Has someone else been talking to you?" he asked, taking a sudden step toward me.

"No…well, kind of. My mom believed in spirits too, or something like that."

"Oh," he said, exhaling and moving back a little.

"So?" I prompted, keen to steer him away from the subject of my mother. "Do you believe these other *beings* or whatever are good?"

"Maybe. But with all things there has to be balance. You know, light and dark, sun and moon, yin and yang…So where there are entities that produce good, there must also be those that don't."

"You mean evil?" I asked, feeling confused.

"Maybe it's not as clear-cut as that. Maybe it's the very presence of one thing—light or darkness—that necessitates the existence of the other. Think about it—people couldn't become legendary heroes if they hadn't first done something to combat darkness. Doctors could do no good if there weren't diseases for them to treat." His eyes focused on me, willing me to understand. When he saw he wasn't about to be rewarded, he gave a half laugh and smiled, putting a hand out to pull me up from the floor.

I stood and took the paintbrush from his hand. "Is it okay if I say I have absolutely *no* idea what you're talking about?"

"You will," he said softly, turning toward the kitchen before I could see his face.

After he helped me clean the brushes and I helped him tidy up the kitchen, I grabbed my bag and he grabbed his keys at the same time, and we paused to smile at each other briefly. I loved that we had this—whatever it was. We didn't have to talk about things; we had our own little routine. I knew without asking that he would drive me home, and he knew without asking that I would let him.

When he pulled his four-wheel-drive up outside my apartment complex he cut the engine and turned to me.

"I'm okay," I said before he could ask.

He nodded and smiled grimly. "Are we going for a run in the morning?"

"I have an early shopping date with Steph."

I was glad I had a legitimate excuse to get out of a ten-kilometer run for once.

Lincoln gave a smooth laugh. "Aha, birthday shopping."

"Yes, and don't start. I'm relying on you to let tomorrow go by without paying me any attention at all."

"I promise I won't even be nice to you."

He was lying.

"Good."

So was I.

chapter five

"Are you up to your destiny?"

WILLIAM SHAKESPEARE

"It is time for you to know." The words floated through the air, almost surrounding me before reaching me.

"To know what?" I asked disjointedly.

"Who you are."

The man in my dream stepped toward me. I didn't recognize him, even though he seemed so familiar. His face was structured around a chiseled jawline. I would have said he was handsome but for his eyes. They were so distant. They made him look separate from this world, disconnected.

"And who am I?"

I was wearing sweats and a once-white T-shirt that now resembled more of a paint palette. A canvas sat on an easel in front of me. A paintbrush was in my hand.

"You are you and you are me. You are the Keshet."

He was standing by the window in my art studio, looking out at a clouded, gray sky. He seemed disappointed with what he saw. It was normal for me. The weather always seemed a little gloomy in my dreams.

"I'm you?" My voice rang with an echo like bells. My words, like his, seemed to float invisibly and effortlessly between us.

"Partly. You are part human as well."

My hand moved absently over the canvas.

"You're not human?" I could smell flowers. I knew the smell well. I loved lilies, especially white lilies. They were strong and beautiful. I'd always been drawn to them.

"No."

"What are you?"

He glided toward me. It didn't occur to me to move away.

"The question is not, what are we. Rather, what are we to become?" He extended his hand, index finger pointed.

"What are you doing?" I asked.

"Waking you up!" His finger morphed into a claw, lion-like, and lashed out at me. I stumbled back.

He was gone. My hand still held the paintbrush. Before me, a smear of colors. Red at the top followed by orange, yellow, green, blue, indigo, and violet. It reminded me of…a rainbow.

I woke up, disoriented for a few moments. I rolled over to look at my alarm clock—1:00 a.m. I was officially seventeen. Apparently, my first gift was a walk in the world of weird dreams. I rolled back over and sandwiched my head between two pillows. *Happy birthday, Violet.*

When I woke again, it was morning and my shoulder ached. I instinctively grabbed at it, then sucked in a breath and bolted upright. I prodded the angry red scratch with a finger. It was no more than an inch long, but it was raw and weeping and it hurt like hell. Images of my dream kept replaying in my mind. It couldn't be. I must have done it in my sleep somehow.

After a quick shower, I headed straight for the espresso machine. It was no surprise to see that at 6:00 a.m., Dad had already left for the day. *Happy Birthday* written on a Post-It was the only evidence he had been home at all.

I sat down with my first cup of coffee and that's when I saw them. The veins on the inside of my forearms looked different. I peered closer. They seemed darker than usual and there were *more* of them—if that was even possible. I'd never recalled the pattern being that intricate; it was almost as if they were interwoven. I shook my head. First my dream and now this. Maybe I was getting sick? Perfect. I could totally imagine spending the whole day shopping with Steph while feeling tragic.

With my second cup of coffee, I headed to my art studio in the spare room. I tried to start a new canvas, but I kept stopping to look at my veins. In the end, I found myself back in bed, reading my mother's letter one more time before packing it away again and storing the box under my bed.

Out of sight. Out of mind.

chapter six

"*Now the deeds of the flesh are evident, which are immorality, impurity, sensuality.*"

GALATIANS 5:19

I pressed number twelve and looked over at Steph as the doors closed. She bounced up and down, making the elevator bounce with her. My stomach dropped. I hated that feeling.

"I am *so* excited about tonight!"

Why Steph was so excited about my birthday was beyond me. I closed my eyes and leaned against the mirrored wall, wishing it were tomorrow and my birthday were a thing of the past. I'd let Steph drag me around looking at dresses the whole afternoon when all I really wanted was for the day to be done.

"I'm glad someone is," I replied.

"Cheer up! Your dad is taking us to one of the coolest restaurants in town. It's the absolute place to go. God *knows* how he managed to get a reservation," she said, batting her eyelids.

Of course, I knew Steph had helped arrange the booking. Her brother, Jase, was a DJ. He could usually get us in anywhere.

"Plus," she added deviously, "I'm sure Lincoln will be there to give you a birthday kiss!"

I sighed. Even though I'd invited Lincoln to meet us after dinner, I wasn't sure he'd come. He wasn't that keen on social gatherings, and I'd told Steph a million times he wasn't interested in me like that. But she persisted anyway.

"Steeeeeph..." I dragged out her name in warning.

She ignored me. "I know you're crazy about him. And I've seen the way he watches you when you're not looking. There is *definitely* something there."

If only she were right.

"If you want him, you have to, you know...make a move. You need to let him know what he's missing out on. Use your...assets."

She meant my boobs. Steph was always telling me that I had it, so I should flaunt it. But I preferred to focus on other things, like my high cheekbones, full lips, and creamy complexion. And, of course, my long hair, which I could hide behind when I needed refuge.

The elevator doors opened in time for my escape. I wasn't about to start wearing super low-cut tops just to get Lincoln's attention. Steph had her style; I had mine. Admittedly, my "style" meant that I was now suspended in a whopping chasm of nothing-but-friends.

Inside the apartment, I dropped the shopping bags in my room and headed for the kitchen. It was white with stainless-steel appliances that sparkled from lack of use—all except for the espresso machine, which was always switched on and running hot. I set about making us coffee while Steph shadowed me.

"What do you want me to do?" I said, throwing my hands in the air. "He just wants to be friends!"

It was becoming irritating having to explain to people that Lincoln wasn't interested in me. And apart from the obvious reason why there was no way I was going to make a move, I didn't want to risk losing what we already had. If I didn't have Steph and Lincoln, I had no one.

"Well, now that you mention it, I *might* have had an idea," Steph said, smiling a smile I knew all too well. It usually meant disaster.

I rolled my eyes. "Dare I ask?"

Steph made herself comfortable on one of the stools at the breakfast bar. I stared at her, waiting for an answer. She blew on her coffee, stalling.

"Ever heard the phrase, 'candy is dandy but liquor is quicker'?"

Great, she wanted me to get drunk. "Ah…ever heard of *underage*?"

"Where there's a will, there's a way," she said matter-of-factly.

"That's your great plan?"

She put down her cup, shook her head at me, and gave an exaggerated sigh, as if to say, *What am I going to do with you?*

"Just a couple of drinks and you can ask him outright. If he says he just wants to be friends, then sure, it's embarrassing, but you can pass it off as having had a few too many and pretend it never happened and you guys can go back to your weird adventure-sports friendship. *But*, if he says something else, then…" She threw her arms wide. "Voilà!"

I had to admit, it had possibilities.

————

When the doormen opened the black glossy doors for us on our arrival at Hades, I had to confess that despite all my complaining, I was feeling pretty good in my new little black dress. It was the back—or rather, the *lack* of one—that was the feature. It started from just above my butt, daringly low, my entire back bare except for two thin straps. Steph had taken care of everything, even giving me a pair of stick-on boob cups as a birthday gift. At first I didn't believe they'd work, but after a few attempts at positioning that left us both crying with laughter, they actually stayed put and even I was amazed when I looked in the mirror. To top off the outfit, my dark hair was tied back in a sleek ponytail that fell in a straight line down my back.

We walked in to find the place already packed with people. I spotted Dad on the far side of the restaurant, waving like an idiot. Steph eyed our hot waiter as he escorted us to the table, which was nestled beneath countless stunning chandeliers in a section that was rimmed with a mass of long, luxurious scarlet drapes. As we followed, the waiter spun around to catch Steph gawking at his backside. He gave her a wink, obviously well practiced in the art of keeping the customer happy while gunning for big tips. Steph, of course, lapped it up.

Out of the corner of my eye, I noticed a waitress with bright-red hair over in the bar area. She looked familiar.

"You look beautiful, Violet," Dad said, standing up as we approached. "You too, Steph. Red is definitely your color."

Steph smiled. Her red minidress was a tribute to the eighties. She had a knack for making new look retro, and with her slim figure and edgy white-blond hair, she could always effect the dramatic.

"Come on then," Dad chirped at me. "Give us a spin." He twirled a finger in the air.

I turned around with my hands on my waist, lingering to let them appreciate the back view of the dress. When I returned to face them, sporting a mock model pose, I froze. Lincoln had appeared out of nowhere. He wore a sexy smile and looked gorgeous in black jeans and an untucked black shirt. I turned quickly to Steph, who was beaming from ear to ear, totally aware of my shock. My eyes darted to the table and I saw what I should have noticed immediately—four chairs and two open beer bottles.

Dad was grinning stupidly with his "I made her" look. It wasn't that dissimilar from the look he gave buildings he'd designed. "Steph, you did good, kid." He glanced around the room and added, "Would've done even better if you'd managed to find her a shawl too."

Steph rolled her eyes before she leaned over and whispered in my ear. "Oh sorry, did I forget to mention that I invited him to dinner too? Oops." She batted her eyelids innocently.

I looked at Lincoln and he smiled back at me, sending my stomach into a frenzy.

"Hey," I said, failing to keep the surprise out of my voice.

41

"Hey. I was in the bathroom," he said, as if that explained everything.

"Yeah, sure. It's good to…thanks for coming." *"Thanks for coming"? Can I be any more infantile?*

Lincoln looked down at the table and cleared his throat. "You look…that dress is stunning." His eyes flashed up at me and quickly away again. My heart skipped a beat and I blushed.

Dad and Lincoln pulled out chairs for us to sit. While looking over the menu, I took a deep breath. Lincoln and Dad had been alone. God knows what was said before Steph and I got there. I needed to calm down—*big time*. Steph's idea of alcohol was becoming more and more appealing.

After our drinks arrived and we'd ordered, Dad excused himself to go to the bathroom. Steph waited approximately one microsecond before reaching under the table into her bag. She flashed a small bottle of vodka at me along with a wicked grin. After taking a big slurp of her orange juice, she slid it off the table, topped it up with vodka, and then returned it, casually stirring her straw. She looked at me with wide eyes. My turn.

I glanced at Lincoln. A questioning look crossed his face. *What the hell.*

I took a gulp and passed my lemonade to Steph. I didn't look in her direction again but I could feel the satisfaction oozing from her. Given half the chance, she would have jumped up and done a victory dance.

Despite my initial nervousness, everyone chatted easily over dinner. Dad quizzed Steph on her college preferences, and Steph and Lincoln enjoyed their usual teasing banter. The main course was delicious, dessert even better—apart from the embarrassing attempt the waiters made at putting a candle in my soufflé and singing "Happy Birthday." Watching the soufflé sink as they sang pretty much encapsulated the way I felt about birthdays. I was at least starting to feel more relaxed thanks to Dad ducking outside for a phone call, allowing for another heavy-handed top-off à la Steph.

"It's generally not a fifty-fifty pour, Steph," Lincoln said wryly.

"Don't worry, Lincoln," she teased. "There's plenty left. Do you want some?"

He shook his head, but he was fighting the urge to smile as he looked at me. "Someone has to keep up the conversation with Violet's dad."

For a second I worried that Lincoln would think we were immature, but one look at Steph and we both burst out laughing.

As soon as Dad returned, he paid the bill and proceeded to fidget, checking his watch repetitively. Dad was too easy to read.

"Work problems?" I asked.

He nodded. "Do you mind? I really have to get in to the office and sort something out." He was already standing as I nodded to let him off the hook.

Dad said his good-byes, apologizing for his early departure and adding a little theater for Steph and Lincoln's benefit—acknowledging that since he was "officially the oldest person in the place," it may not be such a bad thing. Of course, Lincoln dutifully promised to see me home safely—not that Dad had thought to ask.

We settled into a luxurious chaise and ordered more drinks. Music pumped through the bar area, which faced onto the dance floor. I could see why Jase liked working at this place—the DJ pit was huge, with state-of-the-art decks and a captive audience in the bar. DJ heaven.

"Hi, Violet!" the waitress called out over the music when she delivered our drinks.

I looked up.

Shit.

It was the girl I'd noticed earlier. It was one of those awful moments when, for the life of you, someone's name just won't come into your head. She had been a couple of years ahead of us at school and she'd taken the same community art course as me last year during the holidays. I knew she was a painter/sculptor, that she came from a big family, and was quiet but nice. I stared at her for a moment too long, willing her petite frame and bright-red hair to trigger my memory.

"Hi!" I said, a ridiculous smile plastered on my face before shooting a desperate glance at Steph. She never forgets a name. She never forgets anything.

Steph shimmied forward on her chair. "Hey, *Claudia*!" she yelled.

"So, you work here," I said, relaxing a little.

"Yeah." She shrugged. "I'm working a couple of night jobs, wait-ressing. Good tips, you know."

She piled our empty glasses onto her tray. Her eyes darted to Lincoln.

"Oh, sorry. Claudia, this is Lincoln."

They nodded at each other. Claudia turned back to me with an approving look. She'd obviously assumed Lincoln was my boyfriend. I smiled, enjoying the pretense.

"Well, have a good night." She glanced at our drinks knowingly.

"Thanks," I said, suddenly paranoid we'd shortly be escorted from the premises.

Steph just shrugged it off, saying Claudia wouldn't care, and proceeded to enhance our drinks as soon as she was out of sight. Lincoln, who had now moved on to Coke, seemed less than impressed. When Steph jiggled the bottle in his direction, he just shook his head and leaned back on the couch.

It didn't take long before Steph spotted her brother with some of his friends and went to join them at the bar. Her attempts at subtlety were flawed—as was her balance, I noted.

Lincoln and I were finally alone. This was my chance. I was freaking out. I grabbed my half-filled glass and drained it. Lincoln snatched the empty glass from my hand. I couldn't help giggling.

"What's going on with you, Vi? You've been acting strange all night," he said, sounding older than he was.

"Lincoln," I said in mock disapproval. "It's my birthday! Excuse me if I've *finally* given in and am trying to have a good time."

He looked at me for a moment. "I was hoping we might get a chance to talk about...things."

"Oh." He actually looked sincere, damn it. Defensive banter was all I had going for me right now. I slumped back against the couch and one of my dress straps slid down my shoulder.

Lincoln suddenly leaned forward. "What happened?" he asked, gesturing to my mysterious red scratch. I had forgotten about it, but as soon as he mentioned it, it began to sting.

"Um…I don't know. I can't remember doing it. It's possible it happened in a dream," I said. I realized I was slurring my words a little.

His eyes flickered as he studied me. "Anything else?"

"What?"

"I mean, has anything else…changed since turning seventeen?"

I laughed. "Not really. No wrinkles yet. No, no changes…" But then I remembered. "That is, unless the veins in my arms going a weird color count," I said with a tipsy shrug. The moment I said it, I wished I hadn't.

Lincoln grabbed my arm in a move so fast I barely saw it. He was unusually rough; I was certain it would leave a bruise. He inspected my veins in the dim light. They now looked a strong, steely, aqua color. He ran his fingers over the intricate patterns, studying them until I began to feel vaguely uncomfortable.

I wriggled. "Umm, Linc. I was only joking. Can I have my arm back?"

He released my arm and I held it close to my body a little self-consciously, rubbing the spot he had grabbed.

"Did this happen today?" He sounded worried, and frankly,

now so was I. This conversation was not going in the direction I had intended.

"I think so. Don't worry; it's nothing."

"You're probably right," he said, running his eyes over the rest of my body. He bit his bottom lip and pushed a hand through his hair. I watched, fascinated. He wasn't usually the nervous type.

"Well," he started, heading toward an obvious subject change, "I know you didn't want a birthday present…" He saw the look of horror on my face and held up a hand to stop the protest that was about to fly out of my mouth. "So I'm not giving you anything. *But*…I might have installed a new espresso machine at the warehouse."

I couldn't hide my delight. Badgering him to get a proper espresso machine fell second only to bugging him to let me paint one of his walls. Without thinking, I threw myself into his arms. "Oh my God, I love you!"

His arms instinctively wrapped around me, but I felt him tense as soon as my words registered. He wasn't the only one. My stomach flipped over so fast it was like a spin cycle on a washing machine. Did he hear? *Of course he heard!* Everyone hears *those* words.

He pulled back from the hug. His mesmerizing green eyes fixed on me, searching out the meaning of my words. I did the only thing I could; I looked straight back at him and pretended I'd never said them. His hands slid to my hips and lingered. I could feel his heat through the thin fabric of my dress. My breath quickened as I silently willed, prayed, begged him not to let go. But as I pressed closer, his hands suddenly dropped from my sides, and without further ado, the great walls of Lincoln were once again intact.

"You're welcome," he said kindly as much as cruelly, ignoring the slip of tongue we both knew he'd heard.

My cheeks burned and I looked away. I could sense Lincoln shifting back, distancing himself.

A guy sitting at the bar caught my eye. He didn't look much older than me, though I couldn't see him that well. Dressed all in black, he kind of melted into the dim light. Every girl around him seemed to be turned in his direction but he didn't appear to care. He was watching me. Fixedly. I was, for a moment, entranced, as he tilted his drink ever so slightly in my direction. I blushed even redder. I always felt awkward when strangers looked at me, *really* looked at me, the way this guy was.

I turned back to Lincoln. Steph was right—I needed to take control of this situation before it drove me insane. I jumped up and grabbed his hand, pulling him toward the dance floor.

"What are you doing?" he asked.

"I'm going to dance. I—" I stumbled in my high heels.

Lincoln grabbed my elbow to steady me. "You're a terrible drunk," he said, but he couldn't help the small smile.

I tried for a serious face. "I'm tipsy," I corrected, "and it's my birthday and I want to dance. Come on, Linc, it won't kill you."

When we reached the barrier of people surrounding the dance floor, I noticed again the stranger at the bar, sitting dead still, examining me. The base of my neck tingled.

The dance floor was crowded, but we made it through the crush of bodies to the center. The music had a good beat and it was fun to let go. I slipped an arm around Lincoln's waist. When I looked up, he was watching me. He kept a hand on my bare back, splayed and careful, the pads of his fingers pressing cautiously into my skin. His touch burned and my heart pounded.

I started to move my other arm around Lincoln's waist to bring our hips together. He pulled away abruptly, signaling he needed a drink and disappearing to the bar. Perfect. I bit down on my lip, humiliation flooding through me. Was that my answer?

Looking for an escape, I spun around and slammed straight into someone. I felt a weird buzz run through my body as I put my arm on his to balance myself. I must've had more to drink than I realized.

The stranger leaned his head close to my ear. "I was watching you from across the room. You radiate."

Only then did I realize it was the guy from the bar. His voice, low and dark, sent shivers down my body. He was strangely familiar and I wasn't freaked out by him the way I normally would be by a guy I didn't know. Plus, it was nice to know at least *someone* was attracted to me—though "radiate" wouldn't have been my first choice for a pickup line.

I knew it was childish of me to flirt with someone just to get back at Lincoln, but I did it anyway. "Thanks," I said, looking up at him from under lowered lashes.

Despite my cringe-worthy rejection status, the music started to drown out my thoughts, and dancing with a stranger—albeit one who appeared to be wearing a very floral scent for a guy—was not…awful. I was distantly aware that he was starting to move his hands up from my hips, and when he slid them over my bare back, I couldn't stop the gasp. Everywhere his hands went, they left sparks, like mini electric shocks, that lingered on my skin after his hands had moved on. I knew on some level I should move away, but for some reason I didn't. Before I could work out why, Lincoln was there, ripping the guy off me.

He swore and his green eyes flashed with fury. The guy only seemed amused and took a step toward him. For a second I thought Lincoln was going to hit him, but then he just put his arm around my waist and forced me back behind him.

"Get away from her. She's not interested," he growled, his tone more threatening than I had ever heard him use before. He was right too; I wasn't interested. At least, I didn't think so. I *had* only being dancing with the guy to make Lincoln jealous, hadn't I? But Lincoln was acting like he was actually dangerous.

The guy just stood there smiling, an odd light reflecting off his dark hair. "It didn't look like that to me," he said, completely at ease.

Looking into Lincoln's thunderous face, I was suddenly sobered. *What is going on?*

"I have to go." I turned and walked toward our table. Lincoln was right behind me.

"Where's Steph? I just want to go," I said, unable to look him in the eye. I could sense all my good-time feelings flattening around me like a badly constructed house of cards. Lincoln put his jacket on and shoved his hands in his pockets. Body language 101.

"She left while you were…dancing. Said she'd call you tomorrow. Did you know that guy?"

I could feel the anger radiating from him. "No," I mumbled.

"You shouldn't have let him near you! You need to be more careful. Did he do anything? Say…anything?"

I grabbed my bag and swung around. Lincoln was right behind me. "I…he…" I couldn't think straight with him so close. "I'm going."

I made my way for the door, pushing through the sea of bodies that stood between me and fresh air.

We walked home in silence. I stayed half a pace ahead, sucking in deep breaths of cooling air, trying to clear my head. I'd had enough embarrassment.

"Linc, you can go!" I finally snapped. "I don't need a babysitter. Consider yourself off duty."

He stepped in front of me, blocking my path. "Why are you doing this? Throwing yourself at that…He could've hurt you!" He spat the words at me.

That did it. "I was dancing, Lincoln, not *throwing* myself at him! I was having fun."

He gave a humorless laugh. "*That's* having fun? He had his hands all over you."

A blush crept over me. He was exaggerating, but I knew I'd gotten carried away. It was weird, but it hadn't actually felt like I'd been in control. Not that I was about to admit that to Lincoln, who was standing in front of me, heaving like he was about to blow a fuse.

"I was *actually* about to push him away when you decided to intervene and treat me like a seven-year-old," I said, and then I just couldn't stop myself. "And anyway, what if he *did* have his hands all over me? What's it to you?"

There. The question. Well, as close as I was going to get to it.

Lincoln stared at me with green eyes that deepened to emerald in the dark. I stared straight back at him, refusing to look away, even as I felt my breathing quicken and my heart race.

I waited for what seemed like eternity until he said, "Vi, I...you... don't do this."

I could feel, almost *see*, rejection rampaging its way down the street. He was right. I couldn't do this.

"Yeah, friends. Forget it, Linc."

I couldn't believe I'd let Steph talk me into putting myself out there. Lincoln wasn't interested in me. Now I'd basically made him spell it out for us both. *Bravo, Vi.*

I pushed past him. He grabbed my hand and swung me back toward him. Then he pushed me against the wall and...he kissed me.

He ran his thumb along my jawline and down my throat, hips pinning me to the wall. He kissed me slowly and with intensity, and once I got over the mind-numbing shock and realized what was actually happening, it was incredible. I had never been kissed like that before. We melted together. Every movement of mine was somehow perfectly mirrored by his. My heart was pounding so hard I knew he must have been able to feel it, and I was sure my legs were giving way, but he held me up, pushed me harder against the wall.

I grabbed a handful of his hair, remembering all the times I'd dreamed of doing it. I let my hand drift down his back and pulled him even closer to me. It all happened so quickly. I heard him make a low kind of growl and lean into me. His hand slid down my leg and behind my knee, drawing it to him. I moaned and felt him tense. Suddenly he dropped me so fast I had to freaking brace my hands on my knees to steady myself.

He spun around and walked away, running his hands through his hair. I was glad to see that at least I wasn't the only one who needed a minute to compose myself. Finally, he turned to face me.

"I'm sorry, Vi. I shouldn't have…I just couldn't…looking at you…" He flung a hand toward me. "That dress. Watching that creep put his hands on you. I…Damn it! I'm sorry."

It was hard to know if I should be happy or sad. "I'm not. Sorry, that is. I know you felt that."

"We can't have this conversation."

"Linc, *please*, tell me I'm not crazy."

He looked at me and smiled almost painfully. "You're not crazy. We just…can't."

"Why?" I looked at him, my eyes begging him to hold me again. I was sure, in that instant, he wanted to be holding me too. But as I watched, his face shut down.

"It's complicated. You'll understand soon. Sooner than you realize. I shouldn't have been so reckless, so selfish. I'm sorry." He looked down at his feet like a guilty child. I think it was the third time he'd apologized. Not the most encouraging sign.

"Linc, I have no idea what you're talking about. I actually thought that was kind of unbelievable as far as kisses go." I was glad we were in the dark and he couldn't see me blushing.

He made a sound somewhere between a sigh and a growl of frustration. He pulled me in for a hug, which I fell into, feeling crushed. I had the strangest feeling we were stealing this moment and no matter how tightly I held on, it wouldn't help. Lincoln's next words were soft and perhaps not even meant for me, but they burned their way right into my soul.

"Did you ever think we would be anything other than unbelievable?"

chapter seven

"A lie would have no sense unless the truth were felt as dangerous."

ALFRED ADLER

"OH MY GOD! Then what…?" Steph was hyperventilating over the phone. I cringed and put a hand to my head.

"Then…he walked me home and barely said good night before he bolted."

"What? That's it? Are you holding out on me? I don't understand!" she exclaimed, ramping up the pitch with each question.

"Neither do I."

I wanted to cry. Now, not only did I know I wanted him, but I knew there was a part of him that wanted me too, and together we were amazing.

"Oh, Vi, don't worry, you guys will sort it out one day. Maybe he's just worried about the age difference or he's scared of hurting you or something."

It was a possibility, and I clung to it like the last life vest on the *Titanic*. I didn't buy into the age-difference crap; five years wasn't that much. But the other theory was possible. Maybe after everything he'd found out about me, he didn't know how to be with me that way. Maybe he thought *I* wouldn't want to be with him. It was a stretch, but I had nothing else.

"Steph, I've got to go. I have to go see him. I'm sick of this. One way or another, I need to know what's going on."

"Well, about time! I expect a full play-by-play later. Bye. Oh—take an umbrella."

An umbrella was an understatement. By the time I stepped outside, the rain was torrential. My plan of figuring out my whole speech while I walked to Lincoln's flew out the window as I opened the door to a cab. Suddenly I only had a few minutes to compose myself and map out a quick strategy.

I knew I needed to find out exactly why he didn't want to be with me. Even if it was going to be the most humiliating experience of my life, it had to be done. I couldn't keep pretending this thing between us wasn't there. If he was worried about my past, I knew I could assure him I wasn't scared to be with him. That was categorically one thing I *could* do.

I looked at my watch as the cab pulled up outside Lincoln's. It was midday. I remembered that he and I were supposed to have gone for a run this morning. It dawned on me that he hadn't showed to pick me up—or even called. My stomach twisted with doubt. I considered hailing another cab and just going straight back home. As much as I didn't want to consider it, I couldn't ignore the other possibility, the one I had been trying not to think about. Now that Lincoln knew my secrets, did he think I was damaged goods?

Here I was, in the pouring rain, trying to figure out how to make something happen between us, while he was probably avoiding me. I took cover in the alcove beside his front steps. It didn't really help—even with my umbrella, it was useless. The rain was coming in sideways. My favorite *Alice in Wonderland* T-shirt was soaked. Thankfully, it was black rather than white.

I just needed a moment. I wasn't going to run away, but taking a few minutes to pull myself together was allowed. I rested my head against the alcove wall and concentrated on simply…breathing.

I heard Lincoln's front door click open.

Tucked under the umbrella, I could only see two pairs of feet standing above me, just inside his door. The familiar Adidas sneakers I knew were Lincoln's, and there was also a well-worn pair of black Blundstones. I hesitated at the sharp sound of an unfamiliar male voice.

"She *must* be told. You've gotten too close, Lincoln. Remember *who* you are, *what* you are. Remember what she is!"

Lincoln sounded urgent, pleading. "She's not ready! There are things we didn't know about her. She needs more time."

"Her or you?" the stranger said crisply. "Violet has come of age; she must decide, as we all have. You know this—that's why you're here."

My stomach was sinking. I stayed quiet—apart from my thudding heart—mushroomed under my umbrella like any passerby taking a moment to rest.

"Griffin, her life will change forever. You don't know her like I do," Lincoln said quickly.

Griffin wasn't happy. I heard him tapping the doorframe impatiently. "You're not looking at this properly. You've lost faith in her. Or is it something else? Is it that *you* want to play protector to her, rather than allow her to become a protector?"

"Protector"? What the hell?

They were both silent for a moment and I thought they must have noticed me. I held my breath, but then Lincoln spoke again.

"Fine, have it your way, but not today. Give me a few days. Finding out you're part angel is a lot to take in, let alone the rest. I don't want Violet to panic when she realizes her whole world is going to change."

I couldn't be sure if I was breathing. It was all happening in some bizarre virtual reality and I wasn't in control. I let the umbrella slide out of my hand as I stepped toward the base of the steps. Lincoln was in the doorway, his back to me. The other man, Griffin, saw me instantly and met my eyes with recognition—the kind that said he knew I'd heard everything. The kind that said he knew exactly who I was.

He looked back to Lincoln. "I'm sorry, Lincoln, but today's going to be the day after all. It seems it's now out of both of our hands."

"Well, I won't do it," Lincoln snapped, still not realizing I was behind him. "I won't tell her!" He punched the door so hard it splintered and caused me to flinch.

I took a step up, realizing in that instant that everything had changed. Somehow I knew I could never go back.

"Too late," I said.

chapter eight

"The Angel said, 'Let the one who does wrong, still do wrong,
and the one who is filthy still be filthy; and let the one who is
righteous, still practice righteousness.'"

REVELATIONS 22:11

It felt like hours passed as Lincoln and I stood, staring at each other.
Images of that first day we met, of us just *accidentally* meeting in that
self-defense class, flashed into my head. Had everything been a lie?

I had to get away. I turned and stumbled toward the street. My
umbrella was still open, dangling by my side. I was glad for the rain
now. It covered the tears streaming down my face.

"Violet, wait!" Lincoln called out to me, running down the stairs.

I stopped but didn't turn.

"I can explain!" he yelled over the rain.

It felt like the skies were crying for me. "Fine! Explain!" I yelled
back, still not turning to face him. How could I ever look at him
again knowing that it was all lies—and I was more sure of it by the

second, sure that the whole time he had known me he'd been lying to me.

"We're called Grigori. We are part angel, part human. It happens soon after we're born, but we only come of age when we turn seventeen. The same way you're coming of age now."

I spun to face him, desperate to prove to myself that this was all some sick joke. Droplets of water fell from the tips of his hair and pooled in the crease of his lips. He looked amazing, which just made everything worse.

"You're insane!" I yelled in a shaky voice. Oh my God, was he delusional? What had I missed? Usually, I had a good psycho radar.

"I wouldn't lie to you about this," he said, his eyes pleading.

"No? Just about everything else then!" I spat the words at him, literally, sprays of water flying from my lips as I spoke. I looked around for an escape, for salvation. The streets were deserted; no one was stupid enough to be outside. "How do you know I'm one of these 'Grig' whatever, anyway?"

"Grigori. It happened when you were born and your mother died. If a parent dies within twelve days of his or her child's birth, the combination of new life coinciding with new death creates a gateway for an angel to impart a piece of its essence."

"That doesn't explain how you know about me!"

He looked back at Griffin as if seeking support. Griffin did not move from the shelter of the doorframe. Lincoln turned back to me, arms wide. "I know because an angel told me. I know because we all have a destined partner, someone who is already a Grigori…or will become one. I know because…you're my partner, Violet."

He dropped his head and I knew this was bad.

Bad, bad, bad.

He put a hand on my shoulder. "Please…come inside. We'll explain everything."

I wanted to run, to scream, to cry, to do something, anything, but I needed to know. My brain urged me to call it what it was: *bullshit.* I mean, this stuff just doesn't happen, not in real life, and last I looked, I wasn't in some twisted sci-fi flick. The problem was, my mind was screaming one thing while some other part of me was holding me back, grinding me to a heavy halt. Something in my gut, the place I had learned to trust, that place I had always credited with instinct and intuition. And then there was my mother's letter, her words taunting me: *There are spirits in this world*…Could this really be true?

I pushed Lincoln's hand off my shoulder and moved past him, for the first time not wanting to feel his touch or look into his eyes.

Griffin stood in the doorway, waiting. I stopped in front of him, staring daggers. "Am I what he says?"

Griffin looked straight at me, holding my gaze easily. "We are *all* what he says."

I don't know how or why, but looking into his eyes, I suddenly knew it was true. It was as if he had penetrated the deepest layers of my natural defenses and unearthed a truth buried deep within me. At first it felt like something poisonous was worming its way through me, but then I realized it was the rest of me that felt poisonous—and that small hidden part was more pure than anything else.

This *wasn't* some twisted joke. No hidden cameras, no straitjackets. I felt like I could see my world as I knew it shift, change. It moved away from me.

———

Inside the warehouse, Lincoln gave me towels, which I ignored. Instead, I sat in his favorite armchair, soaking it. He didn't say anything, and after giving Griffin and me coffee, he moved back to the kitchen stools, sensing I didn't want him near.

Griffin sat on the couch, and while we both sipped our coffee, I took a closer look at his face. At first I had presumed he was over thirty, but now I put his age closer to twenty-five. He was pleasant enough to look at. Dusty brown hair, short and neat. Clothes— black pants and blue shirt—well-tailored and freshly pressed, at odds with his old, scuffed boots. It was a conservative look for someone so young. That was one reason I had assumed he was older; the other was his light gray eyes. They were wiser, more knowing than his years could possibly explain. He looked boring; it was the only way to describe him, but I trusted him instantly. Trusted those eyes.

"I don't know if I even believe in angels," I said.

"It doesn't matter. You will," Griffin replied.

I lost count of the coffee refills as he told me the story and history of angels and of the Grigori.

I listened as he explained that angels exist in their own realm.

He went on about some kind of onion. I missed most of it. I mean, I was listening to the words, but I was still stuck on the *Oh yeah, you're part angel* bit! It was something about the universe having layers. The angel realm is one; our world is another.

Angels have no physical form. Their purpose is to observe and guide humanity, but never directly interfere. They work like a governing force over the human world, offering options and even influencing free will as long as they do not directly force action. Angels influence all other creatures and the elements as well—animals, climate, nature—they have a hand in everything.

With humans, angels guide us through dreams, epiphanies, or constructing coincidences. Angels can lead a person toward choices of light or dark, and often somewhere in between. They can encourage envy and lust as much as compassion and mercy. But *encourage* is all they are *supposed* to do. The choice, in the end, still lies with the individual human.

"Light and dark? You mean, good and evil?" I asked. "But aren't all angels meant to be good—like helping from above or something?"

"It's not as simple as that, Violet. Angels *do* help us in the role they play in their realm, but with all things, there has to be balance. Just as there are angels who perform miracles of rain in a drought, there are those who facilitate the drought to begin with. For every angel who encourages someone toward an enlightened path, there is one who entices someone to a path of darkness. It's about keeping a balance of light and dark in our world, without interfering with free will."

As he spoke, my hand went absentmindedly to my shoulder and I thought about the man in my dream who'd told me he was me and then lashed out at me with a claw. Was he an angel?

Griffin continued to explain that angels are forbidden from leaving the angel realm. But there are some angels—both of light and dark—who resent their role of servitude. They believe that because angels are the superior beings, humans should be the ones serving them. The most determined of them abandon their duties and exile themselves from the angel realm, assuming human form to seek power and revenge.

In human form, exiled angels still possess angelic strengths and abilities, along with immortality. But in choosing exile, they abandon all the morals and structure by which they were previously bound. Because they had never had a body before, the atmosphere of their new world eventually overwhelms them. Processing human emotions and adjusting to the physical senses—touch, feel, smell—is all too much. Ultimately, exiles lose their ability to maintain balance and sensibility, and deteriorate the longer they are in human form.

"So, being human works like some kind of disease?" I asked.

"You could look at it like that, like a mental disease," Griffin said.

"But I don't understand why the good ones, I mean...angels of light," I corrected, trying to keep up with all the lingo, "would choose to become exiles in the first place?"

He smiled as if my question had answered itself, which bugged me. "That's because you think of light as only good—it's what you've been taught. But no creature is faultless. Angels are free to make their own choices and decisions, just like humans. It's called free will," he said simply.

"So all exiles are bad?"

"Basically. They do differ in their approach—for exiles of light, having a human body is like giving a cult leader with an insane cause free reign and no consequences. For exiles of dark, it's more like giving a serial killer weekend release from jail and putting a gun in his hands."

I shuddered. Griffin watched me carefully. It occurred to me that he was sizing me up.

"Let me be very clear here, Violet: angels do not belong on earth, no matter what their role once was. There are rare exceptions when an exile will try to coexist quietly among humans. But *most* exiled angels are corrupted, dangerous, and lethal. Their extravagant wars, combined with their need to exalt themselves over humanity, make them the kind of predator most people cannot even begin to imagine."

"They're at war with each other?" It was surreal, hearing myself ask these questions. *Angels, other realms, good and evil*...I was tempted to pinch myself, check if I was dreaming, even though I knew I wasn't.

"Since the beginning of time, light and dark have always been in opposition. In the angel realm, they are bound by their laws—in our world, there are no such restrictions. An eternity of rivalry between the two forces is given the perfect arena on earth. The visual effects of slaying flesh are much more…gratifying than spiritual combat."

Griffin stared at me, his expression grave. "There are only three things both light and dark exiles have in common. They despise each other, they hate Grigori, and they place no value on the casualties of their brutal wars."

Excellent news. Not only was I apparently some weird angel-human combo, but I already had myself a badass immortal enemy.

chapter nine

"Our duty is to be useful, not according to our desires but according to our powers."

HENRI FRÉDÉRIC AMIEL

We sat in silence. Lincoln was looking anywhere but at me. Griffin seemed to be waiting, probably giving me a chance to process. *Like that's going to happen.* I found myself staring at my wall, the wall I was going to have so much fun painting.

"Okay," I sighed. I knew I couldn't avoid this conversation. "So, what are Grigori?"

Griffin snapped to right away. He was well into lecturer mode. "When angels first began taking human form and wreaking havoc on earth, their governing body, the Seraphim, made an agreement. They devised a plan to put what they called Grigori on earth. Originally, angels held these positions. However, the same weaknesses that affected exiles also weakened the angels and they failed. So the Seraphim found another way."

"Humans," I said.

Griffin nodded. "If a child loses either parent within their first twelve days of life, the aura around that child provides a gateway for an angel to impart a portion of its essence. Both angels of light and dark, from all ranks, are able to give their essence to humans—and along with it, many of their unique abilities and strengths." He stopped, taking a sip of coffee and leaning back on the couch.

"How many ranks are there?" I asked.

"Nine. Ten, if you count The Sole. I'll draw you a family tree. It seems complicated at first, but it won't take you long."

I watched as he grabbed a notepad from the coffee table and quickly sketched some kind of hierarchy on the paper. At the top he wrote "Seraphim" and listed the other ranks from there, but at the end I noticed he went back to the top and scribbled "The Sole" above. Some of the names I recognized, like Cherubim and Archangels; others, like Dominations and Powers, didn't ring any bells.

I finally succumbed and grabbed one of the towels from the coffee table to soak up some of the water dripping from my hair. At least mopping up water was something I understood. I let the towel cover my face while I sucked in a few deep breaths and snuck a peek at the front door, teasing myself with the prospect of escape.

Griffin took another quick sip of coffee, watching me. He was waiting for me to say something, but what the hell was I supposed to say?

"Would you prefer a short answer?" Griffin offered.

"Please," I said, relieved.

Griffin spoke consolingly. "Grigori are the gardeners. We clear the weeds. Although the folklore has been distorted over time, the theory is the same. Grigori is translated in some texts as *Watcher* and has also morphed into translations of *Guardian*. Put it with *angel* and you get…?" He sat, patiently, waiting.

My stomach glided up into my chest. I could barely believe the words I was about to say. "Guardian Angels?"

"The short version…yes," he said plainly.

I sat up awkwardly, searching for a way out of this. "If I have this essence in me, why don't I know? Surely I would have felt something by now?"

If I had been able to fly over here on a cloud, I would have saved myself the drenching—or better yet, used it to get the hell out of here!

Griffin gave a half smile and I wondered how many times he had delivered this story, how many people had looked back at him with disbelieving eyes.

"When a child reaches the age of seventeen, the essence is awakened. At this point, he or she can choose to go through the final journey of embracing the gifts. Only then will they have the powers of a Grigori."

There was so much swimming around in my mind. I glanced quickly at Lincoln, then back at Griffin.

"Lincoln said I was his partner or something. What does that mean?" Definitely not the kind of partner I was hoping to become when I left the house this morning, I knew that much.

"Grigori always work in twos, just like everything in the universe. Sun and moon, earth and water, man and woman—you get the drift. The first of a pair is told the name of his or her partner when first becoming Grigori. Lincoln has been a Grigori for nine years, but has always been destined to be your partner. That's why he's been here for the last couple of years. He came to start preparing you."

"It's not the only reason," Lincoln said quietly from the kitchen. Griffin frowned.

I did a quick calculation and focused my reply only on Griffin. "Lincoln's twenty-two. How can he have been a Grigori for nine years when he only turned seventeen five years ago?"

Griffin sighed and gave me a sorry smile. "Oh, darlin'," he said, and for the first time I noticed a slight country twang in his voice. "One of the traits of being a Grigori is that we age at a slower rate, increasingly slower the older we get."

I looked over at Lincoln. He was leaning against the kitchen bench, looking at the ground. Another lie.

My voice was quiet, as I couldn't entirely comprehend the words I was about to use. "Am I"—I felt stupid even asking—"immortal?"

Griffin smiled more genuinely this time and I was immediately embarrassed for asking. "No such luck. We're still half human. While stronger and more resilient than normal, we're still susceptible to injury and inevitable mortality."

It was a sign of how bad things had become that I was relieved— at least death was still a certainty.

chapter ten

"*This is your fate, the destiny I have planned for you…*"

JEREMIAH 13:25

Everything stalled. Not just around me, but in my head. Something wasn't allowing me to process what I was hearing. It's not like you find out you're part angel every day of the week.

Griffin stepped outside to take a call, leaving me alone with Lincoln for the first time. I'd been trying so hard to ignore him, standing in the kitchen watching nervously as Griffin explained why he'd been lying to me ever since we first met. Fresh tears welled in my eyes when I glanced in his direction.

"Tell me, Linc." My voice cut into the silence and he started a little to hear me talking to him. "Why rock climbing, marathon running?" I sounded belligerent and childish. I didn't care.

He straightened up and moved a little closer toward me, still keeping a safe distance away. "Training. It's all versions of what we do when we train to be Grigori. I figured if you could do the work before coming of age, you'd be stronger. I just wanted you to be prepared, have the upper hand..." He looked like he wanted to say more but stopped himself. Instead, he watched me with hopeful eyes.

"The whole time I've known you, you've been lying to me." I felt stupid, thinking of how he had just appeared in my life and I had never questioned it. "Pretending to be my friend. Telling me to trust you..." I felt like I was going to be sick. He'd told me he would protect me. Had that all been more of his lies?

"I told you my secrets." I stood and slowly walked toward him, my legs shaking. "I let you tell me it was okay. I believed you." I felt tears escape, slipping down my cheeks, but I wasn't finished. I knew I had about thirty seconds left before I'd lose it completely and wouldn't be able to talk.

He was silent.

"How stupid could I have been, thinking you actually cared?" I shook my head, half laughing at myself. I was just as mad with myself as I was with him. Almost. "You must have thought I was pathetic. I actually thought I loved..."

I moved my feet apart as tears came pouring down. "You never cared." My hand clenched into a fist, unable to control the fury brewing within. "You just wanted to turn me into some kind of fighter, a warrior for your stupid cause!"

I struck out, hitting him across the face once, but hard, with a closed fist—just like he had taught me in so many of our kick-boxing sessions. Just like he had always wanted me to, but I had been too scared. Too scared to hurt him.

He would have seen it coming, but he didn't dodge it. He just stood there and took it.

"I don't even know you." The words left my mouth devoid of any emotion.

Griffin reappeared out of nowhere and flung his arms around me in a death grip, stopping me from hitting Lincoln again. I wouldn't have anyway.

"You've trained her well, Lincoln," he said, slightly amused. He slowly released me. "I hate to tell you this, Violet, but that probably hurt you a lot more than him."

Like he was telling me anything I didn't already know.

Lincoln ignored Griffin and just looked at me. "It wasn't a lie." He shook his head as he spoke. Trying to convince himself probably. "I just didn't tell you everything. I couldn't. I wasn't allowed. So many times I wanted to tell you. The way you feel…I feel…" He dropped his head, but I didn't miss the guilty glance he flashed at Griffin. "…that has *always* been real. You needed to know the truth first so there were no secrets between us. Violet, it's more complicated than you realize. It's not that I don't—"

I threw my hand in the air to cut him off. "NO!"

I knew where that sentence might have been going and I couldn't hear it. I didn't know if I was strong enough to hear it, didn't know if I would have been able to maintain the small amount of control I was desperately hanging on to. I shook my head and managed to say one more time, "No."

I went to the only place a girl can go. The bathroom. Once

safely locked inside, I waged an internal war between going back out there or just climbing out the window and disappearing.

Remember the rules, Vi—now more than ever you have to be strong. No running. No quitting. Simple. Yeah, right.

I left the light off and lit the candle Lincoln leaves on the wooden shelf above the towel rack, braced my hands on the sink, and stared at myself in the mirror.

"What the hell am I?" I whispered.

Looking back at my reflection flickering in the candlelight—straggly damp hair hanging almost to my waist, blotchy red eyes tearing in the corners, and slightly swollen lips—I gave myself an answer. "Screwed. That's what I am."

I closed the blinds to block out the temptation to escape and climbed into the empty bath. I breathed in the vanilla scent of the candle and willed it to calm me, to stop the tears. It didn't. Had everything I had worked so hard for, everything I had faced, all just been leading to this? Had the normal life I had fought to hold on to ever really been mine to begin with?

I couldn't tell if it was my heart or my mind screaming at me from deep within. Whichever it was, the message was clear: *Liar.* How could Lincoln have lied to me for so long? How could the one person who had helped bring strength and normality back into my life also be the one to ensure it would never be normal again?

The thump of approaching footsteps interrupted my wallowing. They sounded like footsteps of doom. After a quick knock, Griffin spoke.

"Violet, I have to get going soon. If you have more questions, I can answer them, but you'll have to come out. I'm not one for the bathroom chat." I think he was trying to be funny. He wasn't.

After a few deep breaths, I washed my face, pulled my tangled damp hair back into a ponytail, and opened the door. I don't run.

Sitting back in the armchair, I ignored Lincoln, who was now sitting on the couch next to Griffin. It took all my strength not to look at him, not to ask him, *Why? How?* Instead I gave my attention to Griffin and tried to be practical.

"So, who are you exactly?" I hoped the petulant tone hid my fear.

"I'm a Grigori, like Lincoln. For better or worse, I do my best to look after and guide the Grigori in this city."

"So, you're in charge." Honestly, let's just cut the crap, people!

"Yes." He smiled, enjoying my candor. "And should you choose to become a Grigori, I will do my best to guide you too."

"But it *is* my choice?"

He nodded. "That's why you haven't felt too many changes yet—your choice is still to be made. The final journey to becoming a Grigori must be taken through your own free will. It's called an 'embrace.'"

That seemed straightforward enough. "So, I can just choose not to do it?" I caught the look of disapproval Griffin was too slow to hide. I didn't bother to look at Lincoln.

"Yes, but you should know, when we come of age, exiles can sense us, as we can sense them, and we often have a mutual preda- tory reaction to one another. Just as we cannot always sense whether they are exiles of light or dark, they cannot always sense whether we have chosen to embrace or not. If you turn your back on this, that is your choice, but you will be without protection, always at risk of being discovered by an exile who wishes to do you harm."

"Basically, damned if I do, damned if I don't." I tried for sarcastic, but inside I was petrified.

Griffin ignored the comment. "We'll be here to answer all your questions, once you've had a chance to digest what you already know."

He picked up his coat and walked to the door. Turning back to me, he said, "By the way, Lincoln was never asked to dedicate so much time to you. The time he gave you was his choice, not part of some elaborate lie. You're hurt that knowledge was kept from you. Consider how much it's hurt him to have had the knowledge he did, knowing this day was coming."

With that, he nodded at Lincoln and left.

Yeah. My heart bleeds for him.

———————

The veins on the inside of my arms seemed darker again, now taking on more of an opaque quality. The pattern had changed also. If I hadn't known it was impossible, I would have said it looked like they were trying to form something specific. I wanted to ask Lincoln but decided instead to let the silence linger.

He moved to the edge of his seat, leaned toward me without leaving his designated safety zone, and motioned to my arms. "I've never seen anything like it. I think it's a side effect of sorts."

I traced the lines with a finger. It was just another part of me that wasn't really me anymore. Another part taken without consent. I bit down hard.

"Did you…have anything? I mean, any side effects?" I didn't look at him as I spoke.

"Sure, I started to sense things differently, become more aware. It's a bit different for everyone when they come of age. We inherit particular strengths and powers from our angel parent. But we don't usually feel major changes until after we've embraced." He glanced at my arms again. "I haven't seen any physical marks like these before."

"Parent?" I quizzed. The idea of being grounded by an angel popped into my mind and I laughed out loud before I could stop myself. Laughing had to be better than screaming—right?

Lincoln watched me with a puzzled look. I could feel the distance between us now. Like there was an invisible river dividing us that neither of us could find a way to cross. I wasn't even sure I wanted to anymore.

"Well, yeah. Not in the conventional sense, of course, but when we are given an angel's essence, the angel parent has to actually give a part of itself to us. It's something they can only ever do once."

"And what? I should be grateful?" I jabbed. I took a breath to calm down. "Do you know your angel…parent?"

"No. None of us do."

I remembered that Griffin had explained some of this, so I continued for him. "Because we could be from an angel of light or dark. We could be part good or part evil."

He nodded. "Sort of. It's an angel's essence we receive though, not their spirit. We are given their strength and powers, but not their morals or beliefs. That still comes of our own upbringing and free will. It's better that we don't know. It stops prejudice among us."

"How old are you, Lincoln?" The question had come out of nowhere, but I had to know.

"Twenty-six," he said in a strained voice. "The aging process slows more radically the older we get. It'll probably take another twenty years before I look twenty-three. I would've told you my real age from the start, but it would have just led to more questions that I couldn't answer." He looked at his feet. "Can only imagine what your father would say then," he mumbled.

I stared at him for a moment, then looked away again before I spoke. "You said *powers*?"

"All Grigori have enhanced strength and the ability to sense an exile's presence. We can return exiles, sending them back to the angel realm to be dealt with there, or, if the exile wills it, we can extract the angelic powers, leaving the exile fully human. Our other gifts are individual to our angel maker and what abilities that angel possesses."

The only ability I wanted right now was the ability to rewind time, but somehow I figured I was out of luck.

"What type of individual gifts?" I asked, still trying not to look at him much.

"Griffin's parent angel was a Seraphim, which, apart from a few Sole angels, is the highest rank. That means, unless there's another

Grigori from the same rank who is older, he remains our leader in this city. His main gift, apart from leadership, is truth. He can deliver it plainly and see through its frailties."

I thought about how Griffin had convinced me unwaveringly that he was telling the truth.

"So, he can just make people believe him?" I asked, slightly horrified.

"If what he's saying is true—yes."

"What about you?"

Other than the ability to break my heart.

"My parent angel was a Power. I have additional strength and speed. I can also see interference—the shadows that cling to people after their free will has been altered by an exile, the marks they leave behind."

I curled my legs up under me on the chair, wrapping myself up tight. Questions swirled in my mind and I was torn between a need for answers and an overwhelming desire to run. Lincoln was watching me, a concerned look on his face, which only made it worse.

"So, what am I?" I said before I could stop myself. "And…and what did you mean *sense* an exile's presence?"

Lincoln hesitated, as if he needed to choose his words carefully.

"Just tell me!" I snapped.

He stared at me for a moment then looked down at his feet. I could see his shame and it only made me more furious—knowing he *knew* what he had done to me, how much he had hurt me.

I stood up, wanting only to escape. Damn the rules. At some point, even I had to cut and run.

"I have to go." I made a beeline for the door, grabbing my umbrella, which was still dripping in the bucket by the entryway.

"Vi, wait. We have to talk about this. Exiles can sense you now. You need to know how to protect yourself."

"No!" I wasn't interested. I was in flight mode and there was nothing I could do now to stop it. Our eyes locked briefly before I opened the door to make my exit. Just as I saw the pleading fear in his eyes, I knew he saw the anger in mine.

The door swung closed behind me with a heavy thud and I bolted down the stairs, listening for the sound of feet following. There was nothing. I wasn't sure if I was relieved or not.

It was still drizzling, but afternoon sun was breaking through the clouds. I didn't bother putting up the umbrella. I just ran.

chapter eleven

"Man has no Body distinct from his Soul; for that called Body is
a portion of Soul discerned by the five senses, the chief inlets of
Soul in this age."

WILLIAM BLAKE

I ran for as long as I could, ignoring my burning legs, afraid that
if I stopped I'd have to admit I had nowhere to go. I hadn't been
in a situation in a long time where my sanctuary was not Lincoln's
place. I couldn't face going home and just sitting there, alone. I
thought of Steph and knew she'd be waiting to hear from me.

I slowed to a walk and pulled out my cell phone. Steph was
speed dial two. Dad was number three and Lincoln number one.
They were the only ones I had bothered programming.

She answered on the second ring.

"About time! How'd it go? Details, details."

I tried to hold back the tears already stinging my eyes. "Not well."

"Oh, honey. I'm sorry. I never liked him anyway!"

Steph and I had a rule. You always swing with your friends. If they like a guy, so do you. If they break up with that guy, you instantly hate him until otherwise instructed. She was swinging.

"Thanks."

"What happened?"

"He's been lying to me…Big lies." Even as I said it, I still couldn't believe it.

"That bastard. Don't tell me he has a girlfriend." I heard her slap something heavy on a table.

"No, nothing like that." I braced myself to tell her everything. I didn't want to keep this a secret from her, the way it had been kept from me. I opened my mouth to tell her the whole sordid tale, starting with my mom's surprise birthday present, but I was overwhelmed by a compulsion to avoid the subject. I waged an internal battle and in the end all I managed was, "He…he's…just not the person I thought he was."

"He didn't try something, did he? 'Cause if he did, I can get Jase and some of his friends to go round and deal with him. A few of them would have him in a minute."

I wondered if that was actually true, but I appreciated the sentiment. "No. Nothing like that—and anyway, I already hit him."

She burst out laughing and I couldn't help but smile for a moment too. It had been ridiculous of me to try to use physical strength against him.

"Good for you. I hope you gave him a black eye!" she said with false bravado. Steph had never hit anyone in her life.

"I think my hand sustained most of the damage." I flexed my right hand. It was still aching from the ill-conceived punch.

She laughed again. "I'm deleting him from my contacts as we speak."

I nodded in agreement, even though she couldn't see me. "Delete away."

"Why don't you come over for a girls' night?" she offered. "I'm fully stocked: DVDs and mint-chocolate ice cream."

"Thanks, Steph, but I think I need to be alone." I knew I'd be terrible company. Right now, the only person I could stand to be around was myself, and that was only because I had no say in the matter.

For what seemed like forever, I wandered the city aimlessly, wanting to be somewhere else—wanting to be *someone* else. I thought about Griffin's words. There had to be some other explanation, a way out of this mess. But somehow I knew he had been telling me the truth. It was crazy to find out all of this stuff, to discover my whole life had been a lie. But even as I felt besieged by my new knowledge, I knew deep down it was all shadowed by something else, something worse—my heart was breaking.

Eventually, my feet refused to carry me any farther. I turned the next corner and was disappointed to discover I'd subconsciously brought myself close to home.

I took the next turn onto my street and had to stop and lean against a wall for a moment. I couldn't breathe; every time I drew in air, it got stuck until finally I had to bend over, arms around my waist, and hold back the scream.

When finally I straightened and moved through the crowd of people on the pavement loading onto after-work buses, I saw Lincoln standing outside the doors to my apartment building. My heart, which a moment ago seemed to be shutting down for good, bounced all over the place.

I had just spent God knows how long walking aimlessly around the city like a mental patient in the making, and with everything swirling around in my head, one thought kept sneaking back in: *It sounded like he was about to tell me he loved me*. I rubbed my face and pulled on a fistful of hair. Maybe if I had just accepted all the lies, forgiven him, and listened patiently as he explained, I could be in his arms right now. It was enough to make me reconsider my actions for a moment—but only a moment.

He seemed different as I took those final steps toward him. I had never seen him look so…scared.

All his grand plans at stake!

"Go home, Lincoln," I said, trying not to look at him, trying not to stop.

"I know you don't want to see me." He put a hand out in front of me, gently stopping me in my tracks. "But I have something that might help you. Might answer some questions. Can I come up?"

I looked down at his hands. He was holding a small wooden box I recognized immediately. My eyes flashed up and then quickly back down. I didn't want him to know I had seen a box just like it before.

"You can come into the lobby." It was the most I could muster—a big concession on my part as it was.

"I don't think this is something we can do in the lobby."

I raised my eyebrows at him and crossed my arms, daring him to push his luck.

"Whatever you think of me at the moment, I *can* help. My car is over there." He looked across the street to his black, four-wheel-drive Volvo. "Maybe we could talk in there. It won't take long."

I had a mind to say no, but something in me, that increasingly annoying part that somehow couldn't drag itself away from him, overruled.

Weak!

I followed him to the car and we got into our usual seats, though nothing was usual about today. Lincoln adjusted his position to face me, moving a little closer in the process. When he saw the look on my face he shifted back a bit.

"I was going to tell you, Vi. When you came over the other night to start on your mural, I was going to tell you everything. Quietly, properly. But then I bumped into your dad and he told me…" His voice trailed off.

"So it ruined your plans," I said wryly. "I'm sorry it was such an inconvenience for you."

"No, that's not it. I was glad you told me. It meant a lot. I just didn't want to bombard you with all of this…I wanted to give you more time."

I snuck a glance at him from behind the curtain of hair I'd draped between us. His green eyes glistened and I swallowed hard before I shook myself out of it.

"There were plenty of other opportunities, Lincoln. Just say what you came to say."

He took a deep breath. "I don't know what rank you're from or what strengths you will have. You'll only find out when you embrace. As for sensing exiles…I may be able to do better than just tell you."

He placed the small wooden box in my hands. As he did, our fingers brushed ever so slightly and I flinched, moving my hands away. A look of pain swept over his face before he was able to mask it.

I opened the box, which was almost identical to the one Dad had given me two days earlier. It was covered in the same intricate carvings but it looked newer, not as worn down by time and hands. Inside lay two wristbands. Like the one in my mom's box, they appeared to be metallic, but closer inspection showed they were again leather with a silver finish.

"What are they?" I asked, not conceding I had recently seen another one.

"Connectors. We receive them from our angel guides when we embrace. When we wear them, we're able to take away an exile's power if we are locked with them in a physical hold. They also enhance our ability to sense exiles. Most Grigori never take them off…" He stopped. I figured the end of the sentence was something along the lines of—*but then, they haven't been lying to someone every day about who they really are!*

"Try one on," he encouraged.

The words in my mother's letter replayed in my mind. *Believe in the unbelievable.* This was the choice she had known would lie ahead. Had she been a Grigori? I looked at the silver bands in the box that was not my mother's but Lincoln's. Everyone seemed to know what was going on. Everyone but me.

Although I had held the band my mother had left me, I was still nervous to touch these. The thought occurred to me that Lincoln might have an ulterior motive, and my heart tightened at the realization that I had to now consider that.

"What happens if I touch them?" I asked. I placed the box down on the center console just to be safe.

He nodded to himself slowly. "You don't have to do anything you feel uncomfortable with. When a Grigori first holds the bands or puts them on, we experience a flush of the senses unique to each Grigori."

"You *sense* something every time you put these on?"

"Yes—briefly, and then it goes away—unless an exile is near. It may not have any effect until you embrace anyway, but I thought it might help you understand."

I bit my lip, considering just getting out of there. Since I'd already bolted once today, it didn't seem as dire to consider a repeat performance. It was that very thought that forced me to stay. I wouldn't run again. I reached my quivering hand toward the bands, hovering over the closest one. I felt it before I touched it—a vibration, almost a hum of energy around it, like it was reacting to me. I picked it up.

When my fingers connected with the leather, I smelled…flowers, fields of flowers. Like someone had sprayed perfume under my nose. It faded just as quickly as it arrived. Then I heard birds flying, flapping, wings and trees swishing. I looked around for the source of the noise. There was nothing. I couldn't decipher if it felt peaceful or chaotic. Moving my tongue around in my mouth I thought I tasted something familiar…apple? But it was too brief to be sure.

Overwhelmed, I closed my eyes. The inside of my eyelids flashed, like someone was flicking lights on and off. I opened them, but again, there was nothing, just Lincoln sitting in the same place, watching me intently.

The next sensation took me by surprise and my muscles seized. Lincoln moved toward me instantly, putting a hand on my arm. It felt warm against my skin, which was buzzing with a cool heat. It was a conflicting sensation—hot yet cold at the same time. I heard Lincoln gasp and release my arm. He was saying something, but I couldn't hear him over the sound of beating wings. The intensity of the feeling traveling up my arm was building so much that I started to panic. I was about to drop the band when Lincoln again put a hand on my arm. Something like a cool wind blew through my body, starting from within me and working its way out, taking the odd sensation with it. I dropped the band and repeatedly clenched my hands into fists.

"Are you okay?" His voice soothed me.

I took a few breaths and gripped my legs hard. I needed to get control of myself. I needed to be stronger around Lincoln, not show so much weakness, not anymore.

"I'm fine. Does that always happen?"

He was monitoring me carefully. "It's a bit different for everyone. They're designed to enhance our senses, to alert us when exiles are near. Most Grigori will be able to get one sense strongly, like smell or touch; some feel more. What did you feel?"

I ignored his question. "What happens to you?"

"I hear birds and wind. I also smell flowers. Sometimes I think I might feel something, but I'm not sure. It's unusual enough to have two senses so strongly, it would be unlikely I'd have a third. Griffin smells flowers too. We smell combinations mostly, but sometimes he says he can narrow it down a little to help identify an exile he has come across before and whether they are light or dark. It takes time to develop though."

I thought about what I had *sensed*. I had definitely heard the birds and smelled the flowers. I was pretty sure I'd tasted apple, but I wasn't positive. There had also been the weird light flickering and the cool heat at the end, but I didn't know what that meant. I suddenly felt self-conscious.

"Does anyone get all of the senses?" I tried to sound offhand.

He studied me, searching my face. "No. Three is the most I've ever heard of. Two is unusual enough. Vi, tell me what you felt."

"Is it the same with the other one?" I said, looking toward the other silver band.

"Yes." He was getting frustrated. "Violet, you're avoiding the question." He'd used my full name. It made me not want to answer him at all, but then I had been using his full name more and more today as well. I guess the distance was growing.

I considered telling him, but instead all I let myself say was, "I might have heard something. I'm not sure." I looked down at my hands, which were now clenched so tightly I could feel my nails digging into my palms, practically drawing blood. Lincoln reached over and covered them with his own and I couldn't help it—I still wanted him. I relaxed my hands for a minute and he took hold of them gently. I closed my eyes, allowing myself a brief indulgence. Then I took a deep breath, let it out, and pulled my hands away. He let me.

"Violet?" he pushed. He knew me too well, but right now there was no way I could afford to let my guard down any further.

"That's it. That's all I felt. I did what you asked, Linc, now…just… just leave."

I could see him warring with himself as he watched me get out of his car, but I knew he wouldn't fight me on this—and he didn't.

chapter twelve

"There are things even angels desire to look into."

PETER 1:12

On the first day, I sat on my bed and watched out the window. Out of sight. Lincoln stood, leaning against the bus shelter, twelve stories below. Waiting for me. It was exactly 6:30 a.m.—the same time we met every weekday morning. I had made it a condition of our early morning runs that he come bearing coffee and we walk the first kilometer so I could drink it. I hugged my knees tight and watched while, for more than an hour, he stood. Waiting. Coffee in hand. Eventually, he tossed the cup in the trash, looked up toward my window, and left.

On the second day, it was raining, but there he stood, at 6:30 a.m., coffee at the ready. He didn't seek cover under the bus shelter. He stood in the same place as always for more than an hour, watching my window. I sat in bed—I hadn't left it since the day before—and tried, unsuccessfully, to read my book. When he dumped the coffee in the trash and walked away in the drizzling rain, my hand went to the cold glass window. It stayed there until long after he was gone.

On the third day, I stared at my alarm clock—6:30 came and went. At 7:00 a.m., I hauled myself out of bed. In fact, I showered and dressed: T-shirt, leggings, and running shoes, not that I had any intention of going for a run. I paced around the kitchen, made coffee, and didn't drink it. Finally, I grabbed my keys and left the apartment. Outside, it was crisp and clear. It would be hot today. I looked in both directions before I allowed my eyes to veer toward the bus shelter. There was an old lady sitting down, knitting something that looked disturbingly like it would match the horrid green thing she was wearing around her shoulders. But that was all. He'd already gone.

On the ledge, near where he would wait for me, a to-go cup was tucked into the corner. I stepped toward it to make out the words written down the side. Just three words.

"I miss you too," I whispered.

———————

Determined not to spend another day cooped up, hiding away, I went for a walk and eventually wandered into a café. Coffee was one thing that wouldn't let me down, not to mention there was no food at home, unless you counted two-week-old Chinese leftovers. I was starving.

The café, called Dough to Bread, was crowded with inner-city types grabbing early morning goodies and to-go coffees. There were a dozen small tables at the back that were about half filled. I took the farthest one, so I could be as far from the activity as possible but still be able to watch. I needed to concentrate on something other than the crumbling foundations of my world.

I ordered a latte and pumpkin soup with a hot, crusty roll. The waiter gave my selection a disapproving glance from behind his little pad. I couldn't care less what he thought. I needed comfort of some sort and if there was a slim chance a soup and coffee breakfast combo was going to do it, then bring on the ladle.

I sat back and watched the mayhem. I imagined it was probably the same customers in here every week, with the same staff ignoring them, and the same huffs and mutters being thrown around. It was almost soothing to be surrounded by such superficial chaos.

I pulled out my art diary and tried to sketch, but I kept getting distracted by the family sitting closest to me. He was reading the morning paper. She was giving their toddler pieces of toast and jam, which the little girl proceeded to wipe all over her face and the wall behind. The woman laughed as the toddler squealed, and he couldn't help peeking over the top of his paper every few seconds to watch them, admiring the view.

That's what it was supposed to be like. Two people meet, fall in love, and then do normal things. I knew now that I'd never have normal again, especially with Lincoln. He was a Grigori and glad of it. I could see in him that it wasn't just something he did; it was who he was. It was a cruel truth to be faced with, that I had cared so much for him yet had never known the very thing that defined him. I had shared myself with him completely and in return had not even been trusted with the highlights.

I tried to distract myself again and noticed a guy sitting on the other side of the room. He was facing my direction, and I caught him watching me before his eyes darted away. He seemed familiar, but I couldn't place him. I was struck by his hair, of all things—at first look, it appeared black, but then I saw other colors rippling through it, shades of purple and silver. It reminded me of a rough opal. I wondered how a hairdresser could have managed such a complex blend of streaks. It was beautiful and…vain.

He looked straight at me. *Shit*. It was my turn to be caught staring. I averted my eyes to the table and luckily my soup arrived to offer the perfect distraction. Maybe someone *was* taking pity on me out there.

Starving, I dunked pieces of my bread roll and shoveled them into my mouth, only pausing to coat the top of the soup with more salt and pepper, my weakness. I finished the meal quickly, enjoying the menial task of feeding myself and wondering what kind of disgusted look my waiter would give me if I ordered another serving.

When he came over to clear the plates, I settled for ordering another latte. I had nowhere else to go. I chanced another peek at the guy with the opal hair. He was watching me, and our eyes met again. Normally, I'd be quick to look away, but there was something about him.

He stood up, still watching me, and started walking in my direction.

Shit, shit, shit.

My mind raced, thinking of things to say to make him go away. I've always hated these moments. I've never been one for "make nice with the stranger." Then he was there, standing in front of me, and I still hadn't thought of a thing to say.

He was deceptively tall, dressed in jeans and a dark gray T-shirt. He cleared his throat and I blushed. I *was* gawking, but not because I was into him; I wasn't interested in him at all. But his hair...and something else...affected me.

"I'm Phoenix," he said with a knowing smile. "I thought we could share a table." He gestured to the other tables, which were now mostly full. "It seems to be getting busy, and since we're both alone..." He gave a half smile along with a slight squint of his eyes, as if daring me to say yes.

I didn't bite. "Look...Phoenix? I've had the kind of week nightmares are made of. Right now, I'd be the worst company in the world." I looked back down at my hands resting on the table, willing him to disappear.

He pulled out the chair beside me but didn't sit. "I *could* just sit here and finish my coffee. You could ignore me. If you can."

I looked up and he was smiling. He was being nice and...*not* at the same time. One thing was certain: he was backing me into a corner.

"Whatever, but don't say I didn't warn you," I mumbled.

He smiled in victory and sat next to me.

"So, Phoenix?" I asked uncomfortably.

"Yes." He was no longer smiling, but everything about the way he was looking at me said he found me amusing.

"As in the bird? Bursts into flames and reborn through its ashes?"

"It does seem a vicious cycle, doesn't it? Lucky for me, I'm used to a little fire." He winked.

Please.

"Now that you know all about my name, don't you think you should tell me yours?" he said.

"Oh, sorry. I'm Violet."

An uncomfortable silence settled over us. Maybe if I didn't speak, he'd get bored and go away. I started counting the sugar packets in the holder. Twelve white, eight brown, and three Sweet'N Low.

"Week of nightmares sounds pretty bad. If it compares to some of my worst nightmares, it must be terrifying." He spoke conversationally, as if we were old friends. It was irritating.

I tried to sound tough but failed. "You have no idea. I didn't even know terrifying could stretch this far." I looked down, not wanting him to see the tears welling in my eyes.

"You'd be surprised," he said confidently.

Yeah, yeah, everyone has at least one horror story.

"Who is he?"

My head jerked up. "I beg your pardon?"

"Who. Is. He?" he repeated. "No woman can be in this much pain without a guy having caused at least part of it."

I liked that he called me a woman and not a girl, especially since he looked like he was about twenty. But I hated that it was so obvious to a total stranger that I was in pain. Exhibitions of weakness were not my lifelong goal.

"It's not a…" I let out a long sigh. "Lincoln."

"Did he betray you?"

"Betray?"

"Yes. Did he betray you? Mislead you? Was he cruel to you? Has he abandoned you?" He waved a hand from one side to the other with each option. "Of course, I could ask if he cheated, but we both know he didn't do that. Perhaps he lied to you, the kind of lie that changes the way you view everything. You know, the kind that lifts the mask off and only leaves behind the terrible truth. There are many things he could have done…I'm guessing it was betrayal. Am I wrong?" His eyes widened.

How had he known Lincoln hadn't cheated on me? How had he known any of it? It was as if he had looked into my heart and pulled out all of my feelings. Where did this guy come from? *No one* spoke like this.

The waiter arrived with my second coffee, another perfect distraction.

"Thanks," I said.

In more ways than one!

I tore open a sugar packet and stirred it in, stretching out the action. I felt like Lincoln had done all the things Phoenix had mentioned. Of all the things though, betrayal was the most accurate.

"Let's just say I discovered one of those terrible truths."

"And does it change how you see yourself?"

"Yes," I confessed.

"Does it change how you see him?"

"That's a little…personal."

"I agree, but no more than the previous question. I would apologize, but then it's only polite to inquire if you are already taken before I…" He smiled with intent.

A lump formed in my throat. This was not a moment I'd been expecting. I shifted awkwardly in the chair, trying to think of something coherent to say.

Phoenix smiled, enjoying my unease, and recognition suddenly registered, words flying from my mouth before I could stop them.

"You were at Hades the other night!"

He rapped his fingers on the table. "I was wondering when you would remember our dance. Usually I'm a little harder to forget."

I ignored the comment. I wasn't about to be distracted by his ego. "Kind of weird, isn't it? That we meet again today."

"Isn't it," was all he said, completely unfazed.

I curled my hands around my coffee and started to lift it to my mouth, trying to buy time. I stopped short when I felt a hum of energy pass through my body. It was the same as when I'd held Lincoln's wristband. It passed, but just as quickly my mouth watered the way it does sometimes before I'm sick. I quickly put the coffee down and scanned the room for the bathroom. As I did, the sensation passed and was replaced by the taste of…apple, rolling through my mouth like a current. I swallowed and it was gone.

"Violet?" Phoenix asked, watching me curiously.

I took a few moments before I gave a pitiful attempt at laughing it off. "Sorry. I just had this kind of déjà vu."

"What *kind* of déjà vu?" His eyes narrowed.

"Don't laugh, but I felt like I just had a bite of an apple. Weird, huh?" I said, giving a shaky laugh.

He smiled a smile of secrets that made me shiver. "I've been known to have that effect sometimes."

I didn't know if he meant the apple or if he'd noticed my shiver. Either way, my stomach suddenly twisted with unease.

I shook my hair away from my face and sat up a little, forcing a smile. "Can you give me your hand? Just for a second."

I had tried for nonchalance but it came out a little pitchy. He stiffened. Something wasn't right. He tried to cover it with another smile, but it wasn't the same easy, relaxed smile; it was nervous. I'd made *him* nervous.

"Sure…if you give me your word to be gentle."

"What?" Odd was not a strong enough word for this guy. But he sat there and waited patiently, hands in his lap.

"Why do you want to hold my hand?" He almost sang the words.

I gritted my teeth. "I promise to be gentle."

He smiled as if he had won some small victory. He put his right hand on the table, palm up. There was little explanation for why I felt a compulsion to touch him. It wasn't sexual, despite the fact that I could barely breathe in the thick mist of sexual tension surrounding him. It was something else, a suspicion I couldn't explain.

I slowly moved my arm toward his waiting hand. I lowered my hand flat like his. I felt it the instant we connected. The same hum flowing from his hand into mine, the taste of apple so sweet it almost made me gag, trickling down the back of my throat.

I snapped my hand back, accusations flying from my mouth. "Who are you? Are you one of them? Did Lincoln send you?" My still raw anger toward Lincoln rose to the surface. Did he have people *following* me now?

Phoenix smiled, also taking his hand back and rubbing it on his jeans. "One of *them*? You will have to be more specific; there are so many 'thems' these days. But no, Lincoln did not send me, of that you can be sure." I was getting sick of his condescending smirk. I didn't find any of this funny.

I got more specific. "Are you a Grigori?"

"No." He casually leaned back in his chair, crossing his legs at the ankle and stretching them out.

"But I *felt* you." This time I whispered.

He sighed. "Is it truly Grigori you are supposed to have the ability to sense?"

Fear wrapped around me like an old enemy that knew me well. My voice dropped until I was barely mouthing the word. "Angel."

He stared straight into my eyes with a frightening calm, his smile gone. "Once. One who is here only as a friend. I am no threat."

Oh. Sure. I feel so *much better.*

I stood without thinking and the chair fell from under me, clanking on the polished cement floor. Everyone looked up from their tables, collectively eyeballing me. I picked it up quickly, almost tripping over it in the process. I threw a twenty, which was way too much, to the waiter and booked it. I had forgotten my art diary.

Screw the diary!

I cut through the botanical gardens, heading for home. I wanted to run, but forced myself to walk. I didn't want to attract the wrong kind of attention from the small groups of homeless that were scattered along the path. I didn't need any more surprises. I checked over my shoulder intermittently the whole way. No one was following me.

I powered through the lobby of my building and straight into the elevator, never so relieved to press number twelve. The doors opened at my floor and I stepped out.

Phoenix was standing by my front door, swinging my art diary between his thumb and forefinger.

The tension I had only just released came thundering back into me with crushing speed.

How did he get here before me?

"What are you doing here?" I said, still puffing from my speed-walk home. He didn't look rushed at all.

He waved my art diary in the air, smiling with the knowledge that he'd had an excuse to find me again. We both knew it was total crap, but that only seemed to amuse him all the more.

"How did you know where I live?" I pushed. The doors to the

elevator started to close behind me. I wanted desperately to get back in and escape.

He's at my home.

Was he stalking me?

His mouth twisted with guilty pleasure. "I do admit, I have seen you come into this building before. I didn't know what floor you were on, but the doorman was kind enough to let me know."

Great. I was going to give the doorman an earful later. He was a good guy but shit for building security.

"In fairness, I can be quite persuasive," Phoenix said, as if he'd read my mind. "I don't imagine he would let just *anyone* up here." He looked delighted by my panic.

"You've been following me." My mouth was dry, and while I tried for a steady voice, I knew I wasn't fooling him.

"Not following, just waiting for an opportunity to introduce myself. You're not easy to get alone."

He was so relaxed while I was completely petrified, and he knew he had all the power. I did the only thing I could; I welcomed anger.

"Enough! You said you were no threat, but you're an exile!" From what Griffin said, *no* exiles could be trusted.

"Not everything is black and white, Violet. Don't believe everything you've been told. I'm...I don't fit into any of your little boxes. Anyway, if I meant to hurt you, it would be done." This guy had clearly not had much practice in the art of reassurance.

"Then why are you stalking me?" I spluttered.

He raised his eyebrows. "Stalking? No. I sensed you at Hades the other night. I sensed you as soon as you walked in. I was interested to…meet you."

"So you've been following me since my birthday!"

He leaned back against my doorframe. "Yes. And before you ask, yes…I saw. The best kisses are always the ones that take us by surprise." He stared into space, reminiscently. I didn't want to know what he was imagining at that moment.

"You watched?" I was disgusted but also blushing.

"Usually I prefer a more active role but"—he smirked slyly—"all in good time."

He was playing with me, baiting me. I stood tall, staring back at him defiantly. *I don't run.*

His expression changed. I couldn't be sure, but it looked like surprise. His eyes held mine and I couldn't seem to turn away. The longer I stared at him, the more I felt my doubts start to lift. I'd been so sure that I needed to get away from this guy, this *exile*, but looking into his eyes…my apprehension softened to the point where I found myself unable to imagine him doing any harm. I was still aware of my previous concerns, but they were sliding further away with each second. It was confusing, and while I was starting to feel more confidence in him, I was less and less sure of myself. To be safe, I tried to keep my guard up.

"I'm not a Grigori," I blurted. "I just have the essence thing. You need to leave. Now." I returned his glare. He looked down at my art diary in his hand and then slowly lifted it for me to take.

I took a tentative step in his direction, and as I did, reality seemed to waver around me. I could hear the flapping of wings and leaves colliding. It was peaceful, violent, and eerie all at once. Over that, I could hear my heartbeat, pounding like I was listening to it through a stethoscope. I closed the distance and glanced up at him.

His eyes, so brown they looked black, latched on to me and pulled me into his gaze. I saw a flash of sadness. It coursed through my body, enveloping me in sorrow. My heart ached for him as if it were my own. My hand flew to my chest as I recognized the depth of his misery, and I swallowed hard. Then the look was gone and he replaced it with something else. Desire?

It washed the sadness away with a relentless force. I felt it as if it were my own, my desire…for him. I leaned toward him and grabbed the edge of the diary. Through the connection, I felt a hum of energy. Then, somehow, it quieted.

He slowly pulled the diary toward him, giving me time to take my hand away should I choose. Part of me wanted to, knew I should. But I didn't. There was a connection I couldn't explain.

When we were just inches apart, he reached out his other hand and placed it flat on my collarbone. I took a deep breath in. It felt as if he had touched me in the one place that could affect me the most. It seemed more intimate than anything else he could have done. The hum that flickered on my skin was like small lightning bolts, but not painful. Not even close to painful.

I knew he could move his hand up and squeeze. I was sure he had the strength to snap my neck, yet just as sure he wouldn't. He moved toward me, to kiss me. I stopped breathing. Just as his lips were about to touch mine, he stopped, breathed in deeply, and whispered, "You smell of apple. It's so…" His lips were so close to mine. With each word, I could feel the vibration of his voice and the warmth of his breath—it smelled of vanilla. I stood, frozen, waiting. His hand slipped slowly from my collarbone up to the side of my face. I felt my body react and it wasn't helping me.

He whispered again, "I'll not take from you, Violet. You will be the one to kiss me." He stepped back and smiled as if he knew exactly how much he had affected me. "When you want it most."

My legs were so weak I wasn't sure how I was still upright. He released his hold on the diary slowly and moved away, clearing my path to the door with a sweeping hand gesture.

"I'm sorry that I came to your home without invitation. I will leave you in"—he gave a half laugh—"peace." He opened the door to the stairwell.

"There's an elevator," I said on autopilot.

"Too slow." He smiled and added, "You're not the same as the others, Violet. You radiate power. If you hide from it, it will only punish you."

"They said it was my choice," I said quickly.

"Of course. But choice and consequence are not the same for everyone. I suspect your power will not make it easy to ignore. An angel who can impart such a strong essence must have been confident you'd embrace it. Good-bye, Violet…for now." And then he was gone.

I stood, motionless. He had been going to kiss me.

And I was going to let him!

What was happening to me? Those first thoughts trickled into my mind, and they were the pebbles that preceded the avalanche. This day, this week, my whole life roared through my head and tore at my heart. Thoughts I had been trying to ignore crashed through my weakened defenses. Would I ever have my life back as I knew it? Was Lincoln using me? And possibly the worst—had my mother done this to me?

I fell to my knees. I couldn't breathe. As my vision began to cloud, I heard the door open. I had no time to look before there was…nothing.

chapter thirteen

"Every visible thing in this world is put in the charge of an Angel."

SAINT AUGUSTINE

Something cold and wet was suffocating me. I gasped in shock, opening my eyes to a cloudy haze. Someone was trying to kill me. I sighted the figure, still blurred, hovering over me. I needed freedom and acted on impulse. In a move that was a combination of self-defense and kickboxing, I bent my arm and swung to hit my assailant in the face, elbow first. I couldn't see clearly, but I felt the impact. It wasn't my best effort, but it was enough to buy me a few seconds to get in a better defensive position. I got to my hands and knees, crawling as fast as I could.

He was yelling at me, coming after me. He sounded frantic. I felt him getting closer. I looked over my shoulder and my vision cleared. Sounds morphed into words. "Violet, Violet, stop! It's me!"

The living room started clicking into place.

"Dad?" I said, still groggy.

"Yes!" he exclaimed, rubbing his face.

"What are you doing here?" I asked, increasingly confused.

"It's that stupid company golf day. I just stopped in to get changed. Damn, Violet." He opened the freezer and grabbed a bag of peas. "You're going to have to ease up on the martial arts. This is going to bruise."

He looked like he wanted to say more but stopped himself. I was glad. I didn't have any answers for him anyway. Well, none that I could admit to. I wasn't up to exposing my freak-hood to Dad.

Pulling myself together took some time. A shower and change of clothes helped to bring back a little normality to my world. I dressed in comfy jeans paired with a long-sleeved T-shirt to cover my arms. Being surrounded by things that were mine—my choices, my tastes—had suddenly never seemed more important.

I curled up on the couch while Dad watched me restlessly from the kitchen. He kept shifting the sugar bowl, folding the dish towel, pulling pieces of nonexistent lint off his sweater. Finally, I broke the silence for him, unable to bear that I could almost hear the wheels of his mind turning.

"I'm really sorry I hit you, Dad. The last few days have been awful and I was…I'm sorry."

"Violet, there's no need to apologize. I know you didn't do it on purpose. But I'm worried about you. You haven't been yourself lately. I think you fainted. What happened?"

I wanted to cry, break down, and let him look after me. I wanted to call him "Dada" like I did when I was little and scared. I wanted him to say, "It's okay, baby. Nothing can hurt you when I'm here," just like he used to. It didn't matter that we both knew it wasn't true. I still wanted him to say it.

"I...I...It's nothing. I had a fight with Lincoln." It was all I could manage once I opened my mouth.

Dad relaxed. It was a perfectly acceptable explanation from his point of view. "Sweetheart...I'm sorry. If he doesn't know a good thing standing right in front of him, he doesn't deserve you."

A parent's fallback line for everything.

"Yeah...well, I'm going to put some distance between us."

"It might be a good idea." He smiled sympathetically.

I felt bad, but it wasn't *all* a lie, and I just wasn't ready to answer his questions yet, or deal with his emotions.

I couldn't even deal with my own.

———

The next couple of days crept by as I tried to piece together some semblance of a life and pretend that everything was as it had been. The problem was, everything *had* in some way involved Lincoln. Life without him left a gaping hole. It angered me that he had infiltrated every inch of my life, so much so that I didn't know how to function without him.

Apart from hanging out with Steph, I spent a lot of time flying solo. I thought at least that meant I would have time to work on my art, but every time I got halfway through a new canvas, I realized I was always painting with Lincoln's wall in mind. Everything circled back to him. Now I couldn't even escape in the world of paint. It was a first.

Lincoln didn't wait for me by the bus shelter again. He stopped texting too. I couldn't help wondering if that was it. Was that all it took for him to give up on me? *Yep,* called my bitch from within.

You were an idiot to have ever thought he cared!

———————

Over the weekend, I agreed to meet Steph at the indoor rock-climbing center. I was surprised she had offered to go with me. It was a sure sign of how pitiful I must have been. The fact that she'd actually risk breaking a nail and attempt real physical activity to keep me happy was no small sacrifice. It was embarrassing that everyone could see how much Lincoln had hurt me—even if they didn't know why.

Steph was quick to take up position as my rope safety, thereby avoiding doing any actual climbing herself.

"You know, you might even enjoy it if you give it a go," I said, while tying my sneakers.

"And *you* might enjoy it if we go and see a movie instead. Either way, I guess we'll never know." She pointed to the wall in front. "So, climb," she ordered.

I clicked on the safety rope and turned back. "Thanks, Steph. I'm glad you're here."

She beamed at me. "I know, I know, I'm fabulous."

"You're a good friend," I reinforced.

"To be honest, I'm just scared you're running out of people to hit. I didn't want to be next in line. Now climb so we can get out of here!" She threw me a smart-ass smile and tugged on her end of the rope to move me on.

I laughed and felt lucky that at least I still had her.

Climbing was therapeutic and it felt good to do something physical. I'd been avoiding all the usual sports and activities that Lincoln and I had done together, and I was really missing them.

From the top, I looked down to see Steph chatting to a guy from our school. I knew his name was Marcus. She'd been drooling over him for months now. She finally looked up at me and gave a little wave before returning to her conversation. *Now* she was happy we'd come rock climbing.

I started making my way down quickly, in the hopes of starting a new climb while Steph was being entertained. And then it happened. I missed a footing and slipped. My hands scrabbled to keep hold of the wall, but it was too late. It was one of those moments when it seems like you have forever to think about what is happening in a split second. As I fell, I realized: *Steph isn't watching. She won't be able to hold the safety rope. I miss Lincoln—I miss him so much.*

The arms that caught me were strong and confident, absorbing my weight as if I had just slid into bed. He cradled me and I knew it was him instantly. I heard Steph screaming and moving toward me, but it was all secondary to the apple that drenched my taste buds, the humming of energy running through my body and somehow flowing back to him as if powering itself back and forth. My eyes were closed, but I could still see the flashes, like lights flicking on and off, almost like going from day to night in a heartbeat.

My arms exploded with cool heat. It shot up into my chest like I had just swallowed the most powerful mint ever.

I opened my eyes. I heard birds flying and could still taste apple pulsing through my mouth as I looked into his eyes. They pierced through my exterior, so intense and serious it felt like he was willing something of me. I felt the senses subside and his gaze softened, releasing me. Everything in my immediate surroundings suddenly came to the fore. Steph was standing next to us, yelling, and I was still cradled like a baby in Phoenix's arms.

"Umm…Thanks," I said.

He smiled down at me. "You're welcome." His tone dropped as if we were sharing a secret. "It was only a matter of time before you fell into my arms." The corner of his mouth twitched.

Steph was hysterical. "Violet! Oh my god, I'm so sorry. The rope just flew out of my hand. I am *so* sorry. I wasn't paying attention. Please don't hit me!"

"It's fine, Steph. It was my fault. I lost concentration." I gave her my best reassuring smile and wriggled uncomfortably. Phoenix got the hint and put me on my feet.

"Violet's right. I was watching and she wasn't concentrating at all. I'm surprised she didn't fall sooner," he said.

My smile faded as Steph's grew. She looked at me with wide eyes and mouthed the word "hot." It wasn't subtle at all.

"Well, if you say so," she swooned. "Aren't you just the perfect angel? Right there at the right time." Her words almost made me fall over. Phoenix gave a knowing smile, enjoying himself.

"I guarantee you, I'm not perfect. As for angel? I've had my moments." He was snickering at my discomfort.

I found my voice and quickly jumped in before he got carried away amusing himself. "Steph, this is Phoenix. We met the other day." I turned to Phoenix, eyes narrowing. "Thanks again. You really *were* in the right place at *exactly* the right time. Almost like you'd been waiting for me to fall or something."

Or you're still stalking me.

"Anyway, we really have to go, so…see you round."

I moved past Steph, expecting her to follow. After a few steps, I turned to see her in the same spot, looking guilty.

"What?"

She screwed up her face in gleeful guilt. "I kind of told Marcus that I would go get coffee with him."

"Right. Sure, no worries. I'll catch up with you later." I didn't blame Steph. There was no point in both of us being miserable.

Still wanting a quick exit, I grabbed my bag and turned for the door.

"Wait, Vi. You can't go on your own, not after that fall. You could go into shock. I'll tell Marcus I can't go."

"No, I'm fine. Really."

"I can't just let you go on your own," she persisted.

Phoenix stepped forward, already smiling. "I could take you home."

Steph saw a green light. "Oh, that would be great. Are you sure that's okay?" she asked, looking up at him.

"Of course. I would love to," he said.

I coughed, breaking up their little powwow. "Actually, I don't need anyone to take me home. But thanks. I'll be fine."

Steph gave me a desperate look. "Vi, I can't leave you alone. You could have a delayed reaction or something. But if you let Phoenix take you, I'd feel much better...*Please.*"

Damn! I looked at Phoenix. Part of me wanted to run, knew I *should* run. But another part of me remembered that day outside my apartment. The way he'd made me feel...just the memory made my stomach flip.

Phoenix watched me, smirking as if he knew exactly how things were going to pan out. It was annoying. Mostly because he was right.

"Fine! Phoenix can take me home. Now go catch up with Marcus."

Steph didn't need any more convincing. She kissed me on the cheek and left me with the exiled angel.

chapter fourteen

*"The virtue of angels is that they cannot deteriorate; their flaw is
that they cannot improve. Man's flaw is that he can deteriorate;
and his virtue is that he can improve."*

HASIDIC SAYING

"Are you hungry?"

We hadn't spoken since the rock-climbing center, and Phoenix's
words cut awkwardly though the silence.

"Oh, I…umm…not sure," I said, sounding like a three-year-old.

The truth was, I was starving. Steph and I had planned to
get lunch before going climbing, but she'd been running late.
She swears she never gets up before midday during break, but
her brother once told me she just uses that as an excuse to hide
her innate geekiness. My bet was she was getting most of her
reading for next semester out of the way. Of course, she'd never
admit that, or her Einstein status for that matter, and I'd never
make her.

It was starting to get dark and I hadn't eaten all day, unless you counted two cups of coffee that morning.

"You should eat something. I wouldn't want you to *faint* or anything."

His comment sounded innocent enough, but I knew it wasn't. My head snapped up, mortified at the thought he may have hung around the other day at my apartment and seen me pass out.

"Food can only help—you've barely eaten anything all day. And I promise to be good." He put three fingers in the air in a Boy Scout salute. His eyes promised the opposite.

"You've been following me…again," I accused, wrapping my arms around my waist. It was creepy to think that he had just appeared out of nowhere to catch me. I had no idea how he could have reached me so fast.

"Sorry?" He tried for shocked but it was only for my benefit. I got the feeling Phoenix knew exactly what he was doing.

"How do you know what I have or I haven't eaten?" I growled. I was getting tired of his games.

He brushed it off. "Let's get some food. I'll explain then."

He walked close to me, but when our arms brushed, I quickly moved aside.

I didn't want to go anywhere with him. The last person…well, the second-to-last person I wanted to be hanging out with right then was Phoenix. Then again, he *had* just offered to explain what was going on. Maybe I could make this work in my favor.

"Fine," I said. "I'll get something to eat as long as you promise to answer all my questions. And you're buying."

———

The pizza place was packed, always a good sign. I didn't need the tip-off though; I had been there once before with Lincoln. It was one of those pizza places that had real wood-fired ovens. It smelled of charred dough, melted cheese, and garlic. The waiters were rude and mostly spoke in Italian. I don't speak Italian, but I knew enough to realize they weren't using terms of endearment.

The only free table was wedged in a tight corner near the kitchen door. It wasn't near the pizza oven, which at least meant I wouldn't be sweating the whole time. But as a consolation prize, there was a good chance of getting knocked out at some point by waiters slamming in and out of the swinging door. Phoenix wasn't perturbed and glided across the room, following our fat Italian waiter who dropped the menus on the table and walked away without asking if we wanted a drink or anything to start. He was sweating so much I almost wanted to let him have my seat while I found *him* a drink.

When I spotted a red-haired waitress finally moving in our direction, I sank into my chair.

How could this be happening to me again?

I racked my brain as she closed the distance. She was wearing the customary waitress outfit—white short-sleeved shirt and black skirt—but tonight her hair was out, waving to just below her shoulders. As she drew close, I spotted the gold name badge pinned to her collar. I smiled, trying not to focus on it too obviously.

"Hey, Violet," she said, flicking her hair back, clearing the view to her name badge. *Claudia!*

"Hey, Claudia. So this is the other place you work." I felt terrible for always forgetting her name.

"Yeah, unfortunately." She leaned toward me, lowering her voice. "Shitty tips and crap boss, but it's work." She shrugged.

I remembered my manners this time. "Claudia, this is Phoenix." I wasn't exactly sure what I was introducing—exile, stalker, or freaky friend?

Phoenix seemed totally uninterested. He lifted his eyes from the menu. "Pleasure," he said, lingering over the word, looking only at me.

My body tingled and I had to clasp my hands under the table, pressing my nails into my palms for distraction. I glanced up at Claudia, who was swooning over the table. I imagined she would have fallen over if Phoenix had actually looked at her.

"Hi," she squeaked. "Can I take your order?"

I ordered a diavola pizza, much to Phoenix's amusement. He ordered the same and a glass of red wine. I stuck to water. Once Claudia was out of earshot, I saw no point in delay.

"You said you'd answer my questions." I knew my only chance was to take control of the conversation, steer it in the direction I needed it to go.

"I did." He stretched his legs out and leaned back in his chair. With all that had been going on, it surprised me that I found it hard to stop my eyes from drifting over his body. Then again, just because everything had gone belly up in my world didn't mean I was blind. Phoenix was pretty damn close to a perfect brooding hottie—that is, if I hadn't already seen total perfection in someone else. His dark hair fell around his face, shimmering with waves of purple and silver, and his physique looked like it was made to be in Calvin Klein underwear ads. Not that I was thinking about what he would look like in underwear. At least, I was trying not to. He didn't make it easy, sprawled out in front of me.

Crap, Violet, get it together.

"Why are you still following me?"

"You leak power," Phoenix said. His eyes were drifting around the room. It irritated me the way my question seemed so insignificant to him.

"Great, well that explains nothing," I grumbled.

He gave a dramatic sigh, finally looking at me. "Everywhere you go, you leave a trail. You haven't embraced your angel part, but you still radiate. You're like red in a world of bulls."

"Okay, so what? That still doesn't explain why you're being all stalkerish."

"Others who mean you harm won't have difficulty finding you. You are so obvious, it would be more subtle if you took out an ad in the paper." He made quote marks in the air. "*Powerful Grigori in the making. No powers, no defenses, easy to find.*" He shook his head. "When they find you—and they will—there'll be nothing you can do."

"Right. So, you just want to look out for me?" I said. And pigs might fly.

"I was bored." He shrugged, like it was no big deal.

I held his eyes, determined to get more answers.

After a waiter delivered our drinks, Phoenix sighed again. "I saw you…that night at Hades, you were so…unaware. I could sense what you were, even though you clearly didn't know. Normally I wouldn't care. Believe me, Grigori are the very last thing I'd want to…" He quickly looked away and then back again, a smile playing on his lips. "But it worked out, didn't it?"

I couldn't help it; I felt myself smiling back.

"Yeah, it worked out." Without planning on it, my tone had softened. If I was honest with myself, I was oddly glad to know that he was around. "So…what's it like? Being an angel?" I asked.

"Ha! Such an obvious question. I was hoping for something more original."

"Okay. What's the first thing you did when you became human?"

He laughed. "Hmm, much better." His eyebrows lifted suggestively. I was suddenly red hot and sure I had asked the very, very wrong question.

"It's okay. I can imagine," I said quickly. "How about this then, why did you leave your realm? I mean, you chose to, didn't you?"

He looked past me toward the wall. "Sort of."

"Why?" I prodded.

"Think of it as being born into a culture with arranged marriages. And divorce is definitely not allowed. Playing caretaker to mankind can be…" His voice trailed off. Wherever he was, it wasn't here. And there was a lot he wasn't saying.

"Do you miss your friends? Did you have friends? I mean…"

He gave a soft laugh. "There were some minds that I enjoyed the presence of, but it's not like it is here. Angels have no corporeal form. Human flesh is considered a lesser form, a vessel with so many frailties."

He saw my confused look and elaborated. "A prison of flesh, a heart that relies on lungs that in turn rely on oxygen to be ever-present. An intellect that relies on senses of the flesh to feed it knowledge. That's why most of our powers, even after we take human form, are still centered on intangible things: imagination, memory…the passions."

"Passions?"

"Emotions—love, hate, desire, fear, hope, despair—the things that lead people to their ultimate bliss or eventual downfall." His words sounded with regret and there was some longing in them too.

"So, if we're so frail and angels are so powerful, why take human form?" Someone had to stick up for us mere humans.

"The very thing that overwhelms you," he said, opening a hand toward the crowded room of diners.

"I'm lost."

He swirled his glass of wine, the liquid clinging to the sides before trickling back down to the bloodred pool. He tilted the glass toward me. "This. For one. Our knowledge is immeasurable, our power beyond compare. Yet I could only *know* what wine tastes of; I could not sip it or roll it on my tongue. I knew the tartness of a lemon, but could not wince from it. It became unbearable to witness the sun's power and watch it strip a desert dry, burn a forest bare, and yet I could not so much as feel it warm my skin. It's why you feel physical senses to alert you that we are near. Those senses are humans' defining strength—and their weakness."

Like flicking a switch, he returned to his more familiar, seductive tone. "There are some feelings, some touches, some sensations…" He inhaled and exhaled slowly, lingering, I was sure, for my benefit. "*Flesh* against *flesh*. No knowledge, no matter how great, can understand *those* touches. Only humans." He didn't blink once.

His eyes, oh my God. He hadn't said anything R-rated, but that didn't matter—he still made it sound so…steamy. My heart was racing and I didn't know where to look. How had he gone from seeming so genuine one minute to exploding with sexual innuendo the next? How did I go from being all *I'll ask the questions* to *Someone get me water 'cause I'm burning up!*

I fixed my eyes on the kitchen door swinging open and shut. I forced myself not to look at him, not to look into his eyes. I didn't need to anyway. I knew without looking that he'd have that same smirk on his face, reveling as I squirmed.

I gave myself an internal count to ten to pull myself together. I made it to seventy-five before I spoke.

"So…" I wrapped my hand around my glass and took a sip. It was empty. I snuck a look at him. He was shaking a little, holding back a laugh.

"So…?" he prompted.

"I was just wondering. I mean, I'm not exactly religious…but have you met…Do you know…?"

"God?" he jumped in.

"Yeah." I never thought I would have to resort to God as a change of subject.

Claudia returned with the pizzas. I ate quickly, using my hands. Phoenix ate slowly and I felt him watching me intently. It should have bothered me, but strangely I was starting to feel more and more comfortable around him. For the first time all night, I felt myself physically relax into my chair.

He half laughed, as if he knew what I had just thought, then carried on with our conversation. "It's not like what humans say in fairy tales, Violet. In some ways it's even harder for us to know the answers to those questions than for humans." He was far away again. When he let his facade drop, it was easier to see his other-worldliness, see the depths of his eyes, the stillness of his features.

He noticed me studying him and his tone lightened. "Anyway, the existence of a being so powerful that it could create life and worlds doesn't need to be revealed to any other being unless it chooses to do so."

"And does he? I mean does anyone know for sure?" I asked.

"Apparently."

"So who, then?"

"Only angels who have taken actions so momentous that they would not have been possible without the knowledge and perhaps help of a higher power. They are known as the Sole, the few who have been elevated beyond their normal rank to…something else. There are only two that I know of."

"Okay. I'm listening." What? Did he need a drum roll?

"The Sword Michael and his opposite, the Star Lucifer."

I swallowed the lump in my throat. "As in…the devil…Lucifer?" I spoke quietly, afraid that the nearby tables would overhear.

"If that keeps it simple for you," he said, shaking his head a little.

"So there is a Hell?"

"No…and yes. It's a nice perspective that humans have of good and evil. It would be easier if it were right. If it were so basic though—to break it all into one or the other, Heaven or Hell—it would mean that angels of *Heaven* could do no wrong and angels of *Hell* could do no good, effectively leaving angels with no free will, and that is not the case. Within the angel realm, angels of light and angels of dark exist equally. For every angel who offers a bridge to walk over, another angel is there to entice someone into troubled waters. Without this, free will would not be possible."

"But I thought evil only existed after Lucifer fell from Heaven." I was no expert, but I had been forced to sit through over a decade of religious studies in school.

"I bet you thought angels had wings too." He raised his eyebrows a little.

I pursed my lips in a vain attempt to defend myself, but of course he saw right through it.

"I can't explain everything. This isn't something that can be summed up over just one pizza. Trust me, evil has always existed. The very story humans tell of creation, its first line, gives it all away." He put on a formal voice. "*Let there be light, yada yada yada…*But consider this: how could *light* be needed if *darkness* had not preceded it?"

I don't know why, but I felt sad for Phoenix as he spoke. I didn't know where it came from. It was as if his sadness was leaking into me somehow. I instinctively reached across the table and placed my hand on his, offering comfort. But I almost jumped out of my chair when we touched. Apple. I had forgotten the senses. Sparks flared between us and I reacted quickly, starting to move my hand away, but he grabbed it before I could. Birds' wings started flapping as if there were a swarm of them inside my head. I pulled at my hand to release it from his grip, but he just pulled back. I stared daggers at him. This wasn't a game. But when our eyes met and locked, a wave of calm flushed my body, like being doused with a bucket of cool water on a sunny day. After a few seconds, the senses were gone and I was just holding his hand.

I bit down on my lip. The corner of Phoenix's mouth curled and he gave my hand a small squeeze before releasing it.

For the first time since all of this happened, I wanted to know more. Knowing that he had actually lived, existed, whatever, through all of this was bewildering.

"Will you tell me more?" I asked as I watched him dutifully pay the bill. I idly wondered where he got his money from and then decided I didn't want to know.

He nodded. "Tomorrow. When I take you to the new art exhibition at the Contemporary Museum."

My eyes narrowed. "You looked through my diary," I accused, feeling violated. I never let anyone look through my art diary.

"Your little notebook? No."

"How did you know I love art then?"

"I just did." He smiled, shifting his gaze down to my hands.

I laughed. There was still yellow and orange paint in the cuticles of my fingernails.

Before we left, I looked around for Claudia. She was nowhere to be seen.

chapter fifteen

"If then we have angels, let us be sober, as though we were in the presence of tutors; for there is a demon present also."

SAINT JOHN CHRYSOSTOM

Phoenix insisted he walk me home, despite my mediocre protests that I was fine. We walked out of the pizza place onto a now quiet street. The silence was quickly uncomfortable.

As soon as we reached the alley that ran behind the restaurant, I sensed it: the tangy-tart flavor of green apples. It reminded me of biting into those liquid-filled pieces of chewing gum. I hated those.

Phoenix stiffened beside me.

"That's not you, is it?" I whispered, my heart racing.

He didn't answer. He didn't need to.

"Phoenix?"

He snapped to, spinning toward me, bracing his hands on my shoulders. "Stay here." He shook me. "I'll be back in a minute. *STAY HERE!*"

I nodded. He turned and walked into the alley, leaving a waft of white musk in his wake. There were no streetlights. It was one of those narrow lanes, not wide enough for a car to drive down. Garbage bins lined one side and odd bags of spilled trash and food scraps from the restaurants in front were piled beside them. After a few steps, the darkness swallowed Phoenix's silhouette.

It was hot, steamy even, but I still wrapped my arms around my waist, feeling a chill.

I strained my eyes but couldn't see anything. Then, over the sound of wings flapping, I heard the muffled scream of a girl. The next scream wasn't muffled. It rang loud and clear. A scream that held absolute desperation. My feet were carrying me into the darkness before I even realized.

Phoenix was standing in front of what I could instantly tell was another exile. He was tall and slim, but broad through the shoulders. He was dressed all in black with glowing white-blond hair. He had hold of a girl, restraining her with an arm around her neck. She was kicking out, trying to get away. Her bright-red hair caught my attention. Then I registered her uniform. The shirt was ripped open and the black skirt was still there, though it was clear it wouldn't be for long. Her gold name badge winked at me in the moonlight. Claudia.

As I walked toward Phoenix, she saw me and screamed, "Violet! Thank God! VIOLET! HELP ME!"

The blond exile tightened his grip around her neck and put his other hand over her mouth, silencing her.

I stopped beside Phoenix.

"I told you to wait. Go back!" he growled at me. I didn't have time to respond before he turned his attention to the blond. "Release her." He spoke quietly, the threat stronger without the volume. A shiver ran through my body.

The blond flinched and threw Claudia down. Her head hit the ground so hard it bounced.

"Kneel before me," the exile sneered at her.

To my horror, I watched as Claudia crawled onto her hands and knees. Blood was flowing freely from a gash above her left eye. She stopped at his feet, kneeling before him as he had commanded.

"Beg me to take your life," he ordered, as if talking to a rabid dog.

Claudia shook with fear but couldn't stop the words. "Kill me. P-p-please," she cried.

"No! Let her go!" I screamed. "Claudia! Claudia, run!"

But she didn't. And instead of letting her go, the blond exile put a hand on either side of her face.

"If you want her, come and get her," he hissed, looking at me. "*Grigori!*"

He lifted Claudia, holding her out to us. Her feet dangled in midair. Before I knew what I was doing, I was running. I felt the sweep of Phoenix's hand at my back as he reached out to stop me. Arms outstretched, I ran, even though I knew I was too slow and he was way too fast.

His arms moved with swift precision. Such a small movement,

but the force was distinctive. Claudia's neck snapped to the side with a life-ending crack. An unmistakable sound imprinted upon me for eternity.

I was there less than a second too late. But it may as well have been hours for all the good it did. He released her, dropping her into my outstretched arms. Her dead weight crumpled on me like a massive rag doll and I fell under her. The exile inhaled a deep, satisfied breath, holding it for a moment before looking straight at me as I struggled desperately to free myself. His face was stone—no remorse.

"Your turn," he said with a smile, as if offering me a go on a Ferris wheel. He lunged toward me.

I didn't stand a chance, but then, I didn't need to. He barely made it within an arm's length of me before Phoenix was there, barreling into him like a freight train.

They exchanged blow after blow, all at lightning speed. If I hadn't seen it, I wouldn't have believed it. The blond was so fast, sending his fist into Phoenix's face with punishing force, throwing him across the width of the alley and into the brick wall. Amazingly, it barely slowed Phoenix, who was back up faster than I could track with my human sight. Phoenix didn't hesitate in his retaliation. He was a beautiful, lethal machine, lithe and fluid as he weaved and dodged the exile's blows.

It was soon clear they were matched in strength but not in skill. With fierce precision, Phoenix maneuvered the blond into the end of the alley, pounding his fists into him over and over again.

Finally, the exile slumped to the ground. Phoenix knelt over him. I couldn't see clearly in the dark and I was glad. One God-awful thrust, then the wet, sticky sound of something being torn and snapped. It was not a sound I'd ever heard before, nor did I want to ever hear it again.

Phoenix was quick to lift Claudia off me and help me up. He wiped the tears from my eyes and pulled me close. The senses were still affecting me, but I didn't care. I held on to him as tightly as I could. As I did, I could feel his exhaustion…and something else. He was rigid, tense.

"What happened?" I stuttered, moving back a little.

"He's dead."

"How?"

"Grigori have their ways; exiles have their own."

"I heard. You ripped his heart out?"

"Yes," he said.

The most frightening thing was, I didn't mind a bit. "How did he make her ask to die?" I was shaking my head even as I asked the question. It was impossible.

"Imagination. He had her seeing one thing but saying another. She was weak and he took her will easily."

I thought yet again of my mother's letter, which I had now read countless times. *Imagination is their highway; free will is ours.*

My mind was racing, reliving the moments.

I was almost there.

"He called me Grigori," I said. "He killed her because she called to me." My breathing tightened with the thought. Had I been the reason Claudia was killed? *Please, no.*

"He would have killed her anyway, just not so fast."

I pulled away and got my first good look at him. He was breathing fast—not with exhaustion…but with adrenaline. His eyes were so…alive…wired.

"He was an exile of dark, a Cherub. Never liked Cherubs, not here or in the realm." He wiped his hands down his jeans as if dusting them off. "His only goal was to inflict pain. You just saved her the torment."

"Her name was Claudia." I needed to say her name out loud. I would never forget it again.

"We need to go," Phoenix said, looking around.

"No. We have to do something. Call the police," I said, horrified that he was willing to just leave her in the dirty alley.

"Someone else will find her." He tried to push me toward the main road. I refused to move and eventually he sighed and nodded.

When the police arrived, we answered all their questions. I felt terrible lying, but Phoenix made it clear there was no choice. At least there was only Claudia's body to explain. The exile's body had disappeared. Not a trace left behind. The police took our statements, accepting all too quickly that we had caught a glimpse of a woman's body lying on the ground when we walked past the alley on our way home from the pizzeria. Phoenix careened through their questions with disturbing ease. I wondered if he was doing something. The officers were too obliging, and the whole process was over in a matter of minutes. I felt an awful pang of guilt that Claudia's family would never know the truth. Though, I was learning, the truth was not always better.

After walking me to my building, Phoenix stood awkwardly on the pavement while I fished through my bag for my swipe card to the main doors. The silence had dragged as I hiccupped and sobbed most of the way home. Any other time, I would have been embarrassed, but for now I was settling for a kind of numb.

"Violet?"

"What?" I tensed, worried he might ask to come up to the apartment. But it was worse than that.

"You should see Linc—"

"No!" I shook my head hard, trying to throw off the whole conversation.

Phoenix put his hands in the air defensively. "Hey, I don't even know the guy and I don't like him. But things out there are… you saw yourself. You need to learn how to protect yourself. Think about it."

That's exactly what I didn't want to do. Thinking about it made me want to fall apart, and I couldn't, I wouldn't, do that.

"Maybe," I said, just to make it go away.

Images of Claudia's body circled in my mind and thoughts of Lincoln stirred close behind—pain and love and loss. All too much to comprehend.

"I have to go." I swiped my card on the doors with too much vigor and had to try three times before they clicked open.

"You can't just pretend he doesn't exist," he murmured.

I spun, heat rising through my body. "Actually, I can! And if you want to see me again, so can you!" My heart twisted at my words as I stormed through the doors.

"We'll see."

I didn't bother turning. I just kept walking into the bright lobby, leaving him on the dark street. When I heard the doors close behind me, I breathed a sigh of relief.

chapter sixteen

"You can do what you will, but in any given moment of your life you can will only one definite thing."

ARTHUR SCHOPENHAUER

I was a little surprised the next morning when Phoenix buzzed the intercom. I had forgotten I'd agreed to go to the art exhibition with him, I was so blindsided by everything that had happened last night. But now, more than ever, I realized I needed to understand this world. Phoenix probably knew more about it than anyone, and for some reason I trusted the things he told me. Claudia's death had taught me that exiles clearly knew what I was, and if that could endanger innocent people, well, I needed to make sure I wasn't responsible. *But I'm innocent too.* I couldn't help my next thought: *Yeah, and tied to the damned.*

When I joined Phoenix in the street, it struck me how unfazed he was. I felt puffy and stale from the night before. I was dressed in comfy clothes and had barely taken a brush to my hair. He looked fresh and minted, invigorated almost. When he looked at me, his chocolate brown eyes stirred, and before he could mask it, a smile formed within them.

"How long have you been here? On earth, I mean?" I asked as we walked toward the bus stop.

"Too long to count. We could take a taxi if you prefer?"

"No. Bus is good." I preferred to take the bus to a taxi when I could. I had a habit of getting carsick in the back of taxis.

Phoenix stood aside when the bus arrived, letting me on first. He really was on his best behavior.

I gave a huff as I took a seat and considered his earlier comment. "What? Are we talking hundreds of years?"

"I guess," he said as if it were no big thing.

My mouth fell open. "Do you miss the angel realm?" I wasn't sure if it had seemed like home to him.

"Sometimes."

I turned to look at him. Glimmers of purple floated through the black base of his hair, and as the sun caught different angles, a few strands sparkled silver.

"Your hair is…amazing."

He smiled and shifted in his seat. "You don't strike me as the hair type. I had you pegged for eyes."

I felt exposed that he had figured me out so quickly. "Do you all have hair like that?" I said, trying to ignore his comment.

He laughed, sounding more relaxed than I had heard him before. "Not exactly. It was more something I inherited. It resembles a natural stone. It's—"

"Opal."

"Yes." The smile he gave me was different, genuine. I knew instantly it was a smile not often seen, and something else was apparent too: I was smiling back.

When we arrived at the Contemporary Museum, the doors were closed, a sign out front explaining that the exhibition didn't open until tomorrow.

"That's annoying," I said.

"Not really. It's better this way. We get the whole place to ourselves." Phoenix didn't stop at the front doors. Instead, he went around the side and knocked on a smaller, more inconspicuous door marked EXIT.

"Phoenix, you can't—"

The door opened. A short balding man stood just inside. When he saw Phoenix, he moved aside, widening the door in invitation.

Phoenix looked at me with a sly grin. "As I said. Not so bad." He held his hand out toward the door and then followed me in.

The bald man shook Phoenix's hand and told us we had an hour until the next shift arrived. Then he left us alone.

"Wow. This is amazing. Who was he?"

"Someone who owed me a favor," Phoenix said, and I knew he would tell me no more. I guess I didn't really need to know, not when there were so many other, more pressing questions.

The exhibition was amazing. Some pieces were still in crates waiting to be hung, but we got to see most of it.

"So, you like contemporary art?" I asked as we moved through the abstract sculpture section.

"To be honest, it's not my favorite. I prefer Renaissance." He watched for my reaction. "But I knew you would like it. I'm sure you've been to a million exhibitions with your Grigori friend, but I knew there was a good chance you wouldn't have seen these pieces."

I forced a smile but didn't respond. I was too embarrassed to admit I'd never been to an exhibition with Lincoln. I hadn't really been anywhere with Lincoln. We were always training.

"Is it my turn now?" he said, as we continued to walk through the oversized rooms.

"For what?" I asked, suddenly nervous.

"To ask a question."

I frowned. "I guess."

He pushed up each of his sleeves. He was so casual and normal in his movements, yet they all looked so precise. I wondered how much practice it had taken and about the transition from angel to human. Did he feel more angel or human now?

"Why are you so afraid to be more than ordinary?"

My eyes instinctively flashed down. Of all things to ask. I felt tears well up and worked furiously at holding them back and getting control of myself. I tried to focus on other things: the twisted bicycle sculpture, the intricate cornice, the stray bits of crate stuffing scattered on the ground.

"I'm not, I just…don't want to be singled out, on display."

"And you think that being a Grigori will put you in that position?"

"I just want *my* life. The one I've been working on for the last seventeen years. I have plans, plans I like, and he…they…had no right to…" I shook my head. I couldn't tell him how much it hurt that Lincoln had lied to me, pretended to be my friend, had known my future and not told me. I didn't add that I now included my mother in the "had no right to" category.

"He? Lincoln, your Grigori?" Phoenix was not letting it go.

"He's not…mine."

"Good to know," he said, walking on to the next sculpture of a naked woman in flames.

I felt like slapping him. Instead, I put my foot down. "We are not talking about him."

On the couple of occasions I'd considered broaching the subject with Steph or Dad, about what was happening to me, I didn't seem to be able to form words. I'd thought it was just me but Phoenix took his time inspecting the burning woman before answering. "Look, Violet, here's the thing. Grigori are not usually…*friends* with exiles. In a way, we're natural enemies…Nonetheless, saying this as *your* friend, you need to stop acting like a lovesick child. Whether you like it or not, you're in this world now, and exiles are very good at sensing power in other exiles and in Grigori."

"And you can sense me," I said, choosing to rise above his other comments. For now.

"Some part of you must be able to feel how powerful you are."

I wanted to deny it, but I couldn't. "When I touch you, I'm swamped. I can't control it."

"I know. Through you, I can feel part of it too." He gestured to a wooden bench in the middle of the room.

I remembered how the sensations had subsided when he looked at me in the pizzeria. Somehow, when I was around him, they seemed to stop. "You controlled it, calmed it down."

He nodded. "I took away some of your anxiety and gave you a little of the emotion you needed to control it."

"You *gave* me emotion?" I said, my eyes widening.

"I'm an empath. It's something some angels…exiles can do. One of the reasons we are dangerous to humans. We can read and influence emotions—intensify some, eradicate others. It's one of my strengths."

I immediately thought back, replaying the time I had spent with him, trying to think about what emotions I'd had.

He seemed to know—or *read*—how I was feeling.

"Violet, I only did it to try to help you find control. You'll learn to do it yourself in time. I meant you no harm."

I looked at him suspiciously. "The other day, at my apartment…"

He looked down. "I *might* have given you a little of my own emotion. In my defense, I didn't take advantage of the situation, no matter how much I wanted…" He didn't finish.

"And last night?" I pushed, increasingly agitated by this invasion.

"I just tried to help you get through what happened to the girl, take the edge off."

My eyebrows shot sky high. Now that I thought about it, I had been coping better than I would have expected considering what I had seen. "Is that all?" I asked, my voice filling with accusation.

"I've been a little…clumsy. I apologize." He shrugged through a smile. "It can be very difficult to contain myself around you."

I was angry at being influenced and blushing at his words. I held on to my anger. "What about today? Now?"

"Hardly anything," he said, waving a hand through the air as if we were talking about whether he had taken an extra cookie from the cookie jar. "Now that you know, don't think you can use it as an excuse to deny the very real emotions you feel for me." And presto, he was back to being his usual arrogant self. "Everything you felt last night and today has come from you. I should know. I've felt it." His smile widened.

Even though I wanted to die, knowing that he had been able to feel every one of my emotions, he wasn't going to deter me. "How will I ever know if what I feel when I'm around you is real or not?"

His smile faltered and he looked worried. He leaned toward me a little. "You'll be more aware of it now. If you ever caught me doing it, I know you'd never trust me again. I wouldn't risk that."

He was right: I wouldn't. But would he?

My eyes subconsciously found the exit door. Force of habit. But I got the feeling that if I ditched Phoenix right now, he'd only be waiting at my doorstep again when I got home. I ran my hands through my hair. The fact was, I was running low on allies. If I pushed him away as well, where would that leave me?

"Okay, but don't…" I warned, trying to quash my flight instinct and muster as much threatening emotion as I could to reinforce my words.

"I won't," he promised, hands in the air in mock surrender.

———————

The next day, I went back to the alley where Claudia had been killed and left a bunch of sunflowers at the entrance. There were already piles of wilted flowers she would never see and cards she would never read from her friends and family.

"I'm sorry, Claudia," I whispered.

Now that I knew Phoenix had been altering my emotions, it seemed easier to look within and find the sadness and—most of all—the guilt. The sound of her neck…the very last look on her face when she knew what was about to happen. I had seen her blue eyes before they were whipped to the side under a blanket of red hair. I had seen the pure fear.

Before I left, I turned back to look down the empty alley.

"I'm so sorry I couldn't save you," I said through the awful lump in my throat and the terrible realization that this might only be the beginning.

———————

Phoenix called as I was walking home and talked me into having lunch with him. I was tempted to refuse when he told me we were going to "our café," which turned out to be Dough to Bread, but he promised to behave after I explained to him that *we* didn't have an *our* anything.

Surprisingly, spending time with him was becoming increasingly easy. Even the senses were less intrusive. They still came and went, but sometimes I seemed to notice them more than others.

I wished I could say being with Phoenix filled the void left by Lincoln, but the closeness, the completeness I felt when I was around Lincoln could not be replicated. It was disheartening to consider that the connection I'd felt so strongly may have just been a result of our angel components and, even worse, that I may never feel it again. At least with Phoenix it was honest…to a point.

We still hadn't talked much about what had happened to Claudia. I got the feeling I wasn't the only one uncomfortable about it. I hadn't even told Steph everything, just the same story we'd given to the police. There was no way to tell her more without having to explain the whole thing, and I still didn't seem able to do that.

On the couple of occasions I'd considered broaching the subject with Steph or Dad, about what was happening to me, I didn't seem to be able to form words. I'd thought it was just me but Phoenix explained that angels in their realm could compel people to say or not say certain things. This level of interference was generally against the rules for normal humans, but it seemed I was no longer in that category. He figured this was probably the reason I wasn't able to share more with Steph or my dad. Apparently, it was standard procedure for a still-undecided Grigori.

"Why are you different?" I asked Phoenix when our food arrived. I thought back to how he'd told me he wasn't like an ordinary exile.

"Just lucky, I guess." His sarcastic tone didn't exactly sound convincing.

I wrapped my hands around my mug of coffee, glad to have the comfort of my old dependable. "Why are you so evasive when it comes to talking about yourself?"

He didn't respond.

"You're not going to tell me, are you?"

"Have I proved to you that I'm not here to hurt you?" he asked through raised eyebrows. Phoenix didn't drink coffee. He didn't seem to have any little rituals like me. Everything he did was always so different—and extreme. He would order the strongest-tasting food, the sweetest or the most unusual he could find. Today he was eating a steak sandwich with beets—because he liked the color—and a side of pickles and fresh chilies. I almost wished the same waiter who'd turned his nose up at my breakfast soup and coffee combo were here.

"Yes. I think so," I admitted, crinkling my nose as I watched him eat a small red chili in one gulp.

"Then can't that be enough for now?" he asked. I watched him as the impact of the chili hit his system. To my disbelief, only the smallest lift in the corner of his mouth gave it away.

I didn't think that I would ever accept a relationship that involved secrets again. After everything that had happened with Lincoln, it seemed hypocritical to accept that Phoenix should be allowed to keep the truth about himself a secret. But then again, it wasn't like we'd been hanging out for long. I couldn't expect him to trust me with everything instantly—not unless I was willing to do the same.

"Will you tell me one day?" I asked, suddenly realizing I saw Phoenix as a part of my world now, part of my life.

He smiled and I could see he was reading me. I blushed and smacked him on the shoulder.

"You know, if you were a Grigori, you would pack a lot more punch." He laughed aloud and the sound made my heart beat a little faster.

Who would've known—it still beats after all!

"One day, Violet"—he stood and then pulled me up to leave, entwining his fingers with mine and tugging on the tip of my baseball cap—"I'll tell you everything."

————

After a couple days of Phoenix following me around, I let him into the apartment. It was no small thing for me to let him into my private space. The only outsiders I had ever invited in before were Steph and Lincoln. But Phoenix's pestering had worn me down. He seemed so enthralled with me, so interested in me. I knew on some level it was because of the whole Grigori thing, but a lot of the time I was around him, it just felt like hanging out with any other friend.

Phoenix had little regard for my personal space—something that left me rethinking my decision to permit entry on more than one occasion. It took less than a day before he started lounging around in my bedroom, reading my limited selection of books, and messing with everything as if it were his own. I did, however, stand my ground when he tried to follow me into my art studio. No one, not even Dad, went in there. But I couldn't deny that having Phoenix around made me feel better. I knew it might just be because of his empath abilities, but there was also another reason: I liked him.

I asked him a lot of questions. He gave me a lot of answers too. Not always full answers, of course, and often they only led to more questions, but he tried and asked me questions in return. I answered some and avoided a lot. Every now and then he would try to encourage me to go see Lincoln, saying it was for my own good. I still hadn't seen or spoken to Lincoln since storming out of his car a couple of weeks ago. He didn't even know about what had happened to Claudia. I considered, briefly, calling him to tell him, but hadn't managed to pick up the phone yet. All in all, I had ignored the issue as much as possible…until now.

It was mid-morning and Phoenix had come over to take me to the movies. We were sitting in the kitchen eating breakfast when Dad walked through the door.

"Hey, Dad. Is everything okay?" I asked.

"Morning, sweetheart." He kissed me on the head. He smelled of shaving cream and aftershave. He had been loyal to the one brand for as long as I could remember. "Just popping in on my way to a client. I left one of the blueprints here last night."

Dad's attention drifted to Phoenix and then back to me.

"Oh, sorry. Dad, this is a friend of mine, Phoenix."

Dad's hands froze on the pile of papers he was rifling through as if he had just realized two things: someone else was in the apartment and that someone else was male.

He straightened and squared his attention to Phoenix. "Hello, Phoenix, nice to meet you," he said, though the look on his face said otherwise. He was giving him the cautious berth that only a father can.

"You too, James," Phoenix said, barely looking up from the magazine he was casually flipping through at the breakfast bar.

Dad and I shared a brief look before I quickly broke the father-daughter telepathy. Phoenix was the first of my friends to ever call Dad by his first name. Even Lincoln called him Mr. Eden, though Dad had told him to call him James. Somehow I didn't think Dad would have offered the first-name basis to Phoenix had he not just assumed it anyway.

"Coffee?" I asked. Diversionary tactics 101.

"No, thanks, I have to go, but you do remember we have that fund-raiser tonight. You're coming, aren't you?"

I had actually forgotten. It was a project Dad had been working on for a while. His firm had become a big contributor to a charity group for homeless kids. They designed buildings and houses on a pro bono basis that were built on the outskirts of the city where there was cheap land. Once kids were allocated a home, they then had to work with the building crews to put up the next one. It gave them a home, a job, an income, and a purpose. It was a good system.

"Yeah…of course," I said, fumbling a bit.

"You forgot," Dad said.

The look of guilt on my face ruined any chance I had of lying. "Don't worry. Steph is coming round later so I can borrow a dress.

I'll be there." I had a sudden thought. "Umm, Dad?" I put on my sweet voice he knew all too well.

"Yes," he said, raising his brow.

"Do you mind if I bring a couple of people?" I didn't see why I should have to stand around all night on my own. Dad and I both knew that he would be busy entertaining colleagues and clients. I was just there to show the united family front.

Dad looked at me, then at Phoenix. He sighed. "Who?"

"Just Steph and Phoenix," I said.

Phoenix looked up, showing his first glimmer of interest in our conversation. He was trying to hide it, but I saw the smile.

The look on Dad's face wasn't so elated. "I guess that will be fine. I'll let them know."

Dad grabbed his blueprints and slowly headed for the door, jangling his keys by his side. He took hold of the door handle but stopped before opening it. "Vi, you should probably know that the organizers sent through their guest list yesterday."

"And?" I said, taking a bite of stale croissant and spitting it back out. I really had to get out and do some grocery shopping.

"And I noticed Lincoln's name was on it."

"What?" I screamed, jumping off my stool.

"I swear I didn't know until yesterday," Dad defended.

"Well, I'm not going."

"Violet, you know I wouldn't ask you if it wasn't important. It's a really big event. You probably won't even see him."

I couldn't believe this was happening. The hardest part was, Dad hardly ever asked anything of me. The last person in the world I wanted to see was Lincoln, but I couldn't let Dad down. I couldn't push him away as well.

"Fine, fine, I'll go," I said.

"Thanks! I'll see you…both there." He darted out the door.

I stood staring at it. Phoenix started moving toward me, but my mouth was so dry I couldn't even tell him to leave me alone. He put a hand on my face. Tiny sparks of energy flickered between us like little electric shocks.

I was still staring at the door, trying to make sense of what had just happened. All my hard work at avoiding everything that reminded me of Lincoln, everything that could put me at risk of bumping into him, had just gone out the window.

It wasn't until Phoenix's lips actually pressed against mine that my body shocked me into the here and now. As soon as our lips touched, any control I had of the senses was ripped away from me. The cool heat hit my entire body. He tasted of apple, and my eyes instinctively closed. The flashes of light intensified, and I was almost sure there were split-second images of day and night rotating through my vision.

Then there was Phoenix, kissing me. He was surprisingly gentle. Unlike Lincoln's intensity, this was vulnerable and frightened me more. I was kissing him back…I think.

Before I could pull away, I got a flash of his desire…for me. I stumbled back, dizzy from the combination of sensory overload and my own head screaming at me.

"I…I…You said *I* had to be the one to kiss you."

"I lied." He said it so easily, not repentant in the slightest, that it struck a nervous chord.

"You're enthralling," he continued. "It's as if you become each of the senses and can affect them in me. Through you, I feel birds flying around me and even feel morning and evening manifest their power."

That got my attention away from my creeping sense of guilt. "Is it day and night?"

"In a way. It's the power that creates them."

"Like the sun?" I prompted.

"No. Like the force that creates and powers the sun."

"Wow," I breathed. How could I be feeling these things? How could my body be reacting this way?

"By the way"—he stepped toward me, closing the distance I had just created—"it's okay." He ran a finger down the line of my face.

I looked away, suddenly very self-conscious. I didn't know what he was talking about, but I dreaded what was coming.

He didn't give me time to prepare myself. "You're allowed to like kissing me." His expression was so penetrating. His usual cocky look had gone, replaced by something totally male.

I gave a shaky half laugh. "You're reading me?"

"Just enough." He ran his finger down the opposite side of my face and then slowly to my neck, following the line of my collarbone. I didn't know if the tingling down my whole body was the senses or just me…or him.

"You promised you weren't going to do that." My words were breathy.

His mouth curled at the sides, pleased with my reaction. He spoke slowly. "What I *said* was that I wouldn't influence you and…I haven't."

I blushed, wanting desperately to get out of this conversation. I had no idea what that kiss meant to me—or him, for that matter—but I knew it wasn't something I could try to figure out with an empath reading my every emotion.

I stepped back again, breaking our contact. It helped clear my mind enough to stumble quickly through my next words. "Can we just…go to the movies?"

It was pathetic, I knew, but it was the most I could muster.

"Sure," he said, heading for the door and holding it open for me.

As I walked past him, he rapped his fingers on the doorframe. "Well, that went well anyway. I think your dad likes me."

chapter seventeen

"It is an awful, an appalling thought, that we may be, this moment and every moment, in the presence of malignant spirits."

RICHARD WHATELY

The day sped away from me, leaving no real time to prepare. I was glad, and worked at keeping busy so I didn't have to think about seeing Lincoln that night.

Phoenix left during the afternoon, promising to return to pick up Steph and me at seven. We had successfully managed to avoid talking any further about our "moment," and I was relieved he'd let it go…for now.

Steph turned up with a ton of dresses cradled in her arms. For the past six months, she'd been collecting invites to formals from all the nearby schools. She called it a hobby. Needless to say, her wardrobe had expanded greatly and I suspected that had been the driving motivation. This wasn't the first time I would benefit as a result.

After setting aside the dress she was planning to wear, she laid out the rest for me to pick from. The choice was easy when I saw she had included the black strapless one I had been eyeing for months. I had tried to fight it in the past—mix it up, wear colors—but the fact was, I liked black and black liked me. The dress was simple, but I knew that with my curves and the sharp slit up the side, I would look about as hot as I could manage. When Steph dangled a pair of strappy black Jimmy Choos in my face, I said a prayer of thanks we were the same shoe size.

Steph's father was constantly away on work, and one of the perks was that he always had his PA arrange gifts for her and Jase on his return. Steph was now great friends with her dad's PA. She basically supplied her with a shopping list of designer clothes and shoes and presto: packages laced with this season's best would arrive on her doorstep.

"Are you sure you don't mind if I wear these?" I asked, even though I had no intention of giving them up.

"No problem!" Steph called out from the bathroom, where she was applying her final touches of makeup.

"Thanks. So how are things going with you and Marcus?" I asked, feeling guilty I hadn't been paying more attention to what had been going on in Steph's life. It was time to start being a better friend.

She came whirling out of the bathroom into my room. "Great! What else do you expect? He's gorgeous, smart, sexy, and going places. Not to mention his family is about as high up as you can get." Her tone was so matter-of-fact, I couldn't help but laugh.

"Okay, but I meant more along the lines of, do you care about him?"

She looked at me like I was missing the point completely. "Violet, honey, I just said he's hot, smart, and full of potential. What more is there to make me feel all warm and gooey inside?"

I couldn't argue there.

"Anyway, enough about me. What's going on with you and Mr. Catch-a-damsel-in-distress?"

I prepared myself again to tell her everything. I wanted to be able to confide in her, but like before, when I actually tried to physically tell her, I couldn't muster the words.

"We're *friends*," I said finally, sitting on my bed, buckling my shoes.

"Uh-huh."

"We are."

"So you're telling me you haven't had any warm, tingly feelings when you're around him?"

"No. Okay, yes…maybe." I shook my head, as much at myself as at Steph. "I'm not looking for that kind of thing anyway."

"Yeah, well, want it or not, you got something," Steph said.

I gave a moan, dropping my face into my hands.

"Vi, it's okay if you like him. Why don't you just try having a bit of fun? It won't kill you."

"Yeah, maybe. I just can't stop thinking about…" I couldn't even bear saying his name.

"Then it's probably a good thing you're going to see him tonight.

You've just built Lincoln up in your mind, like he's some god, but he's not, Vi. When you see him tonight, you'll see."

Yeah…that's exactly the way it's going to go.

I sucked it up and put on a brave face. "You're right. I can do this."

"Yes, you can. Plus, with *you* in *that* dress, he'll probably fall flat on his face when he sees you." She stood in front of me and sprayed me with perfume a couple of times. "It's marginally annoying that you look better in my own dress than I do."

I looked in the mirror. She wasn't lying; the dress definitely highlighted my assets. Steph was thin and beautiful with rich olive skin and shoulder-length blond hair, always perfectly styled and edgy. But she had nothing up top. She always joked about it, but I knew she envied my curves.

"And," she continued in her scheming voice, "if all else fails, you'll have Phoenix there as the perfect jealous accessory."

I hadn't thought of that angle. I didn't know if that was a good thing or not, but I couldn't deny I liked the idea of having extra ammo.

Phoenix picked us up at seven on the dot. He was annoyingly punctual. When we walked into the lobby of Dad's building, it was like walking into a wonderland. The entire place had been draped with millions of tiny white fairy lights. They blanketed the ceiling and shimmered down toward the ground like stalactites raining down on the crowd. There was a band playing in the corner with a woman vocalist singing in a husky, sweet voice. Waiters glided around the room in white tuxedos, balancing tray upon tray of champagne. A sea of glamorous people filled the room, covering the entire ground floor and spilling out onto the terraces, which had been opened up for the night. All the guests were dressed in way too much of everything. I had a flash of self-consciousness and hoped I had dressed up enough, feeling a little bare with no jewelry and my hair down.

As if on cue, Phoenix whispered in my ear, "You're so sexy, I'm struggling to keep my hands still."

I stopped fidgeting and smiled. The whole reading-my-emotions thing did have its benefits, I guess.

Steph fit right in, wearing a stunning emerald green silk dress that floated around her olive skin. The fact that she had an elaborate string of pearls around her neck made her stand out even more.

Phoenix looked hot dressed entirely in black. No tie or jacket, but he still managed a cool elegance. The outfit accentuated his hair and made it look incredible—the deepest plum, almost black, with splices of dazzling silver.

Wherever he walked, women turned their heads, blinded by his otherworldliness. It was like he left a lingering aura behind him that attracted them. He was aware of it, but seemed unimpressed—and while he paid Steph and me all the right compliments, his eyes never left me.

We mingled and Phoenix brought us a glass of champagne each.

Dad found us not long after we arrived. After a quick hello to Steph and barely a nod to Phoenix, he dragged me off to meet and greet all the people he'd wanted me there to see. It didn't take long for the formalities to be over and I was free to return to Steph and Phoenix. I considered just grabbing them and leaving, but I knew Dad would probably want me for a second sweep of the room later.

The idea of seeing Lincoln dominated my every thought. My head turned at the smallest sound. Every time I heard a man laugh or felt someone walk behind me, I spun to look. I hated that I was vulnerable and hated even more that he would be able to see right through me.

Just when I thought maybe Dad had been right, maybe Lincoln wouldn't turn up, I saw him. A group of people beside us started to move away, clearing the path that led straight to him. He was barely ten feet away from me.

My legs almost gave way right then and there. It was like seeing him for the first time, and my breath caught in my throat. Even after everything that had happened, he was still simply the most beautiful person I had ever laid eyes on.

He was dressed in a perfectly tailored suit, crisp white shirt, open collar, black pants and jacket. Leaning against one of the polished concrete pylons in the center of the room, hands in pockets, he looked incredible. But also different. Even from a distance I could see that his face was a little gaunt and his eyes seemed tired, like he hadn't slept in days.

My body started moving instinctively toward him, like one magnet being pulled toward another. But as the rest of the crowd parted, I froze in my tracks.

Lincoln was not alone.

A woman was with him. As I watched, she leaned in close and brushed the top of his shoulder, tidying him up, as if she were the person in his life who could assume this role.

I hated her.

Lincoln looked over through the space now open between us and saw me. I stopped breathing. He straightened.

I felt emotion surge through me—jealousy and something else I couldn't be sure of. All I knew was that it was very intense—and it wasn't mine. I glanced at Phoenix still standing beside me. I wanted to reassure him, but my eyes darted back to Lincoln. I stared as he too looked at Phoenix and then back to me. He said something to the woman he was with and then started to walk over. My heart was pounding so hard I could feel it thundering through my body. Phoenix inched a little closer. I tried to block out the emotion he was leaking into me.

I expected Lincoln to be businesslike. Actually, I don't know what I expected, but I thought it would be awkward. But when he neared me, he just kept coming through the polite personal boundaries I'd expected him to maintain. He grabbed my hand, pulling me into him, hugging me tight. In surprise, my natural instincts took over and my body melted. For the first time in weeks, I exhaled completely and I hugged him back. He pulled me tighter until I couldn't breathe, but I didn't care.

Oh God, just this moment. I need this. I can't let go. Not yet.

"I've missed you," he whispered in my ear. Tingles ran down my spine. I wanted to get closer, hold tighter, never let go. Then I remembered—grabbed some semblance of my mind and remembered the pain. I stepped back and he let me go.

Phoenix took my hand. It wasn't the hand I wanted, though I tried hard to hide it.

Lincoln straightened and visibly composed himself, tugging slightly at his jacket. He cleared his throat. "I'm sorry, I'm being rude," he said formally, looking at Phoenix through narrowed eyes. "I'm Lincoln. I believe we met briefly on Violet's birthday."

Shit.

I'd forgotten about that.

"Phoenix."

Lincoln put out his hand in offer to shake. When he extended his arm, the sleeve of his jacket pulled back, revealing the silver band secured snugly around his wrist.

Phoenix remained still. He saw it too. I got the distinct impression that was what Lincoln had intended.

"I'd rather not," Phoenix said.

Lincoln's eyes darted from Phoenix to me. "I knew it! Violet, he's—"

I cut him off. "I know what he is. He never lied to me about who he was, Lincoln."

I looked him in the eye, the first of my uncooperative emotions threatening to spill over. Steph shot me a questioning look. I just shook my head; I couldn't deal with her questions right now.

Lincoln turned his attention to Phoenix. "What are you doing with her? Why are you so hard to sense? Is this a game for you?"

Lincoln's whole demeanor had changed; his presence was now strong, threatening.

Phoenix tightened his grip on my hand. "It's no game. Violet needed someone to help her through this time. I'm sure you're aware she's more powerful than most. Were you not concerned for her safety?" I could feel his anger rising.

Lincoln returned it with interest. "Of course I was concerned! But I respected her right to be left alone until she was ready."

People were starting to look.

"You were careless. She's like a walking neon sign. You weren't there for her. I was." Phoenix tried for matter-of-fact, but none of us missed the territorial testosterone oozing from his words.

Lincoln laughed. "And she's supposed to feel safe with *you*? What? You have a crush on her? She'd *never* be with someone like you!"

Phoenix didn't say anything for a moment; he just looked straight at Lincoln, a dangerous smirk creeping onto his face. He swung the hand that was holding mine in the air a couple of times and shrugged.

"And yet..." He tilted his head, looking at our joined hands.

Lincoln's jaw was clenched so tight it looked like he was about to pop a vein.

"Stop!" I almost yelled. Things were getting way too heated way too fast. It was a bad idea putting these two in a room together.

"Look." I took my hand from Phoenix. "I don't need a hero protector, so you can both just stop!"

Steph, who was still standing silently on my other side, stepped in. "Umm, guys, I hate to break up the testosterone-fueled standoff, but people are starting to stare." She looked at Lincoln. "And by the way, nice to see you too, Lincoln." She gave him a tight-lipped smile.

"Hi, Steph. Sorry," Lincoln said, looking ashamed. So he should be. Then again, he hadn't been the only one puffing out his chest.

"Yeah, yeah," Steph continued. "Clearly, I have no idea what is actually going on here." She shot me an accusing look. I had a lot of explaining ahead of me. "*Clearly*, I'm out of the loop, but here's the thing. There are two of you and only one of Violet and, bless her, she just wasn't built to handle two guys at once."

It was me who shot her a look this time. She just smiled and directed her attention to Phoenix. "Why don't you and I go and have a drink at the bar? Violet can come and find us when she's ready."

At that moment, I loved Steph beyond words. Phoenix grudgingly followed her, but not before entertaining himself. He planted a slow kiss on my cheek followed by a departing smile at Lincoln. It was annoying, given that Phoenix had been the one bugging me to see Lincoln for the last couple of weeks.

We walked in silence out to the back terrace. Fresh air seemed like a good idea, and increasing the distance between Lincoln and Phoenix an even better one.

"You look beautiful with your hair down," he said, without looking at me. His voice touched that part of me that only he could, and I wanted to surrender, to dive into it, but I reminded myself that that time had passed.

"You've seen it down a million times." I blew him off, tucking my hair behind my ear.

"And a million times I've wanted to tell you how beautiful it looks." He turned and looked straight into my eyes and then deliberately dropped his gaze to the neckline of my dress. It was subtle compared to the way Phoenix forced his emotions on me, but it hit me like a wrecking ball anyway. I wanted so much to reach for him. He had never allowed himself to look at me like that before.

"Don't," I said instead.

"Okay," he said a little defensively. "If you just want to get back to your boyfriend"—he swung his arm toward the doors—"don't let me stop you."

"He's not…you have no right…Damn you!" I couldn't even put a sentence together around him.

Lincoln put his hands in his pockets and looked down. While he wasn't watching, I took a few deep breaths to steady myself.

"Sorry," he muttered. "But I've been going crazy not seeing you, not knowing how you are. I've tried to respect your space, but then you turn up here with *him*."

"I'm sorry it's been so hard for you," I replied sarcastically. "What are you doing here anyway?"

"The fund your dad's company is supporting tonight invited me. I'm one of their main contributors."

"Just another thing I didn't know," I said under my breath.

"It was a trust fund, set up when Mom died. It's not something I think about often. I wasn't keeping it from you."

He had never talked about his parents much. All I knew was that his dad died in a car crash a week after he was born and his mom died of cancer when he was seventeen. Apparently she'd been some kind of entrepreneur, and since Lincoln was an only child, I'd gathered he inherited a fair bit of money, enough to buy the warehouse, at least. The spare room in his place was filled to the ceiling with boxes of his mother's old company documents. He never went in there, always saying he was going to clear it out and turn it into a gym, although I knew he never would.

His tone dropped. "You shouldn't trust him."

"I shouldn't have trusted you," I said, matching his tone.

He grimaced with the pain of my words and it looked genuine, but I wasn't convinced.

"Have you decided what you want to do?" he said, turning away from me, bracing his hands on the railing. "About becoming a Grigori?"

"No. To be honest, there's still a lot I'm figuring out about the whole thing."

"Will you let me help you?" he almost begged.

The truth was, seeing what had happened to Claudia—the way that exile had forced her to kneel before him and ask for her death—had done something to me. Watching her will torn from her impenitently. I didn't know anymore if I really *could* turn away from my fate, knowing I could possibly prevent that from happening to another innocent person one day.

I also knew there was a part of me that was still so incredibly hungry to be around Lincoln, I couldn't resist his offer. I put my hands on the railings, and we both looked out into the night, standing shoulder to shoulder.

"Okay," I conceded. "But that doesn't mean that we're okay."

"Okay," Lincoln said.

Great. Everything was *okay*.

The woman who'd been with Lincoln inside materialized at his shoulder. Her willowy figure and wavy blond hair were complemented by a slinky, cream designer gown. I gritted my teeth. Perfect, now I was going to have the pleasure of being dumped for this beautiful creature.

She gestured for him to speak with her privately. Instead, Lincoln said, "Violet, this is Magda. She's Griffin's partner."

Magda looked at me and smiled, but it was the smile one woman gives another when she's sizing her up. Her eyes were cold. It made me feel a little better for disliking her instantly.

She extended her long, slim arm to me, which matched the rest of her perfect figure.

"*Grigori* partner," she clarified. Three guesses why. "It's nice to finally meet you, Violet. I'm sure we'll get a chance to get to know each other soon, but I'm sorry, we have to go." She had a faint accent. It wasn't foreign, more of a you're-beneath-me accent.

"Why?" Lincoln sounded a little irritated.

Magda glanced suggestively from Lincoln to me then back.

"It's fine, Magda. You can speak in front of her. There'll be no more secrets."

I scoffed out loud and they both looked at me. If they thought I was going to apologize, they would be waiting a while.

She hesitated then gave a brief nod. "The group that followed up on our lead today was ambushed. Griffin's expecting us."

Lincoln's jaw clenched. He looked at me. "I have to go. I'm sorry."

Out of nowhere, I blurted, "I want to come."

Now it was Lincoln's turn to let his eyes dart from me to Magda. She gave a slight shake of her head. Yep, she and I were never going to be besties.

To my surprise, Lincoln ignored her. "She has a right to see this, to understand." He turned to me. "Okay, but you have to promise to stay with me the whole time."

I nodded. I wasn't really sure what I was doing, but I had a guilty suspicion a green-eyed monster had just made my next move.

I leaned my head against the window in the backseat of Magda's car. There'd been no time for good-byes, so I sent Steph a text to let her and Phoenix know I'd had to leave. I was secretly glad for the excuse to escape. Since witnessing Steph's hard stare and Phoenix's brilliant chemistry with Lincoln, I hadn't been looking forward to dealing with the explanations tonight. No doubt I would pay for it tomorrow.

In the front, Magda and Lincoln talked about things I didn't understand, people I didn't know. A trickle of jealousy ran through me. I was being faced again with the harsh reality that there was a big part of Lincoln's life I was clueless about. It made me angry that I had been so stupid, so naïve.

A few other things were abundantly clear from w

He was relaxed and clearly felt at ease around her. Even

she was driving, she fidgeted constantly, adjusting her hair, playing with her necklace. She inched closer to the center console, to him, any chance she got. It was clear how she felt. The question was, how did he feel about her?

What I gathered from their conversation—aside from my complex breakdown of their body language—was that there had been a confrontation between a number of exiled angels and Grigori. The Grigori had tracked the exiles to their hideout but had been ambushed and outnumbered.

"So explain to me again why they hate Grigori so much?" I asked from the plush leather seats in the back of the Audi wagon. Of course Magda had an expensive European car.

Lincoln turned to face me, leaning over the center console. I noticed Magda didn't move away to give him space. Instead, their arms were now touching from shoulder to elbow. I gave a mental eye roll.

Please, could she be more obvious?

"Because we're the only thing that stands in their way," he said.

"To *what* exactly?"

"To power." He smiled wryly. "They want to rule over humanity. They want power and they want to strip our right to free will, turn us into slaves. They can make humans do almost anything. Some are erratic, irrational…Others are more organized. Either way, with that kind of power, it's bad. They want to destroy us

...cause we're the only ones who can stop them and...we're the only ones strong enough to fight them." He shook his head as he spoke. "Sometimes that's the worst thing about it. Knowing that they enjoy hunting Grigori so much...that it's become entertainment, a sport to them."

"But they don't *all* want to cause harm," I said. "Griffin said there were exceptions."

Lincoln knew immediately who I was referring to. He turned back in his chair, no longer looking at me. "Every now and then an angel that has chosen to exile just wants to live quietly among humans. We call them 'silents' and we leave them be, as long as they don't cause trouble. But *most* exiles are riddled with pride, desire, and the need for power. There's a reason they leave the angel realm to come here, and it rarely ends well for humans."

Magda parked outside an old warehouse block. The area seemed familiar. I was sure we weren't far from Lincoln's place. A pang of something like homesickness shot through me. I wanted to slap myself.

I followed as they walked slowly into the deserted building. It looked like it was scheduled for demolition, or should be. Almost all of the dirty windows were broken. There were some old flattened cardboard boxes that looked like they had been used as makeshift beds.

At the far end of the warehouse was a small group of people, huddled around something. We walked toward them, my heels clicking on the floor. The ground was covered in a thick layer of dust, highlighted by a scattering of recent footprints and scuff marks. Steph was going to kill me when she saw the state of her Jimmy Choos.

I felt out of place, like I was a kid getting smuggled into an R-rated movie. I kept expecting someone to single me out. Magda glanced at me out of the corner of her eye. It was obvious *she* didn't think I should be there.

Griffin broke away from the group and walked toward us. On seeing me, he smiled and I let go of a breath I hadn't realized I'd been holding.

"I was beginning to wonder if I was going to have to send out a search party," he said.

I smiled. He was kind of awkward in his attempts to be funny.

"Well, here I am," I replied.

"Yes." Griffin shot a look at Lincoln. "I had hoped you wouldn't have to be thrown into the thick of it like this…" He was still staring at Lincoln. "Still, I'm flattered that you dressed up."

I zeroed in on him. "It was my idea to come, so you can lay off with the accusing eyes."

Griffin's face registered his shock. I'd probably gone a bit too far, but I needed to reassert myself. The last time he'd seen me, I'd been a blubbering mess. I couldn't have him thinking I was always such a girl.

Lincoln started to laugh. I spun around to see him shaking his head.

"What?" I spat the word at him. Griffin was looking equally unsure.

"Nothing, I've just never seen Griffin so taken by surprise. Usually he can see people coming a mile off."

I turned back to see Griffin's reaction, but he was starting to laugh himself.

Magda gave a huff. "Is this really the place for mental breakdowns, people?" Then she stalked off.

I didn't know whether it was her words or her attitude that made me laugh, but either way, for the briefest of moments, we were all smiling.

Lincoln was the first to remember why we were there. He frowned and turned to Griffin. "What happened? I thought tonight was just supposed to be about reconnaissance."

A look of regret crossed Griffin's face. His eyes were shadowed and weary. I could see that he felt the burden of being a leader.

"It was. We still don't know what happened. How they could have been…It doesn't make sense, Linc." He was shaking his head in disbelief.

"How many did we lose?" Lincoln asked, looking toward the far end of the wharf building, where all the other Grigori were gathered.

Griffin brushed his hands across his face. "Three. We thought it might be the same group we've been tracking, but now…we're not so sure. Tom's dead, Linc. They were ready, organized."

Lincoln stiffened. I wanted to comfort him, at least put a hand on his shoulder, but I held myself back.

"Why don't you think it was the same group?" he growled. "It must have been! Why aren't we going after them?"

"Because our people were killed by light *and* dark forces. We thought at first they'd been caught in a skirmish between the two sides. But this has a dark exile's stamp all over it. It's possible they are forcing light exiles to do their bidding. It wouldn't be the first time one side has taken hostages from the other."

"Could they be working together?" I butted in.

"Light and dark? No. They don't work together," Griffin said.

"Why do they take hostages?" I asked.

"Because when they have to use their powers for extended periods of time, it can weaken them. If they can force other exiles to do the dirty work for them, it leaves them always at full capacity," Lincoln explained.

Griffin rubbed his face again. "I know it's hard to believe, Violet, but exiles kill without a second thought. We're losing good people."

"Actually, it's not. I saw for myself." I bit down on my lip.

Confession time.

"What?" Griffin and Lincoln both exclaimed.

"A girl I knew. She was killed by an exile." My eyes welled up at the memory of Claudia being dropped into my open arms. "He broke her neck, right in front of me." I looked at Lincoln. "Her name was Claudia. You met her on my birthday."

He stepped toward me and gently put a hand under my elbow. "What happened? How did you get away?"

"Phoenix. He…killed him."

Lincoln and Griffin exchanged a glance. Lincoln didn't look back at me for a few moments, but Griffin smiled apologetically and gave a nod. "So you see, there's a good reason we're supposed to be divided by realms of reality and space."

I nodded, understanding more and more that exiles were not really angels anymore. They were misguided egos with power. Shitloads of power.

In that same moment, I found new respect for Griffin…and Lincoln, and maybe even my mom.

"I get it," I said.

chapter eighteen

*"The willing, Destiny guides them. The unwilling, Destiny
drags them."*

Seneca

"Violet," Griffin said, "I need to show Lincoln the bodies. He might
see something I missed. If you don't mind, you can wait here."

What I should have said was, *Sure, I'll wait here.* What I stupidly
said was, "I want to see too. If this is part of what being a Grigori
is, then I think I have a right to see."

Griffin put a hand out, gesturing for me to walk with them as
he spun on his dusty black boots. "I won't lie—two were killed by
sheer brutality, the other by…something even worse. None of it is
peaceful in any way."

I nodded, wondering what could be worse than sheer brutality.
The three of us walked toward Magda and the other Grigori. There
were no police or officials, no police tape, nothing to mark it as a
crime scene.

"Will you report this to the police?" I asked Lincoln.

He looked at me sadly. "No. It's too dangerous to involve normal humans in all of this. Plus, there's no way to explain the injuries without raising suspicion. We have Grigori who usually stage another scene that will alert authorities to the deaths but cover the circumstances."

"Like what?" I was horrified but strangely understanding.

"Different things—car crashes, fires, you know."

"Christ," I said. I noticed he only mentioned the kind of accident scenes that left carnage in their wake.

As we got closer to the area, I started to feel a small hum vibrate through me. I tried to control it. In hindsight, this would have been a good point to cut and run. Hindsight's a bitch.

I saw the first body and relaxed prematurely. It was awful but not horrendous, just an inert form. My attention was drawn to the other two victims, and my hand flew to my mouth. I wanted to be sick. They were both women: young, beautiful, and naked. There was already a strong smell emitting from them, a combination of raw flesh and salty blood drying in the heat. I tightened my hold over my mouth when I saw the holes in their stomachs. Beside them was a pile of…organs, I think—like a hand had torn into them and pulled out their insides, dumping them beside the empty carcasses. It was monstrous, a scene of utter destruction.

I wrapped my arms around my stomach, trying to ignore the most frightening sensation that was welling up inside me, pushing at the very fibers of my being: pure pleasure. Whoever, whatever, had done this had experienced ultimate joy in the process. And I could feel it too.

Desperate to avert my gaze, I switched my attention back to the other body. This time I *really* saw it. I'd heard of it before, the way a person's mind can somehow protect them from processing things that are too disturbing. The male, still dressed and moderately undisturbed, lay in a state of emptiness—not like he was dead, more like he was lost. Dead bodies are supposed to look like they are finally at rest, but I knew now what Griffin had meant when he said we would find no peace. There was none to be had. I stared at each one, horrified, my heart crying for them. I felt suffocated.

As soon as I tasted apple on the tip of my tongue, I knew the rest of the senses would follow. I stumbled a few steps, trying to get away. It was futile.

Images of morning and evening flashed before my eyes, blinding me. It was…violent. Painful. I dropped to my knees and screamed. I heard Lincoln cry out, though he didn't touch me. I wanted to stop it, but I couldn't. Cold heat rushed through my body. I felt like a rigid statue of ice with a volcano erupting from within. I could hear my screams—worlds away.

My back arched, my arms falling behind me, dangling to the ground, my knuckles grazing the concrete floor.

An arm encircled my waist, holding me up as I arched back even farther. Another hand gripped the side of my face, keeping me still. I felt myself slipping away, losing myself to the senses. I tried to concentrate, tried to remember what Phoenix had told me.

Emotion. I needed to control my emotions. Or distract them with something that could totally consume me.

I hoped it was Lincoln's arm around my waist.

"Kiss me," I whispered.

The hands on my face froze. Another wave of the senses pummeled through me.

"Kiss me, please!" This time I was screaming.

He slammed into me, crashing through the barriers. So perfectly molded to my mouth, he pushed my lips apart and...we melted. The same cool, pure breeze I had felt after Lincoln had touched me when I first held the wristband galloped through my body, through my soul. It blew the overpowering smell of flowers away like a breeze through a field. I felt the apple fade until all I could taste was his very real mouth. My body poured the cool heat and humming energy into him, until he had absorbed it all. The birds circled us and flew into the distance.

He pulled me closer. Kneeling in front of me, he kissed me intensely and I felt...right. Morning and evening slipped away. It was just us. Silence surrounded us. My heart leapt and I kissed him back, knowing so truly that I loved him. My heart cried and I pulled away, knowing so truly that he had betrayed me.

I fell to the ground.

He fell to the ground.

I cried.

He screamed.

Slowly, the room and people around us came back into

perspective. Griffin was by my side, asking me a million questions I couldn't register. I didn't know if the pain rolling through me was real or not. I looked over to my side and could see the dead bodies lying around me. It was like I was one of them.

"Lincoln?" I croaked. "Is he okay?"

Magda was bent over Lincoln where he lay on the ground. I crawled the short distance to him. I didn't miss the accusing look she shot me before she moved away. With all the violence that had just coursed through my body, I had to fight off a momentary inclination to smash her face with my fist.

"Linc." My voice cracked as I tried to control my tears.

He looked at me, trembling.

"Are you hurt? Did I hurt you?"

He was breathing fast. "A bit more like overloaded. I've never felt anything…Violet, your…" He turned from me to look at Griffin, now also kneeling beside him. "Did you see that? Feel any of it?"

Griffin was calm. "I saw it, but didn't feel it. Tell me."

Lincoln looked to me. "Can I?"

At least he'd asked my permission. I nodded silently. I couldn't keep pretending these things weren't happening.

"I felt all five, Griff. She hasn't even embraced yet and she has all five senses, each stronger than any I have ever felt. When I touched her, she fed them to me. I felt them completely. It's as if she…she doesn't just sense them, but…she *becomes* them."

Yeah, like I'm freaking possessed!

Griffin was silent, then asked, "Why the kiss?"

Good question. Lincoln looked at me.

Please don't make me try to answer this.

"I think it's because she couldn't control it, couldn't make it stop. When I kissed her, it acted as a conduit. Like we could share the senses and give them somewhere to go. Once they moved through me, they left."

Griffin looked curiously at me. "So, someone just has to kiss you to control it?"

I saw Lincoln's eyes flash as he waited for my answer. I knew he was wondering if I'd tried out the theory before.

"No." I blushed. I couldn't say what I knew. Couldn't say that I had kissed Phoenix and it *hadn't* stopped the senses. "I…I'm not sure," I lied.

"Right, so we need to have Lincoln on hand in case this happens again." Griffin looked grave, but when he saw the panic on my face, he softened. "I wish I could give you the answers, Violet, but I don't have them. I've never known another Grigori to possess all the senses or to be so acutely aware that she can sense exiles in the wake of their destruction. It may be that it's just temporary and Lincoln is the only one who can help you because he's your partner. You are designed to complement one another, though such close physical contact is not…"

He and Lincoln exchanged a look.

"Not now," Lincoln said. They were keeping something from me. I felt my defenses go up. I didn't want to be lied to again.

"For now, at least, we need to find out what happened here

tonight. I have some contacts who should be able to let me know if any exiles of light have been taken—we can start there. We need to know what we're dealing with, especially if they have numbers."

"Agreed," Lincoln said. "But we should get Violet out of here in case the senses return." He was already getting up, brushing himself off.

"Good idea." Griffin turned to me. "Lincoln will take you home. We can talk tomorrow, discuss what's ahead for you."

I stared at him. I couldn't contemplate a future like this. I'd been beginning to think that maybe I could face this life, maybe it would ease the guilt over what had happened to Claudia. But I couldn't…My whole body was still shaking from what had just happened. I'd had no control whatsoever, and control was one thing I was not willing to relinquish. I didn't want to be overcome by these senses, especially knowing that the one person who had betrayed me the most was the one person who could stop them.

"Actually, I'm fine," I said. "Look, I understand, I do. What you do, it's important. It's just…I'm not that person." I looked around the room and spotted an exit door. "I'm sorry. I have to go."

I headed for the door and walked straight out without looking back. I kept going until I hit a small park at the end of the road. I hadn't made it far, but my legs were still shaky and I wasn't great in high heels to begin with. Yes, I was a wimp and running was against the rules, but I'd had to get out.

I sat on a worn-out park bench. It was late…or early. It looked as if dawn was creeping into the sky. I heard footsteps. I knew it was him without turning. He sat beside me and reached for my hand, but I pulled it away.

"I'm sorry I hurt you," I said. "I don't know how to control this stuff." I wondered how painful it had been. His scream had sounded pretty bad.

"I was glad to help. *Wanted* to help. It's not the senses that hurt anyway." He put his head in his hands, resting his elbows on his knees. He took a deep breath and blew it out. "Kissing you is…I tried so hard, for so long, to deny myself. I tried to do the right thing. But ever since we kissed on your birthday…I knew once I started I'd never be able to…even though we can't."

"You keep saying we can't. It's just an excuse, Linc."

"It's not."

"Then why? *Why* can't we?" I knew I was probably just hurting myself more, having this conversation with him, but I couldn't help myself.

"We're destined partners, Vi. Like Griffin said, our powers are complemented by one another, our souls affected. Grigori partners, they can't ever be together…like that. It's too dangerous. It weakens our powers, makes us vulnerable to exiles." He ran his hands through his hair. "That's why I always tried to keep my distance, stay away, be professional. But now…"

"Now what?" I asked, struggling to process what he was saying. We could never be together?

Not if I become a Grigori…

He shook his head. "Now every time I look at you, I can see you can't bear to be around me and I can't even make it right."

I was silent. I didn't tell him it wasn't true, that I did want to be near him, desperately, that more and more I wished I had it in me to just…let go.

"Will you ever forgive me?" he asked.

My mother's letter had requested the same thing: understand. I could try. Forgiveness always seemed harder.

"I think my mother was a Grigori," I said, avoiding his question.

"What?" He seemed genuinely surprised, which was a relief. Part of the reason I hadn't told him about this before was because I was afraid it was yet another thing he already knew and was keeping from me.

"Dad gave me a box that she'd left behind for my seventeenth birthday. It was the same as the box you have and inside was one of the silver wristbands and…a letter."

"Jesus. I didn't know; I swear. I've never known of another Grigori who had a Grigori parent. What did the letter say?"

"That spirits are real and sometimes they need to be returned…and to forgive her."

"Oh."

Silence spoke volumes until Lincoln finally broke it. "I know I failed your trust. When you've embraced and you're a Grigori, there'll never be the need for secrets. I promise I'll never keep anything from you again."

"I'm sorry, Lincoln, but are you goddamn insane? Do you *really* think I want to become a Grigori? After what just happened? What will happen to me once I actually embrace this thing? I can't even cope now!"

His brow furrowed. "What are you saying?"

"Let me spell it out for you. I. Don't. Want. To. Be. A. Grigori. Now or ever! I'm sorry you had these grand plans, but I just want to go to school and live my life. Just my normal *human* life." As I said it, I knew it was true.

He stood and started pacing around me. I stood too.

"You can't, Vi. You're not like other people. Even Phoenix said it. Your power attracts too much attention. You need to learn how to harness your Grigori powers to keep yourself safe."

"No, I don't. I've made my choice. Remember: free will. You can tell Griffin."

He hunkered down in front of me, his head in his hands, then he sank to his knees. "Violet, *please*. I can't stand by and watch them hurt you. Hate me forever, but please don't do this. They'll find you and…they'll kill you."

Wow. Nothing like a little death threat to brighten your night.

I stood while he remained at my feet. In that moment, it seemed ironic. It had always been me kneeling at his feet, worshipping him.

"I'll take my chances."

He stared at the ground, but when he spoke his voice was steady. "Do you really think that exile can protect you? Are you really sure he isn't the very thing you should be running from?"

I half laughed. "That smacks of jealousy, Lincoln."

He didn't look up. "Of course. Isn't that what you were aiming for?"

Stabbing myself in the eye with a toothpick would have been easier than forcing myself to turn and walk away. But somehow I did it. I left the man I would have once never willingly turned from, kneeling in the wet grass.

chapter nineteen

"Yet he was jealous, though he did not show it,
For jealousy dislikes the world to know it."

LORD BYRON

I woke to find Phoenix sitting at the end of my bed. Seeing him there, uninvited and in my personal space, should have upset me. Instead of being annoyed, I felt calm.

"Are you influencing me?" I asked, clearing my throat between words.

"No."

I wasn't sure that was entirely true. He smoothed a hand over my bedspread, only to ruffle it again in a clenched fist. He was sulking.

"I'm sorry about last night," I said, rubbing my face awake. Mascara came off on my hands, alerting me to the fact that I now had panda eyes. I hadn't even bothered to wash my face when I got home last night, or rather, this morning.

He didn't respond. He just watched me. I was sure he was

reading my emotions. "*You* were the one who said I needed to talk to him," I tried, reaching for a tissue.

"Talk?" He raised an eyebrow.

I couldn't stop the blush as last night's kiss replayed in my mind. I quickly set about dabbing my eyes, hiding behind the tissue.

"No one feels that guilty about a conversation," he said quietly.

I pretended I hadn't heard him and kept busy with the hard-to-budge mascara.

"I can sense your memory, Violet!" He slammed his hand down on the mattress, and the whole bed, with me on it, bounced. "More than words were exchanged."

He stood and walked over to my bookshelf, pretending to rifle through it. "And the regret you feel isn't regret for whatever you *did* do."

I tried to focus on nothing, tried to control my emotions and block him out. He glared at me, totally pissed.

"Look, Phoenix, if you're going to read me, then at least get your facts straight."

He looked confused. I sat up in the bed, suddenly conscious I was wearing a *Lion King* T-shirt and most likely had bird's-nest hair.

"There was a…" I didn't know how to describe what I'd seen. The idea of those people lying there with their insides ripped from them. The man who had been beyond lifeless, completely lost. Just the memory made me nauseous. I wrapped an arm around a pillow and pulled it close to my body.

"Grigori were killed. When I saw the bodies, I…It was…painful.

I couldn't control it. I was desperate and had to find a way to stop the senses. So I…"

"Used your feelings for Lincoln?"

I looked down, embarrassed. "Yes."

"And it worked?" he pressed.

"Yes."

A look of pure fury swept across Phoenix's face. I shuffled back in the bed until I hit the wall. I was shaking, but I held his eyes.

After a few minutes, he walked to my bedroom door. "Take a shower, get changed. I'll make coffee." His voice was distant.

I lay back in bed and pulled the comforter over my head, not knowing if I was supposed to feel relieved or more worried.

I scavenged around my room looking for clean clothes—something that was becoming an all-too-frequent habit. Normal things, like laundry, just seemed so unimportant these days. I threw on an old pair of jeans that were loose around the waist. I rarely wore them because I constantly had to tug them up. Plus, it was about eighty degrees outside. I knew I'd be hot, but nothing else would pass for clean. While crawling around on my hands and knees in search of a belt, my mother's box, which I'd stashed under my bed, caught my eye.

I pulled it out and emptied the contents across my bed. As I tipped it upside down, I saw on the bottom a faded inscription I hadn't noticed before.

Evelyn bar Semangelof
Magen of Will

I picked up the baby necklace with the small amulet. Dad had told me the amulet was some kind of good luck charm to be worn for a baby's first twenty days. He'd put it on me every day for six months, just to be sure.

I held the amulet in my hand. It depicted three figures standing with their hands outstretched. I could see the faint outline of wings behind them. I flipped it over in my hand and there was another engraving on the back. It was small and faded. I could barely make it out.

S.S.S. Protect

Apart from sounding like the name of a naval ship, I had no idea what it meant.

Had my mother truly been a Grigori? Had everything been a lie? Did she even really love Dad? Or me for that matter?

The sound of a thump on my door startled me.

"Coffee's ready," Phoenix called out. He was obviously still grumpy. I took a deep breath and ran my hands through my hair, a futile attempt to relieve stress.

I put all of the contents back in the box, trying not to touch it or the silver wristband more than necessary. I didn't need another unwanted attack of the senses. My hand lingered on the envelope that held my mother's words before it too went into the box and back under my bed. "Out in a minute," I yelled.

When I reached out to open my door, I noticed my arms and stumbled backward in shock. My veins had wrapped around my wrist like a thin bracelet. I looked closer at the markings and realized they weren't my veins at all; they were something else. The color was almost gray or even...*metallic?*

I inhaled and closed my eyes.

Breathe, don't panic. Breathe, don't panic.

I reminded myself that I was a master at putting things into the deal-with-later section of my mind. This was no different.

The smell of fresh coffee hit me as soon as I walked into the kitchen wearing a long-sleeved T-shirt over my baggy jeans. Yeah, not my best look.

"You'll be hot in that," Phoenix said, barely looking up.

"It's fine."

He looked at me and raised an eyebrow. I kept my emotions as calm and neutral as possible. His eyebrows rose higher, but to my relief he didn't say anything.

I drank the coffee Phoenix had made for me. I was sure it would be the first of many that day. I thought about the previous night and the decision I'd made. For the first time in a long while, I felt like I was getting back some control. Since that day at Lincoln's, I'd been losing myself bit by bit to the fear and panic of it all. The truth had shattered my sense of equilibrium, but I wasn't going to let someone else's idea of my destiny ruin what I'd worked so hard for. For better or worse, this was right for me. So what if I had a few weird marks on my arms? I could live with that.

"You're fooling yourself," Phoenix said out of nowhere, breaking my trail of positive thoughts.

I pouted, determined not to have my moment ruined. "Stop

reading me. It's rude." I skipped to the fridge and pulled out a tub of yogurt.

"I can't ignore you when you're flashing your emotions around like that," he snapped. He wasn't happy, but I was guessing my cheerfulness wasn't the key motivator for his angst.

I was losing patience with his foul mood. "Don't look at me like that. I've made my choice. If you really care about me, you'll respect it. Unless, of course, you only wanted to be around me because you thought I was going to be some kind of super powerful Grigori."

I was joking, but his eyes darted away. I moved toward him, standing in his line of sight. "That *isn't* it, is it, Phoenix?"

He walked toward me and took my hand. The senses started to hum around me.

"It would certainly help in preventing your death, so yes, but…" He lifted his head to meet my eyes and I saw the conflict that raged within him. "It's not why I'm here. Not anymore." He leaned in to kiss me.

He stopped at my lips and whispered, "Tell me to kiss you."

In that moment I almost craved it, but I also remembered my kiss with Lincoln. I stayed where I was and whispered back, "I…I don't want to hurt you."

Something overcame him; he let out a small cry and hung his head, resting his forehead on mine. We stood like that for a minute. I felt the weight of eons of pain pass through him.

Then, rather than waiting for me, he kissed me. I could feel the sense of resolve in his action. I tried to ignore the senses, but as I opened myself up to him, they all merged into one sparking energy, like a firework crackling between us. He felt the change and drew me closer. Then he stopped, pulling back just enough to speak. "Can I do something?" he asked.

"What?"

He half laughed. "Trust me?"

It was a bigger question than he realized. "Okay," I said softly.

He slid his arm from around my waist and took hold of one of my hands. I felt the sparks of energy flare between us just as before, and then he kissed me again, but this time he *really* kissed me. He pulled me tight, arm still wrapped around my body. His other hand slowly crept up my arm, fingers trailing lightly. As his tongue moved into my mouth, the flavor of apple was pushed aside as he brought something else: the taste of pure…seduction.

The sparks of energy flickered and then stopped. I could feel them building, like millions of tiny water balloons filling up. He felt me tense. "Let go," he whispered into my lips.

I wasn't sure what to do and I considered pulling away, but he drew me closer and then it exploded. Millions of bubbles of emotion washed over me. Incredible desire, lust, *love* poured through my body. Every part of me was completely aware of every part of him, and as he kissed me, it was as if he opened a portal to himself. I knew he wanted me, knew he wanted all of me. I felt his jealousy and possessiveness; it was all-consuming and…scary. But there was no denying, as he bled into me, that I wanted it too, wanted him, was completely seduced by his emotions. In that moment, I would have done anything he commanded of me.

I tugged at his T-shirt and he complied, pulling it off in a microsecond. I was barely separated from his lips. I ran both hands down his sculpted back. He lifted me, hoisting me onto the kitchen counter, never breaking contact with my lips. Everywhere I touched, it was like tasting a new flavor of emotion, but always there, lingering, was the taste of seduction…jasmine and vanilla.

Somewhere, far away, part of me was screaming for control, but I didn't care. The part of me that was under Phoenix's influence was relishing the freedom. He scrunched the back of my top in his hands. He was pulling at it, tugging and tightening it around me, but not taking it off. I could feel how much he wanted to, could feel his struggle. I wanted him to take it off—*rip it off* if he had to. The wave of desire rolling through me empowered me. I knew it wasn't all my emotion, but what *was* me was intensified and without boundaries. It was…bliss.

I grabbed at my shirt, to take it off for him. He gripped my hands, holding them down by my side. I felt him shaking as he fought for self-control. He made a deep growl, and then, defiantly, he took a breath and I felt the emotion slide away. He slammed the barriers up between us. All my other emotions—guilt, self-consciousness—rushed back. It was a nasty comedown. A big part of me just wanted him to turn on the tap again and take me back to bliss. But then there was the other part.

"What did you do to me?" I couldn't control my breath.

He took a moment, picked up his T-shirt, and turned around as he put it on, tugging it down over his pants. I blushed when he turned to look at me.

"It wasn't all my emotion, you know."

"That doesn't matter! You took away my control."

I set about making more coffee, trying not to look at him. As soon as I reached for a clean cup, I felt myself launching it across the kitchen. The white ceramic shattered into tiny pieces, ricocheting over the floorboards.

He was surprised but didn't avert his gaze. He kept watching me, piercing me with his dark eyes. "I know you enjoyed it," he said in his familiar seductive tone.

"That's not the point. I couldn't stop you!" Before he could open his mouth, I added, "It doesn't matter what you think you know, Phoenix. You don't know everything about me!"

I got the dustpan and brush out of the cupboard and started to sweep up the mess.

Phoenix made no move to help. I don't think it even occurred to him. He grabbed an apple from the fruit bowl and rolled it in his fingers, watching me.

"I'd never let you make a choice on a kiss and then let that lead to more than what had been agreed. It would be…"

"Bad?" I offered, as he struggled for a word. He didn't get it, didn't realize how important it was to me to have control. Only one person ever truly got it.

He smiled. "Violet, I hate to tell you this, but *bad*?" He raised his eyebrows. "Bad can be a lot of fun. No, the word I was looking for was…cheating."

I blushed and suddenly felt *very* young and inexperienced. "Just don't do it again."

chapter twenty

"*I will send rain on the earth forty days and forty nights; and
I will blot out from the face of the land every living thing that I
have made.*"

GENESIS 7:4

I holed up in my art studio. It was the one place I could go where
I knew Phoenix wouldn't follow me. After our disastrous kiss—or
rather, my disastrous reaction to it—I expected him to just let
himself out. So I was surprised to find him still sitting in the living
room when I emerged a while later.

I didn't have the heart or the energy to tell him to go, so I just
ignored him. I really should have been studying—exams were due
to start after break and I'd barely picked up a book. In the end, the
overwhelming need to crawl up on the couch with a fluffy pillow
and blanket and watch the movie channel, while gorging on salt-
and-vinegar chips, won out. Apart from everything else, not having
Lincoln around had caused my diet a great disservice.

I barely had the remote in my hand before Phoenix asked for a play-by-play of last night's murder scene. I was tempted to just tell him to go away. I wasn't impressed by how his "trust me" request had worked out, but I could also feel myself starting to calm down. Then I realized Phoenix was probably responsible for that. I made a frustrated sound and buried my head in my pillow. "I'll tell you if you cut the empath crap!"

He didn't say anything, but I started to feel more like myself—angrier—so I knew he had backed off.

It didn't seem to matter how much I wanted to move on with my life; everything kept circling back to Grigori and exiles. I was starting to get a bad feeling that no matter what, I wasn't going to be able to escape it.

I told Phoenix about the three dead Grigori, that they'd been murdered by exiles, not just light or dark but both. As I told him about Griffin's theory, he started to shift uncomfortably in his seat, moving cushions around as if distracted by them.

I lost my patience. "What?"

He sighed. "The rules have changed, Violet. Your people need to open their eyes." He was shaking his head.

"What do you mean?"

"I shouldn't be talking about this stuff."

"Grigori are dead. If you know something, you have to tell me."

Phoenix's eyebrows shot up. "I'm *sorry*, you're confusing me with someone who gives a damn. Grigori are the enemy of exiles—of *all* exiles, including me."

"Then why have you been helping me? Why did you kill that exile the other night?"

"I killed him because he was going to rip your head off if I didn't."

"Otherwise what? You guys would have gone out for beers?" I was getting angrier by the minute.

His eyes flashed dangerously. "No. I'd never go anywhere with a Cherubim. I told you I don't like them." He clenched his jaw, watching me. "I thought you didn't care anyway. You don't even want to protect your own. Why would you think that I would, when they'd only plan to kill me later…or worse?"

"I never said it was okay for them to be murdered," I said defensively. I was getting so angry. I wasn't the only one; Phoenix looked like he could breeze out on me at any second.

"Look, you're right. I shouldn't expect you to care," I said, between deep, calming breaths. "But you *are* here and you *did* save me from the Cherubim. I know you don't care about other Grigori…yet you want me to become one of them. But what would be the point if the others are all dead? Please, Phoenix."

"Stop it," he growled. I knew he was referring to my emotions, to the fact I could *feel* that I had him.

"Annoying, isn't it?" I said, flashing him a smart-ass grin.

He put his hands in his pockets and stalked around the living room for a bit, eventually disappearing down the hall. I let him have time to think. We weren't arguing over pizza toppings.

When he took up position again on the couch, he slumped

down, leaned his head back to look at the ceiling, and gave a weighty sigh.

"Okay. You need to understand there was a time when exiles were rulers on earth, a time when they were able to come here and take what they wanted and do as they pleased. They took men for slaves and women to bear them children. They didn't hesitate to kill any who opposed them, and mankind fell under their rule swiftly."

"They wanted humans to serve them," I said, remembering what Griffin had told me.

Phoenix nodded. "I'm sure some of this has been explained to you. The way some angels came here to kill and conquer, while others came for the bodies. You see, the realm can sometimes seem like two opposing countries filled with propaganda and inevitable war. Unlike here though, it's not much fun being at war with no corporeal form." He gave a wry smile. "It lacks the dramatic rewards."

Aka blood and guts. I shuddered.

"In those days, Grigori were a rank of angels," Phoenix continued. "They were not so much fighters as sentinels who watched over humanity and reported back to the Seraphim. But they'd been living on earth for thousands of years and had become weakened by their human form, susceptible to temptation and desire."

"Griffin said exiles can suffer the longer they're human," I said, choosing my words carefully.

"That's true, though I've told you I'm not like other exiles," he said, answering my unspoken question. "Anyway, the exiles threw women and power at the angel Grigori, who were too weak to resist. They joined forces. Together they were unstoppable. Humans cowered under them, and those who didn't were relegated to hiding in mountain caves."

"So what happened?" Clearly we were not living in caves anymore.

Phoenix stood up and started pacing the room. He kept playing with the buttons on his cuffs, undoing them and doing them up again. He was wearing a navy shirt that highlighted his hair, and every time he walked under the downlights, it shimmered.

"Eventually, the Seraphim sent a legion of warrior angels—of both light *and* dark—to earth. For the first time in eons, light and dark had called a truce in order to give earth back to humans. The warrior angels swarmed over the earth like a great flood, destroying everything they touched. They wiped out the tainted humanity, destroyed exile progeny, and seized the exiled angels and all who had broken angel law. As a final message to any angels who considered making a similar choice, they parted the Red Sea, revealing the pits of damnation, and banished them to an eternity of torment and pain."

"Hell," I whispered.

"You can call it that if it keeps things simple for you."

"Wait. Is that where all exiled angels go?" He knew what I was asking. He didn't answer. Instead, he refocused on his cuffs.

"The Seraphim agreed that humanity should have a chance to survive without the direct interference of angels. And, of course, the role of angels depended on the continued existence of humanity, so everyone's survival rested on finding some kind of solution. They knew they couldn't risk putting more angel Grigori on earth and the same thing happening again."

"So no more angels on earth," I said.

He nodded. "Angels were never again permitted passage to earth, unless for spiritual visions—dreams, illusions, crap like that. But they couldn't stop angels who chose to banish themselves permanently from the angel realm in favor of the earthly realm. And they still needed a power that could police these exiles, a power that could carry light and dark strengths in one entity." His hand went out to me. "Human Grigori."

His version was definitely more informed than Griffin's story. "Okay, but I still don't understand what that has to do with these murders."

Phoenix nodded and walked back to sit beside me. "I know it's complicated, but try. Exiles know that before the existence of human Grigori, they were unstoppable."

"Not good for Grigori."

"No. And exiles have evolved. The group your people are tracking are organized. The reason it *looks* like they were killed by both light and dark exiles is because they *were*. They've joined forces against a common enemy." He leaned forward on the couch and grabbed both of my hands.

"Violet, they've called a truce and they have a plan."

"To kill all Grigori," I finished for him.

He didn't respond. He just looked right into my eyes.

F.F.F.F.F.F., recurring!

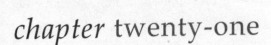

chapter twenty-one

"From the crevice of the great deep, above, there came a certain
female, the spirit of all spirits, and we have already explained that her
name was Lilith. And at the very beginning she existed with man."

ZOHAR III, 19A

Lincoln didn't answer his phone. I left a message and was already
halfway out of the apartment when Phoenix grabbed my arm.
"What are you doing?"

I shook him off. "I have to find Lincoln," I snapped.

He stood beside me as I waited for the elevator. When I raised
my eyebrows at him, he shrugged. "There's no way I'm about to let
you go out there alone. Especially back to him."

He sounded a little childish and I rolled my eyes, but my heart
wasn't in it. The truth was, I was relieved to have company.

I half walked, half ran to Lincoln's place, Phoenix trailing
behind. I pressed the buzzer for a good five minutes, and when I
started banging on the door, he put his hand over mine to stop me.

Lincoln wasn't home and I had no idea where else to go. I didn't know where Griffin lived or where he might be. I silently cursed myself for never getting his number from Lincoln.

The only other place I could think of was the warehouse from last night. I knew it wasn't far from Lincoln's but couldn't remember in which direction. After a quick explanation to Phoenix, I raced back down Lincoln's steps and started taking streets at random, getting increasingly disoriented. Even though I was setting a good pace—no doubt thanks to all my long-distance training—Phoenix had no trouble keeping up.

Finally, he dropped behind. "Violet, you obviously have no idea where you're going!" he called out.

"I know that, Phoenix! Thanks for your help!" I yelled back, slowing to a walk. Panic and fear were riding me hard and I couldn't fight the creeping onset of doom.

"If you want my help, all you have to do is ask." He had stopped, now resigned to yelling to me from the other end of the street.

I turned to look at him, throwing my arms in the air in frustration. "What does that mean?"

"It *means*, if you stay still for a few minutes, I can try to track the activity that went on last night."

"Oh," I said, feeling stupid. "I'll stay still."

I waited and watched, trying not to inhale any of the rotted garbage smells that were wafting my way in waves of heat. Phoenix tilted his head every now and then in another direction, as if trying to hear the far-off song of a bird. He started walking in the opposite direction. "It's this way."

I had to run to catch up. When we were out of sight of passersby, Phoenix stopped again.

"Come on, we have to find them!"

I was panting and jittery and out of patience. I knew he was just trying to help, but at that moment he was also the only outlet I had for the terror that was raking its claws through me. Something was wrong.

Phoenix grinned calmly, which only aggravated me more. He wasn't even breathing fast. "I was going to offer a little timely help, since you spent the first half hour running in the wrong direction. I *thought* you were in a hurry."

I glared at him from where I was bent over with my hands on my knees, sucking in air.

"Take my hand." He smiled, as if daring me.

I held out my sweaty hand. He scrunched his face when he saw it.

"What?" I asked, exasperated.

He kept an eye on my hand until I gave an exaggerated huff and wiped it on my jeans.

"I told you that you'd be hot," he said with a smirk.

"Yeah, well, have I told you that you can be very cold sometimes?" I snarled at him. He only seemed amused and took my hand when I held it out again.

Without warning, I felt the sensation. Like we were moving at great speed and yet standing still at the same time. As if we had become the wind, and the world moved around us. My clothes remained still; my hair barely wavered. We were at the warehouse in an instant. *Now* I understood why Phoenix never bothered with the elevator.

Adrenaline flushed through my body, but I was otherwise bizarrely calm. As if I had never moved.

"Do you go everywhere like that?" I asked.

"Angels are not confined by space, only by time. In our original form, we only have to stop applying our powers in one place and focus them on another in order to be there. In human form, we're not quite as fast."

"That was more than fast. Can people see us?" I said, looking around for witnesses.

"Most exiles have to be careful not to expose themselves, but I move faster than average. Let's just say it's one of my strengths. When I move, it's not like being particles caught up in the wind, but like becoming the wind itself."

It was cool. Of course, he was totally aware of that.

"From now on, we go everywhere like that!" I slapped him on the arm playfully.

"Yes, boss." He grinned.

The warehouse was empty. There was no sign of the violence that had taken place last night. No vestiges of the dead bodies. It had been cleared and cleaned in an eerily pulp-fiction way. I could have cried. I didn't know where else to look.

I turned to Phoenix. "I don't know what to do. Can you find them?"

"Not without having some way to pinpoint them. There are too many power sources floating around that might lead us in the wrong direction."

I dug out my phone impatiently and checked for new messages. Nothing.

I tried to call Lincoln again.

Nothing.

I threw my phone on the ground. It smashed.

"Perfect!" I stormed.

"Violet?" The voice from behind me sent shock waves up my legs.

I spun awkwardly and almost fell into Griffin.

"Griffin. Where did you come from?"

"I just sent off the last cleanup team. What are you doing here?"

He looked exhausted. He was wearing the same pants and shirt as the night before. I wondered if he'd had any sleep since I last saw him.

He looked at me, then at Phoenix, who had distanced himself a little by moving over to look out of the broken windows. Griffin nodded in his direction. "Consorting with *his* kind is not generally what we do." He looked baffled. "It's funny though; Lincoln was right: he's not as obvious to sense as most."

"Griffin, he has information," I snapped, partly annoyed at him and partly annoyed at Lincoln for talking behind my back.

"And what's that?"

"The exiles are working together. They've called some kind of truce. They're combining powers so they can kill Grigori."

"That's impossible. Magda spoke to a source today who said that exiles of dark had taken three exiles of light captive and were using their powers," Griffin replied.

"Your source lied," Phoenix said. He had moved closer without me realizing. Griffin was taken by surprise too, by the look he gave him.

"That's easier said than done. Why would we believe you, anyway?"

"Because I'm telling the truth. Surely *you* can see that. I have nothing to gain. I have betrayed my kind and shown favor to humans…to *Grigori*." His upper lip twitched. "It's not something to be done lightly."

As he said it, I could see the battle within him. I also couldn't stop the surge of guilt as I wondered if he was doing this for me. I didn't know if I would ever be able to give him what he wanted in return.

Please, don't let him be reading me!

Griffin was shaking his head. "You *believe* you know the truth—I can see that. But that doesn't make you right. Light and dark have always stood in opposition. Their very egos prevent them from consorting. They don't work together. *Ever*." He was slipping into his country-folk accent and I wondered who he was trying to convince.

Phoenix just smiled and drifted to the windows again. He looked out toward the sky as if preoccupied by something I couldn't see. "Coming from a Grigori, that's stupidly naïve," he said condescendingly. "Do you forget that you are the very creation of their truce of old?"

Griffin stiffened but did not respond. Phoenix chuckled to himself and turned to me. "Is *he* truly your leader? I'm disappointed."

He was relaxed and almost swaying in an eerie way. As I watched, a shadow seemed to surround him, but there was something else…Fine, long strands of gold were weaving through it. It faded as he drew closer again, and I wondered if my mind was playing tricks on me.

"Is it so hard for you," Phoenix went on, "so *difficult* to consider that Grigori would once again cause a truce between the forces?"

"The truce was between angels of light and dark," Griffin said. "Exiles do not represent the angelic realm." He stood tall, but his voice had begun to waver.

"True, but do you really find it such a leap that exiles have finally coordinated their mutual goals? They've simplified…for now." Phoenix shrugged. "Believe me or not, but we both know you see my truth."

We all stood silent for a moment, Phoenix looking smug and Griffin looking annoyingly stubborn. Frustration overtook me. How could they both be so petty? The growing sense of urgency within me was only getting stronger. I could feel something wasn't right. Meanwhile, these two looked like they were about to start measuring things.

"Griffin?" I snapped. He looked up, realization dawning on his pale face. "Where's Lincoln?" I asked.

"They've gone to meet Magda's source, a silent exile. But they're not expecting to deal with more than one. And if what you say is right…Christ!" He shook his head, angry with himself. "They're walking into a trap,"

Phoenix didn't seem concerned at all.

"Where are they? We have to go!" Panic raced through my body and into my heart.

"Down by the pier." Griffin was already running toward the door. "I'll get the car," he called over his shoulder.

"Wait!" I yelled back. "Phoenix, can you take us both?"

He nodded. "But I want assurance of safety first."

"What?" I spat out, giving him my own version of a scary look. The thought of Lincoln in danger was too much.

"From him." He jerked his head toward Griffin. "If I help you, I want his word I'll be left to exist as I am in this realm."

I wanted to throw something at him but my cell phone was already gone. Pleading did not cover the look I shot Griffin. I just wanted to go. "*Griffin!*" I yelled. "Just tell him what he needs to hear!"

"For *now*," Griffin said. "For now, I'll give you my word. But it will not hold if you become a threat."

Phoenix nodded. "I accept." He held out both arms. "Take my hands."

I slapped my hand into his instantly. Griffin was a little more hesitant.

"For Christ's sake, Griffin, take his hand!"

Griffin took his hand, mumbling something about never damn well singing "Kumbaya" with exiles.

We moved like still wind.

———

We arrived at a huge, old wooden building on the pier. It looked normal enough from the outside—definitely no signs: *Danger: demented exiled angels inside!*

Once we entered, however, it was clear that the ordinary facade had been a mask. The interior was decadent. Priceless antiques blended with stunning pieces of modern art. If I wasn't in complete freak-out mode, I would have enjoyed taking my time.

We ran through the open lobby area, Griffin and Phoenix impossibly fast compared to me. We stopped at the top of a set of stairs. Griffin and Phoenix both stood completely still, as if they were focusing on some point I couldn't see.

"What are you doing?" I asked.

"Looking for them," Griffin murmured, concentrating. I turned my attention to Phoenix and caught a small but definite widening of his eyes. Something he'd sensed had caught him by surprise.

Though I had no idea what I was doing, I decided to see if I could sense Lincoln. The second I concentrated on him—his piercing eyes, the scent that was only his—I felt a pull. I fought a spell of dizziness, but I knew exactly where he was. I had no comprehension how. But I knew.

"Downstairs," Griffin said before I could. We moved quietly. I couldn't even hear Phoenix, who trailed behind me. At the bottom of the stairs, Griffin stopped again.

"In the room to the right," I whispered.

He looked at me, judging. "How do you know?"

I was in no mood to hand out explanations. I had no idea how I knew anyway. The same way I had no idea how I knew Lincoln was in trouble—the really bad kind. I pushed past Griffin without thinking and pulled open the door.

The room beyond it was bare. Unlike the foyer, there was nothing lavish here. In fact, there was nothing at all. Cement walls and floor and a candelabra in the corner with two candles flickering. There was a woodsmoke scent in the air that reminded me of cigars. On top of that…flowers. I squinted into the dark room, looking for what I could sense. We were not alone. My body seized with the cool heat racing through my blood, so much energy humming through me, I felt it would lift me off the ground.

"Griffin. How nice of you to visit." The voice pulsed through the room. I shivered and my body tensed as if something venomous were trying to seep into it. I couldn't tell which direction the sound was coming from until a figure started to materialize.

"Who is your friend, Griffin? She is…" He revealed himself slowly. He was less than ten feet from where I was standing, which was just plain creepy. I wanted to back up, but instinct told me to hold my ground. It wasn't easy.

He brushed his hands over the lapel of his well-tailored suit, making a fuss of adjusting and straightening. If he hadn't been so damn scary, I would have said he looked decidedly campy. However, rippling just beneath the surface of his vain exterior emanated a very distinct brand of evil.

He purposely let his eyes travel down my body. As he did, I felt a sensation like hundreds of spiders crawling over me, scurrying to every corner. I had to fight the crushing desire to run flat-out, or at least drop and roll.

He's doing it on purpose, Vi. Don't let him psych you out!

I might have been new to this game, but I *was* in high school. He was just another bully. Who the hell was this guy, anyway?

"What do we have here?" he said in a voice that sounded too young to match the wickedness reflected in his black eyes, which looked like they were rimmed in eyeliner.

"There is no need for the others to hide, Onyx, either behind the light or in the shadows. We know you're working together." Griffin spoke with such an even tone, it made him sound immediately more formidable. Yet again, my opinion of him grew.

Three figures appeared from the corner of the room where the candles flickered. It looked like they had just emerged from the pulsing light. Another two came into view from the opposite corner. I blinked a few times. I could have sworn they had walked out from the dark shadows of the wall. Oh. My. God…Or not.

"I can sense our people, Onyx. Reveal them!" Griffin demanded, unfazed by the additional exiles who had simply appeared.

"Oh, I'm sorry. How rude of me." Onyx skimmed his hand parallel to the ground, and it was as though a cloud of gloom lifted.

Lincoln and Magda lay on the floor. I could see the blood pooling around Lincoln. It was seeping outward, still fresh. My heart leapt into my throat. Magda moved a little. She was alive, but definitely not in a good way. She couldn't even lift her head to look at us.

"Lincoln!" I screamed. He didn't move.

Onyx stood over them, amused. "I must admit, you have arrived sooner than we had planned." He looked down at Lincoln regretfully. "It will be a shame not to have the extra time."

One of the exiles who had emerged from behind the candelabra moved over to stand beside Onyx while the others remained in opposite corners of the room, keeping watch.

Onyx motioned toward Lincoln. "Strong, this one, but distracted." He smiled at me. "I wonder…Are you the distraction?"

I blanched as his words sunk in. Had this been my fault?

Onyx raised a brow. "What is your name?"

"Violet," I said quickly. "Is he alive?" I knew I wouldn't be able to say much more without betraying how scared I was, but I had to know.

"Not for long." He tilted his head at me. "Violet? Ah…The Seventh Ray. How fascinating. You appear like a Grigori, and yet…you are something…new." He extended a hand to me. "Come," he said quietly.

"No," I said, but my body took a step toward him into a virtual thicket of floral aroma. I couldn't stop myself. In that moment, I knew I would be utterly compelled to do anything he asked of me. I closed my eyes and tried to gather whatever internal resistance I could, sick of other people trying to control me.

When I opened my eyes, he was right in front of me, barely anything between us. All I could hear was the flapping of wings. I didn't know if I had gone to him or him to me. I suppose it didn't matter. What did matter was that I was now within his striking zone.

He towered over me, and while he was instantly intimidating, he also struck me as oddly…elegant. He had short, styled black hair that had seen more than its fair share of hair wax. He was suave-looking, in a proud-to-be-evil kind of way, with high cheekbones and delicate features that made him look young, no more than twenty. As I choked on mouthfuls of invisible apple, he appeared to be merely entertaining himself, studying me like a bizarre science project.

"Get away from me," I said.

He laughed a high-pitched cackle. It caught me by surprise; it was not the deep laugh I'd expected him to have. "You have clout, girl, I'll give you that. But you're unfinished. Look at me." His last words resonated through my mind. My eyes flicked up toward him without my permission. "You are still in molding," he said ruminatively. "Your clay is still wet."

I had absolutely no idea what he was talking about. I was no expert in psychobabble. I wanted so badly to look at Lincoln but I forced myself not to. It wouldn't help.

Where the hell is Phoenix?

Onyx continued to stare, looking into me like he was searching my mind for my innermost thoughts. It was an uncomfortably invasive feeling. I saw his eyes flash.

"You deny your destiny. Oh…" He clapped his hands together playfully.

"What?" I said, sounding every bit the defiant teenager I wished more and more I could be and yet seemed further and further away from.

Instead of answering me, his attention was caught by something over my shoulder. His demeanor quickly changed. He straightened and cleared his throat, drifting slightly away from me.

"Hmm…I will never tire of the drama that surrounds humanity." He spoke lightly but couldn't completely hide his surprise. He'd been caught off guard.

I snuck a quick look behind me to see that Phoenix had finally joined us. He was standing straight and silent. He was relaxed and looking straight at Onyx as if he were nothing more than a try-hard bully. I envied him his control.

"Onyx," Phoenix addressed him.

"Phoenix, she is yours?" Onyx glanced at me.

The way they were standing had me positioned as some kind of monkey in the middle. I didn't know why Phoenix had waited until now to come into the room. I also didn't know why he wouldn't just come and stand beside me.

"I lay claim for now," Phoenix said. I could hear a familiar smirk in his voice. I told myself that now wasn't the time to argue over his possessiveness.

"Interesting…" Onyx said wistfully. "I don't suppose you'd care to enlighten me?"

"Not really. But it does appear that exiles aren't the only ones evolving," Phoenix said.

"She does exude something...extra," Onyx said, contemplating me briefly. "But you're still interrupting my soiree." He feigned a look of hurt.

Phoenix didn't respond, and I was too afraid to turn my back on Onyx again to look at him. Amid the silence, I could sense a surge of power in the room. I almost retched with the overpowering taste of apple, and I struggled to maintain any sight through the bombardment of morning and evening streaming through my vision. I blinked maniacally, straining to focus; it felt like I'd just walked inside after staring directly at the sun.

"Fine, fine." Onyx waved a hand through the air and the intensity of power subsided. Whatever had been going on between them clearly didn't require words. "I will release them to you...if you stay for a story." Onyx smiled wickedly.

The exile standing beside him grunted. "That was not our agreement, Onyx. We will not release them."

He looked no older than me, eighteen at the most. He was dressed like any other guy I went to school with: jeans and a blue T-shirt. He looked too normal to be an angel...exile, whatever.

"Malachi, I have delivered everything I promised, have I not?" Onyx queried.

"You have, but letting them go is out of the question."

"We will have other opportunities." Onyx waved his hand dismissively.

"Do not confuse me with your followers, Onyx. Should it come to a fight, it would not be a certain outcome." Malachi's tone intensified with each word. It was obvious he was an exile of light and their precarious relationship a product of this new truce. It was also easy to see why exiles of light and dark had never made a truce before.

Onyx sighed theatrically. "That is true. But then again, I should enjoy the kill a great deal more than you."

Malachi moved so fast I barely noticed the time lapse between him talking with Onyx and me being hoisted midair with his hand wrapped around my neck. His fingers dug into my skin. I couldn't even draw enough breath to scream.

"You said it yourself. She's powerful and not even finished." His grip tightened. Energy buzzed between us as Malachi steadily increased the pressure, working to finish my life. His eyes penetrated mine with resolve. Growing weaker by the second and pathetically gasping for air that would not come, there was little I could do. I swung my legs out to kick him and struck him in the ribs twice. He barely flinched.

From the corner of my eye, I saw Griffin moving in. I pushed forward into Malachi's hold—which hurt like hell—braced my hands on his face, and jammed my thumbs into his eyes as hard and fast as I could. It had been one of the first moves Lincoln had taught me. It was enough to distract him, and Griffin moved with lightning speed, grabbing hold of Malachi's free arm and wrenching it behind his back at such an awkward angle, I heard a snap. Malachi's eyes went wide and he unclenched his hand from my neck, dropping me to the ground where I gasped like a fish out of water.

When I looked up, Malachi and Griffin were locked together in combat. A mist surrounded them, a spectrum of glistening colors.

Griffin had Malachi in a death grip, holding him in some kind of immobilized state. "Make your choice, if you have one, and make it fast!" he ordered.

Malachi fought against the invisible force holding him. Griffin pulled a long dagger out of a sheath hanging from his pants that I hadn't noticed before. "Choose humanity or I'll return you!" he yelled.

"I would rather be a rodent in the pits than will humanity upon myself," Malachi said with disgust.

"Have it your way." Griffin drove the dagger into Malachi, just under his ribs, pointing it toward his heart with unwavering force. He had clearly done this before. A lot. There was no poof, no bang, no melting flesh; Malachi was simply gone. As if he had never existed.

I stood, holding a hand around my neck. It was burning, but there would be time for whining later. I snuck a quick glance at Lincoln, who looked like he was taking shallow breaths. Alive. Phoenix was still standing, unmoved, expression unchanged. Nice to know he cared.

Onyx had also remained still throughout the struggle. The exiles standing behind him had moved closer but seemed more tentative now, eyes fixed on Griffin.

Onyx cleared his throat and made a *tsk-tsk* sound. "Too often they forget, Griffin. You do look so…lacking. It is a cunning mask. It will not help you in the long run, of course, but for today, as I said, your freedom for my story."

"No stories." Phoenix spoke softly. "We all know that once you start, no one can shut you up." A shiver ran up my spine. His voice held more than just words.

"Why don't we let our little rainbow decide?" He looked at me and gave a dramatic bow. I gathered I had somehow acquired a new nickname.

Just what every girl wants.

"You'll let them go—*both* of them—and your lackeys won't try anything either?" I said.

Onyx looked amused at my words. I realized I had made a faux pas by calling *all* of the exiles his lackeys. The already buzzing tension in the room increased.

"Yes, I will even try to keep it short."

Yeah, but I was betting it wouldn't be sweet. I looked to Griffin. He didn't seem to have a better suggestion and gave a small shrug. It was up to me.

"Tell your story," I said.

"Humans are so predictable, aren't they, Phoenix?"

The silence from Phoenix made me nervous, but he was still behind me and I was too afraid to turn my back on Onyx. Griffin remained quiet. I could see him focused on Magda and looking around for any other trouble.

Onyx sauntered around the room and then began to talk theatrically. "Many, many years ago, this earth and man were created. There are many opinions as to who or what created them, but that is not today's story. Man—we can call him *Adam*, if you like—was given a garden in which to frolic. For a time, it was perfect. Do you know the garden I speak of?"

"Eden. The Garden of Eden. You said a story, not question and answer." With my surname, this was a story I had heard more than once.

He pulled on his tie, straightening it. "I did. My apologies. Well, you see, I'm sure you understand that if man were to have free will, then he must have the presence of choice and opposition. Angels, being entrusted with this responsibility, used their powers to create one of their own—a rare angel, for it was a woman. In all ways the opposite to Adam, except that they were both immortal." He looked at me and raised his eyebrows.

"Eve," I said, frustrated. "I've heard this story before."

He smiled at Phoenix. "Has she *really*? I think not. Not Eve, little rainbow; she was created later, during the cleanup. Before her, there was another. Oh, now I can't seem to remember her name…What was it, Phoenix?" His smile widened. He was clearly enjoying himself. I was almost surprised he wasn't handing out popcorn.

"Lilith." Phoenix barely spoke, but again my body shivered like someone had just walked over my grave.

"Yes! Lilith, how could I forget? Well, Lilith was created to bring balance to this unbalanced world. You see, she represented everything opposite to the untainted man, and brought with her all of my favorite things: temptation, lust, seduction, deceit, anger, fear, persuasion, you get the drift. Anyway, Adam was enraged with Lilith when, after a while, she refused to lie beneath him." He swept closer to me and whispered like he had a naughty secret to share. "Being created as equal opposites did cause a few marital problems. Let's just say, they bickered—and of course their fights were magnificent. Adam had not yet tasted that pesky apple, so he was just as strong, powerful, and immortal as *our* Lilith." He took a deep breath, feigning reminiscence. "Finally, Lilith abandoned Adam and the garden, choosing instead to be absorbed into her own darkness. Three angels were sent to return her to Eden. They threatened her, she threatened them—you know, the usual. But she refused to go back."

Why this psycho was getting kicks out of telling me a story about some whacked-out angel was beyond me.

"Are you finished with your story?" I said curtly. I tried to keep focused on Onyx so as not to give him the satisfaction of knowing how worried I was about Lincoln. At the same time, I could feel Lincoln growing weaker. It was torment, knowing that every minute this deranged angel kept talking was another minute I couldn't help Lincoln.

"Almost, almost. Where was I? Our Lilith went on to bear many children of dark, all of whom perished in payment for her sins. All but one. Lilith's *first* child, the only child conceived with Adam, survived and was an angel…of sorts. The child was taken from her and returned to the angel realm, where a ranking was issued, just like all other angels. Of course, the angel took after its mother and chose the dark. Became a Throne, a dealer of punishment, and was very…efficient."

My eyes darted over to Lincoln again. He was all I could think about. He still wasn't moving. When I looked back at Onyx, he was right beside me.

"Perhaps, on reflection, it was not the best placement. The child enjoyed it a little too much, and eventually the Seraphim imposed banishment from the angel realm, claiming absence of purity, branding the angel as one of the abyss. They sent the angel to its place of creation." He slowly pointed a finger to his feet.

"Earth," I said, rolling my eyes at him.

"Yes, earth. I wonder, do you think the child of Lilith walks among us now?" Onyx gazed around the room, looking happy with himself. "It is a quandary, isn't it? The possible product of man in his most powerful form and the *first* of the dark exiles. It would be a frightening force, wouldn't it? Violet?" He turned his attention back to me, a Cheshire grin on his face so wide it must have hurt. I glanced at Lincoln again. We had no more time for this.

"Lucky it's just a story." I tried to hold his gaze as if I'd been paying attention to his stupid tale, not wanting to let him get the better of me.

"Of course." He threw his arms wide. "Aren't they all?"

He looked back at Phoenix and started to walk toward him. I was finally able to see them both. Like at the warehouse with

Griffin, I noticed that there was some movement around Phoenix's body, a wave of shadowing and something else that looked like tiny threads of gold.

"Things are not as they once were," Onyx said to him. And then, he just walked out the door, closely followed by the other exiles.

I turned to Phoenix, a million questions in my head. But one thing was clear: Onyx feared Phoenix. Somehow, him being there had saved us, and right now that was all that mattered.

"Will he come back?" I asked Phoenix.

"No," he said, showing no emotion.

Griffin was already with Magda. I ran to Lincoln. He was breathing, but there was blood pouring from his side and he still wasn't moving. I tried to stop the bleeding with my hands, but they quickly became slippery and I knew I wasn't helping.

"I…I can't…the blood, I can't stop it. No, no…I need help." I was rambling and crying to myself.

A hand reached down holding a bundle of cloth. I looked up. Phoenix had taken off his shirt. I balled it up and put pressure on the wound.

"Linc, can you hear me?" My voice was so crackly I could barely hear myself. I forced an internal check. I needed to be strong right now. I gently shook his shoulders. "Linc!" I cried. He moved a little and his eyes flickered open.

"Hey," he whispered, "little rainbow." I tried to smile but couldn't. He was delirious. Why was everyone calling me *rainbow*?

Griffin came over, supporting Magda under his arm.

"You're okay?" I said, surprised to see her walking.

"Griff healed me."

Oh, great, no one told me Griffin could do that.

"Well," I almost screamed, "heal Linc, it looks like he's been stabbed or something."

Griffin leaned over and put a hand on my shoulder. "I wish I could, but as Grigori, we only have the power to heal our partners. I can't heal Lincoln."

"Well then, who the hell can?" I snapped. But the answer was already ringing in my mind.

"You," Magda offered, while kneeling on the other side of Lincoln. She was assessing his wounds with much more skill than I had.

"But I'm not a Grigori. I can't." I shook my head.

"You *can* if you embrace. He's been stabbed by his own dagger." She picked it up off the floor. It was covered in blood. Lincoln's blood. Lincoln's *blood*.

"It can't be healed with modern medicine. There's only one way to heal him and you're it." She looked at me, shaking her head, as if sure I would fail him. Perfect.

Griffin scanned the room. "We need to move. We don't know how many more might be out there. Let's go."

chapter twenty-two

"Sacrifice still exists everywhere, and everywhere the elect of each generation suffers for the salvation of the rest."

HENRI FRÉDÉRIC AMIEL

I stood, utterly immobilized in Lincoln's kitchen. My shirt was now sleeveless. I vaguely remembered Magda ripping off the sleeves to use them as blood mops. What was left of my top was soaked anyway. My hands were stained red and disturbingly sticky as blood congealed between my fingers.

Phoenix had insisted we come back in a taxi. He wasn't sure how Lincoln's injuries would cope moving at his speed. After carrying Lincoln to his room, Phoenix and Griffin headed straight back out to get medical supplies. I knew Phoenix was uncomfortable and it wasn't just because Griffin and Magda looked at him like he carried the plague and made it painstakingly clear they didn't want him around. Something had happened back at the pier that had him uncharacteristically on edge—but for now, all I could think about was Lincoln.

Magda had thrown me out of his room, ordering me to clean up and change. She said there was more blood on me than left in him and I wasn't helping. She was right. I was no help at all. My hands shook as I swallowed some aspirin with a quivering glass of water.

The next rational step was to take a shower, but I just stood, frozen. I couldn't ignore the voice in my head singing, taunting, teasing, *He's going to die, Violet.* We all knew it. Even Lincoln, when he came around briefly in the taxi, had it in his eyes. He knew. They knew. I knew. I knew…what I had to do. Hope and dread vied for attention, and I threw myself over the kitchen sink. I vomited until there was nothing left and then some more. My hand grasped at my bruised neck. I relished the pain, found some relief in the brief distraction.

Lincoln needed me to be strong and I was behaving anything but. It was unacceptable. I could fall apart later, I told myself. Much later. I stumbled to my feet, grappled with the water, and swallowed some more aspirin.

Later. Much, much later.

By the time Phoenix and Griffin returned, carrying with them everything but a hospital bed, I was showered and on the couch wearing a pair of Lincoln's sweats and one of his T-shirts. I had also managed to make a latte on the still-sparkling espresso machine sitting in pride of place on the kitchen counter. The espresso machine was about the only thing that was clean. The entire warehouse looked like a disaster site. There were books slung everywhere, the couch had been turned into a makeshift bed, and the kitchen was cluttered with dirty plates and leftover food scraps that couldn't fit in the overflowing trash can. It wasn't like Lincoln at all.

"Magda's with him. She needs space." I offered my poor excuse before they asked. Right now, knowing where this was all leading, I couldn't see him.

I focused on Phoenix. "If Grigori powers come from angels, does that mean you have the power to heal too?"

He looked down and shook his head. "I'm sorry. I can't help you."

"Few exiles are able to hold on to their abilities to heal when they take human form, Violet," Griffin said, putting a duffle bag down on the dining table.

"Why didn't Lincoln tell me partners could heal each other?"

"He didn't want you to make your choice based on anything other than what you wanted."

I was sure I wasn't the only one who found that statement ironic. "What happens to a Grigori if his partner decides not to embrace?"

Griffin opened his mouth, but before he could answer I put a hand in the air. "Actually, it doesn't matter."

"Violet?"

I nodded. I'd made my choice. "We need to talk," I said. There was no more time.

Griffin gave the supplies to Phoenix and asked him to take them to Magda. When Phoenix walked past me, he shot me a look of sympathy. I could tell he was reading my emotions. I turned away.

Griffin sat at the kitchen bar with a bottle of water. He took a few slow sips, playing with the lid, rolling it through his fingers. "You don't have to do this. He'd never ask it of you, not like this."

"I know."

I joined him at the bar, trying to be brave. "We don't have much time. Tell me what I need to know."

"It's a leap. A commitment. You can't undo this once it's done, Violet."

I ignored him. "A leap. *Shit*, Griffin, that sounds dangerously like a leap of faith."

"In a way, it is."

"Well, we're all royally screwed. Right now, I can't even open my mind to the possibility of there being a God."

"It's about faith, Violet; it doesn't have to be about God. You just need faith."

I clenched my jaw and moved on. It still sounded like a damn God thing to me. "Fine, where do I leap?"

"There's a process of declaring yourself. You have to go to the wilderness and remain for one night. There is a mountain to climb with a cliff at the peak. At the first moment of dawn, you jump. From there, the journey is yours. Only one thing is the same for us all: you will go to both the powers of light and dark. There is no exception."

I took a deep breath. I had to jump off a cliff.

"Does anyone die?" I wasn't sure I really wanted the answer, wasn't sure it would change anything anyway.

"Not that I know of, but some have returned and have been affected…mentally."

Great, insanity awaits.

I looked out the window. It was almost dark. "Can I go tonight?"

"Maybe…" Griffin said, but he didn't look too sure.

"Maybe?" I prompted.

"*Maybe,* if Phoenix could get you there, but we still don't know him, Violet. Something happened back there with Onyx that we don't understand yet, and no other exile I've ever seen can move as fast as him and…well, you should know, I can't get a lock on him. I can't read his truth. That's never happened before."

"But you read him at the warehouse."

"I know. I think he can control it, like opening a door if he wants to. But he can also keep it shut. He seems to be able to do the same thing when we try to sense him. It's as if sometimes he allows it and other times not. I just have a bad feeling."

I sucked in a deep breath and blew it out through tight lips. "Stuff your instincts, Griffin. They haven't really paid off all that well today." Any other day I would have been more diplomatic, but as I was learning, life can be a bitch.

He put both hands on the kitchen counter and dropped his head. "You would need to leave now," he conceded.

"I'll take her." Phoenix's voice came quietly from the edge of the kitchen. I wondered how long he'd been listening.

Griffin took my hands. "Lincoln is like a brother to me, but you don't have to do this. You have to want it for the right reasons."

"Yeah," I half laughed. "Reasons are reasons. It stopped being my choice the second he was hurt."

"A terrible freedom." He smiled mournfully and squeezed my hands.

"Yes." I barely got the word out. I couldn't have agreed with him more.

"He's lucky to have you."

I looked over at Phoenix, who had recovered his ever-present equanimity. Despite what anyone might have said, he'd been there for me since all of this began. He hadn't pressured me or forced me to do anything, *be* anyone. I pulled my hands out of Griffin's grasp.

"He doesn't have me."

I knew Phoenix would read the resolve in my emotion. I may have lost my choice in this. I may not have been able to stand by and let Lincoln die. I may be forever tangled in this twisted reality of angels and Grigori, good and evil—but everything else was mine. I felt foolish to have ever thought Lincoln and I could be together. There had always been something in the way. Now, doing what I was about to do would just ensure there always would be.

Grigori partners can never be together.

Magda walked out and threw a pile of bloodied towels into the laundry and then moved into the kitchen where she proceeded to open and close cupboard doors, searching for something...or nothing.

Finally, she spun to glare at me accusingly.

"This is all your fault! He's been so worried about you, he hasn't been able to function. He doesn't eat." She wrinkled her nose at the dirty plates. "Well...not to his normal standard. He hasn't slept in days. He blames himself for everything. That's why it was so easy for Onyx to overpower him. Even now..." She pushed aside a plate in the sink so she could fit a glass under the tap, and it set off a domino effect, the whole pile of plates shifting and clunking. I heard a crack. She persisted anyway, blasting water into the glass and slamming it on the counter after barely a sip. "He's asking for his *rainbow*," she scoffed.

"What is it with all this rainbow crap?" I asked, turning to Griffin and ignoring Magda. It was either that or giving her a one-fingered salute.

Griffin looked up from where he had been showing Phoenix a map. "I think it has something to do with your power. We all have individual strengths; yours seem to reflect a rainbow in your aura. Lincoln can see the shadows that cling to people after they've been altered by an exile. It's possible that in his weakened state, he can also see your aura more clearly too."

"Great. So he gets super strength and powers of Sight, you get to be some kind of human lie detector, and I get my own float at Mardi Gras." I put my hand on my hips and took another deep breath to center myself. I looked at Phoenix, who was watching the room with mild interest.

"Let's go. I have to make a quick stop on the way," I said. Then I turned to Magda, who still didn't seem to want to look at me. "Tell him...not to die."

She stared at me in disbelief. "You're going to embrace?"

I gave her my best don't-mess-with-me look. "Just keep him alive until I get back."

"Aren't you going to see him?" she said accusingly.

"No. We have to go." I couldn't tell her that I didn't know if I could face him at the moment, not while I felt my life as I knew it slipping away.

Phoenix slid up and took my hand, sensing my need for escape. "Where to?"

"Home. I need something."

chapter twenty-three

"If it is nothingness that awaits us, let us make an injustice of it;
let us fight against destiny, even without hope of victory."

MIGUEL DE UNAMUNO

I changed into a pair of black cargos and a gray tank top and tied a sweater around my waist. Survival 101 at its best. I rummaged through my drawers filled with paintbrushes, pens, and junk jewelry and found my old banged-up phone. I put in the sim card I'd removed from the phone I'd smashed earlier and turned it on. Miraculously, the screen showed two bars of power. There were probably a lot of things I should take with me. Weapons wouldn't have been a bad idea, but I didn't have any. At the last moment, I shoved my baby necklace in my pocket along with the poem Mom had left for me.

There was a knock on my door. "Coming!" I called to Phoenix. I raked my fingers through my hair and yanked it back into a pony-tail, then grabbed my hiking boots and pulled the door open. Dad stood on the other side.

"Hi honey," he said. He looked preoccupied.

"Dad, hi. I thought you were Phoenix."

"He's in the living room." He nodded his head in that direction and added, "You guys seem…close."

I started to pull on my boots while Dad was there. I didn't have time for this conversation. "Yeah, but we're just on our way out."

"Vi, are you okay?" he asked, noticing my impatience.

"I'm fine," I said. Then I thought of something. "Dad, I know this might sound a bit weird, but when I was born, did Mom say anything…" I hated doing this to him. Just the mention of her caused a ripple of pain over his face. "Anything weird?"

He smiled at me and relaxed a little. "She named you. She said, 'She is the heart of the Keshet, James. She is Violet.' And then she told us both that she loved us and that everything would be okay."

I saw his eyes fill with tears and I wanted to reassure him, but all I could manage was a loud gulp. I had heard that word before—in my dreams.

"What does *Keshet* mean?"

He pressed his lips together and closed his eyes, shutting out the world from his thoughts for a second.

"*Keshet* is Hebrew for 'rainbow.' Your mom loved rainbows. She used to say they were the link between us and everything else, the reminder that we are not alone. She said they are the perfect showering of light and shade, and as long as we have rainbows, there is hope for the world. Violet is the innermost color of the rainbow, the heart. It's beautiful really." He was far away.

I smiled at him and then gave him a hug, partly because I wanted to give him one, partly because I needed one, and partly to hide the look on my face.

What did my mother do to me?

He was a little surprised; normally I shied away from being too affectionate. When I didn't pull away immediately, he gripped me tighter, like he used to when I was a little girl.

"Vi, something's wrong."

I held on to him and desperately wished he wasn't right.

"It's okay. I…I've just had to make a few tough decisions lately."

"This wouldn't happen to revolve around the men in your life?"

I almost laughed, wishing it were that simple. Guy problems would be a welcome dilemma in comparison. "A little."

"Will you be okay?" he asked, and from the way he said it, I could swear he knew things might be about to change forever. I could hear the fear start to move through him. I couldn't bear it. There was no point in us both going through this.

"Sure, Dad. Hey, let's have dinner together one night next week. We can talk then." I did my best to sound upbeat.

"Vi, it's late. Where are you going?"

I wriggled out of his arms but he still held my hand.

"Somewhere with Phoenix. Dad, please. I know it's late and I know things are crazy, but I'm hoping you'll trust me when I say, I *have* to go." I looked at him and held his eyes. Today was not the best day for him to pull the father-of-the-year act.

With a sad smile, he let me go, as if he didn't know how to start imposing rules now. Selfishly, part of me wished he would. Part of me wished he was one of *those* dads, the type that would lock me in my room and take away my choices.

I hated myself for even thinking it.

———————

I was surprised to see my phone still had coverage. It felt like we were in the middle of nowhere. Phoenix, who had received instructions from Griffin, had brought us here in a matter of seconds. There was no sign of civilization, and it was so dark away from city lights and pollution that all the stars had a chance to shine. Owls hooted and creatures I really didn't want to meet rustled in trees nearby. I was grateful there was at least a half moon that shed a glimmer of light. Without it, we would have struggled to see our hands in front of our faces. A canopy of trees curled above us, the branches stretching out like ominous arms with long, deliberate fingers.

I told Phoenix I needed to call Steph, so he gave me some privacy and said he would collect a few supplies. I had no idea what that meant. I couldn't imagine him gathering wood.

Steph answered on the first ring. I knew I'd be in trouble; I hadn't spoken to her since ditching the party the night before. It was odd to think how much had happened in twenty-four hours.

"Vi! About damn time! Where the hell have you been?"

"Hell," I answered, using her own word.

"What's going on? Your phone has been going to voicemail all day. I even went round to your place earlier, where, by the way, I found my shoes covered in dirt! I was actually starting to freak out that one of the men in your life had finally lost his mind and kidnapped you. Are you okay?"

"In a way. Sorry I haven't called, and sorry about the shoes. Lincoln was hurt and we had to go help him."

"What do you mean *hurt*? And what do you mean *we*?"

"He was hurt in a fight…kind of. It's a long story. By *we*, I mean Phoenix and me."

"That sounds healthy. Could things get any weirder in your love life? Honestly, I require some big time hole-filling on the story here. Is Lincoln going to be okay?"

Yes, as long as I forfeit my life as I know it and ride to his rescue.

"I'm working on it."

"How?" she asked with a heavy dose of suspicion.

"Look, Steph, I don't want to lie to you, but I can't tell you at the moment."

"Is this something to do with Phoenix?"

"Yes and no. It's complicated."

"Well, duh, I figured out that much. Where are you now?"

"The middle of nowhere. I'll fill you in later."

"Well, when are you going to be back?"

It was a good question. I wondered if I would ever truly return.

"Soon. I'll call you when I'm home," I promised.

"I hope Lincoln's okay."

"Me too."

"You don't have to be his savior, you know." She waited silently on the other end for my response.

"Bye, Steph," was all I could squeeze out.

"Bye, babe," she said, sounding worried but letting me off the hook. I really hoped I would get the chance to explain everything to her.

I sat on a rock, playing with the buttons on my phone. The screen light came on, shedding a little glow on my surroundings. Trees, dirt, and rocks. As long as the creepy-crawlies stayed away, I could cope.

The light faded from the phone and I had a moment of complete darkness. I was sure I could actually hear my heart cry. When I pressed one of the buttons to relight the screen, it was wet with my tears. Funnily enough, the moment I had the light again, I didn't want it. Right now, I preferred the darkness.

Lincoln was bleeding to death while Magda played nursemaid. It was stupid that it bothered me, but it did. In fact, everything bothered me. Steph and Dad had no idea what was going on. I'd lost my friendship and anything else I'd once imagined there might be between Lincoln and me. Becoming a Grigori meant a chance to save him but it also meant giving him up—it meant giving *myself* up too. And though I wanted to deny it, I had a growing feeling that I was missing something very important about Phoenix.

I couldn't help but feel cheated. I'd worked so hard to keep normality in my life since the attack. A month ago, I was actually normal, happy. Now I was about to do the very thing that ensured I would never have that again.

My breathing became shakier and I fought the urge to throw myself on the ground and sob. I didn't hear Phoenix approach, just felt his hand on my shoulder. He didn't say anything and I was relieved. I couldn't put on a brave face right now. I sat, with his hand on my shoulder, and cried until I started hiccupping.

Eventually I stopped and Phoenix stood. "Come on. I've set up a camp for the night."

"With what?"

"A few things." I couldn't see his face but I could hear the smile in his voice. I was glad he was there. I gripped his hand tightly.

"What's going to happen to me when I embrace? Do you know?" I wiped my eyes and tried to pull myself together.

"I don't know. I've heard it can be pretty physical."

"Will I have to fight someone?"

"Perhaps." He pulled me to my feet. "Come on."

Setting up camp was an understatement. Phoenix had a fire roaring. He'd also positioned gigantic logs—that would normally take three men to lift—as seats. And a bed. An actual bed—well, a mattress at least, but it had linen and pillows.

"I was going to get a tent, but it's clear tonight and I figured we wouldn't really need it."

I looked at the bed. "It's…it's…" I really didn't know what to say. Of all the things I'd been expecting, it wasn't this.

"I know there's only one bed, but I have another mattress. I just haven't blown it up yet."

I bit back the "how convenient" remark.

"How did you…?" *Possibly get all this stuff here?*

He just smiled and sat on the other side of the fire, where one of the logs had been perfectly positioned away from any drifting smoke.

"If I'm going to have to fight someone, maybe we should practice," I said, catching him by surprise.

"No. We shouldn't." His tone was final. I got the distinct impression this was a closed subject.

Of course, I plowed ahead. "Why not? I'm sure you could teach me a thing or two."

He launched through the fire, catapulting himself at me so fast he looked like a comet. He barreled into me and I fell back onto the ground under his heaving body. His hand was wrapped taut around my neck.

"Lesson number one," he growled. "Never fight with someone you can't beat."

His eyes flashed dangerously. I felt his body rise and fall with every intense breath, reminding me that, despite what he might have thought, there were parts of him that were *all* human. Lying under him, the wind knocked out of me, I knew he wasn't thinking about fighting me.

"Okay, okay." I surrendered. He kept his hold on my neck.

Why do they always go for the neck?

I opened my mouth to speak again, but he tightened his grip enough to strangle my words and make me gasp. Slowly, he softened his grasp and ran his hand down my neck to my collarbone, watching me with his dark eyes, smiling when my breath quickened.

"I do like your neck…very much," he mused, and then he rolled off me and somehow glided to a stand.

I hoisted myself onto my elbows. "Yeah, well, if I ever come back as a Grigori, *then* I'll kick your ass."

"You'll come back, and you'll be a Grigori." He spoke with such certainty, it made me smile. "I doubt very greatly, however, that you'll kick my ass. But I and my ass will enjoy your efforts."

I threw a handful of dirt at him. He blew right through it and was standing behind me, helping me up, before the dirt had even hit the ground.

After I had brushed myself off, I sat beside him on the log and let my eyes glaze over as I watched the campfire. Phoenix elbowed me in the side and handed me a white to-go box with chopsticks sticking out the top. "Chinese?" he offered.

The way he said it, it was as if we were sitting at the dining table, no different from any other night. I started to laugh.

We ate cold chicken chow mein, and although I couldn't stomach much, it was comforting to have food around. I was grateful that Phoenix was there. I'd never needed to be looked after so much, and for someone who was not completely human, he was surprisingly good at the job.

"Fortune cookie?" he said, throwing me another white box.

I threw it back. "No thanks." I didn't need anything else telling me my future.

"It'll all work out, Violet. You'll be safer once you have more tools to defend yourself. You'll be strong, and they won't be able to take you by surprise."

I knew they were words of encouragement, but I had the sneaking suspicion he was also pleased about what this was doing to my relationship with Lincoln.

"I guess you think I'm happy about all of this."

It was like he'd read my mind. I shot him a look of accusation.

"It's hard not to read how you're feeling," he said with a shrug. "I'd be lying if I didn't admit I don't mind a bit of distance between you and Lincoln."

The fire flickered and my mind skipped with it, dancing between moments. Finding out what I was, feeling the betrayal. Learning about the senses and discovering my freaky vein-ridden arms. Meeting Phoenix. Kissing Lincoln. Kissing Phoenix. I remembered how much it broke my heart to be with Lincoln, and I remembered the feeling of distance, the bliss of unawareness, that came with kissing Phoenix.

I walked over to the mattress and sat on the edge. The hardest thing was knowing that, even if this worked and Lincoln was healed, nothing would ever be okay again. This choice was going to change me forever, and there was a part of me that questioned if I could ever forgive him for that.

I felt a tingling sensation and knew Phoenix was probing into my emotions. I avoided his eyes, guilty that once again I had let Lincoln rule my thoughts. I'd made a choice to be with Phoenix;

I needed to stand by it. Things would never be the same. *I* would never be the same. Griffin even said that some people came back unable to live normal lives.

When I looked up, Phoenix was watching me. He was deathly still. Then he spoke, warningly. "I am not like other people, Violet. I know where your emotions are leading."

That was the whole point. He wasn't like other people, and right now that was precisely what I needed. "You told me once to tell you…when I wanted it most."

He knew exactly what I was talking about. "*You* told *me* once never to do that to you again."

"I've changed my mind."

He dropped his face into his hands and I prepared myself for rejection. A lump lodged in my throat. But when he slid his hands away, the face he revealed was not one of refusal. It was resolved, even resigned. He stood slowly and studied me. My heart raced. With each step, the look of desire smoldering in his eyes intensified.

The smoke from the fire followed him as if it were attached by an invisible thread, drawn to him. As he neared, something within me screamed, but he put his hand on my face and it stopped. Silenced by his touch.

He leaned toward me slowly, giving me time to change my mind. Then he touched my lips with his, trembling, and I knew control was on a tenuous string. But it still wasn't enough. If I couldn't have the control I wanted, then maybe I'd be better off with none at all.

"More," I pressed.

"Tell me what you want," he said.

"Take me away."

And with that, Phoenix released an onslaught of emotion. I sank into passion. An eternity of desire and temptation drenched me. Deep within it was a feeling of despair so old it was almost musty. On top of that, layers of new hope shimmered. I sucked it all in, even the waves of pain and ripening anger, which rippled into the mix. I took it all, just happy it wasn't mine, relieved to be feeling something other than my own private hell. Phoenix let the emotions run and siphoned the flow, pushing aside what he did not want me to feel and covering it all with an impassable layer of lust.

He supported me like I was a feather and laid me on the mattress. He kissed me softly, his mouth moving down my neck, never breaking contact. His hand hovered at my waist, playing with the bottom of my tank top, pushing it up a little then pulling it back down, trembling with want.

My body ignited as cool heat turned to fire and ice within me. The smells of the dense forest and smoky fire were drowned out by the smell of white musk. I tasted apple—green, tart, tangy apple. "Take it off," I cried.

"No," he grunted.

He hovered over my mouth. I could feel his quick breath on my lips.

"Please."

He didn't move for a moment, but then he let out a dark growl that belonged in the wilderness more than anything else he had brought with him.

He lowered his body onto mine and pressed the length of it against me, covering me. I moved his T-shirt up around his chest and he pulled it over his head.

His hand went back to the bottom of my top. This time he didn't play with it. One minute it was there; the next it wasn't. I didn't know how, didn't care.

Then something happened that I hadn't prepared for. It was as if releasing the pain that had consumed me created a void to be filled. My memories traveled to my birthday, when Lincoln had kissed me. With Phoenix's body pressed against mine, I remembered the feel of Lincoln. I remembered the desperation of wanting him closer. The way we had melted together. The way I had always felt so intensely drawn to him.

I felt myself pull Phoenix closer, tighter. He hesitated and then pushed against me. I wrapped my arms and legs around him, but I knew it wasn't him I was desperately trying to hang on to.

"I can read your emotions, Violet," he whispered into my ear. "I should stop." But he didn't pull away.

"Don't stop, don't stop," was all I could muster. Even as I said it, I knew it was cruel, knew it must hurt him to know I was longing for Lincoln's touch.

I opened my eyes a little when he didn't respond. He was looking straight into mine, waiting for me. He battled with himself, but I could see that desire was winning. I knew I had the power. I shifted a little and then arched slightly in invitation. He grabbed a fistful of my hair and wrapped it around his hand till it was tight against my neck, then he pulled me up to meet him and kissed me without restraint, recapturing my focus.

He kept a firm hold on my hair, his hand at the base of my neck. Each time I let my mind wander to Lincoln, he tightened his grip on me, pulling me back to him until all other thoughts had been subsumed under the all-consuming layer of Phoenix.

The campfire erupted in a million sparks of light, creating a canopy above us, a fiery-domed ceiling. The shadows I had seen around Phoenix earlier returned, along with the thin threads of gold that reminded me of never-ending strands of hair wrapping themselves around him…and me. It was like being spun in toffee.

Between the images that surrounded me and the emotions that Phoenix bled into me, I could barely form coherent thoughts, yet I felt a growing sense of unease. This wasn't how it was supposed to be.

I lay in his arms after. Quiet. Pushing creeping thoughts of Lincoln from my swirling mind. My homeroom teacher used to rattle off a quote at the end of school every Friday, before we all headed off to act like out-of-control teenagers over the weekend. It kept playing through my mind.

Remember, all passions start from love or hate. But beware—you never know whether they will end with delight or sorrow.

I was acutely aware I was lacking in the delight department. In my struggle to escape the constant downpour of emotions, I now felt as though I had only succeeded in sinking deeper into the chasm. I told myself that most first times aren't all that great and that, physically, Phoenix had been beyond amazing, guiding me gently the entire time. But that nagging voice inside, the one that always points out the truth even when you're in denial, was singing hauntingly at me, *Silly, silly Violet...*

We were both silent as he stroked my hair. I pretended to be asleep for a while. So did he, I think.

"I should get going," I said finally.

"I could walk with you to the top," he offered.

"I get the feeling it has to be a solo trip." I leaned over the mattress, searching for my clothes, keeping the sheets up high for cover. "Thanks, though."

Phoenix threw the sheet off himself and stood up. He was butt naked. It was dark, but my eyes had adjusted enough and I couldn't help but look. His body was truly incredible, and I felt a pang of guilt that I hadn't given it the sole attention it deserved. Images flashed through my mind, glimpses of fire flaring and shadows hovering, that made me shiver.

He collected my underwear and cargos and handed them to me. Then he passed me my tank top.

"How? I thought you ripped it." I held it up, intact.

"Imagination. I think it probably got away from us both a bit. I'm sorry if..." He looked down and I felt awful. I braced myself for his leaking emotions. It was times like these, when he was vulnerable, that I felt them most acutely. But nothing came to me, not even the slightest trace.

I quickly threw my top over my head and shimmied my undies and pants on while still under the sheet. I crawled over the mattress and sat beside Phoenix, who was on the far edge. I was relieved that he was now wearing pants too. I wasn't up to the challenge of nakedness and conversation right now.

I put a hand on his shoulder as he had for me just a few hours ago. "I asked you to be there for me and you were." I *really* didn't want to be having this conversation.

"That doesn't mean it was what you needed. I couldn't stop myself. I wanted to be your first." He was shaking his head regretfully and wouldn't look at me.

"That obvious, was it?" I cringed.

"No." He stood up and paced a couple of steps, picking up a stick and throwing it into a tree. I heard it slice into the bark, like an axe splitting wood. "No, I just know, Violet. I can sense it." He sounded angry at himself, tired of his abilities. "You were...I've never been so...consumed."

It was odd he'd used those words. I thought of the campfire, the way it had flared around us and become all-consuming. Had he seen it? Had he put it there? Had I? I had no idea if it had been a manifestation of his power or my own imagination working overtime.

I stood. "Let's just get through today. Then we can talk."

He accepted this with a nod.

I gave Griffin a quick call and he told me Lincoln was just holding on. I could tell how grave the situation was by the tone of his voice. I put my phone in my pocket and almost fell into Phoenix when I turned around to look for him.

I stepped back a little to put some space between us. "Sorry, I didn't know you were there," I said. I looked down and saw he had my mother's necklace dangling from his hand.

"I found this on the bed; it must have fallen out of your pocket." His tone was icy.

I reached to take it from him, but he swung it into his fist.

"Why do you have it?" he asked.

"It was a baby necklace."

"Do you know what it's for?"

"No. Do you?" I asked uncomfortably.

"Just an old wives' tale. Nothing important." He released the amulet into my hand.

"Oh," I said, relieved to have it back in my possession. Again, I had a nagging feeling I needed to know more about Phoenix. "Do you remember you once said that you'd tell me everything someday?"

"Yes." He looked suspicious.

"When we get all this sorted out, I'd like answers to some questions I have."

He turned from me and walked over to the mattress. "That's fair," he said, not looking at me. He came back holding out a bottle of water and I felt like a bitch—he was still looking after me.

"Don't happen to have a flashlight in your bag of tricks, do you?"

He shook his head. "Griffin said you have to travel in true light."

I looked at the mountain above us. I could barely see the outline. "Any other instructions?"

"Just to get to the top. You'll know what to do when you get there." He pulled me close for a brief second and kissed the top of my head. "Be careful. I'll be waiting." His hand ran over the back of my head. It felt bruised from where he had gripped my hair. I guess it hadn't *all* been gentle.

My old friend guilt niggled at me while I walked away. I wished I could be what Phoenix wanted, but I had a feeling I couldn't give him what he wanted most.

chapter twenty-four

"As for courage and will — we cannot measure how much of each lies within us; we can only trust there will be sufficient to carry us through the trials which may lie ahead."

ANDRE NORTON

It was a relief I had my sweater, more for protection than anything else. The terrain was dense and there were no visible paths to follow. The air was thick with sappy, woodsy smells.

Though my eyes had adjusted to the faint moonlight, at a stretch I could only see about thirty feet in any direction. I hoped the sounds I was making, bashing through the trees and stepping on dried leaves and sticks, would deter any wildlife from investigating rather than provoke them. It would be just my luck to get eaten by some wild animal on my way to jump off a cliff.

I realized too late that taking the most direct route up the mountain was probably not the smartest idea. I pulled my hood over my head to help guard against the thorny branches and random dead sticks that stretched out from trees, lashing me as I passed.

I stopped only once for a drink of water. It felt surprisingly comforting to have a clear destination and task at hand. I didn't want to keep stopping and break my momentum; it only gave me time to ponder things I couldn't change. Hiking turned out to be a welcome distraction.

By the time I reached the top, my ankles, which had been exposed between the tops of my shoes and bottom of my pants, had been ripped to shreds by flying sticks and jagged rocks. The backs of my hands had suffered a similar fate. My face had escaped relatively unharmed, with only a few minor scrapes on my forehead from a particularly nasty thorn bush. I was grateful that even with my lack of preparation, I had at least picked up a sweater with a hood.

It had been a little more than an hour's hike, but when I stood at the top of the slope bent over, bracing my hands on my knees, I allowed myself a moment of conquering pride.

Then I straightened—and saw the cliff.

It stood tall. A giant, mocking me with its inevitability. Any sense of self-accomplishment I had allowed myself to indulge in skittered away.

Mother…

From below, you wouldn't even know the peak was so gigantic it resembled Mount Thor. I swallowed despite my dry mouth and wondered what waited for me on the other side—or was that at the bottom?

Bells rang in my ears and my stomach tightened as I remembered Lincoln's words. *I just wanted you to be prepared, have the upper hand.*

No wonder rock climbing had been on his list of must-dos. I thought back to my most recent attempt with Steph. I couldn't afford to be so reckless today. No safety rope and no angels waiting to catch me. I was quickly rethinking my hasty refusal to let Phoenix escort me. I glanced at my phone screen; just over an hour till sunrise, too late to do anything about it now.

I surveyed the cliff face as best I could, looking for the most suitable route and assessing backup paths. A little reluctantly, I settled for working my way up the right-hand side of the escarpment. It appeared to have the best footing, as far as I could see anyway. Of course, there was a catch. The top third looked like vertical suicide. I knew it would be a tough climb, but the other paths didn't look as doable, with big crevasses cut out of the middle sections. With no buddy and no ropes, they would be impossible.

I pulled off my sweater and stuffed my phone into my pocket. After trying a number of arrangements with the water bottle, I gave up. I drank what I could and left the bottle along with my sweater at the base of the rock.

The first third of the climb was relatively straightforward, and I kept a steady pace. But there was no avoiding that after already climbing the mountain, I was tiring quickly. I tried to take short breaks, but hanging on in midair soon felt like more of a hindrance than a help.

At about the halfway point, the rock face shifted in angle, becoming a more severe slope. Foot- and handholds became harder to come by and I slipped a couple of times, but managed to stay on course. At the base of the vertical rise to the top, there was a narrow landing where I could stand. I took the opportunity for a brief rest and also wriggled my phone out of my pocket to check the time. I had about twenty minutes till sunrise. My hands were so sweaty, a slippery film had formed over my fingers. I did my best to give each hand a thorough wipe on my pants while keeping balance on the tiny ledge. I was running out of time, not to mention if I fell at this point...Let's just say I wouldn't be up for another try in a hurry.

I surveyed the next section carefully and picked out as many footholds and handgrips as I could to map out my path. *Come on, Vi. You can do this. Easy.* I sucked in a breath of champions and I was on my way.

I may have been able to fool my mind for a short while, but my body wasn't having it. My arms shook, weary from overuse and supporting my entire weight; I didn't have long before they would start to give out on me. Nausea swept through me as my muscles burned and knotted with lactic acid. My mouth was rapidly oozing saliva that tasted of thin, metallic-like blood as my system tried to flush it through.

When my right hand finally grabbed at the top of the rock face and struggled to find a grip, I couldn't stop myself from wildly reaching, desperately seeking an end to the physical torment. My hands worked with a jerky urgency and my fingernails bent back and snapped as I scratched at the top of the rock until I found a good hold. My foot followed nicely into a previous handgrip and I levered myself up, folding my body over the top. Once I got my knees onto the landing, I crawled frantically into a safe zone, desperate to be away from the edge.

I barely had time to pull myself onto all fours before I threw up.

Lying on the cool hard surface, I focused on what was most important at that moment: remembering how to breathe. Though every muscle in my body screamed at me, I managed to stand and walk to the opposite edge of the cliff top. Strangely, I wasn't even shocked when I saw the death drop that lay before me. Looking down, the canyon was as deep as the mountain had been high…and then maybe more. The leap would be certain suicide. Things weren't looking up and it seemed I was only going down. A noise escaped my lips. I wasn't sure if it was a laugh or a cry.

My phone no longer had reception but the screen still lit up and reported that it was three minutes till sunrise. The sky glowed with the promise of daybreak, and birds throughout the forest below were starting their morning songs. I looked out over the surrounding forest. It was beautiful. I waited a moment, soaking it all up before I allowed acceptance to sink in. No matter how picturesque it looked, no matter what kind of peace I could draw from it, nothing was going to change the fact that I was about to leap off the biggest mother of a cliff I had ever stood on. Nope, I was all alone and I was screwed and…I knew it.

With only seconds left, I tried to clear my head and stop the panic. I let go of all the inhibitions I normally forced upon myself and my thoughts drifted to Lincoln. The sound of a beating heart thrummed through my mind. *Da-dum, da-dum, da-dum.* I knew it was his, knew he was still alive. I closed my eyes, concentrating on the too-slow rhythm of his heart, taking a deep breath, readying myself. I may not have had faith in much right then, but love or hate Lincoln, I had faith in *him*.

I slowly opened my eyes. The sun speared its first bright rays of golden orange into the sky and I leapt from the cliff with the sorrowful knowledge that no matter what the outcome, at the very least, part of me would die that day.

chapter twenty-five

"For your sake, I hurry over land and water;
For your sake, I cross the desert and split the mountain in two,
And turn my face from all things,
Until the time I reach the place
Where I am alone with You."

AL HALLAJ

I couldn't breathe. I was face down in something. Something gritty. Thoughts of being buried alive burned through my mind.

I flexed a hand; more grit slid through my fingers. I pushed some weight onto my elbow to lift my heavy head, but my arm slid out from under me, sending me back for another ground kissing. I gasped for air and spat grit from my mouth, the sweat on my face providing the perfect glue for it to cling to. I forced my eyes open and glimpsed a slice of burning light before shutting them tight against the glare.

That voice, the one that you're *really* supposed to listen to, screamed at me, *Get up, get up, open your eyes. GET UP!*

I managed to get on all fours and twist into an awkward sitting position. I opened my eyes again gradually. The burning light I had seen was the reflection of the blazing sun at full height, bouncing off the sand. Sand…but no beach, just desert. No trees, no cliffs, no rocks, no dirt, just sand and…me.

Right on cue, just when I thought I was completely alone, came the sound of someone clearing his throat. Discovering a reserve of energy I had thought long gone, I found myself on my feet within a nanosecond.

To my right stood a man. He looked like he was on his way home from a formal beach party—black pants and white shirt open at the collar and untucked. No shoes. I tried to make out his face while squinting against the sun. He was handsome, with honey-brown hair falling to his shoulders and what looked like a two-day stubble on his chin.

He was observing me patiently. He didn't smile or frown; he simply stood there, watching, feet resting lightly on the sand, hands by his sides.

He cleared his throat again, focusing on my stance. I was still holding a defensive position: feet apart, knees bent, hands at the ready. It took effort, but I slowly relaxed my pose, straightening my body, bringing my feet closer together, and letting my hands hang at my sides. It was less obvious, but I knew I still had a good footing. If I had to move quickly, I still had a fighting chance.

He just watched, expression unmoving.

Silence stretched and my already frantically beating heart found that it could, in fact, pound even faster. Was I supposed to say something? Frenzied thoughts collided in my head. *Did Griffin tell me I was supposed to say something? Should I introduce myself? Should I run? The sun is high—Lincoln! How long have I been here? How long have I been gone?*

"May I assist?" the stranger said. He didn't have an accent so much as he carefully enunciated each word.

"I...umm...I...what?"

While I grappled for something to say, a mist, not unlike the one I had seen fall over Griffin and Malachi, seeped out of him and drifted slowly over to me, showering me in a glory of colors. As the tiny particles touched my skin, they disappeared.

The stranger's power, for I assumed that's what it was, surrounded me and continued to grow. The logical part of my brain demanded, *Run, run, run.* Of course, I just stood, a poster child for all things dazed and confused. Then...calm hit me like a river, running through my body, extinguishing the anxiety that had taken over. My heartbeat quieted, my breathing slowed, my muscles loosened. I exhaled, basking in the instant relief.

"Thank you," I said hesitantly. This wasn't going to be the smoothest conversation of my life.

"You have come to embrace?"

I swallowed. "Yes."

"You hold unique power within you. You are not like the others."

His eyes twinkled with curiosity. I didn't respond.

"You are not grateful for your gift?"

The way he said it annoyed me. He may have calmed me, but it clearly wasn't an endless supply. "I had plans for my life and they didn't involve dealing with AWOL angels." I threw my hands in the air. "But here I am."

He stepped forward, still allowing for a polite distance. The sun was beating down unforgivingly and my skin blazed as he inspected me.

"Perhaps that is why he chose you. My name is Uri. I am an Angel Elect. I believe you refer to me as an angel of light." He extended his hand in offer. I hesitated.

"It is quite safe," he reassured me.

I took his hand. Unlike my dirty calloused one, it was soft and tender. I could feel the senses buzzing around me, but it was as if they were muted.

He released my hand and stepped back, flawlessly assuming his previous stance. Sand glided over his feet like ripples of water. "So, you have found a reason suitable for your choice."

"Did I ever really have a choice?" I asked, thinking about how everything had kept circling back to this question, perhaps to this moment.

"Of course. You chose how, why, when…even *where* to an extent."

"What about *if*? Did I get a say in *if*?"

He bowed his head, as if slightly impressed with my question. "There is an element of your existence that was predetermined," he confessed. "It is not that you did not get a say, rather that the foundations of your very being denied you the ability to reject your destiny at any cost. It was simply a matter of the right question being laid before you so that you could, in turn, make the right choice."

"And if I hadn't? If I'd let Lincoln die?"

"I cannot tell you what is not possible." He tilted his head toward the sun, looking right into its glare, and his eyes stayed wide and unaffected.

"I don't understand."

"It is beyond your comprehension. You should not try."

"Well, I want to know!"

He turned back to me, showing mild interest at my snappy tone. It lasted about three seconds.

"Your destiny was laid before you at the time of your birth. For that destiny to have changed, it would require a significant event that was not of your path and not of your own doing. You have only ever experienced one such event, and though it has caused a slight change in the fabric of your true nature, it was prevented from causing irreparable damage."

His expression didn't change or give away any more information. If anything, his eyes seemed less and less focused.

"Someone interfered," I said, mimicking the words Lincoln had used when I first told him about the teacher who had crossed the school for no reason and saved me from the attack. Everything started making sense. "Who was it?" I asked.

"Your angel maker, who appears to be willing to break our laws for you." His lips twitched ever so slightly. I couldn't tell if it was approval or disapproval. "Your essence lies in you like the seeds of a forest. Not one, but many."

Over the years, school had taught me the value of a blank face. The one that says, *If it's easier for you, I won't ask, but in truth, I have no idea what you just said.*

"Is that good?" I asked, wiping the beads of sweat trickling down the side of my face.

"Your will is strong—so strong, in fact, it appears to have the power to overcome the will of others. Whether that is good or…other? That is up to you."

Brilliant.

"Answers in riddle? A bit clichéd, don't you think?"

"Perhaps, but riddle is all we have. If comprehension lay at your feet, there would be no need to walk in search of it." He was silent for a time. He looked vacant, like he wasn't really there. Then, as if someone had turned a light back on, he focused on me again.

"You have given your heart to one and your flesh to another."

I blushed and looked down at my feet.

"Let us hope the truth will release you," he said.

"More cryptic stuff?" I said defensively. I don't know what I'd been expecting. I mean, I wasn't naïve enough to have thought I'd see halos and magic tricks, but I hadn't counted on evasiveness either.

He held his hand out again. "May I see the amulet?"

A tingle of fear ran down my chest. "You had me bring it?" Even as I asked, I knew the answer. I took the necklace out and placed it in his open palm. "It was my mother's. Was she a Grigori?" I wished now that I'd pushed Dad for more specifics about her past. All he had told me about her family was that both of her parents passed away when she was very young and that she had been raised by an aunt she didn't like.

"I will not answer that. However, I can tell you that this amulet was never hers and always yours. There is a reason this message rests on the back of it." He raised his eyebrows a fraction. "You may wish to consult some of your histories if you want to know more."

"Why don't you just tell me?" I asked, relaxing my stance further and putting a hand up to try to block the sun's glare. I was now sure he had no intention of coming closer than was necessary. He actually appeared repelled by me. It was a good thing too. If it had come to a fight, I would have been in trouble.

"My knowledge is not meant for you, only my guidance."

He didn't speak for a time. Then he gave a small nod. "You have many virtues and you will need them all. Your essence will be embraced."

He made it all seem so simple, but I knew it was anything but.

"So…how do we do this?" Visions of being struck by lightning bolts came to mind.

This time, his mouth actually curled into the smallest of smiles. "A journey. You will find your powers within you on your return. Use them carefully, for they are plenty, and know that even the greatest bringers of justice will only find salvation in surrender."

I showed him a blank face. He started to turn.

"Wait!" I yelled. "What rank does my angel maker come from?"

Confusion tainted his perfect features. His hands twitched ever so slightly. "I…do not know."

He began to walk away.

"Do I follow you?" I called.

"Not today. You have somewhere else to be. You seek water and must allow yourself to find it."

He was gone.

I was alone, in the middle of nowhere, surrounded by millions of tons of sand and dust. My only company was a searing thirst.

chapter twenty-six

The obvious questions came to mind first. *Where am I? How long have I been here? Will I die out here?* And then the ones a little further back started to seep in. *Will anyone truly miss me? Will I resolve things with Lincoln before one of us dies? Is this the angel of light's doing or an angel of dark's?*

The questions kept coming as I staggered through the never-ending desert. The sand was deep and soft, and the scenery was unchanging. Even after walking for hours, I felt like I was still standing in the same spot.

The questions that drifted into my mind simplified. *Where did I leave the water bottle? Can anyone see my water bottle? Is that…blood?*

The last one snapped me out of my delirium enough to allow

me to put a hand to my mouth and feel the wetness running from my nose, mingling with the grains of sand stuck to my face. Dehydration and fatigue were taking over. I let some of the blood trickle into my mouth to wet my tongue, so desperate was I to escape the dryness. My body retched in penalty. Maybe that's what all of this was: punishment.

I went to check my phone again, even though I knew there would be nothing on the screen, that the battery was dead. When I pulled my hand out of my pocket, a piece of paper floated to the ground. I bent to pick it up and fell to my knees. I didn't try to get back up.

It was the poem my mother had left for me. I looked at it, trying to see the words through my blurred vision. I managed the first four lines.

> *You must love no-thingness,*
> *You must flee something,*
> *You must remain alone,*
> *And go to nobody.*

I sat, blinking my eyes, trying to keep a little moisture in them. I *had* turned toward this path to emptiness, nothingness; I *had* fled from myself and those who loved me; and I remained *completely* alone. I thought back to how I hadn't been able to confide in Steph or Dad. Something clicked. I blinked again and refocused on the poem.

You must be very active
And free of all things.
You must deliver the captives
And force those who are free.

If taken in the literal sense, I'd been active as all hell, delivering *myself* as a captive to my will. Maybe forcing those who are free meant the task of returning exiles for judgment and protecting free will. I tried to swallow but my mouth was too dry. *Is this why my mother left me the poem? Was it to help me find a way out? Please, please, please!* Every hot breath I inhaled scorched my throat, roasting it from the inside out. I could hardly make out the next lines.

You must comfort the sick
And yet have nothing yourself

Lincoln's injuries and leaping to certain death pretty much covered that.

You must drink the water of suffering
And light the fire of Love with the wood of the virtues.
Thus you live in the true desert.

I understood enough to know that it didn't matter what drink was on offer; I'd take it. And if it was suffering they were after, they had it. Right now, I didn't know if I *was* in the true desert. And love and virtues seemed far away.

Staggering back onto my feet, it was obvious the rest had not helped. I stumbled, tripping to my knees every few steps. I was coming to the end.

I lifted my head and looked before me to the expanse of nothingness and resolved that no matter what my life had in store for me, I would rather *that* than this.

From within the mirrors of sand emerged a lion, magnificent and wild. He padded lightly across the sand, leaving a small gust of wind in his wake. This was not a good sign. I was hallucinating.

I watched in fascination as my lion quietly paced out a wide circle. When he reached the place it had begun, he padded into its center, stopped, and turned to face me. Golden fire roared in his glistening eyes as they remained fixed on mine. I wondered if I should be afraid, but then remembered it was a hallucination. So I stood and stared back into the vivid eyes of my lion, for I knew he was *my* lion in every way, an extension of myself.

The lion watched me for what seemed like forever, studying me with the kind of interest a lion does not normally show. I stared back, transfixed, and observed as his tail began to sway again, bringing with it a breeze that floated across my face.

It was like a breeze of life. I closed my eyes and took a breath, trying to draw in every last bit. When I opened my eyes, a living wind surrounded the lion like a tornado, whirling around him, lifting the sand higher and higher until I could no longer see him.

Unable to hold myself up, I dropped to my knees and slid down until I was lying on my back.

A blanket of new dust covered the area, covered me. I thought of Lincoln, heard the faint *da-dum da-dum da-dum* of a straining heart, *his* heart. I clambered wearily back to my knees and tried, but failed, to stand. I remained kneeling as sand rained down on me.

Finally, I forced my feet to work, to hold my weight. I pushed myself forward. One step, two steps. I walked right into the tornado to meet my lion, and I knew then that my virtue was never letting weakness rule me. Sand whipped across my face. I screamed—not for the burning pain, but for the icy knowledge that my virtue was also my vice. I wouldn't give up on him.

It was calm in the center and the lion was nowhere in sight. I marveled as I tried to comprehend what I was looking at. I was standing before a pool of water. I fell to my knees and reached for it, fearing that this too was a hallucination, a cruel mirage. Cool water claimed my hands, and when I scooped them toward my mouth, the water came with me. I would have cried in delight if I hadn't been so busy drinking between coughs.

The third time I put my hands into the water, it wrapped around my wrists and pulled me under like quicksand.

There was nothing I could do but hold my breath as I plummeted into the pool and beyond. It seemed hasty to accept the inevitable demise. I suspected death would be the easier outcome, and therefore was nowhere in sight.

Dozens of reflections surrounded me, manifestations of…me.

From different times in my life, different moments. Some I remembered; some seemed like they came from other people's memories. I could see myself in the eyes of others. I saw those others too—my mother, my father, Steph, Lincoln—and I saw people who had hurt me—the elementary-school bully, the horrible ballet teacher, the girl squad from my old school that always had that knack of making me feel so inferior. And finally, the teacher who had attacked me. He appeared time after time, taunting me like contorted mirrors in a fun house. The old fear I knew so well rushed back and I felt anger that he could intrude on my life at every point, even this.

My lungs burned with the need for oxygen, my vision blurred, and I couldn't hold on much longer. I was spent. I closed my eyes. All movement stopped. The water stilled, and when I could no longer wait, I inhaled…warm, damp…air.

chapter twenty-seven

"You remind me
Define me
Incline me.
If you died
I'd."

Lemn Sissay

I landed on something hard. My eyes shot open while I continued to suck in more sharp, burning breaths. Tiny droplets of water misted my face. I was half sitting, half lying back in a wooden-slatted...deck chair?

Dark, ill-omened night encircled me. I blinked to adjust to the dim light.

Did I pass out? How did I get here?

My surroundings slowly came into view. A stainless-steel table was to my right. On it, a glass of water. A light rain was falling. I was saturated. Had I imagined the water pool and was only wet because of the rain? Uncertainty enveloped me. I sat up, swinging my legs to the side. As I did, another chair came into view—and on it, a man, instantly familiar.

Anger sparked. "Is this some kind of game to you? How you get your kicks, playing with my life? Well, congratulations. I found your stupid water and almost died in the process!" I screamed between coughs and splutters.

I could see him smile through the darkness, teeth startlingly white. My hands gripped the side of the chair and my stomach prickled. Uri had not smiled.

"I see you have met my brother. He sent you looking for water, did he? Sounds like something he would do. Predictable." His upper lip twitched at one corner.

I squinted into the dark. He looked exactly like Uri, but on closer examination, there were differences. Uri had not shaved in what looked like days; the man sitting before me was clean-shaven. Uri was dressed in casual slacks and shirt; this man looked like he had just stepped out of a boardroom. His suit was black and perfectly tailored. He wore a crisp white shirt that glowed under the moonlight and was tightly held around the neck by a silver tie. I looked down; his patent black shoes reflected the night, and the sand beneath them was perfectly still, like it was afraid to move. There was no doubt he looked identical to Uri, but this was not the same man—and we were still in the desert.

"You're the angel of dark," I whispered, wishing I was in a better physical state to defend myself. But even though I had managed to maneuver myself into a sitting position, I knew I would be hard-pressed to stand up, let alone fight…or run.

"I prefer Angel Malign and, of course, there is always my name. I am Nox." He did not offer his hand as Uri had done. He was repelled by me, the same way Uri had been, but he was worse at hiding it. Or didn't bother to try.

I snuck a quick look over my shoulder at the glass of water on the table.

"Thirsty?" he asked offhandedly.

I wanted to deny it, but I was still desperately parched.

"Yes," I confessed.

"Please." He swept his hand toward the table. "Help yourself."

I leaned forward a little and felt my legs shake furiously. I wouldn't be able to stand without falling.

"May I assist?" he asked. The same words Uri had used, yet this time they caused a crawling sensation over my skin. I wanted to shiver but restrained myself.

"No. It's okay."

"Will you refuse me the same courtesy you gave my brother?" He smiled slyly.

I looked down, feeling tired and beaten. "No. You can help."

Before I even finished my sentence, I saw a mist flow from him to me. A slight dusting of colors shimmered within it like glitter. My muscles suddenly relaxed and I felt rejuvenated. I still ached like I had run a marathon, but it was bearable. I walked to the table and gulped down the water. It didn't occur to me until I had finished every last drop that anything could have been in that glass. The fact was, I would have thrown back a glass of bleach as long as it was wet.

He watched me and sighed. "It's always a little frustrating to be the second visit on a Grigori Trial, though I must say, they are normally in better shape than you. My brother must have shown quite an interest."

I thought back to my meeting with Uri, which now seemed like a lifetime ago, and the total indifference he had shown me. "He didn't seem overly interested."

"Perhaps not to you." He walked over to the table and stood on the opposite side. I strained to see his face.

"You have come to save the one you love?" he said conversationally.

"Yes…No…He's not the one I love, but I do want to help him." I was trying to convince us both.

He made a *tsk-tsk* sound. "And for whose sake do you come?"

"For his." *Uh, duh!*

"Are you *sure?*" The words teased their way through the air, landing lightly like the misty rain and seeping into me slowly.

I thought of the question, of who was really at risk. It was Lincoln's life I wanted to save…because…*I* couldn't fail him.

"For mine." The realization stung.

"Very good. I am sure my brother told you how strong you appear. Did he tell you how very weak you are too?"

I half laughed, but my heart wasn't really in it. "Stating the obvious, don't you think?"

"True and not. Your current state is merely a physical reflection of your strength and your weakness. They compete in a *wonderful* battle within your soul. I wonder which will win…Don't you?"

I swallowed and remained silent.

He chortled lightly. "It is a situation that we must contend with, our exiled flock. I do wonder, at times, if they find their paths fulfilling. I suppose I will never know." He was adjusting his jacket, tugging at the sleeves. It reminded me of Onyx. "I admit, it is quite satisfying being able to enjoy these material objects. Do you like my suit?"

I was a little taken aback. "I…I can't really see it."

He sighed. "Yes, the shadows do like to accompany me when I assume flesh." His next words came abruptly. "Who is the other who seeks claim to your heart and your body?"

How could they know all this?

"Phoenix." My voice cracked as I spoke.

"He is one of us?"

Nothing like you, I wanted to yell.

"He's an exile," I said, resting my hands on the table to help hold myself up.

"Yet you wish to be a Grigori? Will you surrender him?"

"I want to save my friend. I know that becoming a Grigori will mean dealing with exiled angels and I accept it as my future. But I have no reason to surrender Phoenix. He is good and he's my friend."

"What if he gives you reason. Will you surrender him then?"

"I don't believe that day will come."

"I can see that you do not." He smiled widely. "Do you have a question for me before I offer you the embrace and passage home?"

Home? Did he say home?

My mind went blank and I couldn't think, though I knew I had questions. My words stumbled out. "Uri said he couldn't answer my question."

"Annoying, isn't he?"

I smiled a little and delivered the same question. "Was my mother a Grigori?"

"Hmm…Evelyn…She was a Grigori of specific charge." He motioned with his hand toward the deck chairs. I shook my head.

"What does that mean, 'specific charge'?"

"She had only one task. To return one exiled angel for judgment. She was charged with the mission by her angel maker directly. Very rare." He was pondering something as he spoke.

"She knew where her angel essence came from?"

"Yes, I believe she even left you a trinket of theirs."

My hand went to the outside of my pocket, tracing the outline of the necklace. "The names on the back of the amulet."

He just smiled.

"Who did she have to return?" I asked.

"*That* question I cannot answer. I believe the seed is planted…for now."

He returned to his chair and reclined, crossing his legs at the ankles and placing his hands behind his head. He looked like he was relaxing in his backyard—a very dark, desolate backyard.

"Will you send me back now?" I tried to sound like it didn't matter.

"Of course. You need only pierce your way to freedom."

"What?" Dread pumped at the base of my heart.

"Take the dagger from the table; it is yours now."

I looked down to where the glass had sat on the table. A silver dagger lay in its place.

"When the figure appears," he continued, "give it form and pierce it with a killing blow."

"I have to kill someone?" *Is he insane?*

"Details, details. It's really just pretend; think of it as a game. Of course, if you prefer, you could stay here with me." He was enjoying himself. He lay back in his chair and looked at the sky.

I reached out, my hand shaking. One finger at a time, I wrapped my hand around the dagger, lifting it into the air. The cold steel responded warmly to my touch, as if it recognized me. A chill ran down my spine and I flinched. The table disappeared and in front of me stood a figure, neither man nor woman—a blank canvas, just a silhouette.

Nox had said I needed to give it form. I thought of a form, if there would be one that I could kill. Then he stood before me. My hands shook with pure fear and adrenaline.

"Can you speak?" I asked him. My voice was shaky. I realized I was crying. He said nothing, remained still, watching me.

I looked in the direction of Nox; he was still casually reclined in his chair.

"Is there another way?" I called out to him.

"Not one you would prefer," was all he said.

This was it. This was what I had to do to get back—to become a Grigori, to get my powers, to heal Lincoln, to return to Phoenix. My grip tightened around the dagger weighing heavily in my hand.

I had to stab the man who had destroyed part of my world, taken part of my innocence, my trust, who had betrayed me and God knows how many other girls. I took a step toward him, the teacher I had feared more than anything else. Until now. Until these trials, until knowing Lincoln might die, until knowing I might die. I stared at him and I didn't need any more reason. With all the other forces in my life straining to consume me, he had been the first to shatter the perfect prism of my life. I pulled my hand back for leverage; I only planned on doing this once. But when I closed my eyes, I found myself. One moment of simple clarity absorbed me and my decision was changed and made. I opened my eyes and plunged the dagger into the stomach, tilting it up toward the heart, as I had seen Griffin do. Only then did I allow myself to take in the full scene, to lift my eyes to meet those of my victim.

I was staring at myself.

I would ask myself another time if it had been strength or weakness that led me to change the image of the figure.

I heard Nox chuckling. "So, a new chapter has begun."

Blood poured onto my hands as once again I searched within myself for an anchor and heard the faintest thrum of a heart. This time, though, I wasn't sure whose it was that was struggling to beat.

Perhaps it had always been the sound of my own fading heart that I heard.

Vision abandoned me and the darkness consumed me, a willing victim.

chapter twenty-eight

"What was I once, what have I now become…"

My head rolled to one side. To the other.

"Violet. Violet! Wake up!"

Someone was talking. Words. I could hear words. My mind snickered at me when I strained to hear them again, but I was lulled back into nothingness, content in the quiet.

Bam!

My head snapped to the side with hard, fast impact.

"Violet, wake up, damn it! Open your eyes!"

That voice again. Eyes? My eyes? Oh…I opened them a little.

"It's me, it's Phoenix."

Phoenix?

My hazy vision came into focus and I saw his perfect face and opal hair looking down on me from above.

"Phoenix, you look like an angel." My voice sounded gravelly.

"Are you okay?" He patted me over urgently, looking for wounds.

I ran through the inventory. Legs and arms were still working. I knew this because I could feel pain through every inch of them. I also had the pleasure of realizing one half of me was lying on a bitch of a rock, which was digging into my butt.

Phoenix helped me sit up. I took in my surroundings and could see the mountain I had climbed, with its haunting cliff top towering above me. I was in the valley that lay beneath.

"Are you okay? Did you fall?" He was wiping my hair from my face. "There's blood on your hands, your skin—it's red and blistered and…you have cuts all over yourself." He was almost mothering me and I fought the urge to swat his hands away. It helped that I wasn't sure that my arms could move.

Thoughts of Uri and Nox circled my mind. The desert, the lion, the faceless figure.

"I…I…" I started to say that it wasn't my blood. Then I remembered: it was. I threw myself into his arms. I was so frightened I couldn't even cry—I could barely breathe.

He held me tight. "You're safe, you're safe. It'll be okay." I hoped he was right.

"What time is it?" I asked, suddenly remembering, jerking away from him and wincing at the price for such abrupt movement.

"Just after sunrise."

"Oh no! I've been gone a whole day and night?" I asked frantically.

"No, you've only been gone a couple of hours. Violet, what happened?"

Maybe I had fallen? Maybe I had never been anywhere. Had I just been lying at the bottom of the mountain after miraculously surviving the fall?

"Water?" I asked, increasingly lucid. Phoenix disappeared for a moment and returned with a water bottle. He would only portion the liquid out to me slowly, despite my protests. I dropped my face into my hands, struggling to grasp all that had happened.

"Your arms," Phoenix said quietly. I lifted my head and looked at them. The strange markings had converged to create an intricate weaving, which wrapped around each wrist like a wide bracelet. It looked like a kind of mercury, light bouncing off it in a rainbow of colors.

I marveled at the markings. "Steph is going to freak."

Phoenix was watching me with trepidation.

"It felt like I was gone for days," I said, picking up the bloodied dagger that lay in the leaves beside me.

"They can do that—remove reality and make your imagination control you."

It was more than that, though. It had to have been.

I tossed the dagger around in my hand a couple of times, spinning the hilt and then catching it again. Phoenix looked at me dubiously.

"What? It's mine. Trust me, I earned it."

I started to feel much stronger with each passing moment. I rubbed my face, which was stinging on one side.

"Did you hit me?"

"Just a tap," he said, kicking at the red dirt.

"Then why do you look so guilty?"

"I don't," he said defensively, stilling his feet and looking away.

"I think I can walk. We have to go." I tried to start moving and flinched with pain.

Phoenix sighed. "Stand up. I'll do the rest."

———————

Phoenix had to catch me from falling when we walked through the door to Lincoln's warehouse. The dehydration was still affecting me, and though the water helped, it also made me feel sick. Cradled in his arms, I saw him look over me, his worry showing.

"There is something I need to tell you." His voice sounded grave.

My stomach was flipping out on me. My mouth watered, not with apple this time. "Does it have to be right now? I think I need a bathroom."

He bit his lip. "It can wait."

He carried me to the bathroom, where I threw up all the water I had managed to swallow.

When I emerged, Griffin and Magda were in the kitchen. Phoenix was nowhere in sight. They both froze with looks of horror as they took in my appearance.

"Are you…?" Magda started.

"I think so." I held my wrists in the air. "If this is anything to go by."

They stared in disbelief until I broke the silence. "How's Lincoln?"

Magda looked down. "Worried about you. He's dying and all he wants is to see you."

I actually felt a tiny bit bad for her, but I also couldn't help a brief wave of guilty satisfaction.

Phoenix was sitting beside Lincoln's bed when I walked into the room. Lincoln was heaving as he tried to speak to him. I had clearly interrupted something. Phoenix shot up from his seat to help me over to the bed. I looked at him questioningly, but he just shrugged it off.

Lincoln looked like death, but when his eyes found me, he smiled. I clenched my jaw and my heart squeezed with restraint. His brilliant green eyes were dull and tired, but there was no arguing they were still the most exceptional eyes mine had ever taken in.

"Vi, you okay? They t-t-told me you were going to embrace," he said, struggling with his words.

"I'm here, aren't I?" I said, trying to reassure both of us as best I could.

"I didn't want...Not like this. I'm sorry." He was in so much pain. With every word, he grimaced, and I knew he would be trying to hide as much of it as he could from me.

"I know. So...let's see if this healing thing works."

I looked toward Phoenix. "Can you ask Griffin to come in?"

He left the room without responding. Something had upset him.

"Vi, there's some...something you need to...I can see..." He was straining himself too much, looking toward the doorway, making sure we were alone.

"Tell me later. When you're better."

"I...I'm s-sor..."

"I know."

Griffin explained how the healing was supposed to work. In theory, I should have been able to just channel my will to heal Lincoln. As he was my destined partner, it would happen naturally. It all came through the power of the angelic qualities I should now have had and the wristbands—or in my case, the markings on my wrists.

"Okay, so I just take his hands or something?" I asked.

"You need to find your own way to connect with him and open yourself," Griffin explained. He sounded nervous and I could see Magda fidgeting. They weren't as sure as they were trying to make out. They stood at the back of the room, giving us space. Phoenix hovered in the doorway.

Lincoln was drifting in and out of consciousness. He took shallow breaths and his lips were almost blue. Connecting with him had been something that I had been trying very hard *not* to do of late. How could I *open* myself to him? My mind drifted to the dream I'd had, to the stranger who said he was me. Was he my angel maker? With all I now knew, it seemed more plausible that the dream had really meant something. I remembered the painting, the colors. And I remembered the question: *What are we to become?*

I didn't realize I had spoken aloud until Lincoln whispered, "Everything we can."

I took his hands, closed my eyes, and tried to center myself and concentrate on my will, directing it all toward healing Lincoln. After a few minutes, I couldn't stand it. "Nothing's happening!" I snapped at Griffin.

He was calm, like a Zen master, which only irritated me more.

"You have to find your own way to connect. Maybe you need to try a different tactic. Remember when Lincoln helped you the other night, he focused your senses, brought them through you and out. Maybe…"

I cut him off. "You *are* kidding me. You want me to kiss him?"

Griffin just gave me a look of pity, but I could swear there was a touch of amusement mixed in. I caught Magda rolling her eyes to the ceiling. Phoenix, on the other hand, stepped forward.

"No. You can find another way; you just have to tap into it. You need to rest."

But we both knew there was no time for rest.

"He's barely conscious now," I replied. "We can't risk it. Otherwise this has all been for nothing."

Phoenix slammed the wall with his fist and I flinched in shock. I waited for his emotions to bleed into me. They didn't. After he composed himself, he turned to me, his hands clenched tight.

"Fine, but this is the last time."

It was fair enough given all that had happened, but the way he said it was frightening. I looked down, avoiding his eyes. "Maybe you should wait in the living room."

"I'm not going anywhere."

I didn't dare challenge him, but he did step back to the doorway.

"Lincoln." I stroked his hair, trying to get him to come round. "Linc."

His eyes fluttered. "Hey," he said, as if I had just appeared.

I smiled. "I can't heal you like this. I have to try something else. I'm going to kiss you, okay?"

He smiled like he was drunk and took hold of one of my hands, even though it must have hurt him. "I...You don't ever need to...ask. We...loong...gether."

I looked to Griffin, who couldn't hide his concern. Lincoln was deteriorating. Fast.

"It's the painkillers," Magda said flatly.

I ignored her comment, though I could feel Phoenix shifting uncomfortably behind me. Again, I half expected to feel his emotions overflow into me. Surprisingly, I felt nothing.

I placed my free hand on Lincoln's face and took a moment. This would be the first time I had actually been the one to kiss him, to instigate it. Somehow it made it seem different, more intimate. Phoenix huffed behind me. He was reading me. Crap. I just had to pretend he wasn't there.

Before I could think about it anymore, I leaned down and kissed Lincoln's cool lips. My whole body relaxed and contracted at the same time. I could feel the death that was so close to him, hovering eagerly. Stirrings of power came from within me and I hunted it down, searching for its source so I could draw it up. I grabbed hold of it and steered it from me, into Lincoln, as if channeling a river, willing it to flow.

His lips parted, allowing the connection between us to open, and I poured my power into him and he...kissed me back. Lips that were cool became warm. The hand that had held mine limply tightened and pulled me in. He was healing, I could feel it, and it seemed to give me strength too.

The kiss intensified and together we grew strong. Power thrived through my whole being. My connection to Lincoln was like a living thing I could almost touch. His free hand reached out and curled around my waist as he brought his whole upper body to meet me and pulled us together.

We were like one person, giving life to each other. I felt a tear slip from my eye. I wanted to give this to him so much, but I couldn't deny my anguish as I mourned the life I had sacrificed for him. I was bitterly aware that in healing him, I had not struck anyone but myself that final killing blow.

The questions sliced through my mind like shards of jagged glass. *Who was left dying in that desert?* And even more disturbingly, *Who returned?*

"Stop!" An arm wrapped around my waist and ripped me back to reality.

Phoenix stood behind me, restraining me. I looked at Lincoln, now sitting up. Our eyes locked for a moment before I looked away.

Griffin stepped forward. "Well, that way works. Lincoln, how are your injuries?"

I appreciated his efforts at steering the attention away from the awkwardness.

Lincoln lay back down, pushing off the sheet to reveal his wounded torso. The bandages wrapped around his stomach were covered in blood. I gasped. I couldn't believe he had made it to this point. Surely I couldn't have healed that?

Magda moved over and started taking off the gauze. While she did I turned to Griffin. "His injuries are too severe. How does this work?"

Griffin gave me his tutor smile. "We give each other a little life force. It is one of our powers as Grigori. Unfortunately, we can't give it to anyone, just our partner. This should give him enough strength to heal the wound himself…We hope. It sort of restarts his own enhanced self-healing abilities, so that, although still hurt, he should be able to recover at a faster rate than humans."

I fidgeted impatiently. "So, how long will that take?"

It was Magda who answered. "No time at all."

We all looked at her.

"What do you mean?" Griffin asked.

Magda stood up and took a step back. "See for yourselves."

Lincoln rubbed his hand over the wounded area. There was a lot of dried blood, but when I looked closer, I couldn't see the wound. "Where is it?" I asked.

He looked up at me, his beautiful green eyes glistening, bright as ever. "Gone. You healed me, Violet, completely. I feel…fantastic. Like I was never hurt."

Then his eyes scanned my face and body. "You were hurt. When you first came in, you had cuts, bruises. They've gone. You healed yourself."

"That's impossible," exclaimed Griffin and Magda at the same time. They examined me, grabbing my arms, looking for signs of my injuries. My muscles weren't sore, my thirst had gone, my throat wasn't burning. My burned skin had returned to its normal shade. In fact, I felt good. More than that, I felt strong. Powerful. I yanked my arms back.

"He's right. I don't know how, but I'm healed. Maybe Lincoln healed me at the same time."

Griffin obviously wanted to discuss it further, but when he saw the look on my face, he wisely let it go.

Lincoln sprang out of bed. He walked over to me and took my hands in his. "This is what the markings meant," he said, examining my wrists. "The lines running through your arms. They were forming wristbands. They're within you." He marveled at me and I felt his thumbs brush over my wrists. My body betrayed me, reacting to his touch. Just as quickly, I felt a strange surge of anger toward him.

Phoenix moved forward. It was understandable. I dropped Lincoln's hands and took a step back so I was beside Phoenix.

"Violet?" Just the way Lincoln said my name held within it so much.

I stood staring at him, power coursing through my body. I ran my hands through my hair, stalling.

"I'm glad you're better. I…It was more important that you were okay and so I made my choice, Linc. I don't regret it, but…I don't know if *we* can ever really be okay." Even as I said it, I felt the anger still bubbling beneath the surface.

His eyes shot to Phoenix. "Does this have anything to do with him?"

Phoenix stiffened beside me. Lincoln watched as I stood in silent panic. I didn't know how to have this conversation; there were too many people in the room and too much emotion was riding on it.

As his eyes penetrated mine, comprehension flickered. "Something happened. You…Please tell me you didn't."

He looked like he didn't know whether to yell or beg.

Phoenix put an arm around my waist, claiming me. "She doesn't have to answer to you. She just saved your life. A simple thank you will suffice."

Lincoln jabbed his finger toward Phoenix. "*You* don't talk. You son of a bitch! If you touched her, I'll kill you!"

I flinched when he turned his daggered gaze back to me. "Violet, answer me."

I could do this. I had to do this. I'd made my choice. Why, then, did I feel so wrong at the same time?

"Can we have a minute?" I asked quietly.

Griffin and Magda couldn't have vacated the room faster. I think they had already been inching their way to the door. I bet Magda was loving this.

Phoenix, however, remained where he was. "No," he said. "Last time I left you alone…No."

"Phoenix, please, I can't have this conversation with you in the room. I know I've asked a lot of you, I know you must think I'm awful, but please just give me this minute."

His arm dropped from my waist and his other hand went to my face. "I'd never think that of you. You could never be awful. It's just…" His eyes darted to Lincoln. "He's trying to manipulate you and he irritates me…a lot."

He shot Lincoln a hateful glare and then turned his attention back to me. "He loves you, Violet. But I hope he's explained to you that Grigori partners are *not* compatible. There is no way he can ever have you, yet he still wants to stop anyone else from having you. He leaks his love for you everywhere. It's clumsy, it's…messy." He screwed up his face a little. I stayed very still, trying not to react—not even to Phoenix telling me that Lincoln loved me.

"But I love you too," Phoenix went on.

Oddly, I couldn't feel that emotion from him as he said it. The only thing I felt was anger, but it didn't seem to be coming from him—it must have been mine.

"Knowing that," he continued, "tell me it's safe for me to leave you in here with *him*."

Conflicting sensations ran through my body. I couldn't tell him that I loved him, and saying that I would try wouldn't cut it. Worse still, he could probably read my emotions anyway.

I settled for the words, "You can trust me."

He stalked out, throwing a final glare of contempt at Lincoln, who was shooting back a special look of his own.

Lincoln moved over to his wardrobe and grabbed a fresh T-shirt. He didn't say anything, just moved things around, throwing them with excessive force. He unraveled the last of the thick bandages that covered his torso, leaving his chest bare. He took a cloth from a bowl of water on the dresser and used it to wipe away the rest of the dried blood before putting on the clean T-shirt. With his back still to me, he pulled a painting off the wall and hurled it across the room.

"I gave you that," I said quietly, looking at my painting on the ground.

He was breathing heavily. Part of me wanted desperately to run from the room, from the conversation. The other part wanted to comfort him, reach out to him.

"Tell me." He was almost trembling with restraint.

"What, Linc? What exactly is it you need me to tell you?" Familiar defenses were coming back to me and I was grateful. We had only been back around each other for minutes and we were already fighting.

"Did you sleep with him?"

"Yes," I said, determined not to be pushed around and made to explain myself—not after everything that had happened.

He turned to face me, hurt glistening in his eyes. "Do you love him?"

"I...I don't know."

"But you're with him?"

"Yes."

"And what about me, Violet? Do you love me?"

"That's not fair." I looked down at my feet; my pants were covered in dirt and dried blood.

He gave a sarcastic, empty laugh. "A lot isn't fair. It's not fair that I had to be the one to train you to be a Grigori. It's not fair that I couldn't tell you the truth, even though I knew you'd hate me for it. It's not fair that I was dying and became the reason you embraced, which only gives you more reason to push me away. It's not fair that I know how great we would be together, except that we can't. It's not fair that, even though I know I'll never have you, I had planned everything—the candles, the lilies—replayed the words I wanted to say a million times when you and I finally made love. I *get* that it's not fair, but I'm still going to ask because we're on a roll of all that is unfair, so what's one more thing?" He grabbed the wardrobe door and slammed it so hard it almost broke off its hinges.

My mind was boggling at everything he'd just said. "Lilies?"

He half laughed. "White. You don't like roses."

My heart cried out from a muffled place. Only Lincoln would ever know all the little things. But instead of making me feel better, it just made me bitter.

He dropped his head and took a step toward me, closing the distance. "Tell me you love me."

When he looked up, our eyes met and I couldn't stop the words. It was like when I had felt compelled to do what Onyx asked of me, but I knew this time no one else was pulling the strings. It was my own soul compelling me.

"I love you," I whispered, unable to deny the buried feelings.

His shoulders relaxed and he moved closer to me. "We'll work it out. Find a way."

There was a time I had wanted to believe that. But not now. Even as my heart sang, I felt a rush of hatred and rage, overpowering everything else. I was surprised by its vehemence.

Lincoln's hand reached out, toward my face. I stopped it with mine and took a step back.

"Violet, don't, please."

"You can't have it both ways, Linc. I've loved you more than I've ever loved anyone. I just went to hell and back for you, maybe even in the literal sense. And even knowing what I know now, I'd do it again. I'm trying to do this, trying to live up to my end of the bargain and the promises I've made along the way...But you need to know, the part of me that loves you...it also hates you, Linc. I'm with Phoenix and right now that's what I need. I trust him."

The words cut into Lincoln as he took in their meaning. They cut into me too.

"He's not what he says he is, Violet. He's taking advantage of you. You're only young. He's manipulating you."

"I'm only young?" My anger boiled over. It was the wrong choice of words. "But not too young to become some kind of angel warrior? Not too young to jump off a cliff not knowing if I would live or die? Yeah, I'm too young to make a decision about a guy, but when it comes to driving a dagger through myself to become *this*"—I held my wrists in the air, my markings reflecting a rainbow of colors—"I'm old enough for that, right?"

Lincoln looked shocked and I knew why. Admitting I'd stabbed myself had surprised us both.

"What do you mean you *drove* a dagger through yourself?" Worry creased his eyes.

I stared into space, distancing myself from the memory. "Nox, the angel of dark, made me kill someone of my choice before he would send me back."

"And you chose yourself?"

I didn't answer.

"Of course you did…You'd never willingly hurt someone else if you didn't have to. Oh God, Violet, I'm sorry." Rather than taking a step forward, he took one back and ran a hand through his hair.

"I know," I said.

"Look, I know you don't want to hear this right now, but something's not right. I can see a shadow on you, a mark. Surely you feel it?"

"No, don't do this. Don't turn me against him." Phoenix was all I had left.

He stared at me. I waited for him to fight back, but he didn't.

"Okay," he said. Sadness rang in his voice. He was letting me go. He didn't want to, but he would do it…for me.

"Okay?"

His head shook even as he repeated the word. "Okay."

He made for the door, his next words just loud enough for me to hear. "But we both know you're lying to yourself."

chapter twenty-nine

"Take care, then, that the light in you not become darkness..."

Luke 11:35

"Angels!" Steph said, practically bouncing up and down in her chair. "No way! Wait, this *can't* be real..."

We were sitting in the food court at the mall. It had been a strategic move on my part, putting her in her comfort zone.

After the trials, whatever it was that had prevented me from telling Steph and Dad about the whole Grigori thing seemed to dissipate. Whatever—or whoever—had been interfering with me had stopped. I had made the choice to tell Steph and hoped it might help me build up to telling Dad...one day.

At first Steph had laughed. She thought it was some elaborate joke. It wasn't until I'd retold the story, in full, several times and finally pushed up my sleeves and put my arms on the table that she started taking me seriously. The sudden addition of markings on my wrists, which on close inspection proved so inhuman that only the extraordinary was acceptable, left her momentarily stunned. Once she recovered and I swore truth on our very friendship, I sat back and let her mind battle it out between logic, evidence, and trust. I think it was trust that held the winning card, and from there, Steph pretty much took care of the rest of the conversation, asking a million questions and examining my wrist markings in awe. It was a relief to be with her again and out of the intensity that now surrounded almost every facet of my life. A breath of much-needed ordinariness.

"So, let me get this straight…" she said for the hundredth time. "You're part angel and now you have powers and you can *heal people*?"

"I can only heal Lincoln." I glanced around the food court. Kids our age were milling around, not a worry in the world. Well, maybe that wasn't entirely true—being a teenager is tough most of the time—but I was willing to bet not many of them were dealing with my lot.

"Because he's your destined partner," Steph continued. When we'd first sat down, she'd slurped at her iced coffee, attacking the scoop of ice cream bobbing on the top with her straw. But now it sat untouched and Steph leaned forward on the edge of her seat, staring at me with wide, unblinking eyes.

"Yep."

"Holy crap, Vi! If you're bullshitting me, you better say now! You're telling me you actually went on some mystical quest and met a good angel and an evil angel?"

"It's a bit more complicated than that, but sort of…yeah."

"Jesus."

"No. He wasn't there," I joked, trying to lighten the mood. I wasn't sure if I was doing it for her sake or mine. I couldn't believe she had taken everything so well to this point.

"You're not going to go all religious on me now, are you? If you tell me you're joining Sunday school, I don't think I'm going to cope."

"Trust me. Church is way down on my list of places to visit."

"But you *are* going to become a Grigori?"

"It's already done. It's a one-way ticket." I tried to sound on top of it, but Steph could sense my sadness.

"Vi, I can't believe you've been going through all of this on your own. It's kind of shitty you didn't tell me sooner, but I get it too. We'll work it out. Sure, it's not your everyday kind of problem, but that doesn't mean you have to give up your life as you know it."

"I just can't pretend that I'm normal, no matter how much I want to." I rolled my sleeves down, masking the now permanent reminder on my wrists. Steph viewed my markings from a cosmetic point of view and thought they were fantastic. They *were* beautiful. They would be more beautiful if I could take them off, though.

She smiled sympathetically. "You're still *you*, Vi. I know things must seem crazy right now, but maybe doing normal stuff is exactly what's going to give you sanity." Her eyes brightened. "Starting tomorrow night!"

Trust Steph to find a silver lining. "What's tomorrow night?" My words dragged with suspicion.

She gave me her best innocent look, which of course meant the exact opposite. "You and I are going out. There's a party at Hades and my brother has spare tickets." She flipped open her phone and started texting. "I get that things are crazy, but you need to do something fun and forget about all this stuff for a while."

It didn't sound like such a bad idea. "Is Jase playing?" I asked.

"Yep, and he promised me he could put some names at the door if we wanted to go…" Her phone beeped. "And," she said, reading the message, "it's all organized: four golden tickets!" She slapped the phone closed.

I let a smile creep onto my face at the idea of a normal wild night with Steph. "I suppose one night out wouldn't hurt."

"Exactly! I'll call Marcus and see if he can come. Maybe you can bring Phoenix."

"Oh, yeah…"

I hadn't actually seen Phoenix for a couple of days. After the trials and healing Lincoln, I had asked for some breathing space, just to clear my head. It had been good to go into a semi-lockdown at home, to have some time to myself.

"There's probably something I should tell you about Phoenix."

"What? Don't tell me he's a Grigori too. I'm starting to feel like an outcast!"

"No. Definitely not a Grigori." How exactly did I say this? "He's kind of, sort of…an exiled angel," I said, my voice sliding up an octave with each word.

"WHAT? *Phoenix* is an angel? You're *dating* an angel?"

"An *exiled* angel," I corrected.

It took a few moments of frozen shock before she started again. "I can't believe you didn't tell me. Was he good or evil?"

"What do you mean?" I asked, not fully understanding.

"Ah…hello? I mean, when he was all halo and wings."

I rolled my eyes at her.

"You know, was he one of the…whatever you called it, light ones or dark ones or whatever? Which one was he?"

Alarm bells rang as Steph's words hit home. Exiles were exiles. I mean, once they were on earth, they all kind of went into the same bag, but that didn't make their pasts count for nothing. Angels of light and dark were very different beings.

"I never asked." I spoke in a daydream.

"What do you mean, *never asked*?"

There was a pause before I snapped to. "Of course he was light. He's been amazing. Trust me, I've met a dark angel and he's nothing like that. He was an angel of light." Even as I said it, I could feel the stirrings of doubt. I pushed them aside. "Phoenix isn't like other exiles anyway; he's different." Again, I realized I didn't know exactly what that meant. "I'll call him tonight and see if he's free," I said, putting a stop to my runaway thoughts.

Steph watched me for a moment, tapping her fingernails on the table, then blurted out, "Look, I understand why you're so hurt by Lincoln, but are you sure it's the right time to get involved with someone else? You might not have ever really *been* in a relationship with Lincoln, but in some ways you two were like an old married couple. You were in love with him—completely."

I really didn't want to have this conversation. It felt like I *couldn't* have it in a way.

"You're the one who told me I should be having fun. Anyway, right now, the main thing I feel for Lincoln is *hate*." The words had come from my mouth, but it didn't feel like me talking.

"Wow, Vi, okay, I feel the rage. I get it, Lincoln's on the shit list, but does that mean that Phoenix is the one you want to be with?"

It was a question I'd been starting to ask myself before the trials too. But since we'd come back, something had changed. I was less inclined to doubt him now.

"He's good to me, he looks after me when I need it, he's honest, and…we…" I blushed.

"*Jesus, Mary, and Joseph!* You had SEX with him!"

I had a feeling she was enjoying the new slant on biblical references.

"It kind of just happened," I said in a low voice, trying to remind Steph that we were actually in a public place and I didn't want the whole world knowing I had lost my virginity to an exiled angel.

"*It kind of just happened?* The flu kind of just happens; sex requires consensual dirty thoughts and the extensive removal of clothing! I want details, and when I say *details*, I mean the good details, not the gross details." She screwed up her face and we both laughed.

"Actually, it was strange. Don't get me wrong, Phoenix was amazing. He has obviously, you know…Clearly it wasn't *his* first time."

"Yeah, yeah, he's a sex god. Surprise, surprise. So what's the problem?"

"Nothing I guess. It's just…He has this ability to make everything seem much more intense. He takes me away…It's a rush and…kind of scary. I feel like I lose myself to him." My mind drifted to the images of the fire encasing us and the golden strands wrapping around us both.

"Is that a good thing or a bad thing?"

It was a logical question. I answered quickly before I could let the doubt set in. "Good. It was good, I think."

"Well, I suggest you keep it to yourself for now. I wouldn't like to be around if Lincoln finds out."

I covered my face with my hands and sank into my chair.

"No way!" Steph almost fell off her seat in disbelief.

"He figured it out." I cringed, peeping out from behind a few fingers.

"*Christ almighty!*" She smiled at her words. I rolled my eyes.

"Okay, but in all seriousness, what did he do? Was Phoenix there? Did he hit him? Who's stronger out of the two? Is it a fair fight?" She was rambling on so fast I could barely make out her words.

"Actually, it was awful. He told me he loved me and that he had dreamed about how we would be together." I told her about the candles and the lilies. She looked around wistfully.

"*Oh. My. God!* That is so…What did you say?"

"It's a little hazy now, but I think I told him…that I hated him."

Steph leaned forward and actually looked worried. "Wow, not really into subtlety at the moment, are you? That doesn't sound like something you'd say to your worst enemy, let alone Lincoln."

I was a bit confused myself. "Maybe not. But every time I think of him or I'm around him lately, I just can't stop all these feelings of anger and hate. I mean, it was bad when I first found out he'd been lying to me, but since coming back from the trials, it's like I can't escape them, like they're controlling me."

"Hey, I'm all for a little venting, but maybe you should try letting go of some of the hate. You know, deep breaths or something. I mean, it sounds like you're not going to be able to avoid each other for long, while doing the whole save-the-world thing too."

She had a point, and more than that, I actually agreed with her…in theory.

We spent most of the afternoon hanging out. Steph filled me in on her own love life, which was full-steam ahead. She and Marcus were officially a couple. He satisfied Steph's long list of requirements and he pretty much worshipped her. According to her, all was as it should be. She offered to carry on keeping me company, but after the tenth text message from Marcus, I pushed her onto the bus to go meet him.

Feeling the urge to be a little spontaneous, I bought some new clothes. They weren't my usual style, but since everything else in my world had changed, why not my look? I even went and had my hair cut. It was nice to try something different, and it gave me a new sense of confidence.

By the time I walked into the apartment, it was dark. Dad was sitting on the couch reading an architecture magazine. He closed it and sat up a little when I came in.

"Hello, stranger. It seems like we never see each other these days."

I knew I was going to have to explain my lengthy absences. The problem was, I still hadn't figured out what I was going to say. We hadn't even crossed paths since before the trials.

"I'm sorry I've been so caught up with work, sweetheart. I know I haven't been around much, but if you still want to catch up over dinner one night soon, I'd really like that. How about Thursday next week?"

I relaxed and almost laughed. I'd forgotten that Dad pretty much existed in his own world. I decided it was a good thing.

"Sure, Dad. Next week sounds fine. How about we go Italian?"

"Great!" He went back to his magazine.

I made coffee and a potato chip sandwich and headed to my art studio. With a blank canvas, coffee in hand, and Florence and the Machine playing on high, things seemed almost normal. I even managed to fit in a quick call to Phoenix, inviting him to meet me at Hades the following night.

After speaking with him on the phone, I felt much better. Any doubts that had floated into my mind after talking with Steph vanished.

Of course he'd been an angel of light.

chapter thirty

"There is no arguing with the pretenders to a divine knowledge
and to a divine mission. They are possessed with the sin of pride.
They have yielded to the perennial temptation."

WALTER LIPPMANN

I was standing alone as they marched toward me. Death, Doom, and
Destruction in the form of an army of exiles—a promise of pain and
suffering wafting in and out of focus, becoming shadows and then reap-
pearing. They moved like a physical force, almost suffocating everything
around them.

The two that led emitted enormous power. One was slightly elevated
above the ground, still walking but levitating at the same time. It
was Onyx. The other looked at me, burning a hole into my eyes right
through to my soul.

"We can feel your power, rainbow. You are the link that promises
destruction. We are coming for you."

I heard the words, even though he didn't actually speak.

I stood, unable to move, like the nightmares from my childhood where I couldn't run away. I tried getting down on my hands and knees. In my dreams, that sometimes worked. But I couldn't move at all.

"Who are you?" I asked.

"Joel. Once of the Principalities. I will not let you cloud my path. I have played caretaker to man for too long; now this world will conform. It is the only way."

I saw the long, silver sword by his side. He held the hilt and leaned on it like a walking stick. Blood was sliding down the edges. Where had it come from?

"The only way to what?" I asked, now feeling like this wasn't only a dream.

"To take the control we are entitled to. Humanity is weak and wicked in nature. They will serve us or be sacrificed."

"And you're planning to be what? Their leader?" I must have confused him, because he lost his composure for a brief moment before lifting his head high and continuing the sermon.

"Humans have spat in the face of free will and abused their privileges. The time has come for a new order and it is clear that I must succeed where others have failed." He lifted the sword off the ground, still pointing it downward. Blood dripped slowly from the point.

Fear coursed through my body, along with all five senses, though somewhat dampened.

His body distorted, eyes appeared all over him, and wings spread from his back—three wings on each side. My breath caught. They were magnificent. Then they burst into flames, raging red and blue fire, and he just stood there in front of me, his arms slightly apart as he burned. Then he was gone.

Onyx was left standing before me, his minions floating in the background under a cloud of gloom. He looked at me, smiling, tilting his head as he had the last time we met. He looked at me like he knew all my secrets.

"For one who was once of the light, he does have an increasing flair for the dramatic," he said, sounding amused by Joel's demonstration. "It's a slippery slope, the road of sin. Even those with the most noble of causes can justify the need for it. Fabulous, isn't it? He truly believes in his crusade, even as it stains what is left of his soul."

Onyx glided toward me. I struggled for movement in my unwilling body. It seemed to cause him great pleasure.

"That's the beauty of exiled angels, for we all must inherit Original Sin in flesh. It is called concupiscence"—he rolled the word on his tongue—"and it has the most intriguing results in our kind. It makes things so much more...entertaining." He laughed and walked away into the pulsing darkness that enveloped him.

I stood in emptiness, still unable to move, trapped. I could hear Onyx laughing his high-pitched cackle. Even in a dream, the guy was grating.

I could do this. I could free myself from this. It was just a dream. I took a deep breath and tried to center myself and draw on the power that had been given to me. I used it to push the darkness away, peeling layers of it back and slowly surfacing, until the dream started to release me and I was able to bring myself back to—

—a street. No, some kind of alley. My mind took a moment to

catch up with my eyes, but bit by bit, the world around me came into focus. It was still dark, but not the same dark. It was night and I was no longer in my bed.

The senses were all around me now—a part of me, they hummed and buzzed. Apple and flowers encircled me, warning me but not overpowering me. They informed me and departed.

I was standing on my own, all except for the dead body that lay at my feet. A car drove by the opening to the alley, throwing a momentary beam of light toward me, illuminating enough of the body and face for me to recognize it. Lying in a pool of blood, in jeans and what was once a white button-down shirt, was *Marcus*.

What had I done? I didn't know where I was, but I was dressed and it was the middle of the night. Had I been sleepwalking? Panicking, I patted down my jeans pockets and felt the familiar lump that meant I had my phone. When I pulled it out, I saw my hand was dripping with blood that I had smeared all down my clothes.

I called Griffin. I described the area and found a couple of street signs at the end of the alley. Griffin told me he would be there in ten minutes. After I broke into an all-out panic, he promised to be there in five.

I walked back into the dead end where I had woken from my nightmare and found the bloodied body. I braced myself for the awful sight again. Thoughts of Steph rolled through my mind.

But…it wasn't Marcus.

This guy was tall and slim, wearing a dark suit. He would have been about thirty years old. He didn't look anything like Marcus.

I called Steph. She answered, half asleep. "This better be an emergency of epic proportions. I'm talking rising from the dead kind of stuff here. It's 3 a.m."

"Steph, when did you last speak to Marcus?"

"Tonight, why?" she asked, becoming more alert with my tone.

"Can you try to call him for me? I need to know if he's okay." I was doing that thing where I bounce up and down on the spot. It was becoming a habit.

"Okay." She drew out the word as if she thought I was crazy. I was wondering the same thing. "Can I ask why?"

I was freaking out, not thinking straight, so I just blurted it out. "I had a nightmare and then I woke up in an alley in the middle of the city and I was standing over a body and it looked like Marcus and now it…doesn't."

"WHAT! Marcus is dead?" She was hyperventilating.

"Yes…No! I don't know. Can you please just try to call him?"

She hung up the phone without another word.

While waiting for her to call back, I looked in the alley to find something to clean myself up with. I settled for ripping apart a cardboard box. But when I looked down, the blood was no longer on my hands. They were as clean as if just washed. I dropped the cardboard, searching myself for any other signs of the blood. Nothing.

I was losing it. Losing perspective. I started to feel woozy and claustrophobic. I was going to pass out. I walked toward an upside-down crate and collapsed onto it just before my legs gave way.

The next thing I knew, someone was slapping me across the face. Griffin.

"Aww!" What was it with everyone belting the crap out of me when I was unconscious?

"Ah, you'll be okay. You have extra durability now and you wouldn't come round with the lighter slaps." He smiled a little.

"How many times have you hit me?" I asked, alarmed.

"A few," he said, blowing it off and adding, "you're a Grigori now, Violet. You can take a few hits." As if that was the end of it. "What happened?" he asked.

I told him how I had ended up in the alley with the dead body after having a nightmare about Onyx and another exile called Joel. He sighed when he heard the name.

"Do you know him?" I asked.

"Yes, he's an extremely powerful and insane exile, once of light"—he raised his eyebrows at me—"with a particular panache for dream altering. He believes he is on a divine mission, and he leaves a trail of death and destruction everywhere he goes. He is especially vengeful toward Grigori and has always been a hunter of us. We've never been able to get close enough to finish him." He shook his head and frowned. "Acting alone is bad enough. Working with Onyx…" Griffin wiped his forehead then threw his hands in the air. "Honestly, they used to at least have *some* honor. Light and dark working together—there's no integrity anymore." Griffin kicked one of the wooden pallets beside me, breaking it in two. It seemed to calm him down. "Come on. Let's look at this body." He turned toward the end of the alley where it lay.

My phone rang and when I answered, Steph was on the other end, yelling at me.

"Are you insane? You almost gave me a heart attack!"

"Did you speak to Marcus?"

"You mean did I piss Marcus off to no end by waking him up in the middle of the night? Yes! I'll be surprised if he ever takes me seriously again!"

My whole body folded over in relief. "That's great!" I said.

"*No*…it's not great. He thinks I've lost my mind."

"Okay, so I'm sorry about that part, but I'm still glad he's okay."

"You really saw a dead body that looked like him?" She sounded in control but for the little tremor in her voice.

"No. I saw a dead body that *was* him. I can't explain it now. I'll call you in the morning."

"There is some seriously weird stuff going on around you at the moment. You know that, don't you?"

"Yep."

"Well, call me when the sun is up." I could hear her getting back into bed. "Night." The phone went silent.

When I rejoined Griffin, he was leaning over the body and already on the phone, organizing a cleanup crew. I suddenly had a bad feeling. He snapped his phone shut and put his head in his hands, taking deep breaths.

"His name was Angus. He has been a Grigori for more than a hundred years. He was my…mentor. My friend."

I swallowed a lump in my throat. "Griffin?" I asked hesitantly. His eyes flicked up to me.

"I…I had blood on my hands. When I first realized I was here, there was blood all over me. I don't know if…if I?" I didn't believe it, but the fact was, somewhere along the line I had lost time, and when I came to, a dead body was at my feet.

"Killed him?" he offered, looking up at me calmly.

"Yes," I gulped.

"No. This was done by exiles. I'm sure if you concentrate, you'll feel the energy they have left behind."

I didn't need to concentrate. I had already felt it, but I'd still had to ask.

I could hear the pain in Griffin's voice at losing his friend. I gave him some space, returning to my crate halfway down the alley.

I was still sitting there, staring into midair, when more Grigori arrived. I recognized some of them from the last murder scene. It was comforting in a way; their presence seemed to calm the new power that was bubbling inside me. I assumed they were the cleanup crew. A couple of them nodded at me as they walked by, acknowledging me as one of their own.

Magda and Lincoln turned up at the same time. They had obviously come together, but that didn't bother me as much as I would have expected—as if my jealousy were somehow censored. When I thought about it, it actually seemed like when it came to Lincoln, all my feelings were suppressed now—except, of course, for anger. I put it down to coping mechanisms, sweeping it under the carpet, where all things "Lincoln" went these days.

He stayed to talk to me while Magda threw out a half-assed wave and kept walking toward Griffin. *Yep, really feeling the love from Magda.*

"Are you okay?" he asked tentatively.

"Yeah," I said, even though my hands were still trembling.

"Was it really Angus?"

"That's what Griffin said."

Lincoln swore under his breath.

"Did you know him too?"

"Yeah, in fact, I was hoping to introduce you to him. He survived a lot of pretty terrible things. Who did this?"

"Onyx and Joel," I blurted out.

His eyebrows rose. "Together?"

I nodded. "They sucked me into some warped nightmare and when I came to, I was here. It had to have been them. They're completely and utterly psycho."

"Well, at least you're starting to understand what exiles are really like."

I didn't miss the dig intended for Phoenix and immediately felt defensive. I gave Lincoln my best I-couldn't-care-less-what-you-think-and-I'm-pissed-at-you smile and stood up. "I haven't slept all night. I'm going to grab a taxi. Tell Griffin I'll see him in the morning."

"You're just leaving?" He held his hands out in disbelief.

"Yep. I'm tired, Linc, and I don't want to fight with you. I'm going home to sleep. If Griffin needs me, he'll call." And then out of spite, I added, "Don't worry, I'm sure Magda can hold your hand if you get lonely."

I spun on my heels to make my getaway. Like a blessing, a taxi pulled up almost immediately, giving even more impact to my departure.

chapter thirty-one

*"You know that when I hate you, it is because I love you to a
point of passion that unhinges my soul."*

JULIE DE LESPINASSE

I dragged myself out of bed after only a couple hours of sleep. I
was determined to get control of my life, tired of letting everyone
push and pull at me. I was a Grigori now and I needed to know
what was going on. Especially since it appeared I had my own little
renegade-angel fan club.

I called Griffin and arranged for him to come to my place. He
sounded like he hadn't slept at all and slyly remarked on my disap-
pearance, but his heart wasn't in it. I think he was too tired to
bother with a lecture. He knew we needed to talk.

While waiting for Griffin, I put in a load of laundry and tidied
up the apartment a little for the cleaners who were due later. I
considered ringing Steph to start groveling, but then thought
better of it. It was still early and any movement before midday

might be considered a hostile act. I didn't want to risk burying myself any deeper.

When I came back into the kitchen, I saw I had a new text message.

Griffin asked me to come with him. Hope that's okay. Linc.

I looked at the clock on my phone; they were due any second. I didn't have time to prepare myself—emotionally *or* physically. I dropped my face into my hands and more or less laughed. Could things get any crazier?

In that instant, the doorbell rang. I went to the door via the mirror. I knew I wouldn't have stopped if it were only Griffin waiting on the other side.

Damn it.

I paused, bracing myself to lay eyes on Lincoln. I knew that no matter how angry I was at him, the sight of him would still affect me. It always did. I opened the door and his green eyes took me in, as I did him, and…nothing. Maybe I was finally getting over him?

I fixed them coffee, only needing to check with Griffin how he took his. I'd made a million cups of coffee for Lincoln and knew he liked a double espresso with just the smallest dash of milk, and if asked he would say one sugar, but really he preferred two.

Once I settled on the couch, I looked over to see Lincoln staring at me. He was baffled by something.

"Did you put any sugar in this?" He motioned to the coffee he had just sipped.

"No," I said, equally baffled. I moved to stand up, but he stood himself, shaking his head at me.

"Don't worry. I'll get it," he said.

Griffin noticed the tension. "Look, if you two are going to behave like twelve-year-olds, this isn't going to work. In case you haven't noticed, we *are* dealing with a fairly large problem at the moment."

I looked at the floor guiltily.

"Sorry, Griff," Lincoln said from behind me. "We're fine, aren't we, Violet?"

I didn't miss the condescension in his tone.

"We're great," I said, turning around and narrowing my eyes. I was tempted to add that he wouldn't even be able to remember how twelve-year-olds acted since he was so damn old, but somehow I forced my hateful mouth shut. Instead, I turned back to Griffin. "I'm sorry too." It wasn't often I felt like I had received a parental scolding. I was disappointed with myself for letting Griffin down.

We ran through the details of the previous night and I filled in the gaps. Lincoln listened in amazement. It didn't bother me; it was just as unreal to me. Griffin listened intently and didn't interrupt until I had relived the night completely.

"I think you've been tampered with," Griffin said.

"Huh?"

"As a Grigori, your defenses should be stronger. Given what we've already seen of your strengths, you shouldn't have any difficulty being able to stop them from infiltrating your dreams, your imagination. They're using their powers to obscure you somehow," Griffin explained.

"I don't understand. I thought once I was a Grigori, my powers would protect me. Are you telling me these psycho exiles will be able to invade my dreams whenever they want and send me out to discover dead bodies?"

I felt like throwing something—or crying. It was too much to contemplate. After everything I'd been through, it still wasn't enough. Lincoln fidgeted in his seat then stilled. I thought for a second he was going to come to me. I thought for a second that I wanted him to, but at the same time, I was relieved that he didn't.

"I don't know how, but it seems you have some kind of block in your defenses. That's why I brought Lincoln." Griffin stood up. "Can we move the furniture back?" he asked.

My brow furrowed. "Why?" Out of the corner of my eye, I saw Lincoln give a sly smile.

Griffin started pushing the couch back. "We need to test some of your other abilities. Then we can see if there are any other problems. That means a little sparring. Given how volatile you seem to be at times, I thought it best to put Lincoln on the firing line since you can heal him so well." Griffin was smiling too.

I stood up and started to push my chair back. "Fine by me," I said, trying but failing to conceal my delight at the thought of testing out my new powers, not to mention releasing some pent-up aggression toward Lincoln.

Great, we were all smiling. I guess it was an improvement.

We cleared all the furniture to the walls, creating our own little thunderdome. Griffin gave us some general guidelines, which were basically that he wanted me to both give and take blows, testing my strength and durability.

Lincoln and I stood opposite each other, waiting. He smiled and shrugged. "So hit me, Violet. Let's see if you can finally pack a little punch."

That was all it took. I drew strength from within and pummeled my fist into his stomach and then across his face, knocking him back a few steps. There was a time when I would have been mortified, but I felt nothing. I was strong and fast—but then, so was he.

He was back in position within moments; his speed was amazing. He leveraged back and struck out with his foot, landing the impact squarely in my gut. I stumbled back, marveling that I didn't fall over.

I caught Lincoln watching me cautiously. I knew that look. "Stop being a pussy, Lincoln! We came here to test me out, so test!" I yelled, not holding back on my growing hostility.

He rolled his eyes at me, but then stepped forward and struck me across the face. He made contact on the first attempt, but I dodged the second, remembering defense was also important. From there, it was game on.

We struck out at each other; I used every move he had ever taught me and anything else I could throw at him. I was agile and barely had to think of a movement before my body obliged. It was just too much fun. I couldn't believe it, but with power and strength on my side, I thrived. It felt…natural.

After sustaining the blows Lincoln had delivered, I should have been on the way to the hospital. It was surreal, but I barely felt sore. No wonder nothing I'd ever done to Lincoln in our training sessions had caused any impact. We both hit hard, but I was still holding back—and if I was holding back, so was he.

I decided on a different strategy. Without warning, I stepped back and laughed. He looked at me in confusion.

"What?" he demanded, a little breathless.

I spoke between bouts of laughter. "Nothing…I just thought you'd be stronger." I tried to sound unimpressed.

"We're doing what we need to do for the purpose of today." I could hear the condescension in his voice. He thought I was being petty. I simply chuckled again.

"You wanted this, Linc! You wanted me to be strong, *be* a Grigori. What? You're not worried you'll hurt me, are you?" My words held a multitude of digs.

He reacted as I'd hoped, shaking his head. "Fine, Violet," he said, resigned. "Let's see how strong you really are."

I didn't stop to think, *couldn't* stop. I threw all the force I had into one punch, directed at Lincoln's chest. In it was all the hate and anger that I felt toward him.

In a move so fast I didn't even see it, Lincoln caught my hand in his, absorbing the impact and stopping it. My jaw dropped at the awesomeness of his power. His hand, which held mine with surprising tenderness, let go.

Griffin stepped between us. "Enough. We have what we needed. You're strong, Violet, especially for a rookie. I've rarely seen another make Lincoln even break a sweat. Your problem isn't in offense," he said.

I stepped back, trying to process everything, mostly my own attitude, my own hatred. I was starting to feel out of control, literally. The question was, if I wasn't in control, who *was?*

I looked over at Lincoln, who was behind the kitchen island rinsing his face. Sensing me, he looked up. Our eyes locked and I glimpsed pain, just for a moment. Bruises were forming on the side of his face.

I pointed to them. "I could try to heal those."

It was intended as a peace offering, but it was too late. He threw down the towel he was using to dry his face. "Forget it. I'm not in the mood."

It took me a few seconds to get it. When I did, my face burned with mortification. "I…I wasn't offering to kiss…I didn't mean."

"As I said. Forget it." I noticed he hadn't offered to heal any of my bruises.

"So what now?" I asked Griffin. He rubbed his forehead, weariness showing. The circles under his eyes were darkening by the minute.

"I don't know. At last count, Joel and Onyx between them will have a force of about fifteen. That's a lot of exiles to handle, especially since we keep losing good Grigori. They're picking us off one by one and making sure we know about it."

"Is that why they led me to the body...to Angus last night?"

"Partly, I think."

"Griffin," Lincoln interjected, "there's a reason they're targeting Violet. They fear her, but all they did last night was succeed in giving us a heads-up that there's a problem with her powers. We need to find the cause."

"Maybe I'm just defective," I threw in defensively. He didn't bite; instead, he just turned his attention back to the nothing zone. His restraint was impressive, as well as annoying.

"Either way," Griffin stepped in once again, "we should probably arrange to have someone with you so this doesn't happen again. Lincoln? Can you stay with her tonight?"

My mouth flew open. "No!"

Lincoln gave a bitter laugh, shaking his head again. It made me feel about five years old.

"Umm...what I meant was..." I said, trying to regain a little composure, "I've got plans tonight."

"You're going out?" Lincoln spoke quietly, but his disapproval came across loud and clear.

"Yeah. I mean...Steph roped me into a night out. She says I need some balance."

"Steph and balance? I'd like to see that. So, I take it you've filled her in."

I still wasn't sure if that was allowed, but no one had told me otherwise. I shrugged. "I'm not going to keep secrets from my best friend."

He was quiet. It occurred to me that I may have hurt his feelings...again, since I'd accused him of so many secrets...I was more and more aware of how some of the hateful things I was saying to him must have been affecting him. Not that it was going to stop me. After talking with Steph and then Phoenix yesterday, my anger toward Lincoln was in overdrive.

"It was different," Lincoln mumbled.

I didn't say anything more and Griffin didn't get involved in this one. I was just relieved he didn't object to me having told Steph. Instead, he started meandering around the apartment, looking at the art. He stopped in front of one of my favorite pieces of photography in the living room: an open field in pitch-black night lit by a bolt of lightning, which illuminated the silhouette of the field and a small white gatehouse in the distance. I was glad Griffin appreciated its beauty.

Eventually, Lincoln broke the silence. "You should still have someone with you," he said coldly.

"That's fine. Phoenix is coming," I retorted.

I tried to cover my shock at my willingness to go straight for the low blows by loading dirty cups into the dishwasher. I had to stop and grip the edge of the counter. I was holding on really tightly and I didn't know if it was due to shame or the need to enforce restraint. Even though part of me realized I was hurting him, I still wanted to.

You're screwed in the head, Vi—absolutely nuts!

Griffin joined us again. "We'll be going out tomorrow to some of the usual haunts to try to track down Joel and Onyx."

"I'll be there," I said before he could ask.

"You will?" Lincoln seemed surprised.

"However I got here, Lincoln, this is what I am now."

"That's settled then," Griffin said. "If you don't mind though, Violet, it might be a good idea if one of us stays around until tonight at least."

I took one look at Griffin and sighed. He was hanging over the back of a chair, so tired he could barely hold his head up. Lincoln was seated on a barstool, looking anywhere but at me. I got the feeling he didn't want to be stuck with me any more than I wanted to be stuck with him.

"I'll stay," he said without looking up.

I knew if I said I didn't want Lincoln to be here, Griffin would only offer to stay in his place. "Fine," I grumped.

Griffin left so quickly it was almost comical. Once upon a time, Lincoln and I would have laughed about it together.

Now, we just moved around the apartment awkwardly, avoiding crossing into each other's designated space, allowing long silences to stretch. Finally, after pacing the hallway for the seventy-fourth time—yes, I was counting—he came back to sit on the couch opposite me, where I was slowly sipping my third coffee.

"You know, you don't have to handle all this on your own. You are allowed to let us help you. We have been through this ourselves."

My defenses reared before I had even realized it. "Yeah, and I suppose when you found out you were a Grigori, you just took it as a greater calling and ran off to do the trials."

"Actually, no."

I didn't say anything else, frightened of what might come out of my mouth if I opened it again. Lincoln stood and opened the sliding doors that led to the terrace. I followed him out. I honestly had a moment where I considered not—for fear that I might lose it and throw him over the edge. *This isn't me.*

"My mom was still alive when I found out, but she was sick and struggling to run her business. Griffin found me and kind of took me under his wing. At first I didn't want anything to do with it. I thought he was some kind of preacher trying to brainwash me into joining a cult."

"Didn't he just use his truth mojo on you?"

"Eventually. He doesn't like using it unless he has to. By the time he did, I had started feeling the senses. Not like you did, but enough to produce that déjà vu feeling. That, combined with Griffin's power, helped me open my eyes to what was going on all around me."

He looked down, elbows resting on the railing, turning his coffee mug in his hands. "My first encounter with an exile was when I realized one had infiltrated Mom's company. She was sick with cancer and, using glamour and control of her imagination, he persuaded her to redistribute the funds of the business. What was once a company that donated profits to children's charities and the homeless became a financier of war and weapons. Mom and her whole company were under the illusion they were making good choices for the right reasons. They couldn't see through all the lies and deceit. Through my essence, I knew there was something wrong. Griffin and Magda helped me work out the rest."

"That's why you still donate to kids' charities."

"It's what Mom would have wanted."

"So…you embraced?"

"Yes, but by that time it was already too late. Her cancer had spread; she was dying. He poisoned her mind and her soul completely. By the time I returned, he'd disappeared, but the damage was done. She died a month later and I…I failed her."

He stared into his coffee as if it were a mirror of his past. He tipped the rest over the edge and walked back inside to the couch. I sat down opposite.

"*That's* why I'm a Grigori. *That's* why I believe in it. No one should have to be controlled by another being. We have free will for a reason."

Instead of saying how sorry I was, instead of reaching out to him the way he had done for me so many times, I curled my knees to my chest, wrapping my arms around myself, and said nothing.

After a while, Lincoln turned on the TV, and desperate to distance myself from him, I closeted myself in the bathroom. Sitting on the edge of the bath counting minutes, I let the shower run. When I finally emerged, he was gone. There was a note on the table.

I'm sure you'll be fine until you meet up with Phoenix. See you later.

chapter thirty-two

"Then you will know the truth..."

JOHN 8:32

I was putting the finishing touches on my makeup when I heard Steph's signature knock on the front door.

"Mother of God! You look hot!" she said when she saw me in my new clothes.

I smiled, feeling confident. "Are you going to constantly throw around the blasphemy from now on?"

"Gotta do what works for me." She shrugged and waved her hand at me. "Explain."

I glanced back at the mirror—skinny black jeans, black jersey silk top with a revealing neckline, and black patent high heels. It was definitely a more dramatic look-at-me outfit than I usually gravitated toward. I couldn't deny it; since the trials and the feel of the power coursing through my body, my confidence had grown. It was vain, but becoming a kickass Grigori had given me a glow.

"It was time for a new look," I surmised.

"Well, no arguments here. You look *a-ma-zing*." She walked over to me, surveying me more closely. "There's only one problem."

"What?" I said. Trust Steph to find a problem.

"These," she said, as she touched the silver bracelets on my wrists. Along with new clothes and hair, I had bought myself an array of bangles to cover my wrist markings. "You're better without them." She raised her eyebrows, but her expression had softened. It didn't take much for her to know how I was really feeling.

"People will notice," I said, looking down, organizing the contents of my handbag. "I don't want to spend all night explaining myself."

"No one will notice, and even if they do, you can blow it off as a cool tattoo or something. Trust me!"

I looked at Steph dubiously, then took off the bracelets to please her. But as we were walking out the door, I quickly slipped them back on again to cover the markings.

There was a line a mile long when we arrived at Hades. Steph spotted Marcus waiting for us. He was looking good, in that preppy boat-shoes kind of way. Steph might like some things a little crazy, but she definitely wants her guys clean-cut. I guess it's another reason we're best friends: we never fight over guys. She elbowed me as we got closer to him.

"He might not be an angel, but that doesn't mean he can't give a girl a taste of Heaven." We both laughed and I linked my arm through hers. It wouldn't be long before those two got a lot closer—in the biblical sense, that is.

Jase had made good on his promise and our names were at the door. It was incredibly satisfying to skip the line and walk right on in.

The restaurant section had been closed for the night and all the tables were gone, making more room for people to stand and drink and dance under the dozens of chandeliers. This, however, also meant that it was only open to over-twenty-ones. It hadn't been a problem getting in since Jase had left our names at the door, but that didn't mean it was wise to start ordering up at the bar and risk getting carded.

Marcus dutifully obliged, readying his fake ID before getting drinks for us all and hauling them back through the crowds. There were people everywhere; the vibe through the whole place was amazing. It felt good to be surrounded by fun for a change. Steph gave me a sip of her mojito. It was lethal and she was sucking it back like a Slurpee. I had visions of dragging her home at the end of the night. Much to Steph's horror, I was just having a Coke. Control was not something I was keen on relinquishing more of right now.

When Steph finished her mojito in record time, she promptly sent Marcus off to get her another concoction from the cocktail list.

"Has he ever actually said no to you?" I yelled over the music.

"He's gorgeous, isn't he," she yelled back, oblivious that I was teasing her. I couldn't blame her and smiled back; she was genuinely happy. "If your angel doesn't arrive soon," Steph added, "he might have more than just Lincoln to worry about."

I looked at her in confusion.

"Ah, Vi, you must have noticed that pretty much every guy in here, except for Marcus of course, is drooling over you."

I looked around the room. She had been exaggerating, but there was a good handful of guys watching me. I blushed red hot but couldn't stop the smile.

A breeze drifted in from the open door. Then I felt it. The taste of apple, the humming energy, birds flying maniacally. All the senses flowed through me, but unlike before I had embraced, now I had control. I could move them around, bring them forward, focus on them—and also push them back and silence them. And most importantly, I knew who it was. I was pretty sure it wasn't normal for Grigori to be able to sense exactly *who* the exile was, but I was beginning to accept I wasn't ordinary.

"Phoenix is here," I said.

"Where?" Steph looked around.

"Close. I can feel him."

"You can *feel* him?" She was wide-eyed in disbelief.

I turned around and Phoenix was standing there. He looked worried. I smiled and his face relaxed. He raised a hand to the side of my face. As soon as he touched me, my body leaned into his and I folded into him, yielded to him.

"I've missed you," he said.

"Me too," was all I could manage.

His eyes drifted down, taking in my new look. He bled his desire for me and I knew he was doing it on purpose. His eyes settled on my wrists where the bracelets glittered. He didn't say anything. Finally, he looked away from me and over to Steph. It didn't take long for him to process the look of awe plastered over her face.

"Ahh," he exhaled. "I suppose it's no surprise she told you."

Steph stood, almost hypnotized, staring at Phoenix.

"Steph." I elbowed her. She jumped to attention.

"Sorry, it's just, now that I know, it seems so weird to be standing here in a club with an *angel*."

Phoenix gave a slight smile. "Trust me, it's not that interesting."

Marcus returned with more drinks and that stopped all the angel talk. I could tell Phoenix was relieved.

By about ten o'clock, Steph and Marcus both looked as if they had crossed the line of one drink too many. I cringed for them, as they started embarrassing themselves on the dance floor. Eighties flashback dresses were one thing; flashback dance moves another altogether.

Phoenix and I settled onto a couch in the corner and eased back into being around each other. We avoided Grigori and angel talk as much as possible. He told me about the time he had "climbed" Mount Everest in 1901. It would have only taken him a few seconds had he not lingered at the top to enjoy the quiet and the view. I tried to take it all in stride, but it's hard to stop your jaw from gaping when someone is telling you he climbed the damn thing over fifty years before the first humans ever did. And, oh yeah…he was clearly well over a hundred years old!

Phoenix moved over so he was sitting right beside me. He let his fingers trail up my thigh. "I was thinking..." he said suggestively. My body tingled. With every touch, I felt more and more certain that my future *wasn't* with Lincoln and that forgiveness was not a possibility. I was reminded of just how much Phoenix could affect me, take me away. My breath caught and then raced. The thought of escaping into his bliss was definitely exciting. But as I felt myself leaning toward him, I was strangely reminded of being caught up in Onyx's and Joel's powers. My senses sharpened.

"I need to learn how to block you when I want to," I said, breaking the mood abruptly.

He stiffened. "Why?"

"I need to learn how to use my powers. Apparently, I have some kind of kink in them."

I saw him hesitate and wondered why he didn't seem keen to help. Just as I was about to question him, he smiled dangerously. "We might have to leave to *fully* test out the theory."

I smiled and laughed. "I was thinking more along the lines of a kiss," I said, sounding more nervous than I would've liked. "For now," I added, so he knew I wasn't saying an outright no. I was worried I'd hurt him if I told him I wasn't sure we should rush into the whole sex thing again.

Phoenix moved closer and looked me over. It was odd; he didn't seem to be able to hold my eyes.

"Are you okay? If you don't want to..." I left the words hanging, whatever bravado I had mustered quickly fading.

"It's not that I don't want to. I'd do anything to have you as mine." Then his eyes managed to fix on mine and he pushed the hair back from one side of my face, cupping his hand along my jawline, his fingers stretching into my hair. I could feel in that moment what I was to him, and then he confirmed it in words.

"You're a goddess."

He kissed me. Humming energy coursed through me, and he opened the channels to his emotions and released a torrent of lust. I reached within myself to find my power and built a wall around me, pushing back the surging energy that exploded through my whole body. I didn't know if what I was doing was right; I just followed my instincts.

Gradually, the lust subsided. Phoenix must have felt the resistance from me because he pushed harder. This time I was inundated with desire, total and utter desire. All the right parts—or *wrong* parts—responded to it, my body ruling my mind.

My hands traveled over him as I got lost in the moment, and he pulled me in. I again retreated into my core strength and began to build walls of protection. As I did, the lust and desire receded and I began to feel myself breaking through.

Along with gaining self-control, I was able to see *within* my power. Morning and evening flashed before me, and in them I saw the fibers of my core, my soul. Something that wasn't me was wrapped around them, strangling me.

I realized I was searching for a part of myself that had been locked away. I was trying to break free of something. Just as I drew on my power again to help me, Phoenix pulled away from me, breaking my concentration and snapping me back to reality. I stared at him, a little startled. His hand went instantly to my face, as it did so often, and calm floated over me, dulling everything else.

"You pushed me out. No one has done that before." He was searching my face, assessing my reactions. It made me a little uncomfortable.

"Phoenix…" But I never got a chance to finish. As I opened my mouth to speak, apple flooded it. Everything in my being screamed danger. "Exiles."

Phoenix froze. "There can't be, I can't sense…" Then, reconsidering, he asked, "How many?"

I focused, trying to work it out. I hadn't done this before. "I'm not sure." But as I drew on my angelic powers, I felt a shift—it was something new, as if somehow I was able to push the senses out and search. I managed to do it for just a few seconds, just long enough to get a glimpse. "A lot…Eight…Maybe more."

A series of words that I had not heard come from Phoenix's mouth before rolled out forcefully and then he gritted his teeth. "I still can't sense them. How close are they?"

That much I could tell. "Still outside, but not for long."

He stood. "Wait here. DON'T MOVE!" he ordered.

And then he was gone.

chapter thirty-three

"There are two great days in a person's life — the day we are born and the day we discover why."

WILLIAM BARCLAY

I reached for my phone. Before I had time to think, my finger had pressed speed dial one.

"Violet? What's wrong?"

"They're here, Linc. Exiles, lots of them."

"Where are you?" he said quickly. I could hear the sound of his front door slamming and his feet bounding down the steps.

"Hades."

"Don't move. Don't do anything. I'm on my way." He hung up. He only lived a few blocks away; it wouldn't take him long at full speed.

I looked over and saw Steph hanging off Marcus on the dance floor. She saw me and flailed her hands in the air, signaling me to join her. I thought about warning her, but I didn't want to freak her out. I gave a shake of my head. She tried again, but after a forced smile and a second shake of my head, she gave up on me.

I could feel them getting closer. They were outside the front door. I could *see* them somehow, could almost pinpoint them exactly, like some kind of infrared vision.

I concentrated, trying to figure out exactly how many there were. I realized that there were ten, and two were very powerful, surrounded by what I could only describe as golden auras. Chills, the stabbing kind, ran through my body when I focused on them.

When I tried to use my power to find Phoenix, all I got was a sinking feeling in my gut. I couldn't sense him at all. I didn't know how I could sense the other exiles and not him; it was as if he had the power to block me. But the others…They were inside now. I was sure of it.

I spotted a green exit sign to my right, but I refused to run. For the first time, I realized it wasn't because I wouldn't allow myself to, but because I didn't *want* to. The place was full of humans, unaware and defenseless, just like Claudia had been. I was a Grigori now and that meant I was their only protection. I looked toward the entrance, but there was nothing out of the ordinary.

How in the hell are they inside?

I stood up to get a better view and focused my power on *feeling* them rather than looking for them. Awareness crept through me. They were moving into the room, steadily and all together.

A purple mist, like millions of tiny amethyst crystals, streamed over the room, searching. It was me, my mist, but not multicolored like everyone else's; it was…violet. The mist frosted the room, revealing the truth, stripping away the glamour.

They were there, at least ten of them, moving through the middle of the room. They walked toward me as they had in my dream, and I knew they brought with them the three *D*s: Death. Doom. Destruction.

I blinked, again seeing what everyone else did. It was as if they weren't there. It was like the space they existed within wasn't real.

My eyes darted to Steph, still dancing, none the wiser. At least it seemed she was safe, though I wasn't sure for how long. The two exiles at the front were the ones with all the power. The others, though strong, didn't bother me. Even in their numbers, I had them.

Not that it will do you any good, Vi.

Because the two at the front had me sweating buckets.

My wrists pulsed with cool heat, reminding me of my purpose. Two things flew through my mind: I wished I hadn't thrown my dagger into my bedside drawer instead of trying to find a way to squeeze it into my skinny jeans, and maybe I should have gone with more sensible heels.

I cleared my head, giving me back the *real* view of the room. They were closing the distance, eyes fixed in my direction. I recognized Onyx; he was relaxed in his stride, confidence radiating from him as he swung his sword with every step like a walking stick. The other exile walking beside him was more controlled in his movements, calculated, precise. They were like the positive and negative of a battery. They didn't belong together at all. Although he looked different from in my dream—no wings spreading from his sides, no blue, blazing fire—I knew the other was Joel. He also carried a sword, but held it tightly under his arm, like a soldier with a swagger stick.

Onyx stopped a few feet away and the other angels spanned out in a semicircle around us. They created a wall between us and everyone else. Some were dressed in casual jeans and T-shirts, others in sleek suits, some in old-fashioned clothes that looked like tacky costume wear. I presumed a few had stalled in previous eras. Good to know there were all types of fashion victims in the world. Not one of them looked older than mid-twenties, and a few were no older than me. However, they had a few things in common: not one was human and they were all in their prime, ready to pounce.

I gave myself an internal pep talk.

This is your job now, what you've been given the power to deal with.

It didn't work. I tried again.

For Christ's sake, Vi, you're stuck like this now, so you better figure out how to beat these psycho angels or you're going to die...very, very badly!

It was better.

Onyx looked at me and smiled. "All alone?"

"No, there are plenty of us around. We saw no point in leaving the dance floor just for you," I said, heavy on the smart-ass to avoid showing fear. Onyx's smile broadened. I snuck a look over his shoulder. Phoenix had to be back any moment.

"Are you sure?" he teased. He looked at me in that I-know-something-you-don't-know way, and a wave of doubt washed through me. He laughed, pleased with my reaction.

"Is it the angel or the Grigori on his way to save you?"

"I don't need anyone to save me."

He straightened a little, still amused. "I admit, you do emit a unique aura. But I can see you have no comprehension of the power you carry. My exiles have been sensing your power all over town. You seem to leave a rather large footprint. It's fascinating. You've become somewhat of a talking point." He looked to the exile beside him. "Has she not, Joel?"

Joel stepped forward. He was in a tailored black suit with a dark shirt that had a short collar, not unlike a priest's clerical collar. Strangely, he reminded me of Nox rather than Uri.

"Do you know your maker?" he asked. I felt an immediate compulsion to answer him, so forceful I would have stepped back had I not been compelled to remain where I was.

"No, I have no idea," I said in a trance. Something was very wrong.

Joel's lips twitched. "Are you of light or dark?"

I couldn't help myself. "I don't know," I answered honestly.

"What did you see on your trials?"

I took a step toward him, wanting to please him. "A desert, my guides, sandstorm, lion, water, death, dagger." I tried to stop myself, but the words just tumbled from my mouth.

Onyx and Joel looked at each other. Phoenix had once explained that some exiles retained the ability to speak telepathically after taking human form. I was guessing these were two that could.

While they were silently conversing, I searched within myself and found my power. The first thing it told me was that Lincoln was near. I started to put the walls up, trying to protect myself before they tried to mind-rape me again. I needed to be stronger. They turned back to me, watching in curiosity.

Onyx laughed. Surprise, surprise.

"You should conserve your strength."

I saw Lincoln from the corner of my eye, circling wide, trying to reach me undetected. Then, finally, I saw Phoenix in the shadows. He put his finger to his lips and I looked away, but not before I saw the golden threads encircling him. Why couldn't I sense him if he was that close?

Joel pulled out his sword, the same one that he had been holding in my dream. "Tell your Grigori friend there is no point circling wolves. He may join you unharmed, for now, if that is where he wishes to stand."

I looked over to Lincoln and shook my head, telling him not to come forward. He ignored me, marching right through the wall of exiles to stand by my side. He took my hand briefly and power swirled between us. Then he turned to Onyx.

"Why are you here, Onyx?" He didn't sound in the least frightened, despite the fact that last time they had met, Onyx had almost killed him.

"Lincoln, my friend, you look well…considering." He surveyed Lincoln in surprise, then turned to me. "Your handiwork?"

"It's none of your business." I didn't want to answer any more questions.

He smiled. "That's where you're wrong, Violet."

"What are you doing here?" Lincoln asked again, ignoring Onyx and gesturing at the club. "Even for you, this is a little public."

"Perhaps, but we grow in strength and number. We can create a glamour when we need one," Onyx said.

"It won't be long before we do not need to hide at all," Joel added and then pointed at me. "She is the first step to us claiming our rightful power over humans."

Things just kept getting better.

"What are you talking about?" I demanded.

"You have been created as a weapon for your kind. Destroying you will be a blow to your people and a message to your maker. Your creator sits safely in his realm, leaving you to do his dirty work. It must end…and soon it will. Soon we will know the identity of every Grigori now and in the future."

"That's impossible," Lincoln said, almost laughing.

"Let us see how impossible it is once we have the list."

Dread sounded in my voice. "What list?"

Onyx chuckled. "It's a scripture really. Soon we will have the name and maker of every Grigori, even those who have not yet embraced. It is almost boring to think how easy it will be." He looked off, daydreaming.

I had found my reason to embrace. Saving Lincoln's life had been my choice. Even though I couldn't seem to help the hatred that welled up in me when I thought of him and all that had happened between us, I now knew my choice had been the right one. I'd had a reason to become Grigori. Now Onyx had just given me a reason to *be* one.

I stared at Onyx and Joel with disgust. "You will never get that list. I promise you." As I spoke, I knew I would do whatever it took to stop them from preying on innocents, on defenseless Grigori who didn't even know what they were. It had been hard enough finding out the way I had; the idea of exiles knowing who they were before they did…No.

Joel spoke. "I can see that you believe that. I even admire your conviction, but I'm afraid you won't be around to prevent it."

Lincoln moved his shoulder slightly in front of me, assuming a protective stance. I held back the urge to push him away. Even now, I could feel the anger toward him.

"You came here for her?" Lincoln asked.

"Yes," Joel said simply. The same energy I had felt in the alley when the cleanup crew arrived thrummed through my core. I grabbed Lincoln's hand and spoke quickly, as low as I could. "Griffin and Magda are here. They've brought help."

"You can tell that?" he whispered, surprised. I gave a small nod.

I could feel them on the other side of the circle of exiles.

Lincoln stood tall. "You won't touch her," he growled.

Onyx sighed dramatically. "I could almost believe you, but half the work is already done. She is tainted," he said, as if I had some disease.

"What the hell are you talking about?" I asked.

He smiled. "Allow me to give a demonstration." He opened

both his arms in a grand sweeping gesture and the room slid into a deep red glow.

Shadows emerged from the walls and ceiling and danced toward me. My breathing quickened and I felt my throat tighten in fear. The dozens of elaborate chandeliers hanging from the ceiling looked like they were melting, dripping fire and liquid glass onto the dancing crowd. The crimson curtains draped around the edges of the room rippled maniacally, like a raging sea, devouring everything within their reach. The dark floorboards splintered and flew upward like sharp wooden swords rising from the floor.

People started screaming as they were impaled on the wooden spikes and dripping lava-like glass burned holes in them. I tried to step forward, to run to Steph's side, but I was paralyzed. The faces of the exiles surrounding me had morphed into creatures—animals, gargoyles, ravens, and snakes. Some looked like they had fangs coming from their mouths and began biting into the necks of defenseless humans. Others turned into bright illuminations that burned my eyes. I started screaming, and even though I knew they were tricking me, using my imagination, fear and panic overwhelmed me.

I was aware of Lincoln grabbing my shoulders, trying to shake me out of it. But it was no use. I tried to draw on my power, to build my walls. But Onyx and Joel, working together, bulldozed through it.

A gust of wind pushed at my back as a hand went to the base of my neck. Sparks of energy, little electric shocks, flickered down my spine. In my ear, Phoenix whispered, "Try again."

I reached within, while exiles tore Steph from the floor where she was cowering and dragged her toward me, laughing and ripping at her clothes. I focused all my strength and pulled it into a ball. I wanted to build it, to grow it within me, control it. I concentrated a little of the energy on my body, willing it to move. Twinges of pins and needles pricked my legs and I knew I was breaking their hold.

I took a step toward Onyx and Joel and launched my ball of power, letting it sail over them to the other exiles and beyond to the illusions that lay before my eyes. A cloud of my amethyst mist settled over the room like a blanket, evaporating the horrific illusion and bringing me back to myself.

Fully clothed and intact, Steph was still dancing with Marcus, oblivious to everything that was going on.

"He's broken it!" Joel screamed in fury, looking around. I didn't know what he meant, but I remembered Phoenix standing behind me.

"Phoenix!" Onyx yelled through the club. "Phoenix!" he yelled again.

Lincoln turned to me. "What's going on?"

I didn't respond, but I had an all bad feeling.

chapter thirty-four

"...and the truth will set you free."

JOHN 8:32

Phoenix stepped into the circle. My bad feeling heightened when I saw his face, shadowed and rigid.

"You released her, you imbecile! Why? You had the perfect hold. She didn't even know!" Joel yelled. His insanity was in full swing.

"What hold?" I asked, looking at Phoenix.

"I didn't realize it was going to happen. I swear, Violet."

"What are you talking about?" I asked, saying each word slowly, deliberately.

Onyx seemed to find a new reason to smile. He moved toward Phoenix, separating from Joel. My eyes darted to Lincoln, who took a few small steps in Joel's direction. The last thing we needed was Joel trying something like Malachi had done when Onyx had gone on one of his rants.

"He has tampered with you, weakened you! And given his

heritage, I'd stake that before you embraced, you gave yourself to him in the…physical sense."

I shifted uncomfortably. Did everyone have to know this one detail about me? I tried to keep my cool, but it was flimsy at best. "What does that have to do with anything?"

"Let me guess: you two shared a night of indescribable seduction." He waved a hand through the air. "The world *moved* around you, and ever since, you haven't been able to tell when he has been tinkering with your emotions—unless, of course, he wanted you to know."

My mind raced back over all the moments I'd been with Phoenix since that night. Apart from the heavy dose of desire he had intentionally poured into me earlier, I couldn't remember being aware of him affecting me, bleeding his emotions into me, the way I had been before. I looked at Phoenix. He wouldn't meet my gaze.

"The kink in my power?"

"And the best thing is," Onyx continued, "what *has* he been so busy doing to you since he's had this little advantage? Would you like me to tell you?" He raised his eyebrows.

Phoenix stepped forward. "NO!"

I looked to him again, but he still wouldn't meet my gaze. "Yes," I said.

"Very well. He has given you hate, little rainbow. So much hate that eventually it would have built to the point where it ruined you. He has clouded your judgment and dulled every other emotion with anger, planted it deep within and given it a target."

I looked at Lincoln, who was standing quietly, but I realized his mind was churning as surely as mine, adding everything up. When my eyes fully took him in, it was like I hadn't seen him in weeks. The urge to throw myself into his arms was almost overwhelming.

I looked back at Phoenix. "You made me hate Lincoln." My bottom lip shook and a tear slid down my face.

"I didn't know the connection would form until after it happened." Phoenix's voice was grave. "Even after we…I could *feel* what you felt for him when you healed him. I couldn't risk losing you."

"And my feelings for you? Did you influence those?" Even as I asked the question, I knew the answer. It wasn't just because of Onyx's revelations that my feelings for Phoenix were now dulled. He didn't answer.

"I thought you said that was cheating," I said, waiting for him to tell me I was wrong. He didn't.

Onyx started strolling around us, reveling in the results of his malice. "Now, now, Phoenix, don't be coy. It was quite the feat, given her power. She must have relinquished her body to you completely. Dare I guess she gave you a unique sacrifice?"

"That's enough," Lincoln warned in a threatening growl.

"Jealous, are we? Or is it just denial? Tell me, Lincoln, will you ever look at her in the same way? Knowing she first surrendered her body to an angel of dark?"

The last of my stomach plummeted to the ground. The bad plummet. The kind you don't come back from. A hand went over my mouth.

"Yes, dark! You stupid girl." Onyx was grinding his teeth with anticipation. "Oh, but, Lincoln, you must have wondered yourself. Tell me you didn't have your own suspicions?"

"Don't," Lincoln warned again, but it only encouraged Onyx.

"He *is* powerful, our Phoenix. With a mother like his, how could he not be?"

My mind was racing. Mother? Angels didn't have mothers.

"In your defense, he is actually more difficult than most to sense. Phoenix is one of a kind: son of the Goddess of the Night and of immortal Man. He mingles well, using his human heritage when it suits his purposes."

Onyx walked around Phoenix and then meandered his way back toward me again. I tried to keep my eyes on him; I knew Lincoln was watching Joel, and Griffin had the others covered. Phoenix remained still and silent.

"Phoenix?" I looked at him, begging him to tell me what I knew now he wouldn't.

He looked from me to Onyx, anger flaring in his eyes. "I never had a choice, Violet. All the rest"—he tossed his head toward the circle of exiles—"they made their choice, but I...I was judged before I even began, stuck in the realm, handing out punishment until it consumed me. When it did, they threw me to earth and left me to rot."

Onyx had told me this story. All the pieces were falling into place.

"You have a mother." I could barely say the next word. "Lilith."

"The Mother of Dark," Onyx whispered in my ear. I flinched;

he was standing right behind me. I hadn't been watching him. As I realized my mistake, he drove his blade into my back, driving it all the way through until I could see its point emerge from my stomach. I screamed in pain—both for Phoenix's betrayal and Onyx's blade.

He drew the sword out in a clean movement and I released another bloodcurdling scream. I felt the vibration of the blade as it scraped against the bones in my spine. Blood poured from my body, warming my skin and leaving my insides cold.

I heard Lincoln shout my name and looked up to see him in full battle with Joel. They were all fighting. My eyes panned the room as my legs gave way beneath me. The glamour still held. People were laughing and dancing on one side of the room while on our side there was all-out war. Even Phoenix was fighting, though I wasn't sure whose side he was fighting on.

Onyx stood over me as I writhed on the ground. His smile had changed from amused to ecstatic. The thought of my death brought him pure joy.

"You know, for one so powerful, you're not very smart. I really thought I'd given you enough to connect the dots when I first delivered the tale of Lilith."

He knelt beside me and my thoughts flashed back to the night I had seen the dead bodies that had been ripped apart from the inside. He was rolling up his sleeve. My vision scanned the battle around me. We were losing. I could barely see Lincoln, now buried under at least three exiles.

I thought back to the desert.

My virtue will be my devotion to never give up.

I was free of the chink in my armor. I was wounded—beyond wounded—but not dead yet. I reached up and grabbed Onyx's wrist. I felt the power course through me. He looked down at me, smug.

"I admire your fight, but you have no dagger and those trinkets you wear on your wrists will do me no harm."

Wincing with pain, I leaned over and pushed back my bracelets, revealing the markings that swirled like a reflective river of mercury around my wrists.

Onyx's eyes widened. "You still have no dagger and you cannot leave me only human unless I will it, and I do not." But his voice wasn't so carefree now.

I could feel my power, and this time I didn't reach inside of myself to draw it out. I simply released it. I knew now what it could do. Uri had told me: my will had the power to overcome another's.

"No, but *I* do." I held my voice as steady as I could, delivering him my own dramatic smile through lips now dripping with blood. My mist surrounded us like a bubble and I tore Onyx's angelic powers away from him. He fell beside me. No longer angel or exile, just powerless and human.

"I would rather be dead than left to become rancid in flesh!" he cried.

I spat blood. "Yeah? Well, welcome to the world of not getting much choice in the matter."

I turned my attention to Joel, who had Lincoln on the ground and was pummeling him with a fist of iron. I wasn't close enough to touch him, but I didn't need to be. I dragged my arm across the floor and pointed it in Joel's direction. My wrists burned with hot ice and I felt the link form between us. He was locked.

He stopped attacking Lincoln and turned to me savagely—but I already had him. Just as they had controlled my body with illusion, I could control theirs with the power of my will. I could feel it building. I released it, searching the room and clinging onto all the exiles—all except Phoenix. I stopped them, froze them in a way, but I couldn't drain them all. I could barely hold them for long. Griffin was close to me, working his way toward me.

"I can't hold them much longer," I spluttered through more blood.

Griffin took in the scene, registering what I was doing with astonished eyes. "Return them!" he yelled to the other Grigori.

One by one, I felt the links drop off as Grigori drove daggers into the exiles, returning them for judgment. I watched as Onyx slowly crawled away, cowering and pathetic. He was the least of our concerns; without his angelic powers, he could do no harm.

When only Joel was left, it was Magda who stepped in front of him and drove her dagger into his side. She smiled as his eyes went wide. "I bet when you walked into Hades tonight, you didn't realize you'd never leave."

She pulled out her dagger, blood spraying in its wake. Joel fell to his knees, disappearing, melting into the surroundings. Right at that moment, I almost liked her.

With Joel's departure, the glamour lifted. The mass of drinking, dancing humans suddenly became aware of the battlefield, littered with wounded Grigori. Luckily, I was in the back corner and Griffin quickly dropped beside me, covering me up. But not before I heard a high-pitched scream I recognized instantly.

Steph ran over, dropping to her knees beside me. "Oh no, oh no, oh no, Violet. Oh my God. Tell me what to do?"

Griffin tried to put pressure on the wound, until he saw I was also bleeding from my back. "It'll be okay. Do you have any strength to heal yourself?"

I gave a weak smile. Even if I'd had the faintest clue *how* to heal myself, the fact was, I'd used everything I had to take care of Onyx and hold the others.

"Lincoln will be here soon; he can heal you. It'll be okay." Griffin wiped blood from my face and smiled at me with something like paternal pride. It was weird, given that he only looked about twenty-five.

"You were amazing. I've never seen anything like it. You saved us all."

I tried my best to smile back. I knew that in making the sacrifices I'd made, in becoming Grigori and doing my duty, I now had Griffin's respect...and friendship.

I turned my head in Lincoln's direction. I could see him on the ground, not moving. Magda was shaking him. I knew he was okay, though, could feel his heart beating strongly. I looked up at Griffin. "How old are you?" I asked.

He half laughed. "Eighty-two next August," he said in his

country twang. I was willing to bet he'd been raised on a farm. It suited him too.

"The aging thing could've b-been an upside, I guess." My insides tightened and my vision started to go hazy. Griffin shook me by the shoulders as my eyelids grew heavy, tired.

"Violet, you have to stay awake. Lincoln is starting to move; they'll have him up in a minute. Come on. You know I'll slap you if I have to."

But we both knew. He wasn't going to slap me, and I didn't have a minute.

Steph was at my side, brushing hair back from my face and mumbling. She was praying.

"I thought w-we agreed…no Sunday school," I said, my voice barely audible.

"Well, every-frigging-thing else seems to be real—why not God?" she said, sobbing. The theory held up. The question was, what kind of God was he?

I felt a pressure on my stomach and groaned at the pain, unable to muster the energy to scream. I looked down to see Phoenix kneeling by my side. Shadows moved around him, and tiny lines of gold encircled him. I saw his mist of power flow from him and enter me. I could feel the bones in my spine knitting back together, the muscles in my stomach reattaching. He was healing me…painfully. As I grew stronger, it hurt more and I began to scream. Then the pain just…stopped.

I didn't need to inspect the wound when Phoenix let his hands slide away. I knew he had healed me completely. Though weak from the blood loss, I was fine. Steph started on the Hail Mary.

I lay on the ground and tears leaked from my eyes. Phoenix sat back on his heels.

"You healed me," I said.

"Yes." His hands, which he had been holding in midair, dropped limply to his sides. Defeated.

"You told me it wasn't one of your powers."

"I told you not all exiles had the power to heal." He looked down rather than at me.

The veil had been lifted; truth surrounded me. Ugly, painful truth. And even worse, the awful, unchangeable consequences.

"You...you could have healed Lincoln. You let him lie there while he was dying. You let me become a Grigori even when I didn't want it."

"I knew they'd find you and destroy you. Embracing was your only chance."

"Why did you heal me?"

"Does it really matter now?" His eyes darted to mine for a brief moment before dropping to the ground again. I noticed some blood on his shirt, above his stomach. I didn't know if it was mine or his.

I looked up and saw Lincoln standing behind him. He had a dagger in his hand. He'd heard everything, but I knew he was looking to me. Once again, the choice was mine.

"No," I said softly, looking at Lincoln.

Phoenix spun around and Lincoln grabbed his shirt, dragging him to his feet.

"No!" It was Griffin. "I gave him my word of safety. He has won freedom today." He looked at Phoenix. "But my word is no longer yours."

Lincoln released him roughly, pushing him away. "Leave. You saved her life, but if I ever see you again, I'll take pleasure in driving this dagger through your heart. I don't imagine your judgment will be favorable."

Phoenix looked back at me, still sitting on the ground. "Violet?" he said quietly.

"Leave, Phoenix. Don't come back."

I looked into his eyes and they flickered with pain and...something else. Then, with a trailing breeze, he vanished. I wondered how it was that I had never questioned who, or *what*, he really was. Maybe he had influenced me; maybe I'd influenced myself. Maybe I'd never know how much of myself had been under his spell since the day we first met.

Lincoln dropped his dagger and fell to his knees in front of me. He pulled me onto his lap and rocked me back and forth.

Neither one of us spoke.

chapter thirty-five

"Be thou the rainbow in the storms of life!
The evening beam that smiles the clouds away,
and tints tomorrow with prophetic ray!"

LORD BYRON

I sat in the school library, reading the various versions of the story of Lilith. I really should have been studying. But the whole thing kept niggling at me and I couldn't seem to pick up any other books. Eventually, when I'd exhausted the options on the library shelves, I turned to the Internet, which was not so limited.

She was everything from Adam's first wife to the original demon, the Bringer of Darkness, the Mother of All Evil, the Serpent of Eden, the consort to the Devil. I blushed red hot when I read how she was the incarnation of lust and seduction, and couldn't avoid the flashbacks to the intense time I had spent in Phoenix's arms.

I now understood why Phoenix was so good at a lot of things.

Even moving like wind. Lilith had the ability to create and become windstorms. One of her many names was Lady Air. I was yet to find out if he had inherited her most dominant ability—vengeance—but something about the look he'd thrown me at Hades before he disappeared made me nervous.

All in all, the most consistent theme was that Lilith was credited with a whole lot of pure evil. The next most consistent myth was that she brought death to infants. As I read one of the stories, I found myself staring at the words.

Three angels were sent to bring her back for judgment, but she refused, swearing instead to bring suffering to the offspring of man for all time. She did, however, concede that if she saw the angels' names or forms represented in an amulet, she would have no power over that infant and would spare its life.

The angels sworn to protect humanity from Lilith were: Senoy, Sansenoy, and Semangelof.

I dug through my school bag and fished out my baby necklace. On the back of the amulet was engraved, *S.S.S. Protect.* I remembered the inscription on the bottom of my mother's box. "Evelyn bar Semangelof," I whispered.

"Earth to Violet!"

My head snapped up. Steph was standing over me, slurping on a Popsicle.

"Sorry," I said, looking back down at my baby necklace.

"That's okay, I like being ignored."

"Sure," I said, still staring at the amulet.

"Are you actually in this conversation?" She took a closer look at me. "I know that look. What now? If they're boarding the ark, you better let me know. I have more than most to pack."

"Hmm?" I couldn't break my dazed state.

She gave an overly dramatic sigh. "Hello? You're missing out on some good lines here!"

"Oh, sorry. It's just…I think I know who my mom was supposed to defeat."

"And? Don't go all Bible on me."

"What?" I said, finally looking up in confusion.

"You know, tell us everything but the stuff we really want to know." She raised her eyebrows, urging me on. "Well?"

"It was Lilith."

"*Lilith?* As in Phoenix's *mother*, Lilith?"

"Weird, huh?" I said, still dazed.

"That's one way of putting it. Are you sure?"

"No." I ran my hand over the amulet, letting the necklace slide through my fingers.

"Well, if it turns out your mom and the mother of the damned were…immortal enemies, let's just say it's a good thing you and Phoenix aren't bumping hips anymore. Could lead to one *hell* of a family intervention."

"Good point."

"Look, Vi. He's out of your life, isn't he? I mean, you haven't seen him since that night, have you?"

"No."

"So, do you really need to get caught up in this stuff? You're not even sure it's true. Come on, haven't you earned yourself a little break? At least until after finals."

I stared at the computer screen, then up at Steph. "You're right." I closed the search screen and deleted the history. Then I threw the books on the returns shelf.

"Hallelujah! Of course I'm right. Not everyone needs to rely on divine intervention, you know!" We both laughed.

While we waited at the bus stop, Steph occupied herself texting Marcus back and forth. The two of them were inseparable these days. I worried at one point that she would want to tell Marcus about the whole angel thing, but she assured me it wasn't high on the list of things she wanted to share with him. Apparently, he'd been so wiped out that night at Hades that when the glamour dropped, he was busy in the bathroom throwing up. By the time he resurfaced, most of the drama was under control.

On the whole, it had been eye-opening the way people had just carried on with their night after a few random explanations about gang violence and turf wars. I even overheard one girl say she'd seen that kind of thing at Hades before. The club owner had been quick to assist, keeping our people covered until we had things under control. Griffin thought the owner may have known more about us than he let on and said he'd pay him a visit when things had settled down.

Thankfully, no Grigori died at Hades, though that didn't make it much better. Griffin arranged a memorial service for the Grigori who had been lost in the nights before. Most of them had no family left, so it fell to fellow Grigori to take care of things.

I didn't make it to the service; I had another funeral to attend that day. There were so many people in Claudia's extended family, we could barely fit in the church. It was a nice service, though; they displayed her artwork and sculptures for people to see, and one of her sisters sang "Amazing Grace." Steph had gone with me.

"Study or shopping?" she asked now, breaking into my thoughts.

"Neither, actually. I promised Griffin I'd catch up with him this afternoon."

"*Just* Griffin?" She raised her eyebrows.

"Yes." I knew where this was going.

"You can't avoid him forever. You haven't even seen him since, you know…" She made a stabbing motion at her stomach.

I sighed. Not seeing Lincoln hadn't exactly felt like my choice. While everyone was cleaning up at Hades, he had just up and disappeared. He hadn't said good-bye or been in touch since. If he was trying to send me a message, I was getting it loud and clear.

"He doesn't want to see me," I said. "And after the way I treated him, I can't say I blame him. I'm still having flashbacks to some of the awful things I said to him…If I were him, *I* wouldn't want to ever see me again either."

"Sure, but it wasn't your fault," Steph said sympathetically. "You'll never really know until you talk to him. He's going to be your partner for, like, a hundred lifetimes or whatever. It kinda makes avoidance a problem."

"True."

But just thinking about Lincoln tore at my heart. How could he ever forgive me? I was sure he would know, just as I did, that the hatred Phoenix had used and exploited had all stemmed from my own feelings—even if he *had* amplified them by a gazillion. I'd once thought that friendship with Lincoln was not enough, but now I craved him in my life so badly, I would take anything. I just didn't know if I could bear the rejection.

———

Griffin was waiting for me outside my building. We had been meeting regularly to work on focusing my powers.

"You know, I would still feel a lot better if you'd agree to go to one of our training facilities for a few months. Most Grigori spend some time there, learning our histories and how to control their powers."

Instead of heading upstairs like we normally did, he motioned ahead. We walked along the pavement, sipping the to-go coffees he had brought with him.

"Sorry, but no can do. Not right now, anyway. I have exams and then art school, and I plan on doing both. Anyway, you're practically an encyclopedia on all things Grigori, so I'm sure you can fill me in."

"I *suppose* I could get a couple of senior tutors to visit at some point," he said, pretending I hadn't just given him his favorite kind of compliment.

"Really? But isn't the training facility in New York or something?"

"Yes, but believe it or not, I am actually of some importance. Plus, it won't hurt that you're a Grigori anomaly."

I rolled my eyes. "Thanks, Griffin; you really know how to make a girl feel special."

"Sorry."

"That's okay." As much as I had tried to fight it, I was learning to accept and even welcome my future as a Grigori. Even the idea that there were still so many unanswered questions didn't frighten me as much as it once would have. I knew the answers were there to be found—and I knew I was going to find them.

"So, what about this list they were talking about?" I asked, refocusing on what was now my priority.

"I've got people looking into it. We always thought it was just a myth, but given that both Onyx and Joel were convinced of its existence, they were obviously privy to some information that we have not discovered yet."

"If there is a list or scripture thing out there, we need to find it, Griff." The idea of exiles knowing the identities of future Grigori before they had any idea themselves—let alone the fact they would be powerless—was unthinkable.

"I know. We will."

I stopped midstep. "How do *you* know who's going to end up Grigori if you don't have a list?"

Griffin stopped too. "The guides. They always make sure we know the identity of the first of a pair."

"And then the first finds the second, like Lincoln found me."

"Correct."

"Griff?"

"Yes," he said, like any underpaid, much admired professor.

"When I embraced, my guides didn't tell me what rank my angel parent comes from. Why?"

"I don't know. Maybe because they knew your powers were tainted and they didn't want you to have too much information, be too vulnerable. Or…maybe they didn't know."

"How can that be? Aren't they supposed to know everything?"

He pondered that for a while before he answered. "There is one exception."

"Which is?"

"They cannot know what comes from above. Angels have a hierarchy, as you know. If you carry the essence of a higher angel, it would be within that angel's power not to disclose his identity."

"How many angels can do that?"

"Not many, I suspect."

I remembered the rank of angels who were not part of the hierarchy. "The Sole," I said, thinking aloud.

Griffin nodded. "It's one possibility. But in the end, maybe you'll have to accept that you may never know. At some point, we all have to try to have a little faith that, even in the chaos, there's a purpose."

"It's a nice thought, Griff."

And it was. I just wasn't sure I was ready to buy the souvenir T-shirt.

chapter thirty-six

"*The good man brings good things out of the good stored up in
him, and the evil man brings evil out of the evil stored up in him.*"

MATTHEW 12:35

I had sensed him following me for a few blocks. I stopped, leaned
against a stone wall, and waited.

He headed toward me, more of a sway in his walk than ever
before. I wondered if he had ever truly been himself around me.

"What do you want, Phoenix?"

"I'm going away for a while. I wanted to say good-bye." He
smiled, but it was empty. There was nothing there.

"Fine, good-bye."

"We're connected, Violet. You can't deny it. You gave me something that you can never give to anyone else, not even him, and I
gave you part of myself when I healed you. We share a bond."

I didn't want to get tied up in a conversation about what had
and hadn't happened between us.

"I'm a Grigori, Phoenix. You made sure of that. Now that I am, I won't turn from my responsibilities. If you cause trouble, I *will* return you."

"You mean you'll kill me." His lips twitched and his eyes narrowed slightly.

I held his eyes as I replied. "If it comes to that."

"In many ways, you already have."

For the smallest second, I thought I saw the genuine part of him that I'd convinced myself never existed. But as soon as I glimpsed it, it was gone.

"However," he continued in a lighter tone, "there are advantages to being a phoenix. It seems neither one of us can run from our destiny."

He reached out and grabbed a few strands of my hair, twirling them in his fingers. I pulled my head back, but he didn't let go. His cold eyes flashed at me and I felt a shiver run down my spine. I pulled back again, and this time he let my hair trail over his hand. It reminded me of something.

"The gold strands that wrap around you. They wrapped around me that night."

"A legacy from my mother. Her hair was the first gold."

"Like your hair is opal."

He smiled, but again there was nothing in it, just emptiness. After studying me for a moment, he asked, "How did you know they were coming that night? Did you really sense them from that far away?"

"Why?" I asked hesitantly.

"I've been trying to work it out, how you did it. It wasn't with the normal Grigori senses. You found them with a Sight, didn't you?"

I looked away and remained silent, unsure what I should be saying to him now and whether I knew the answer anyway. Even though I wasn't looking at him, I could feel his glare burning my skin.

"Hmm…I knew it."

I looked up. "What does that mean?"

"It's just a theory. I wouldn't want to burden you with it," he said provokingly.

"I guess I shouldn't be surprised you're keeping secrets," I shot back.

"Yes, we should both have learned our lessons by now. And just as you have embraced your destiny, perhaps it is time for me to embrace mine." He pointed to the building behind me. "Did you really think this would protect you?"

I turned to face the grand stone church. I hadn't even realized I'd stopped in front of it.

When I turned back, he was already walking away. It was a brilliantly clear day, not a cloud in sight, and yet the sun didn't seem to reach his body. He was shadowed and I couldn't help it: I felt sad for him.

————————

Two weeks later, I was standing in a sea of people in short shorts and tank tops. Short shorts should be outlawed. Even on hot guys, they just look wrong.

I sat on a bench near the starting line to tie my shoelaces. I felt him before I saw him. But it wasn't the senses. It was something more human.

"Hey," he said. He sat beside me.

"Hey."

"I wondered if you'd make it."

I smiled. "We said we would, didn't we?"

"We said a lot of things."

"You knew, didn't you? That Phoenix was dark." More pieces had been coming together since I'd been released from Phoenix's hold. It had been like a fog clearing; things I'd been oblivious to at the time were now painfully clear.

"I suspected."

I didn't know if I could ever make things right, but I had to start somewhere. "I'm sorry, Linc, for all the awful things I said…and did."

He inched closer to me, but not so close we touched. "You have nothing to apologize for. It wasn't really you. And even if it was, I would have understood."

I couldn't hide my confusion. "Then why did you disappear that night?"

He pushed his hands through his hair and looked away from me toward the gathering crowd of runners. "I promised you I'd protect you. I promised I wouldn't let anyone hurt you again. I knew something wasn't right about Phoenix, but I just got caught up in everything and he…" He shook his head. "Worst of all, when you were lying there hurt and I could have actually done something to help, I wasn't there and he was. I've failed you time and time again, and I can't keep asking you to forgive me." He slumped forward, his head in his hands.

I turned my body toward him and softly put a hand on his chin, tilting his face to meet mine. Our powers flared through the small touch, recognizing each other. His chin was rough and unshaven. It was sexy as hell. "You never failed me. You're the one person in my life who has always been there. I'm not your mother, Linc. You can't blame yourself for everything." I took a deep breath. "All I know right now is, I want you in my life…if you want me in yours?"

He looked at me, his eyes revealing all the things he couldn't say. "Violet, we—"

But before he could surge into that discussion, the one where he told me we could never be together, I stopped him.

"Linc, how about we just go one day at a time."

He held my eyes and I could see how hard it must have been for him—holding back, never encouraging me—when he knew how I felt. When he felt the same way. But there was no other option for us. We were Grigori partners.

Yet even as I told myself this was the way it was, I couldn't help but hold on to the glimmer of hope within, the one that whispered, *Where there's a will, there's a way.*

"One day at a time," he agreed.

A voice crackled over the loudspeaker, drowning out everything else.

"ALL CONTESTANTS IN THE RACE, LINE UP FOR THE STARTING GUN."

Lincoln stood, extending his hand to me. I took it. Power surged between us, affirming that we were strengthened together. Better together. I could see him suppressing a smile, just as I suppressed my own.

"You ready?"

He pulled me to my feet.

"Yep."

And I was.

Running a marathon when you have enhanced abilities in strength and endurance can be a mighty temptation. But apart from a few healthy bursts of competitiveness, we remained well-behaved. There were more important things in the world than winning a race, and there was too much at stake to risk exposure.

Steph and Dad were waiting at the finish line. I couldn't help but laugh at their faces when they saw Lincoln running with me. More than anything, Dad was just pleased to see it wasn't Phoenix. He'd been in an overly chipper mood since I told him Phoenix wouldn't be hanging around anymore.

After several pats on the back, Dad predictably started making noises about getting back to the office. Before he left, he gave me a hug. "I'm proud of you, sweetheart. You remind me of your mom. She'd be so proud of you too."

I hugged him back and blinked away the sting in my eyes. I hoped he was right.

Steph and I went out for a post-marathon celebratory juice. I was impressed she only complained twice about having to get up before 7:00 a.m. on the first Sunday since exams. When I had asked Lincoln if he wanted to come with us, he'd said there was something he had to do. He'd also reminded me there was a wall in his warehouse with my name on it. Steph rolled her eyes and threw around a few Jesus and Mary exclamations every time she looked at my beaming smile.

When I arrived home, one perfectly bloomed white lily sat at the foot of my door, a note tied around the stem.

Training tomorrow, 6 a.m. x

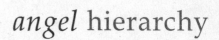

angel hierarchy

The Sole

1ST CHOIR
Seraphim

Cherubim

Thrones

2ND CHOIR
Powers

Dominations

Virtues

3RD CHOIR
Principalities

Archangels

Angels

Can't wait for more?

(Yeah, we thought so.)

Turn the page for a preview of

ENTICED

I looked down the narrow street as far as my eyes would allow. It was littered with homeless people lying on flattened cardboard, the lucky ones wrapped in torn sleeping bags, the rest burrowed in piles of old newspapers. I scanned the dark redbrick walls, which ran at least five stories high on each side. The protection they offered was part of what made this strip so popular.

Lincoln walked slowly beside me, his hand going to my elbow for a moment—a silent reminder that I needed to be alert. I tried to move myself quickly through the flush of heat that came whenever I felt his touch.

I stopped walking and he looked at me, a question on his features. I smiled into his emerald-green eyes before I could stop myself.

"I think I can sense them," I said.

I didn't *think*, I knew. I'd been tasting apple for the past couple of blocks and the sound of birds flying, smashing through trees, was not one shared by others nearby.

"How long have you been sensing them?"

I hesitated. He saw. "Violet…How long?"

I was worried Lincoln would judge me—that the fact I could sense them from so much farther away would be a form of supernatural condescension and alienate me. "Not long. Maybe one street back," I said awkwardly.

Lincoln raised his eyebrows at me.

"Three streets back."

The corners of his mouth curled. He was holding back his Cheshire. I was a fool—he was proud of me.

I rolled my eyes at his twinkling expression. "They're in the street. There are two of them," I said.

He nodded, now refocused. "I can smell them."

I returned his nod. Morning and evening flashed before my eyes as the fragrance of sickly sweet flowers flooded the area so strongly it even overpowered the stench of the street.

He took half a step in front of me and I let him. I might be able to sense them from farther away but Lincoln could size them up and pick the strongest much faster than I could.

They emerged from the darkness, looking human, but not human at the same time. Both were dressed casually, although one had bloodstains all the way up his right arm like a butcher at the end of a long day. I had an awful feeling I knew what that meant. Exiles had a habit of indulging in the internal physical torture of their victims. It prompted me to again take in my surroundings.

While still keeping sight of the approaching engagement, I cast my eyes quickly over the sleeping bodies lining the street. I took in one, then two, then three figures tucked into their sleeping bags, unmoving. Energy hummed through my body and a cruel thrum worked its way up into the base of my ribs.

I grabbed Lincoln's arm. He didn't look back but I had his attention.

"They're all dead. They've killed them all," I said, all too aware that the exiles were moving closer by the second. Agents of death.

"Stay focused. Stick to the plan," he whispered back.

Great. The plan. The one that has me all dagger happy. Except I'm not.

Lincoln and Griffin had insisted that it wasn't enough for me to rely on my power to get me out of everything. I still had to enter combat the same way as all other Grigori. In theory I agreed. But at this very moment—standing smack-dab in the middle of a slaughter zone while two over-stimulated, decidedly unhinged exiles moved in on us—it seemed extreme.

The exiles stopped in front of us, smiling. They were assessing us the way only otherworldly creatures can. A flick of the eyes, showing a defensive mechanism and hunger at the same time.

"You're a little late," said the shorter of the two, the one with the bloodied arm, like he'd been waiting for us.

"You knew we were coming?" Lincoln asked, twisting his body to shield me.

The exile laughed. "I have a message for you."

"And I thought your days as messengers were over."

The jock-looking exile licked his lips, barely restraining himself.

"The reward of getting to kill you"—he glanced at me—"and her is sufficient incentive."

"Well?" Lincoln said, showing no concern.

The exile's smile broadened and he spoke slowly. "Nahilius said to tell you he's coming for what's yours."

Lincoln stiffened. The exile cackled loudly.

"Make your choice," Lincoln growled. There was no denying that when he went into fighter mode, he was lethal. But so were they.

"Choice?" The jock boy laughed. "So kind of you to offer. I think I will choose decapitation for you and something a bit more…fly-by-the-seat-of-my-pants for her."

He lunged toward me, but Lincoln was ready, his arm intercepting the exile, clotheslining his forearm into his opponent's neck, breaking his speed and redirecting his attention. That was all I had time to see before my own creepy exile started throwing punches in my direction.

Why is it that they all know how to fight?

We exchanged blow for blow. I'm not short for a girl, but he was tall for a man, so he had that over me. He got in a few good knocks to my face, but he really favored his right side so I just kept moving toward it, getting nice and close so he couldn't gain any leverage against me. I was getting on top of things, a series of kicks to his legs left him shaky. I hadn't landed one in that magic spot that would blow out his knee, but he was stumbling.

A glow of colors lit up to my right. I knew what it was, but I looked anyway. Lincoln had the jock in a headlock, and as I turned,

I saw him plunge his dagger into the exile, returning him. What I failed to see was the tall exile's fist heading straight for my ear. It was a sucker punch, but then these guys had no morals let alone fighting ethics. I was caught off-balance and could feel the warm wetness that could only be blood seeping down the side of my neck as I fell, now completely aware of the exile coming down on top of me.

My hand went instinctively to my dagger, my fingers wrapped fiercely around the hilt. There was an opening. I was going down, he had launched himself over me, but I had time. If I hadn't hesitated I could have gotten it out, I could have returned him.

Instead, my shoulder smashed into the gravel road and I rolled onto my back quickly in an attempt to evade him. He collided into me so hard I felt the top of my spine being ground into the road, and I screamed. I punched him in the face twice, but he was too close now and had taken the advantage. He drove his knee into my stomach and drew back a clenched fist for what I knew was going to hurt a lot.

But it didn't. He never got his chance.

All I saw was Lincoln's dagger coming through the exile's chest, the glory of his power's colorful mist and then the exile was gone.

––––––––––

I balanced on the edge of the oversized bath at Dapper's apartment, feeling nauseated and nervous.

"I've never had to heal anything this bad before," Lincoln said, sitting beside me. He sounded a little uneasy too.

My eyes took in my reflection in one of the three full-length mirrors in the king-size bathroom. Dapper was totally vain.

"Oh," I said, looking at my bloodied face and neck. My ear was still trickling fresh blood and when I twisted to try to examine the back of my neck, Lincoln stopped me.

"Trust me."

"Oh," I said again. Then, refusing to look too weak, I shrugged it off. "Okay, well…do your thing."

"You know I won't be able to heal these completely," Lincoln said, looking down at his intertwined hands and twisting his fingers. "Griffin…"

When he didn't elaborate, I raised my eyebrows. "Griffin what?"

"He suggested that…" he blew out a breath. "He thought it might be best to see if you can…" but he couldn't find the words and was starting to look like he might up and bolt.

Then I realized why he was looking so impish. *Oh. My. God.* I flashed back to the one time I had healed Lincoln. To the way we connected, the feeling of my power working its way from my body into his.

"You want me to…" I danced a finger between us.

"It might help you."

"Yeah," I agreed, forcing nonchalance. "I mean…we should try. I think it might work…" Actually, I had no idea.

He gave a pained smile. "I want you to be healed and I think this will help but I don't want you to do anything that…Griffin doesn't understand."

He was right about that. No one but us knew how deep the feelings went. How impossible they were to resist.

"So…you don't think we should?" I asked, now feeling the blush of embarrassment.

"No. I think we should. If it means healing you and…if you're okay with it."

I couldn't speak.

My mouth had gone dry and I was already panicking that it would be too dry to kiss—if that was what was about to happen. But then I got it.

He was making sure I wouldn't go all schoolgirl on him—because in the end, we still couldn't be together. But just the idea of having a moment of closeness with him—even if only for medicinal purposes—was too tempting to deny.

"Don't panic, Linc. It's hands-on doctoring—nothing more," I said, trying to muster a believable smile. *Liar, liar, pants on fire!*

Lincoln's eyes nearly burned a hole in me. He was looking to see if I was telling the truth and for a moment I thought he looked a little disappointed.

He reached gently for my face. "Okay," he said, already moving toward me. His eyes were cast down until just before our lips met, and then, as if he couldn't stop them, they met mine…and locked. Eyes are the windows to the soul—they can say so much in just a brief moment.

His lips smoothly met mine and gently his hands went to my shoulders. I couldn't stop my eyes from closing. As if I had to close myself away from the world—just him and me.

Do you close your eyes when it is for healing? When it isn't meant to mean anything…but does?

I could tell he was concentrating on his power, working hard to heal me. I tried to clear my head and do the same. I stopped thinking about his delicious lips that fit perfectly with mine, pushed aside the feeling of heat rising from him and of sharing the same air, and found my power, tucked deep within me, simmering gently.

At first, my power seemed to reach out to Lincoln, searching for any sign of injury or malfunction. Once satisfied, it turned inwardly to me. I could follow it independently, even though it was part of me. When it found Lincoln's power already within me, the two joined forces and became one, accelerating the process, healing me almost instantly.

I felt Lincoln's sharp intake of breath. I pressed nearer, drinking in our rare closeness, craving more. Just a few seconds more, a few precious, stolen moments.

He pulled back a fraction: "Violet."

"Hmm," I murmured, just wanting him closer again.

He jolted back, away from me. "Violet, stop! You're healed."

"Oh," I said, as if it were news to me. I shuffled back, averting my gaze, even though I so desperately wanted to look at him and search his eyes. I needed to know why it had been so easy for him to pull away when it had proved so impossible for me.

The quiet in the room amplified each of my heavy breaths leaving me so…exposed.

Lincoln stood, but then sat back down and ran his hand through his hair.

"You know," he went on, "we can't."

"What?"

"The kiss. It was healing, Vi, and soon you'll learn how to heal without needing to…It wasn't, you know…It doesn't count."

His words were like a sharp slap across the face. I dropped my head. "Yeah. No…I…I…" *Shit, shit, shit.* "I didn't think it… No…I don't want it to…I…"

But before I could talk myself into more of a stupor, his hand went to my face, silencing me. His thumb smudged my cheekbone with just the right amount of pressure to make my heart gallop and my breath catch as it only ever did for him.

He was absolutely right.

The healing kiss doesn't count at all.

I bit down on my lip as he looked at me, my hazel eyes so inferior to his brilliant green, which now seemed unable to hide his desire.

Bang, bang, bang!

"If ya haven't fixed her by now—she's broken for good! Get out of my bathroom!" Dapper yelled.

Lincoln dropped his hand from my face and looked horrified with himself. I swallowed back the pain and feigned sudden interest in my fingernails.

"Vi, I…" He stood up, then spun back quickly to look at me. "You see! This is why! Griffin doesn't understand." He turned on his heel and all but flew out of the bathroom.

I just sat there in my front-row seat.

I wanted to scream when he closed the door behind him.

Why can't we be together?

Discover more at

embracetheseries.com

acknowledgments

This story would simply be no more than a stack of papers jammed into a box somewhere if not for the wonderful people who made it more and turned it into a book.

Thank you to my agent, Selwa Anthony, who has expertly steered me from the outset and never faltered.

I am so lucky to have had an incredible team of publishers in Australia: My sincere gratitude to Tegan Morrison for her tireless work, invaluable input, and belief in the story. Thanks to Fiona Hazard, Katrina Lehman, Kate Ballard, and Airlie Lawson (international rights extraordinaire).

Thank you to my U.S. Publishers and the awesome crew at Sourcebooks who never cease to amaze me with their energy an commitment to the series. Sincere thanks goes to senior edi Leah Hultenschmidt, publicist, Derry Wilkens, project e Kelly Barrales-Saylor, and production editor, Kristin Zelazk

A couple of good men—Graham McNeice and Ia Okeden—who introduced me to Selwa and set the wheels

My friends and family, in particular Mum, whose support is always cherished. Amanda, who gave me the gift that set me on this path. Chris, whose opinion is always so valued and appreciated. A big thank-you goes to: Christine, Nick, Kylie, Liss, Peit, and Joe, and my dear friend Harriet, who gave me the push to put the manuscript out there.

I owe a debt of gratitude to my parents-in-law, Jenny and Phil, for all the research material and countless discussions and without whom this story would not be the same.

Dad...I know it's not your thing, but I love that you read it anyway. You're getting better at pretending!

To my favorite and kindest reader—Matt. Thank you for your unconditional love and support, and for never complaining that there was no dinner.

Lastly, the following songs cannot go without mention: "Falling," "Drumming Song," "Kiss with a Fist," and "Hardest of Hearts" by Florence and the Machine; "Lentil" and "Lullaby" by Sia; "Citizen" and "Trap Doors" by Broken Bells; "All the Same to Me" by Anya Marina; "Love Lost" by Temper Trap.